SECONDHAND HEROES

BROTHERS UNITE

JUSTIN LAROCCA HANSEN

DIAL BOOKS FOR YOUNG READERS

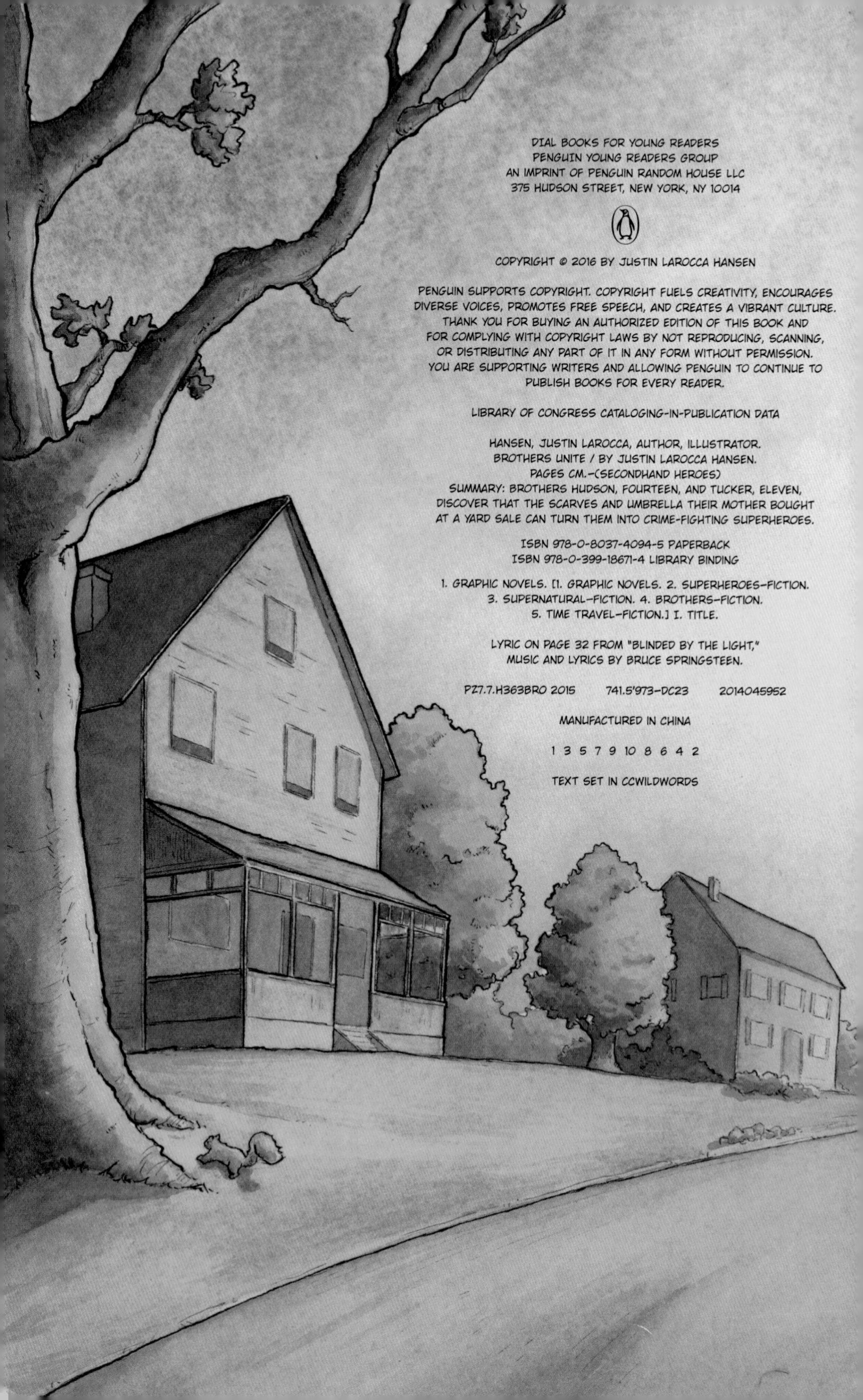

DIAL BOOKS FOR YOUNG READERS
PENGUIN YOUNG READERS GROUP
AN IMPRINT OF PENGUIN RANDOM HOUSE LLC
375 HUDSON STREET, NEW YORK, NY 10014

LIBRARY OF CONGRESS CATALOGING-IN-PUBLICATION DATA

HANSEN, JUSTIN LAROCCA, AUTHOR, ILLUSTRATOR.
BROTHERS UNITE / BY JUSTIN LAROCCA HANSEN.
PAGES CM.–(SECONDHAND HEROES)
SUMMARY: BROTHERS HUDSON, FOURTEEN, AND TUCKER, ELEVEN, DISCOVER THAT THE SCARVES AND UMBRELLA THEIR MOTHER BOUGHT AT A YARD SALE CAN TURN THEM INTO CRIME-FIGHTING SUPERHEROES.

ISBN 978-0-8037-4094-5 PAPERBACK
ISBN 978-0-399-18671-4 LIBRARY BINDING

1. GRAPHIC NOVELS. [1. GRAPHIC NOVELS. 2. SUPERHEROES–FICTION. 3. SUPERNATURAL–FICTION. 4. BROTHERS–FICTION. 5. TIME TRAVEL–FICTION.] I. TITLE.

LYRIC ON PAGE 32 FROM "BLINDED BY THE LIGHT," MUSIC AND LYRICS BY BRUCE SPRINGSTEEN.

PZ7.7.H363BRO 2015 741.5'973–DC23 2014045952

MANUFACTURED IN CHINA

1 3 5 7 9 10 8 6 4 2

TEXT SET IN CCWILDWORDS

FOR MY BROTHER JEFFREY,
WHO WAS AND IS MY PARTNER
FOR ALL THE REAL-LIFE ADVENTURES
THAT BECAME THIS STORY.

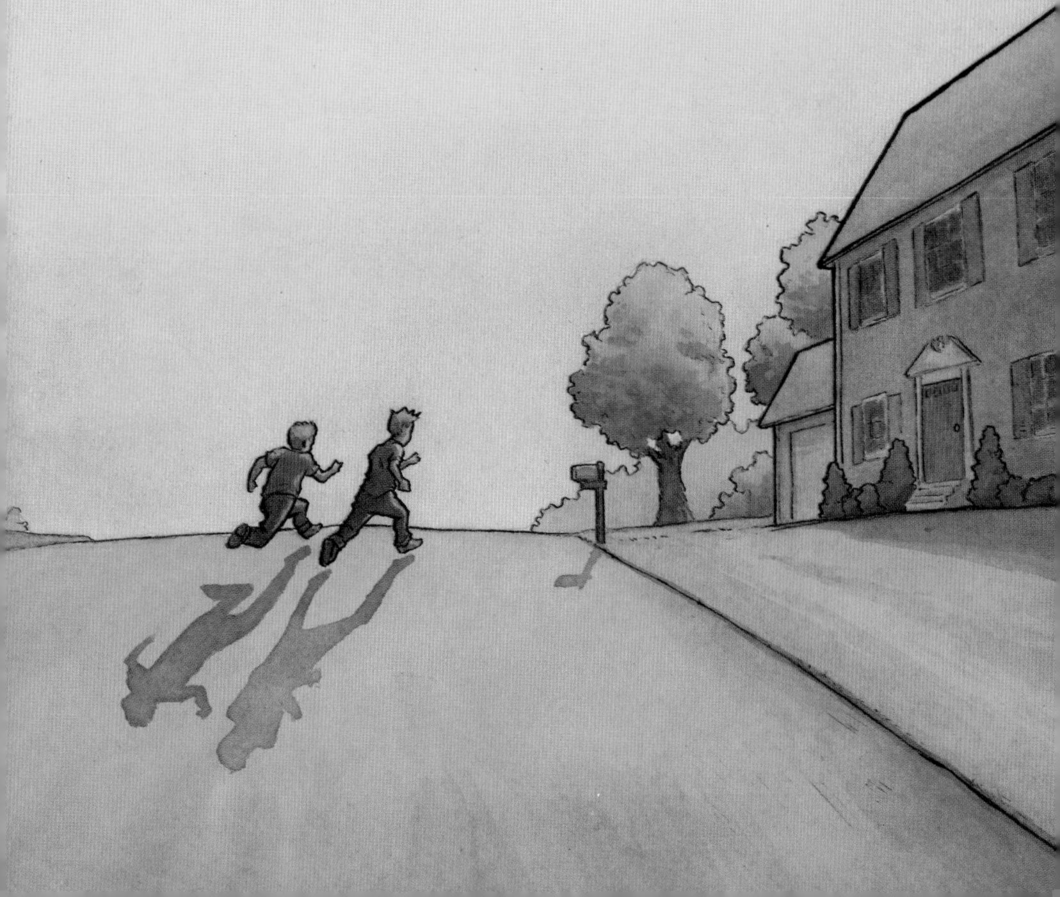

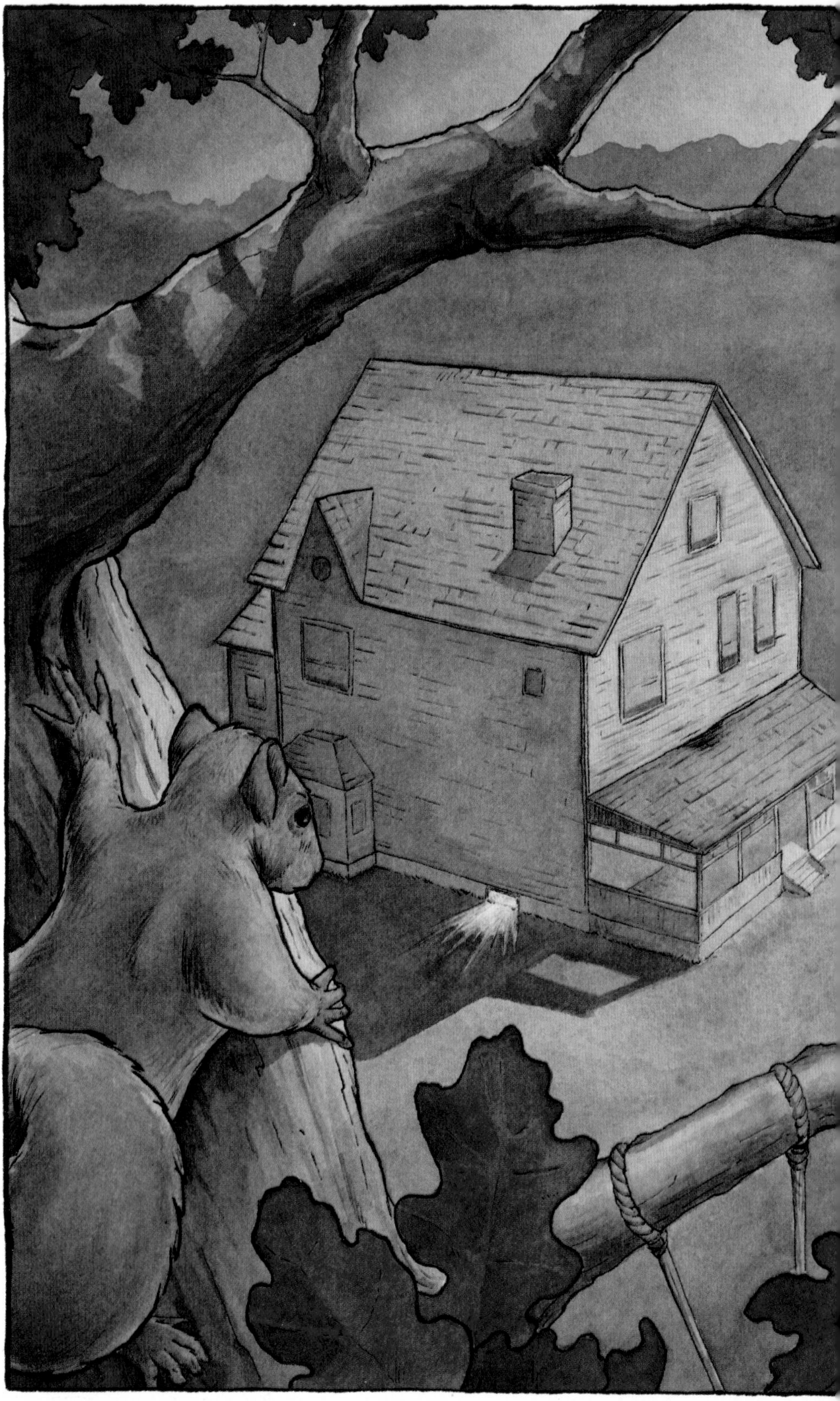

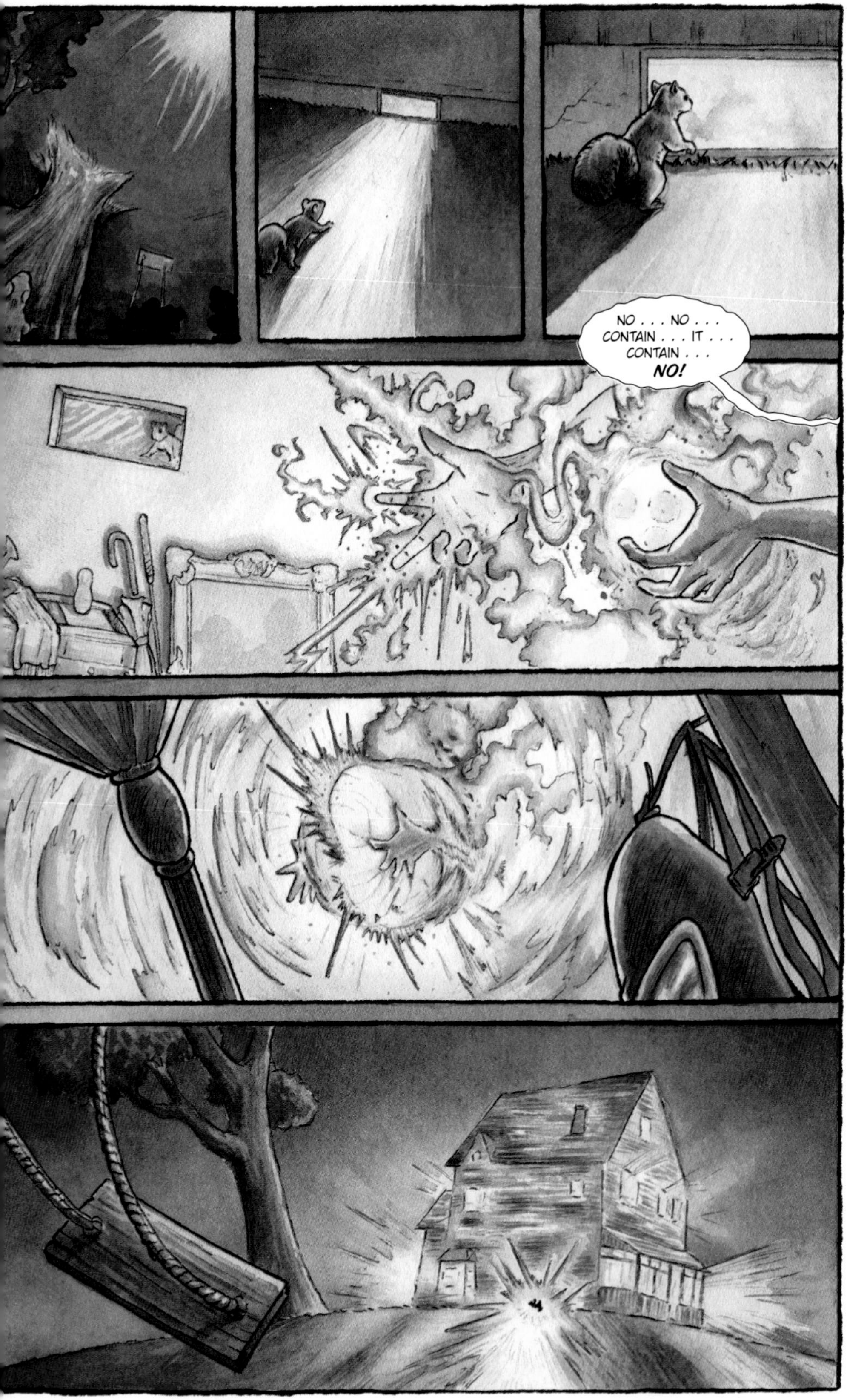
NO . . . NO . . . CONTAIN . . . IT . . . CONTAIN . . . NO!

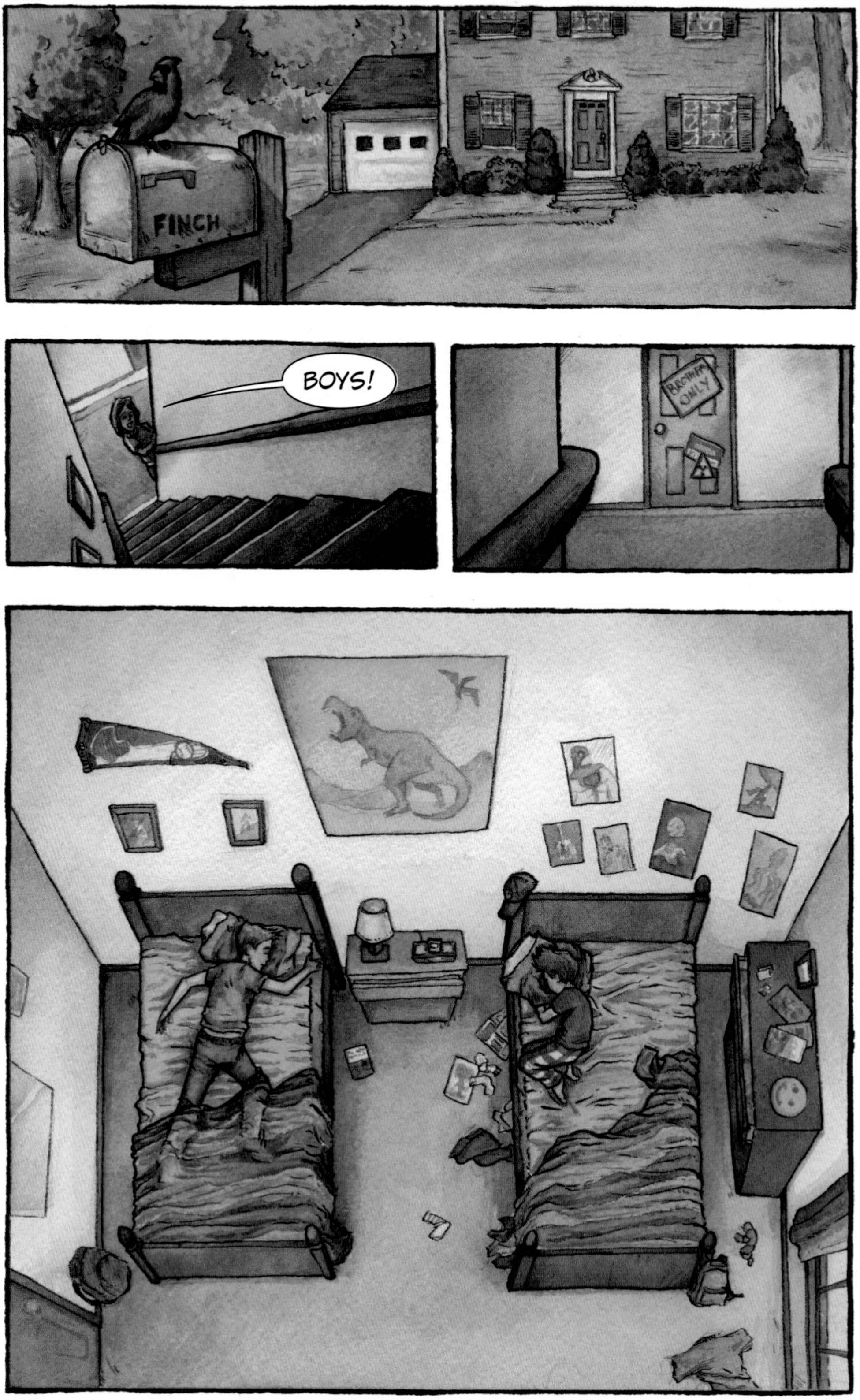
FINCH
BOYS!

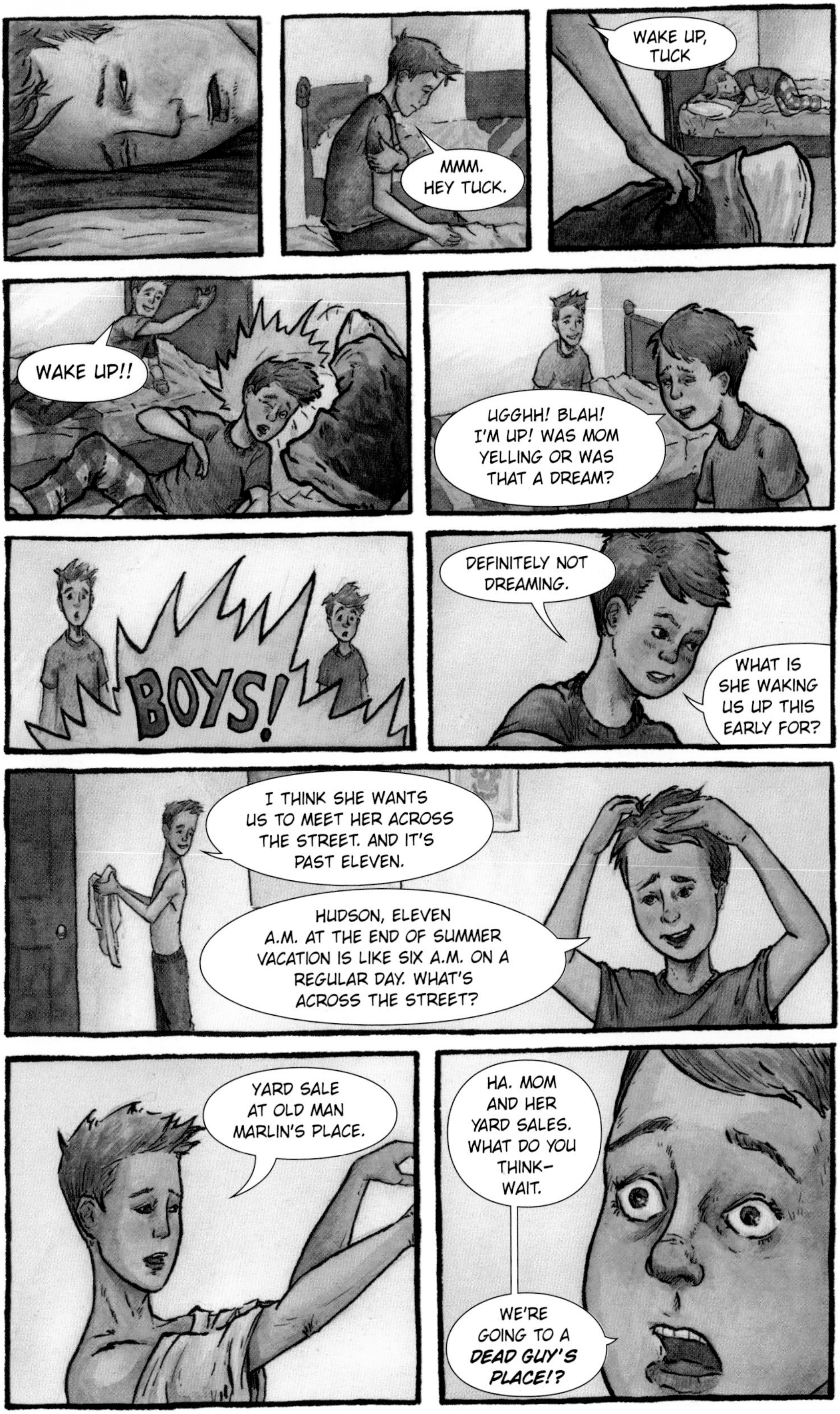
MMM.
HEY TUCK.
WAKE UP,
TUCK
WAKE UP!!
UGGHH! BLAH! I'M UP! WAS MOM YELLING OR WAS THAT A DREAM?
BOYS!
DEFINITELY NOT DREAMING.
WHAT IS SHE WAKING US UP THIS EARLY FOR?
I THINK SHE WANTS US TO MEET HER ACROSS THE STREET. AND IT'S PAST ELEVEN.
HUDSON, ELEVEN A.M. AT THE END OF SUMMER VACATION IS LIKE SIX A.M. ON A REGULAR DAY. WHAT'S ACROSS THE STREET?
YARD SALE AT OLD MAN MARLIN'S PLACE.
HA. MOM AND HER YARD SALES. WHAT DO YOU THINK-
WAIT.
WE'RE GOING TO A *DEAD GUY'S PLACE!?*

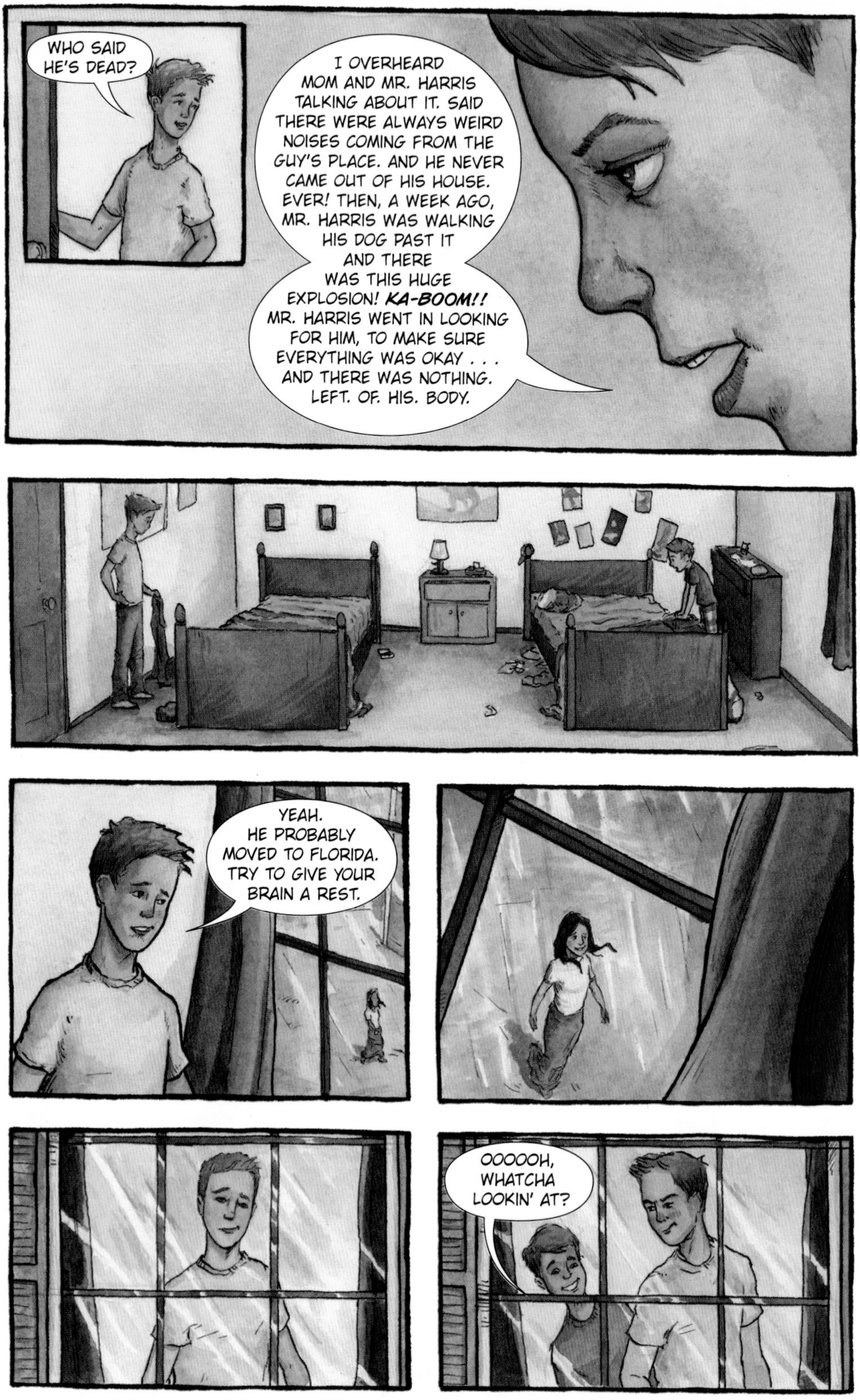
WHO SAID HE'S DEAD?
I OVERHEARD MOM AND MR. HARRIS TALKING ABOUT IT. SAID THERE WERE ALWAYS WEIRD NOISES COMING FROM THE GUY'S PLACE. AND HE NEVER CAME OUT OF HIS HOUSE. EVER! THEN, A WEEK AGO, MR. HARRIS WAS WALKING HIS DOG PAST IT AND THERE WAS THIS HUGE EXPLOSION! **KA-BOOM!!** MR. HARRIS WENT IN LOOKING FOR HIM, TO MAKE SURE EVERYTHING WAS OKAY . . . AND THERE WAS NOTHING. LEFT. OF. HIS. BODY.
YEAH. HE PROBABLY MOVED TO FLORIDA. TRY TO GIVE YOUR BRAIN A REST.
OOOOOH, WHATCHA LOOKIN' AT?

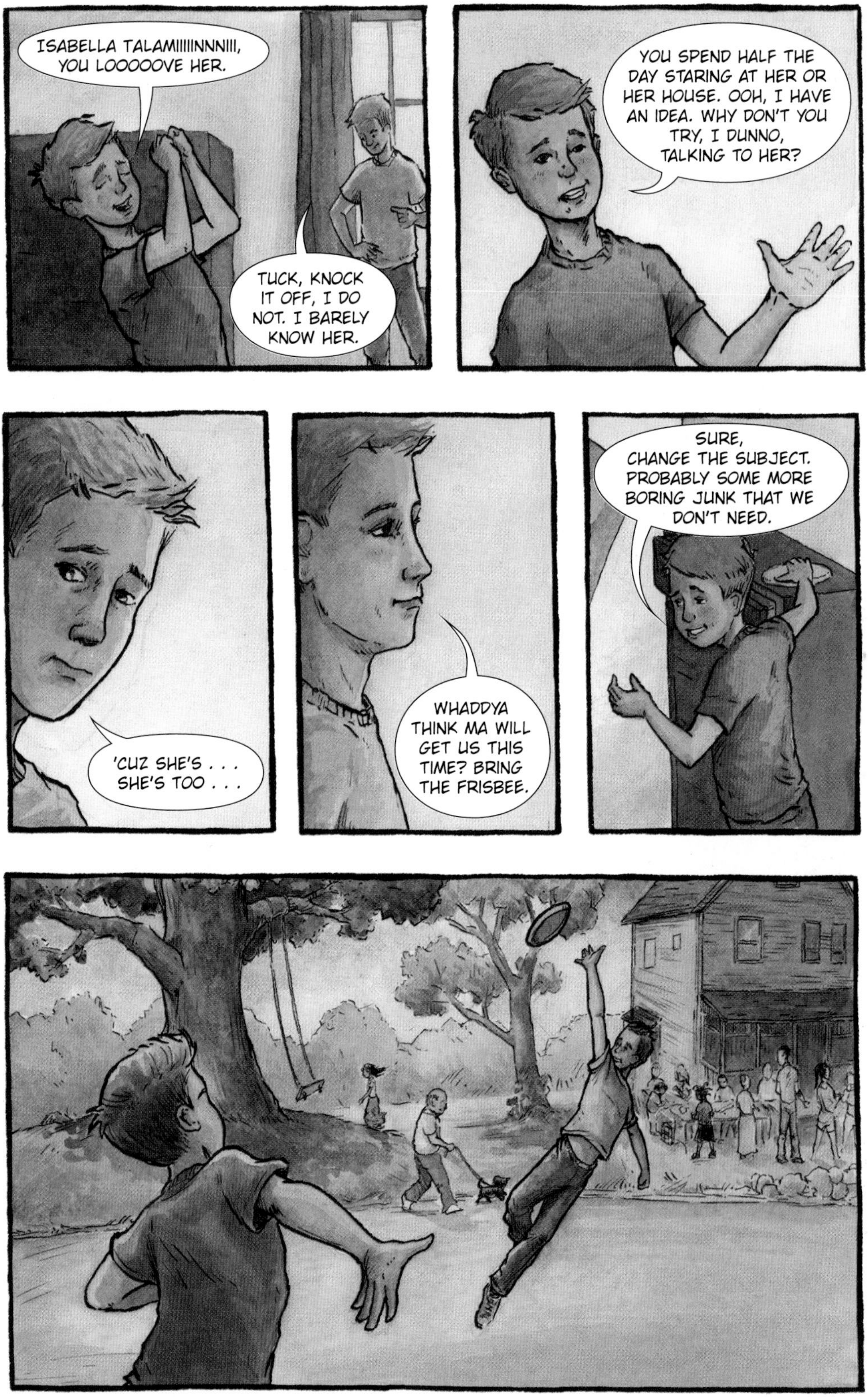
ISABELLA TALAMIIIIINNNIII, YOU LOOOOOVE HER.
TUCK, KNOCK IT OFF, I DO NOT. I BARELY KNOW HER.
YOU SPEND HALF THE DAY STARING AT HER OR HER HOUSE. OOH, I HAVE AN IDEA. WHY DON'T YOU TRY, I DUNNO, TALKING TO HER?
'CUZ SHE'S . . . SHE'S TOO . . .
WHADDYA THINK MA WILL GET US THIS TIME? BRING THE FRISBEE.
SURE, CHANGE THE SUBJECT. PROBABLY SOME MORE BORING JUNK THAT WE DON'T NEED.

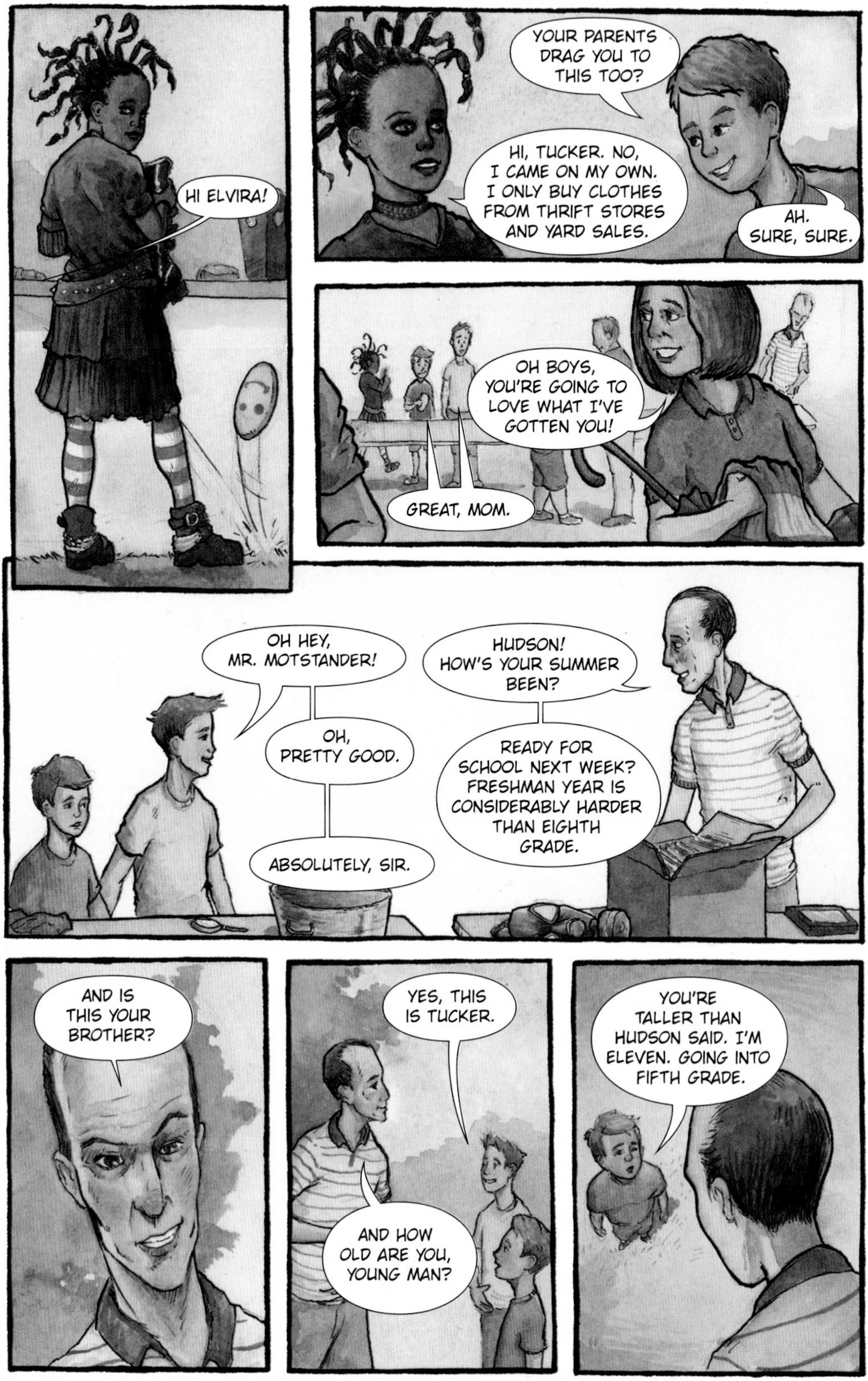
HI ELVIRA!
YOUR PARENTS DRAG YOU TO THIS TOO?
HI, TUCKER. NO, I CAME ON MY OWN. I ONLY BUY CLOTHES FROM THRIFT STORES AND YARD SALES.
AH. SURE, SURE.
OH BOYS, YOU'RE GOING TO LOVE WHAT I'VE GOTTEN YOU!
GREAT, MOM.
OH HEY, MR. MOTSTANDER!
HUDSON! HOW'S YOUR SUMMER BEEN?
OH, PRETTY GOOD.
READY FOR SCHOOL NEXT WEEK? FRESHMAN YEAR IS CONSIDERABLY HARDER THAN EIGHTH GRADE.
ABSOLUTELY, SIR.
AND IS THIS YOUR BROTHER?
YES, THIS IS TUCKER.
AND HOW OLD ARE YOU, YOUNG MAN?
YOU'RE TALLER THAN HUDSON SAID. I'M ELEVEN. GOING INTO FIFTH GRADE.

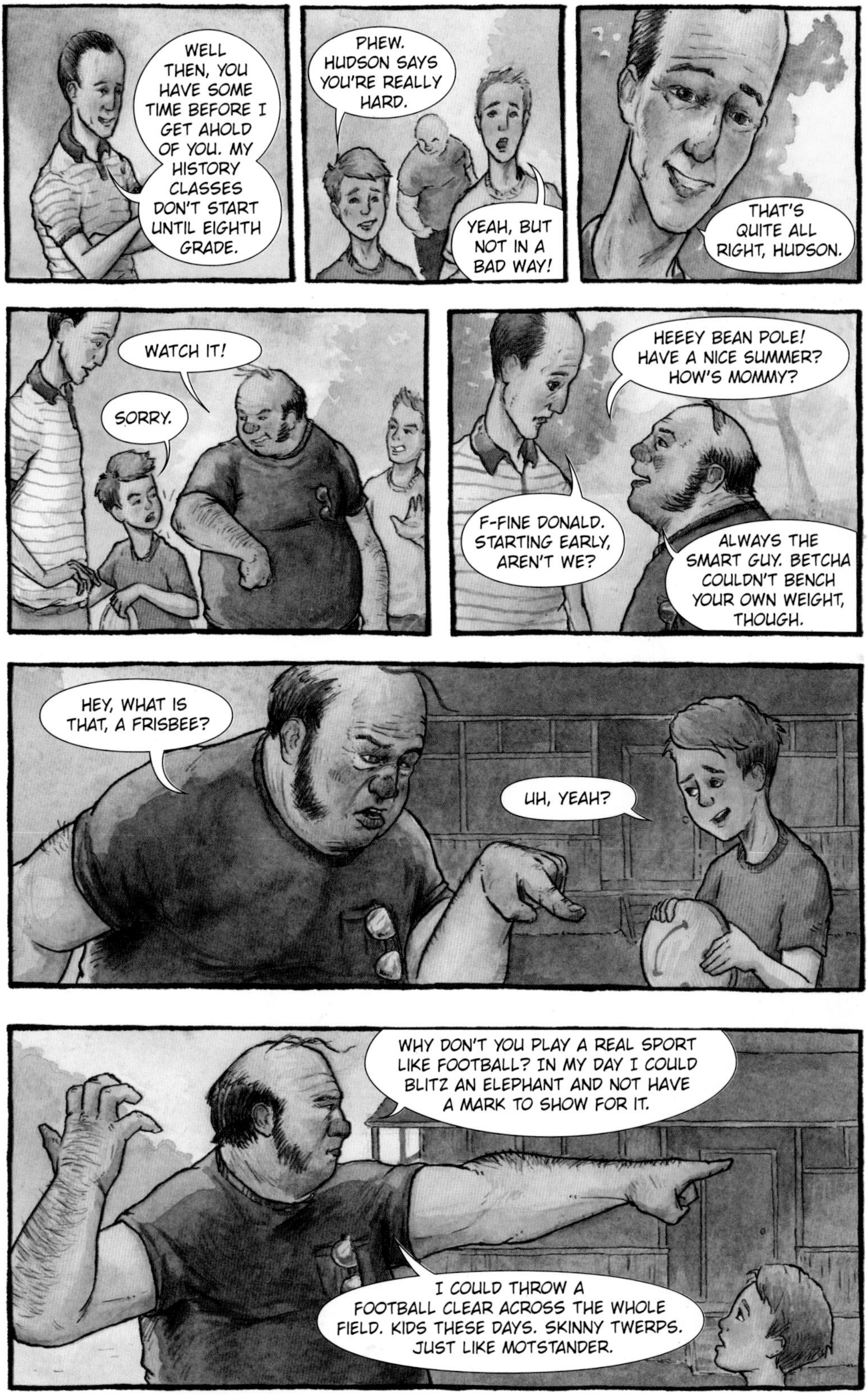
WELL THEN, YOU HAVE SOME TIME BEFORE I GET AHOLD OF YOU. MY HISTORY CLASSES DON'T START UNTIL EIGHTH GRADE.
PHEW. HUDSON SAYS YOU'RE REALLY HARD.
YEAH, BUT NOT IN A BAD WAY!
THAT'S QUITE ALL RIGHT, HUDSON.
WATCH IT!
SORRY.
HEEEY BEAN POLE! HAVE A NICE SUMMER? HOW'S MOMMY?
F-FINE DONALD. STARTING EARLY, AREN'T WE?
ALWAYS THE SMART GUY. BETCHA COULDN'T BENCH YOUR OWN WEIGHT, THOUGH.
HEY, WHAT IS THAT, A FRISBEE?
UH, YEAH?
WHY DON'T YOU PLAY A REAL SPORT LIKE FOOTBALL? IN MY DAY I COULD BLITZ AN ELEPHANT AND NOT HAVE A MARK TO SHOW FOR IT.
I COULD THROW A FOOTBALL CLEAR ACROSS THE WHOLE FIELD. KIDS THESE DAYS. SKINNY TWERPS. JUST LIKE MOTSTANDER.

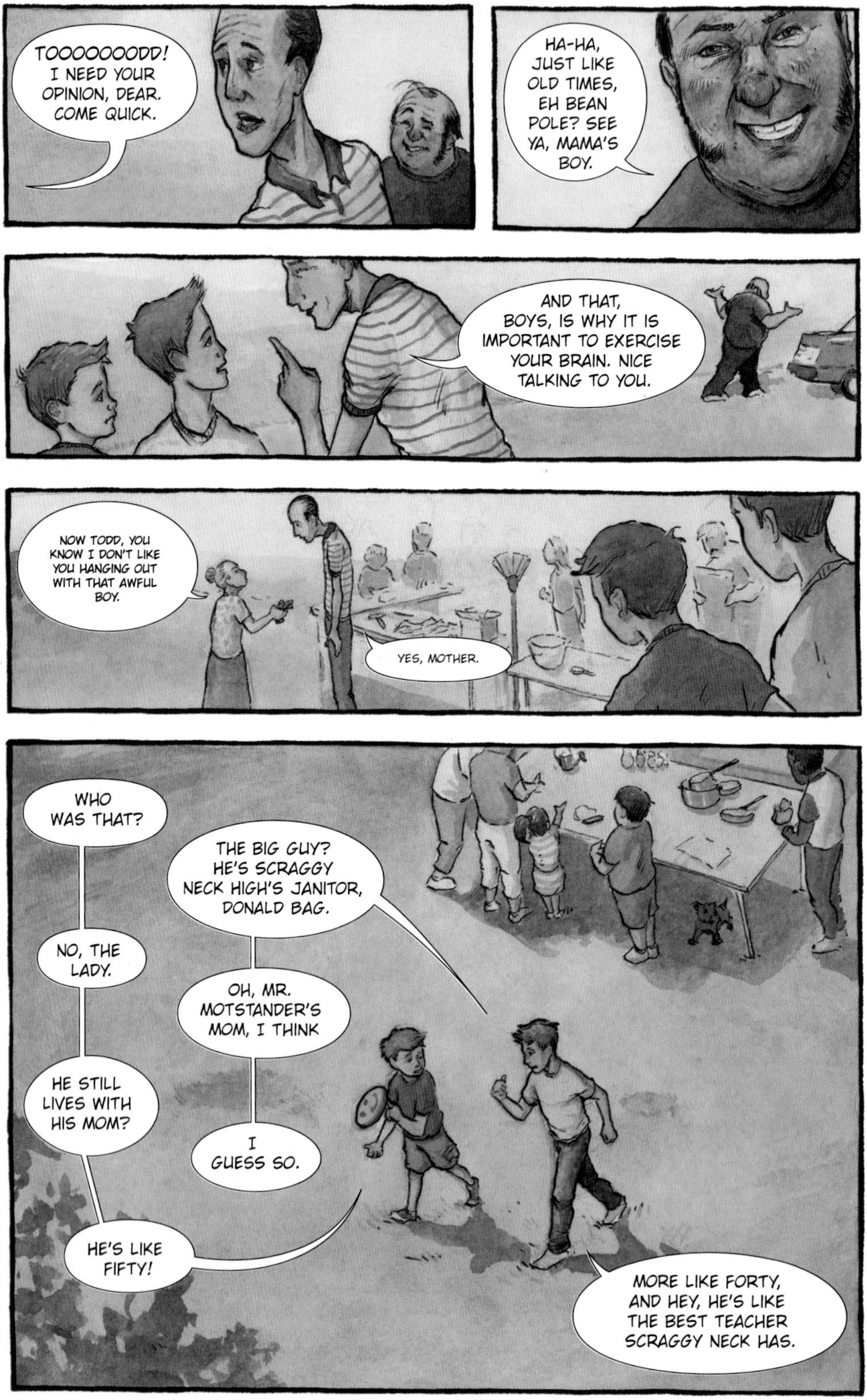
TOOOOOOODD! I NEED YOUR OPINION, DEAR. COME QUICK.
HA-HA, JUST LIKE OLD TIMES, EH BEAN POLE? SEE YA, MAMA'S BOY.
AND THAT, BOYS, IS WHY IT IS IMPORTANT TO EXERCISE YOUR BRAIN. NICE TALKING TO YOU.
NOW TODD, YOU KNOW I DON'T LIKE YOU HANGING OUT WITH THAT AWFUL BOY.
YES, MOTHER.
WHO WAS THAT?
THE BIG GUY? HE'S SCRAGGY NECK HIGH'S JANITOR, DONALD BAG.
NO, THE LADY.
OH, MR. MOTSTANDER'S MOM, I THINK
HE STILL LIVES WITH HIS MOM?
I GUESS SO.
HE'S LIKE FIFTY!
MORE LIKE FORTY, AND HEY, HE'S LIKE THE BEST TEACHER SCRAGGY NECK HAS.

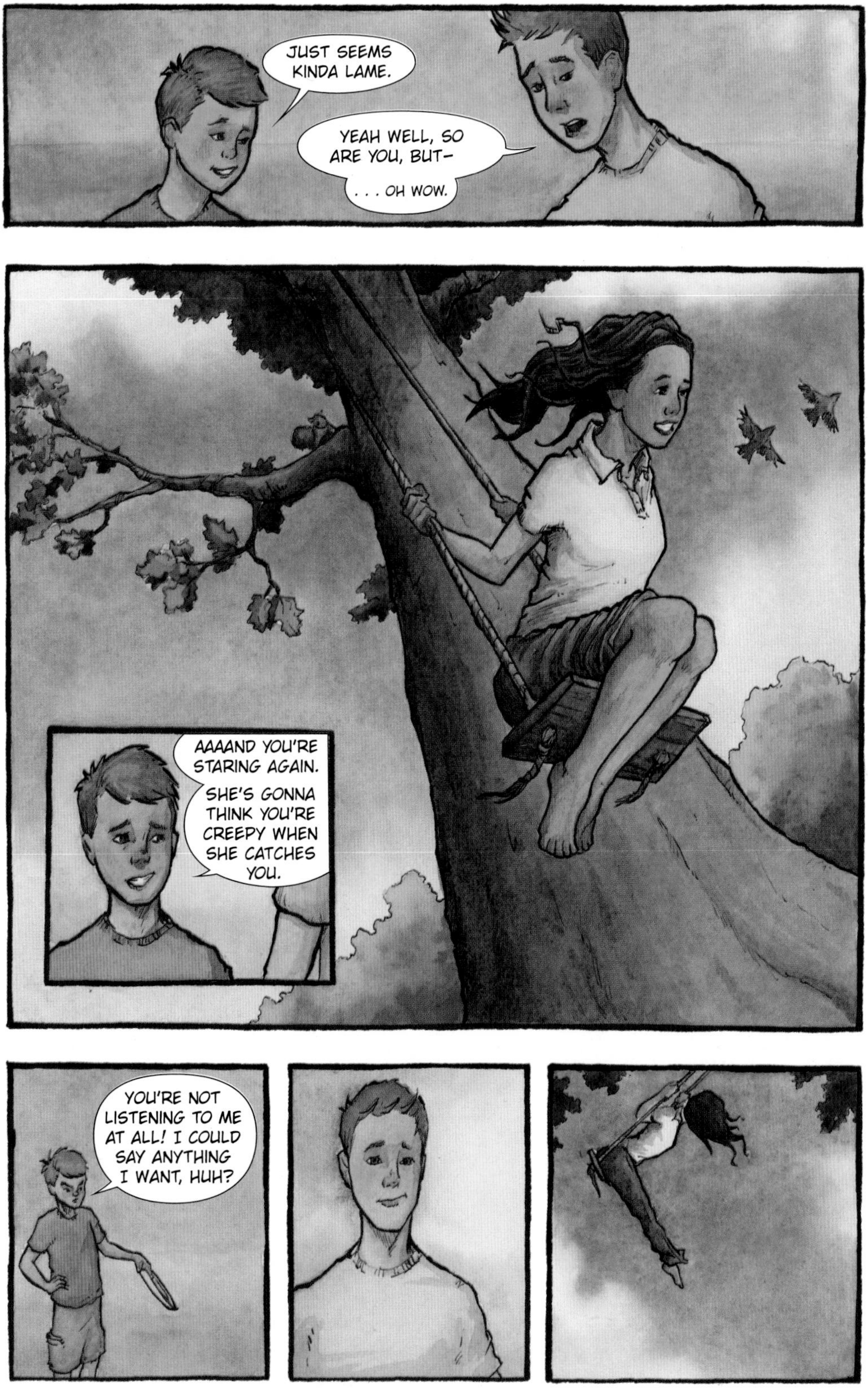
JUST SEEMS KINDA LAME.
YEAH WELL, SO ARE YOU, BUT-
. . . OH WOW.
AAAAND YOU'RE STARING AGAIN.
SHE'S GONNA THINK YOU'RE CREEPY WHEN SHE CATCHES YOU.
YOU'RE NOT LISTENING TO ME AT ALL! I COULD SAY ANYTHING I WANT, HUH?

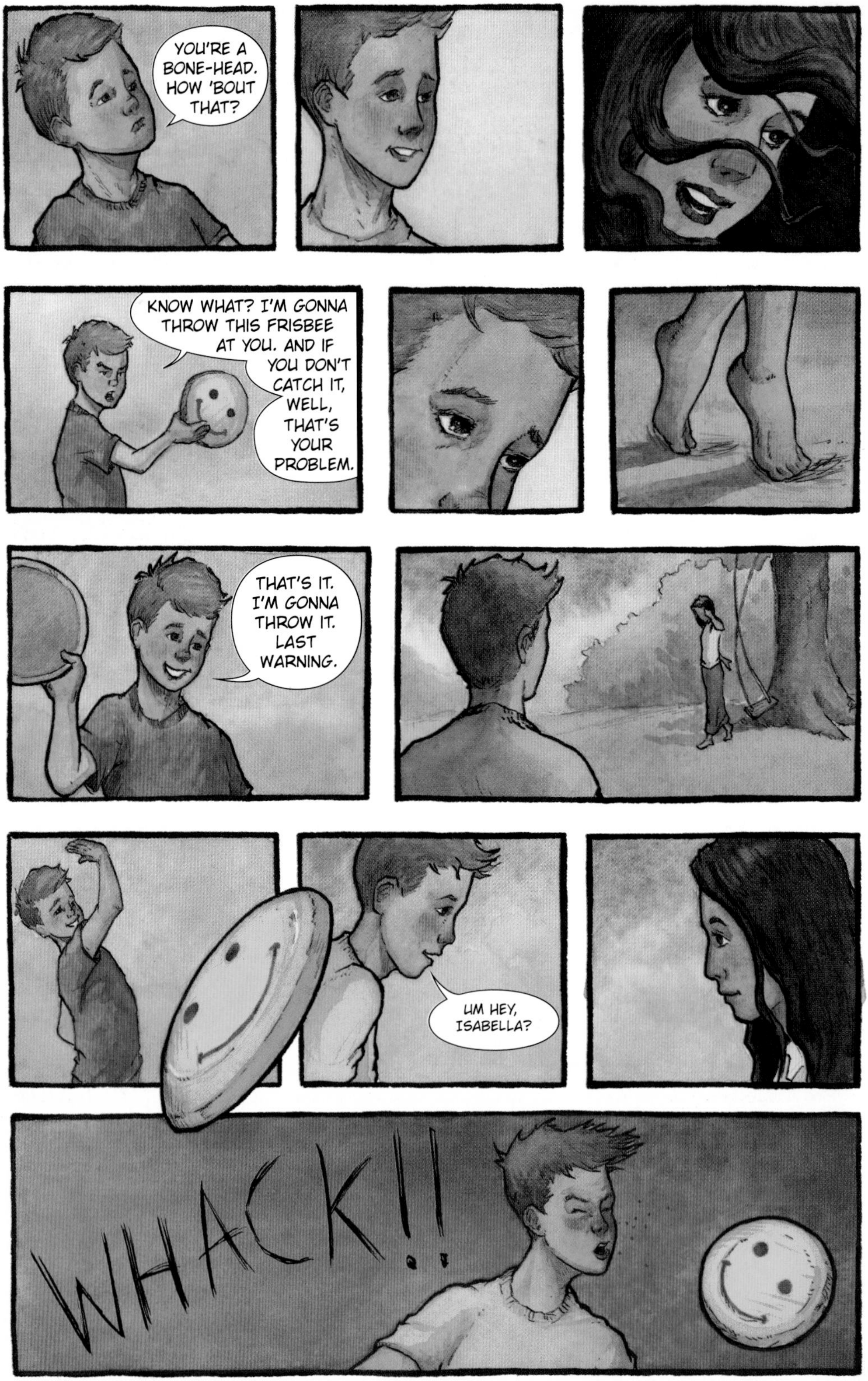
YOU'RE A BONE-HEAD. HOW 'BOUT THAT?
KNOW WHAT? I'M GONNA THROW THIS FRISBEE AT YOU. AND IF YOU DON'T CATCH IT, WELL, THAT'S YOUR PROBLEM.
THAT'S IT. I'M GONNA THROW IT. LAST WARNING.
UM HEY, ISABELLA?
WHACK!!

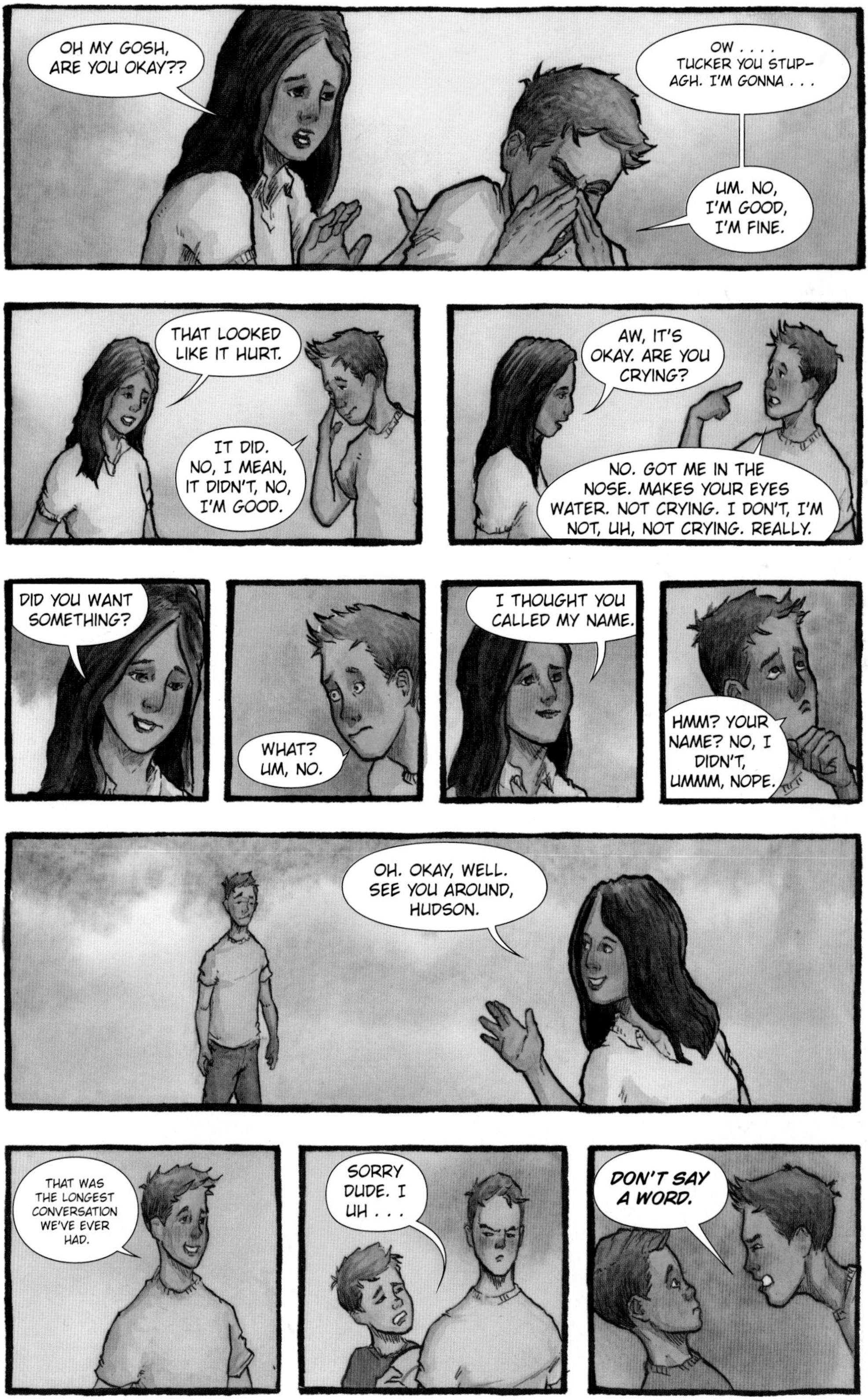
OH MY GOSH, ARE YOU OKAY??
OW . . . . TUCKER YOU STUP– AGH. I'M GONNA . . .
UM. NO, I'M GOOD, I'M FINE.
THAT LOOKED LIKE IT HURT.
IT DID. NO, I MEAN, IT DIDN'T, NO, I'M GOOD.
AW, IT'S OKAY. ARE YOU CRYING?
NO. GOT ME IN THE NOSE. MAKES YOUR EYES WATER. NOT CRYING. I DON'T, I'M NOT, UH, NOT CRYING. REALLY.
DID YOU WANT SOMETHING?
WHAT? UM, NO.
I THOUGHT YOU CALLED MY NAME.
HMM? YOUR NAME? NO, I DIDN'T, UMMM, NOPE.
OH. OKAY, WELL. SEE YOU AROUND, HUDSON.
THAT WAS THE LONGEST CONVERSATION WE'VE EVER HAD.
SORRY DUDE. I UH . . .
DON'T SAY A WORD.

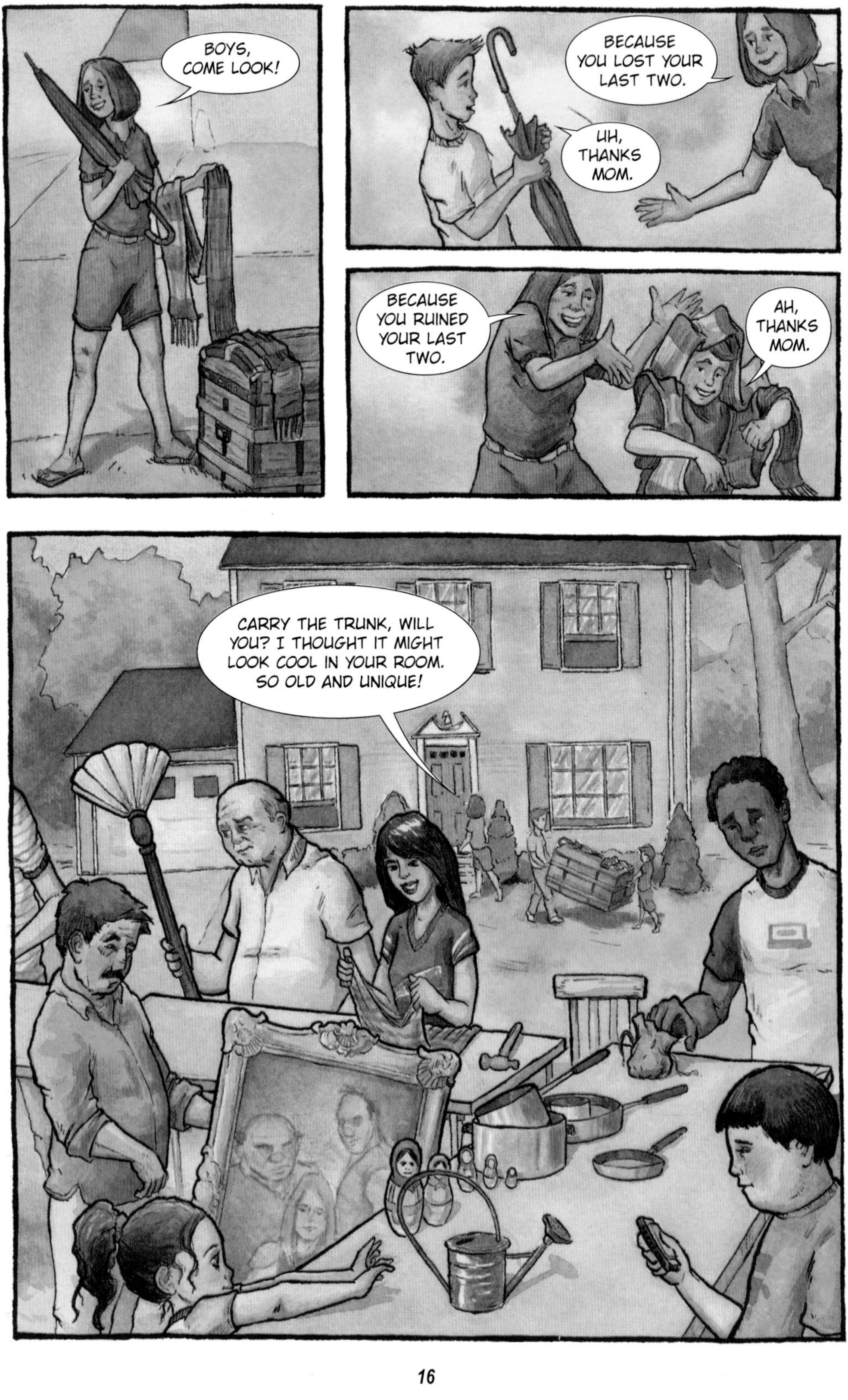
BOYS, COME LOOK!
BECAUSE YOU LOST YOUR LAST TWO.
UH, THANKS MOM.
BECAUSE YOU RUINED YOUR LAST TWO.
AH, THANKS MOM.
CARRY THE TRUNK, WILL YOU? I THOUGHT IT MIGHT LOOK COOL IN YOUR ROOM. SO OLD AND UNIQUE!

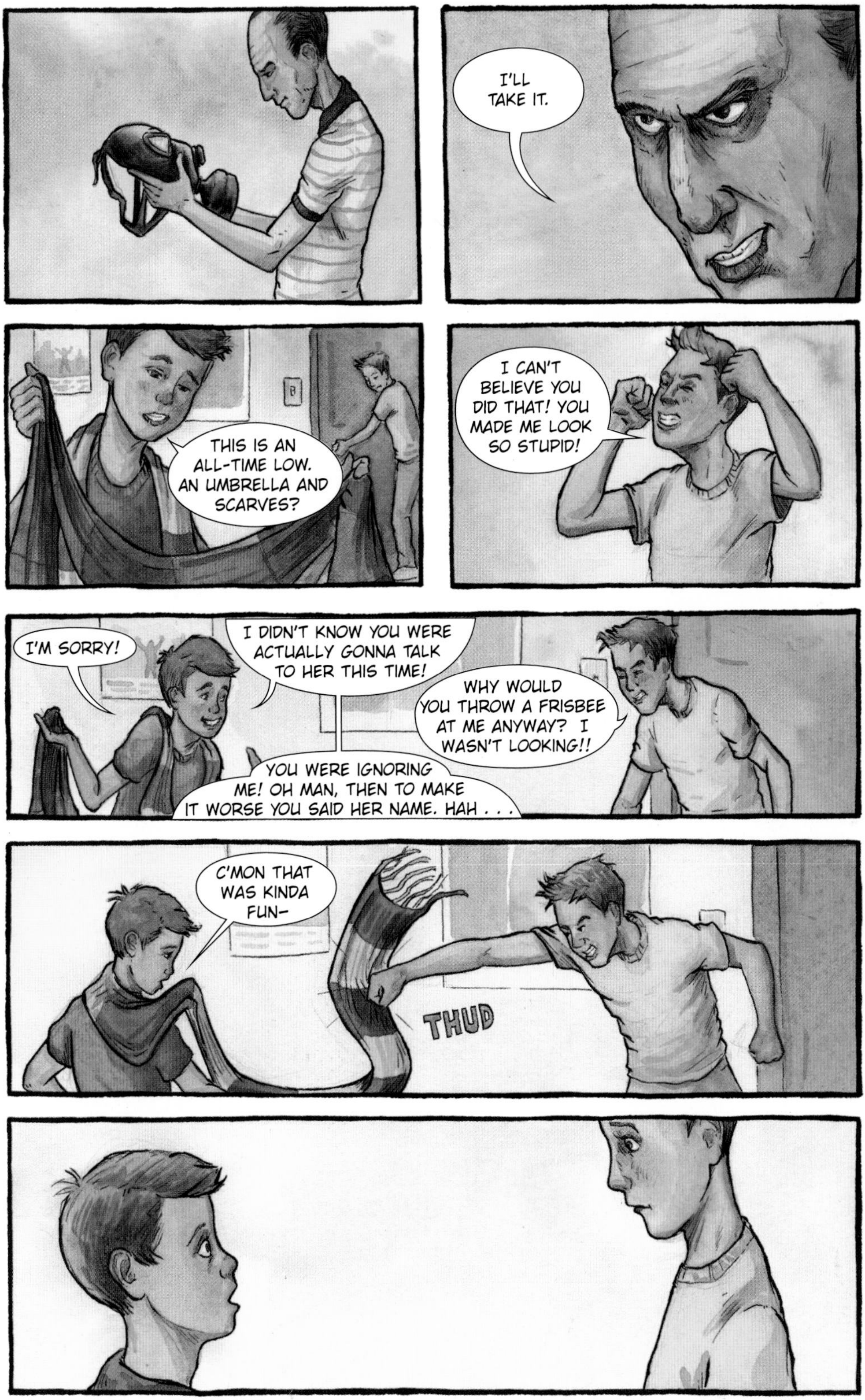
I'LL TAKE IT.
THIS IS AN ALL-TIME LOW. AN UMBRELLA AND SCARVES?
I CAN'T BELIEVE YOU DID THAT! YOU MADE ME LOOK SO STUPID!
I'M SORRY!
I DIDN'T KNOW YOU WERE ACTUALLY GONNA TALK TO HER THIS TIME!
YOU WERE IGNORING ME! OH MAN, THEN TO MAKE IT WORSE YOU SAID HER NAME. HAH . . .
WHY WOULD YOU THROW A FRISBEE AT ME ANYWAY? I WASN'T LOOKING!!
C'MON THAT WAS KINDA FUN-
THUD

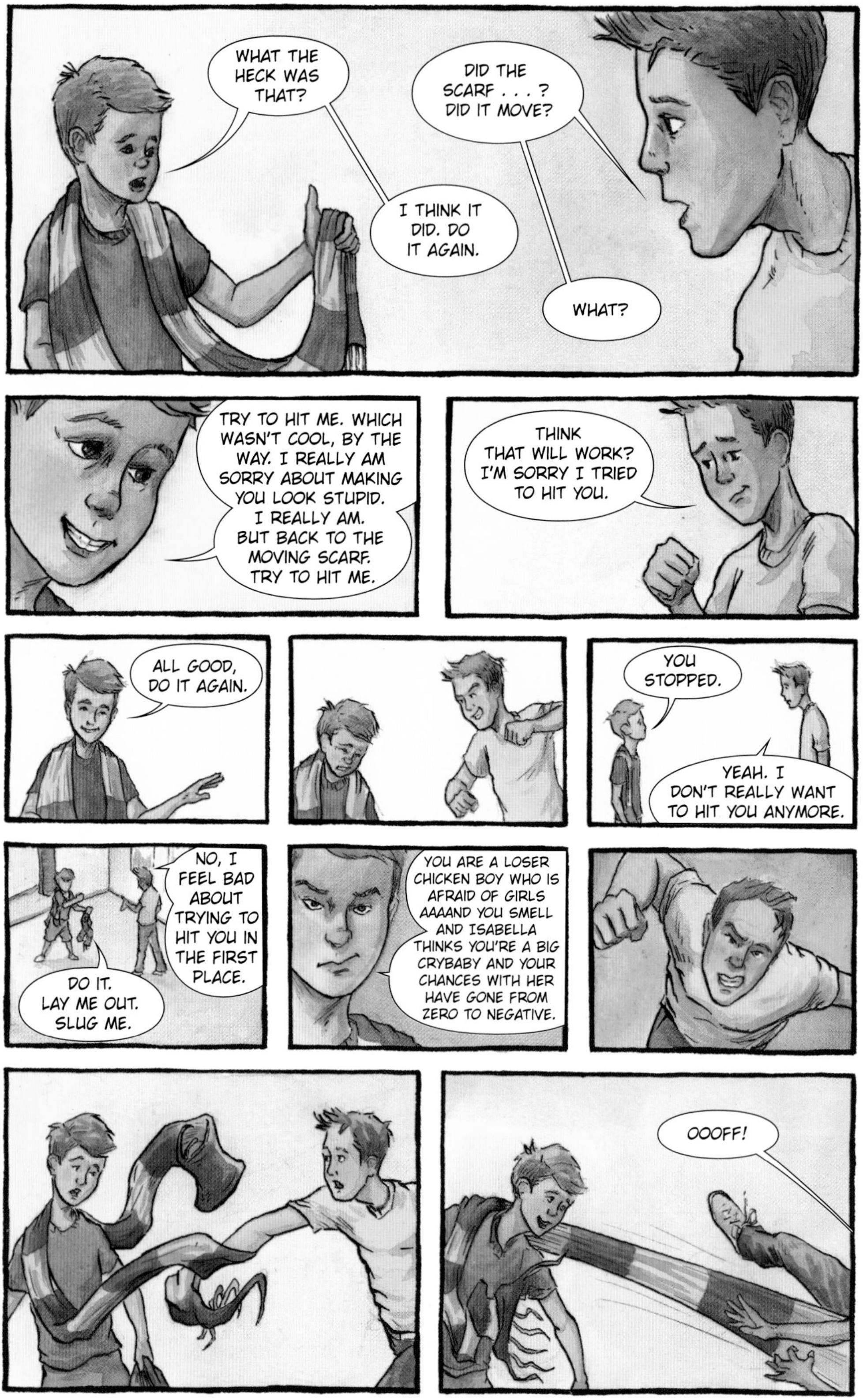
WHAT THE HECK WAS THAT?
DID THE SCARF . . . ? DID IT MOVE?
I THINK IT DID. DO IT AGAIN.
WHAT?
TRY TO HIT ME. WHICH WASN'T COOL, BY THE WAY. I REALLY AM SORRY ABOUT MAKING YOU LOOK STUPID.
I REALLY AM. BUT BACK TO THE MOVING SCARF. TRY TO HIT ME.
THINK THAT WILL WORK? I'M SORRY I TRIED TO HIT YOU.
ALL GOOD, DO IT AGAIN.
YOU STOPPED.
YEAH. I DON'T REALLY WANT TO HIT YOU ANYMORE.
NO, I FEEL BAD ABOUT TRYING TO HIT YOU IN THE FIRST PLACE.
DO IT. LAY ME OUT. SLUG ME.
YOU ARE A LOSER CHICKEN BOY WHO IS AFRAID OF GIRLS AAAAND YOU SMELL AND ISABELLA THINKS YOU'RE A BIG CRYBABY AND YOUR CHANCES WITH HER HAVE GONE FROM ZERO TO NEGATIVE.
OOOFF!

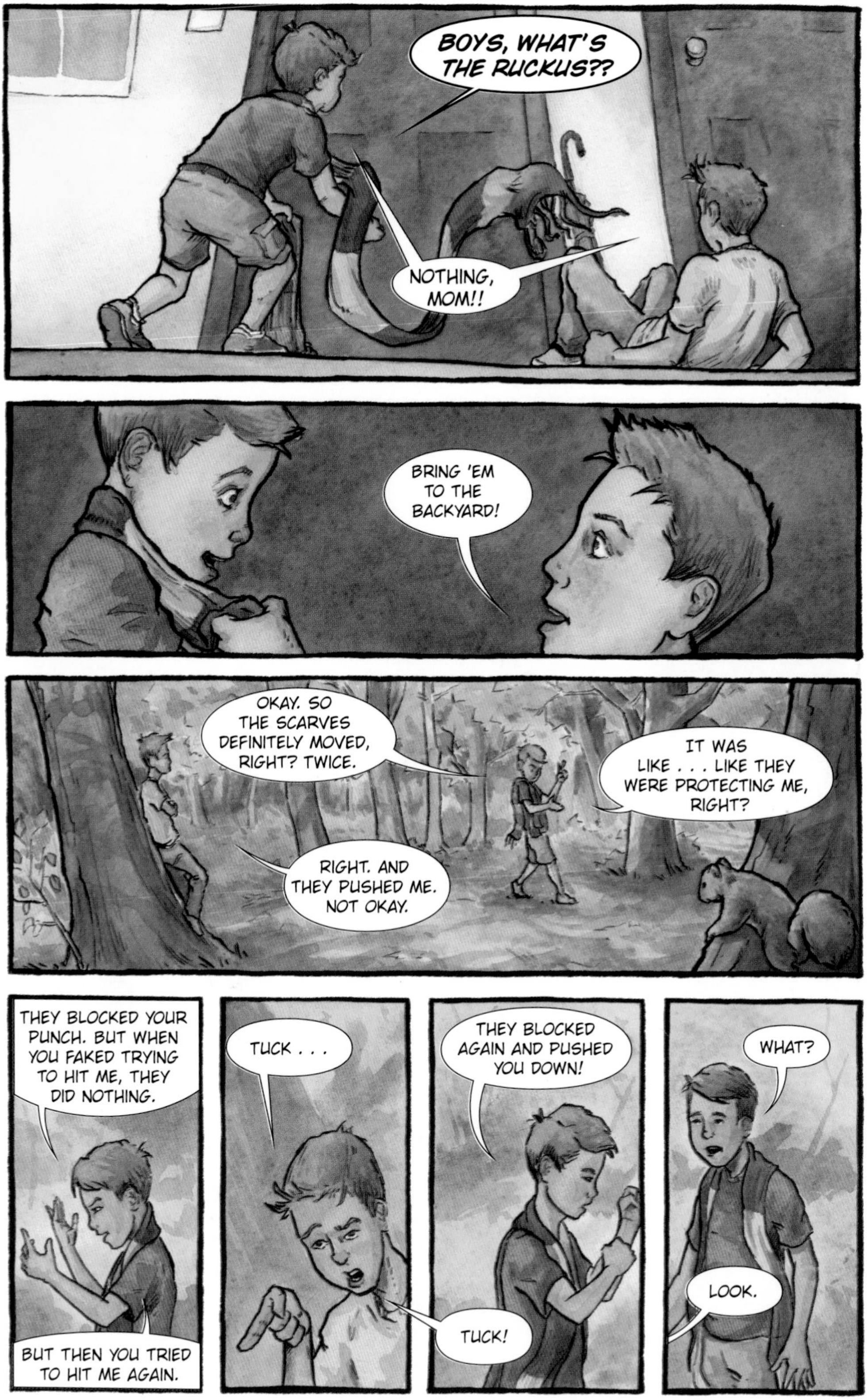
BOYS, WHAT'S THE RUCKUS??
NOTHING, MOM!!
BRING 'EM TO THE BACKYARD!
OKAY. SO THE SCARVES DEFINITELY MOVED, RIGHT? TWICE.
IT WAS LIKE . . . LIKE THEY WERE PROTECTING ME, RIGHT?
RIGHT. AND THEY PUSHED ME. NOT OKAY.
THEY BLOCKED YOUR PUNCH. BUT WHEN YOU FAKED TRYING TO HIT ME, THEY DID NOTHING.
BUT THEN YOU TRIED TO HIT ME AGAIN.
TUCK . . .
TUCK!
THEY BLOCKED AGAIN AND PUSHED YOU DOWN!
WHAT?
LOOK.

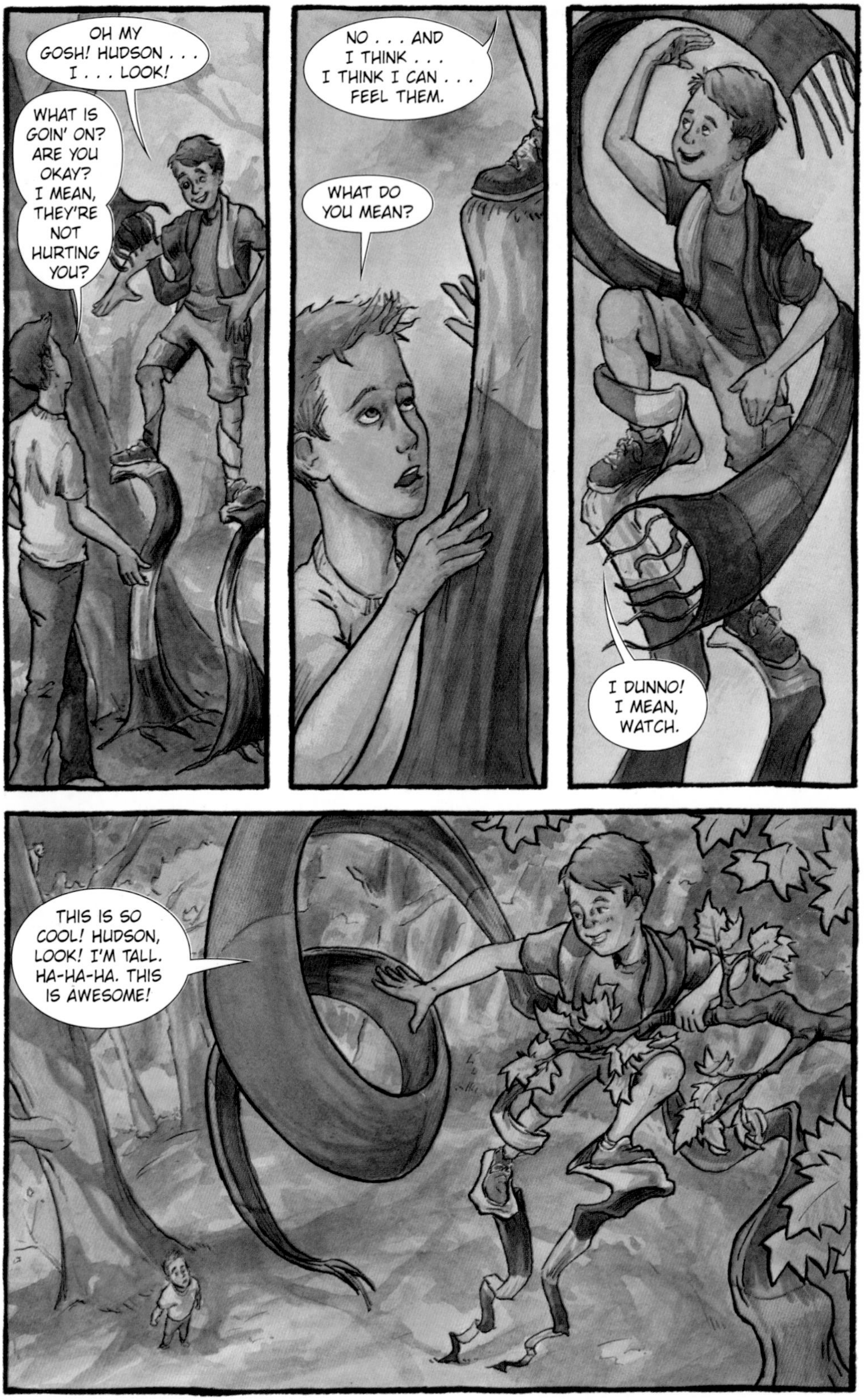
OH MY GOSH! HUDSON . . . I . . . LOOK!
WHAT IS GOIN' ON? ARE YOU OKAY? I MEAN, THEY'RE NOT HURTING YOU?
NO . . . AND I THINK . . . I THINK I CAN . . . FEEL THEM.
WHAT DO YOU MEAN?
I DUNNO! I MEAN, WATCH.
THIS IS SO COOL! HUDSON, LOOK! I'M TALL. HA-HA-HA. THIS IS AWESOME!

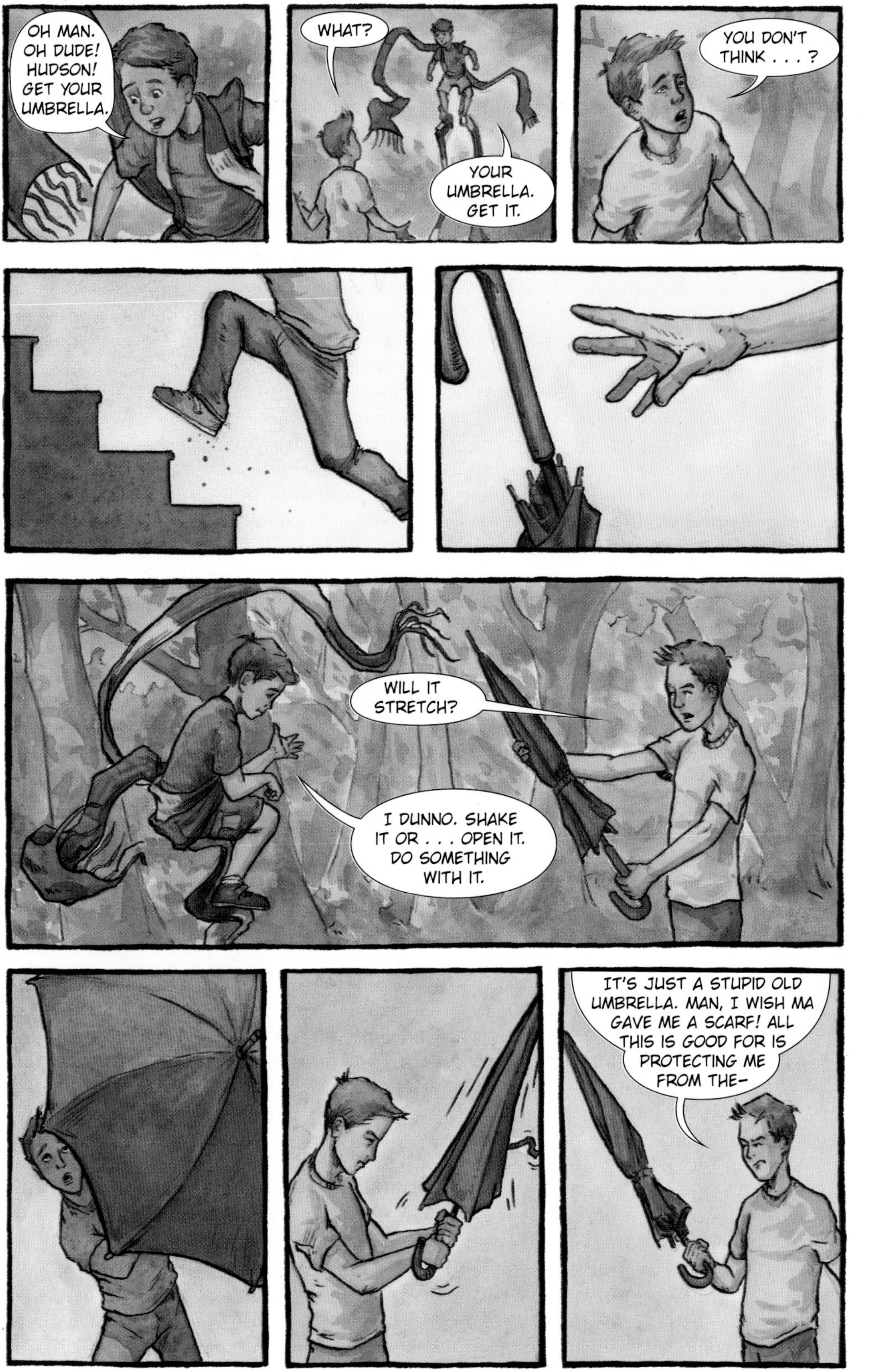
OH MAN. OH DUDE! HUDSON! GET YOUR UMBRELLA.
WHAT?
YOUR UMBRELLA. GET IT.
YOU DON'T THINK . . . ?
WILL IT STRETCH?
I DUNNO. SHAKE IT OR . . . OPEN IT. DO SOMETHING WITH IT.
IT'S JUST A STUPID OLD UMBRELLA. MAN, I WISH MA GAVE ME A SCARF! ALL THIS IS GOOD FOR IS PROTECTING ME FROM THE–

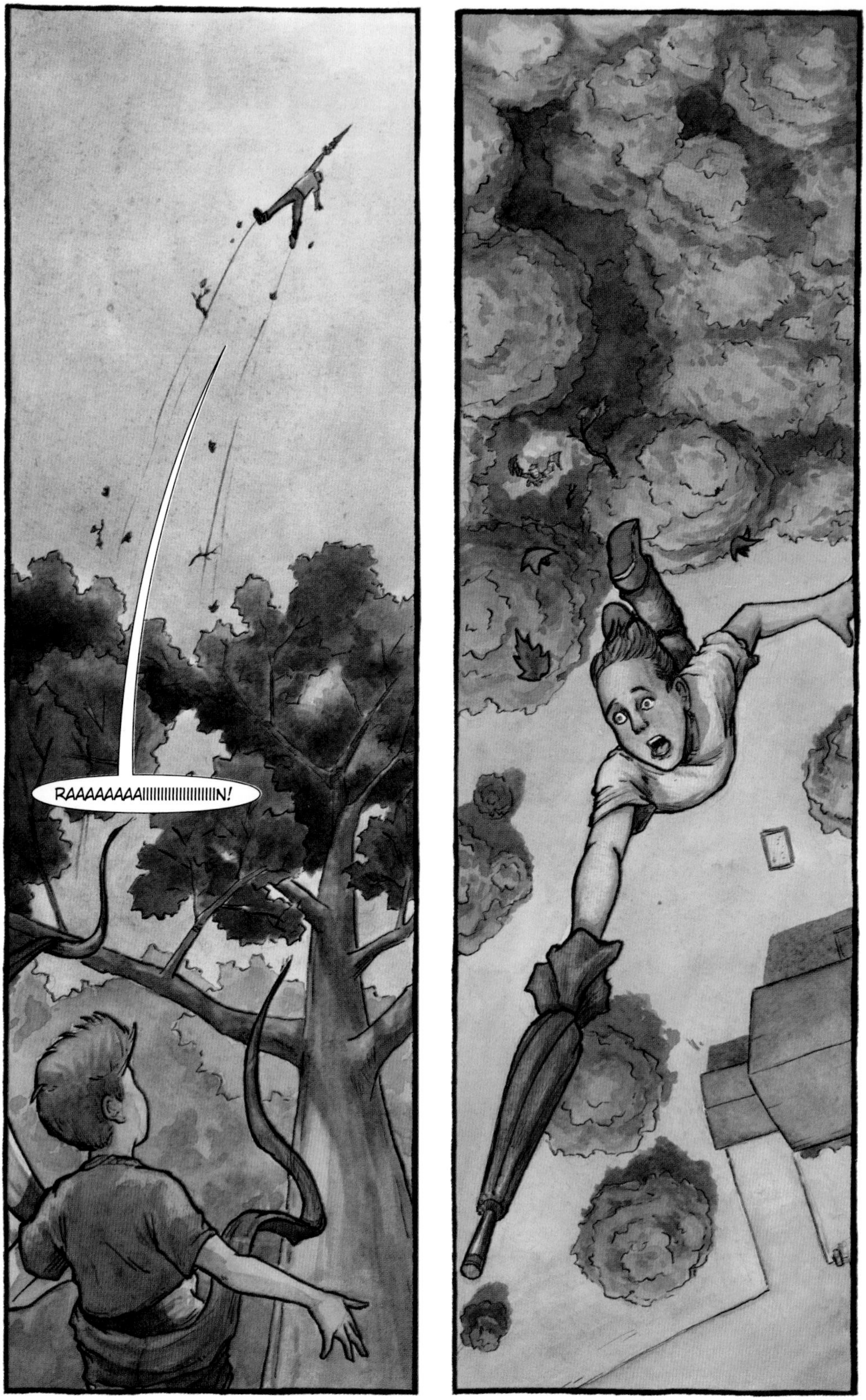
RAAAAAAAAAIIIIIIIIIIIIIIIIIIIIIN!

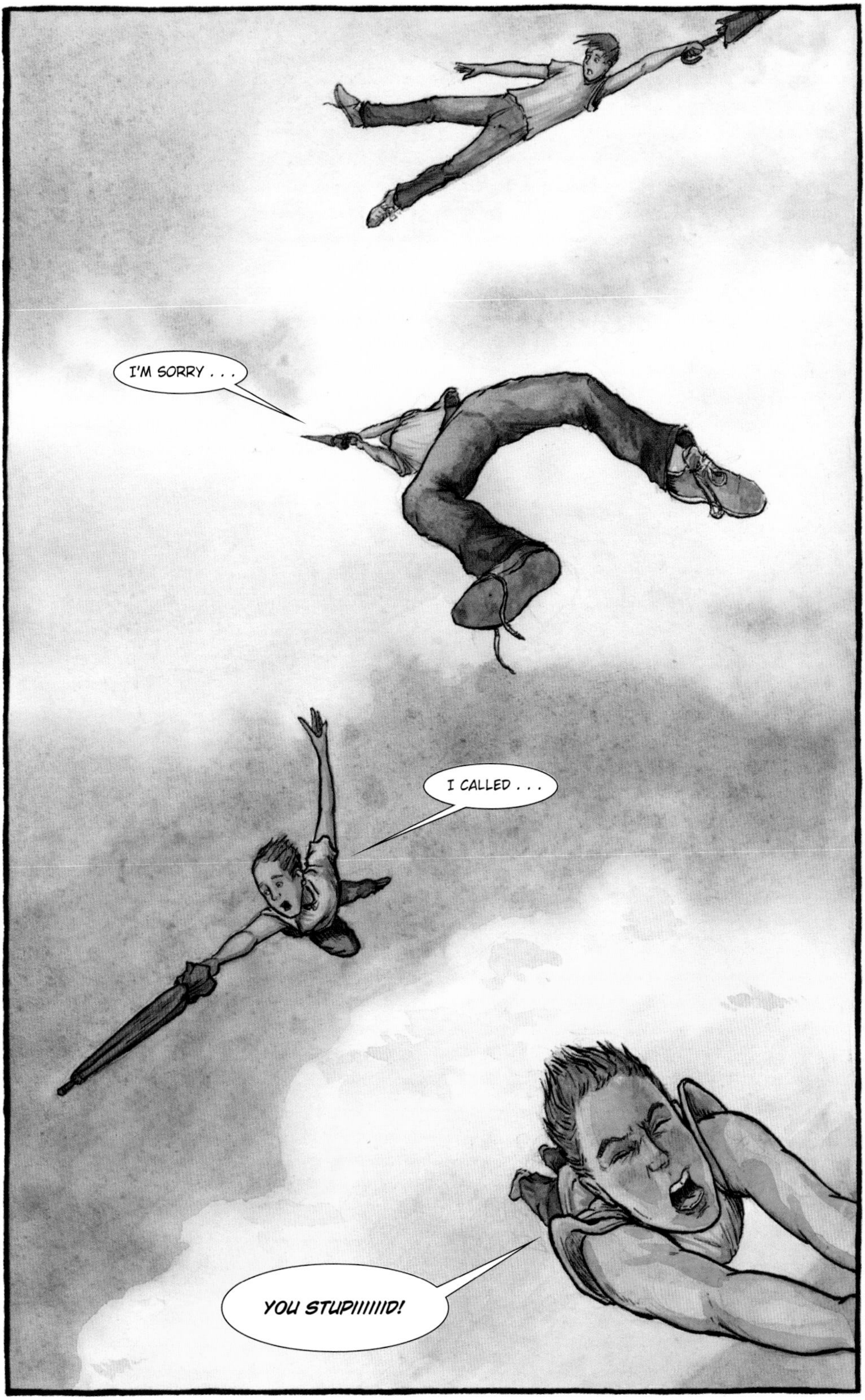
I'M SORRY . . .
I CALLED . . .
YOU STUPIIIIIID!

whup

HUH...HUH...HUH.

THIS IS MY HOME.

TUCKER WAS RIGHT. THIS. IS.

AWESOME!

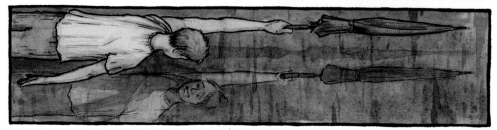

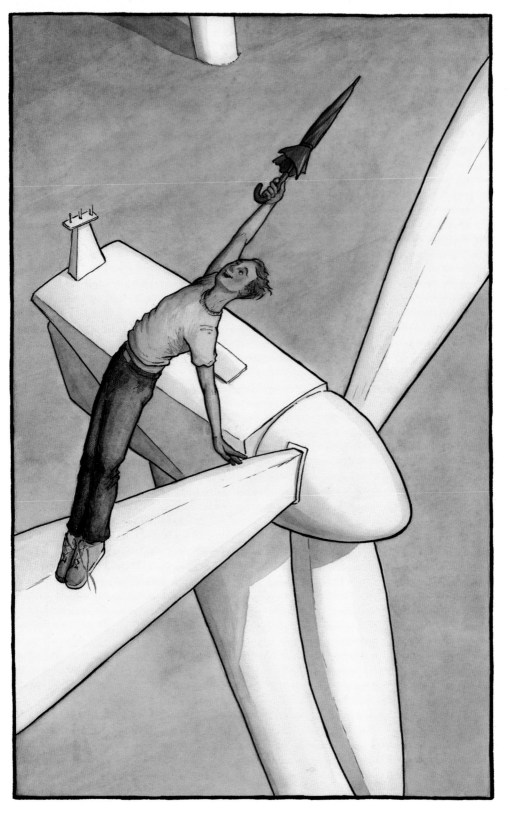

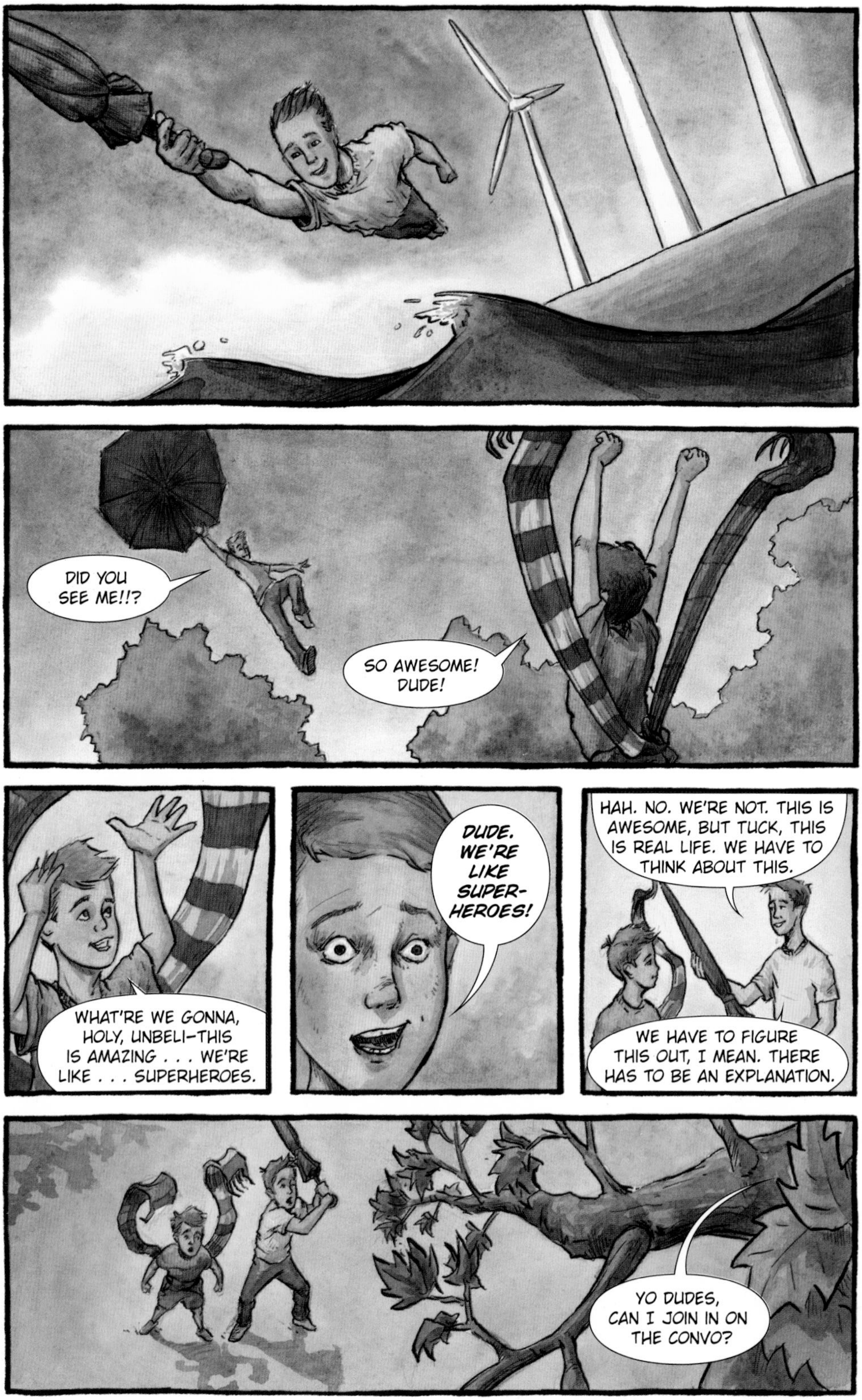
DID YOU SEE ME!!?
SO AWESOME! DUDE!
WHAT'RE WE GONNA, HOLY, UNBELI–THIS IS AMAZING . . . WE'RE LIKE . . . SUPERHEROES.
DUDE. WE'RE LIKE SUPER-HEROES!
HAH. NO. WE'RE NOT. THIS IS AWESOME, BUT TUCK, THIS IS REAL LIFE. WE HAVE TO THINK ABOUT THIS.
WE HAVE TO FIGURE THIS OUT, I MEAN. THERE HAS TO BE AN EXPLANATION.
YO DUDES, CAN I JOIN IN ON THE CONVO?

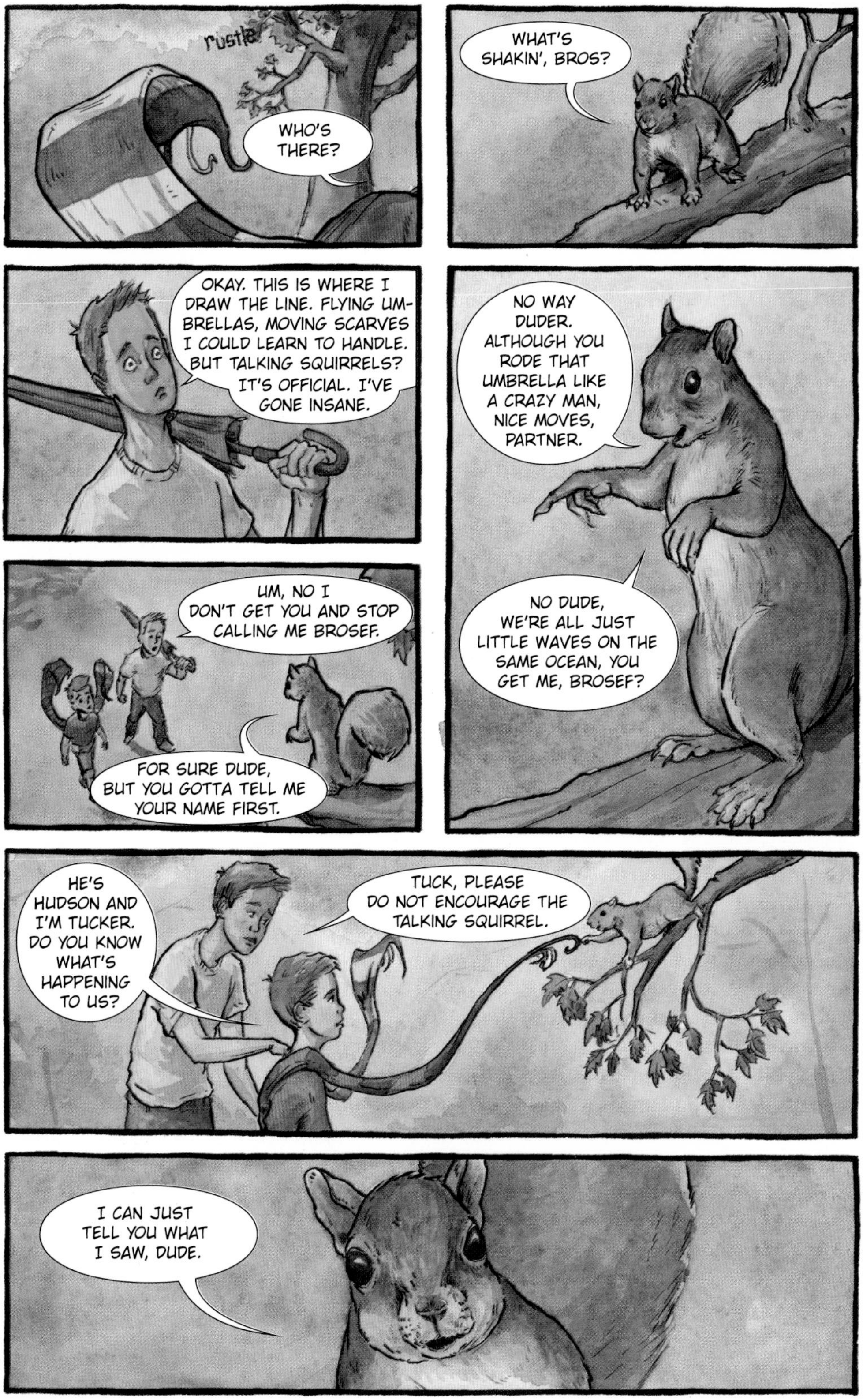
rustle
WHO'S THERE?
WHAT'S SHAKIN', BROS?
OKAY. THIS IS WHERE I DRAW THE LINE. FLYING UMBRELLAS, MOVING SCARVES I COULD LEARN TO HANDLE. BUT TALKING SQUIRRELS?
IT'S OFFICIAL. I'VE GONE INSANE.
NO WAY DUDER. ALTHOUGH YOU RODE THAT UMBRELLA LIKE A CRAZY MAN, NICE MOVES, PARTNER.
NO DUDE, WE'RE ALL JUST LITTLE WAVES ON THE SAME OCEAN, YOU GET ME, BROSEF?
UM, NO I DON'T GET YOU AND STOP CALLING ME BROSEF.
FOR SURE DUDE, BUT YOU GOTTA TELL ME YOUR NAME FIRST.
HE'S HUDSON AND I'M TUCKER. DO YOU KNOW WHAT'S HAPPENING TO US?
TUCK, PLEASE DO NOT ENCOURAGE THE TALKING SQUIRREL.
I CAN JUST TELL YOU WHAT I SAW, DUDE.

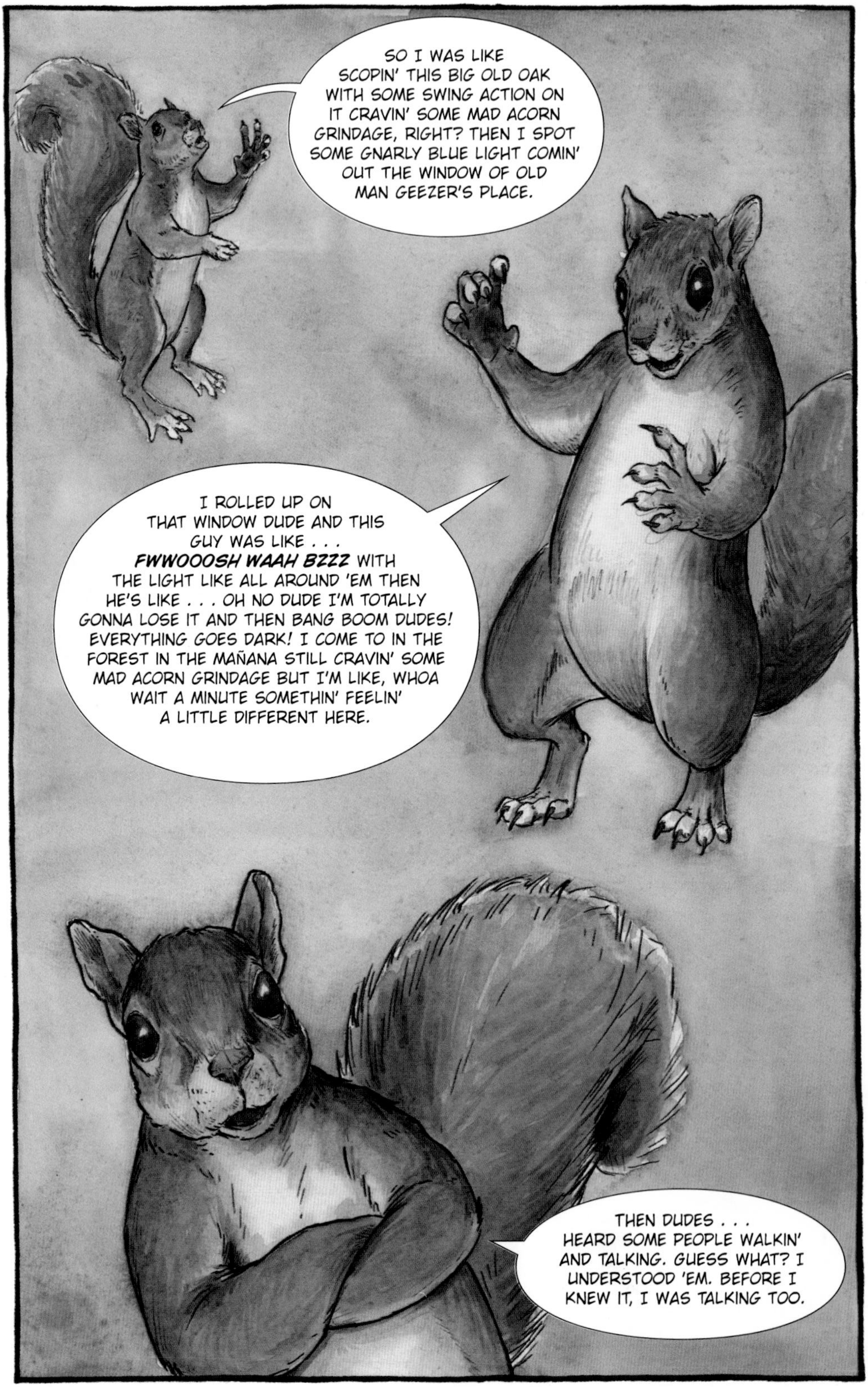
SO I WAS LIKE SCOPIN' THIS BIG OLD OAK WITH SOME SWING ACTION ON IT CRAVIN' SOME MAD ACORN GRINDAGE, RIGHT? THEN I SPOT SOME GNARLY BLUE LIGHT COMIN' OUT THE WINDOW OF OLD MAN GEEZER'S PLACE.
I ROLLED UP ON THAT WINDOW DUDE AND THIS GUY WAS LIKE . . . ***FWWOOOSH WAAH BZZZ*** WITH THE LIGHT LIKE ALL AROUND 'EM THEN HE'S LIKE . . . OH NO DUDE I'M TOTALLY GONNA LOSE IT AND THEN BANG BOOM DUDES! EVERYTHING GOES DARK! I COME TO IN THE FOREST IN THE MAÑANA STILL CRAVIN' SOME MAD ACORN GRINDAGE BUT I'M LIKE, WHOA WAIT A MINUTE SOMETHIN' FEELIN' A LITTLE DIFFERENT HERE.
THEN DUDES . . . HEARD SOME PEOPLE WALKIN' AND TALKING. GUESS WHAT? I UNDERSTOOD 'EM. BEFORE I KNEW IT, I WAS TALKING TOO.

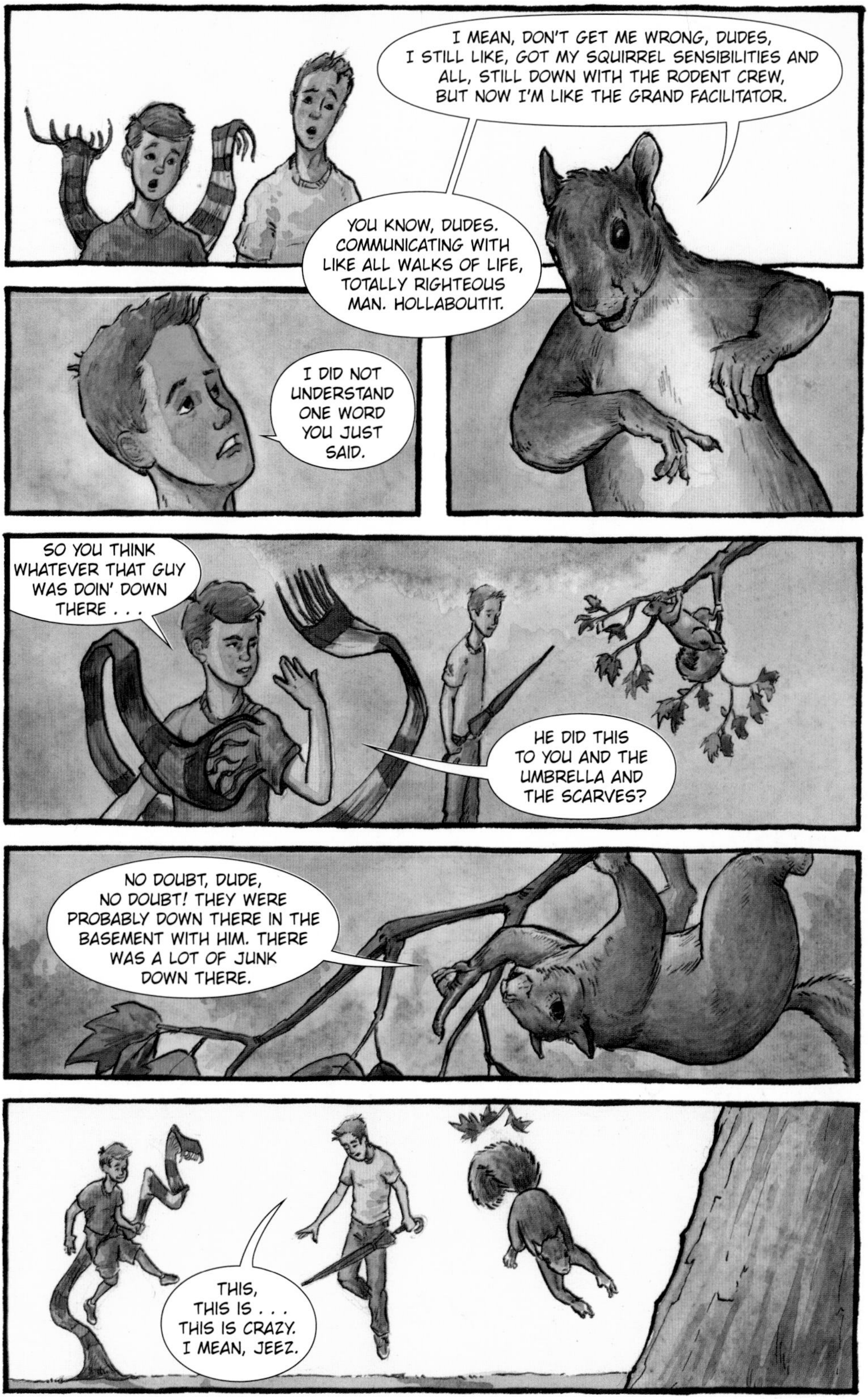
I MEAN, DON'T GET ME WRONG, DUDES, I STILL LIKE, GOT MY SQUIRREL SENSIBILITIES AND ALL, STILL DOWN WITH THE RODENT CREW, BUT NOW I'M LIKE THE GRAND FACILITATOR.
YOU KNOW, DUDES. COMMUNICATING WITH LIKE ALL WALKS OF LIFE, TOTALLY RIGHTEOUS MAN. HOLLABOUTIT.
I DID NOT UNDERSTAND ONE WORD YOU JUST SAID.
SO YOU THINK WHATEVER THAT GUY WAS DOIN' DOWN THERE . . .
HE DID THIS TO YOU AND THE UMBRELLA AND THE SCARVES?
NO DOUBT, DUDE, NO DOUBT! THEY WERE PROBABLY DOWN THERE IN THE BASEMENT WITH HIM. THERE WAS A LOT OF JUNK DOWN THERE.
THIS, THIS IS . . . THIS IS CRAZY. I MEAN, JEEZ.

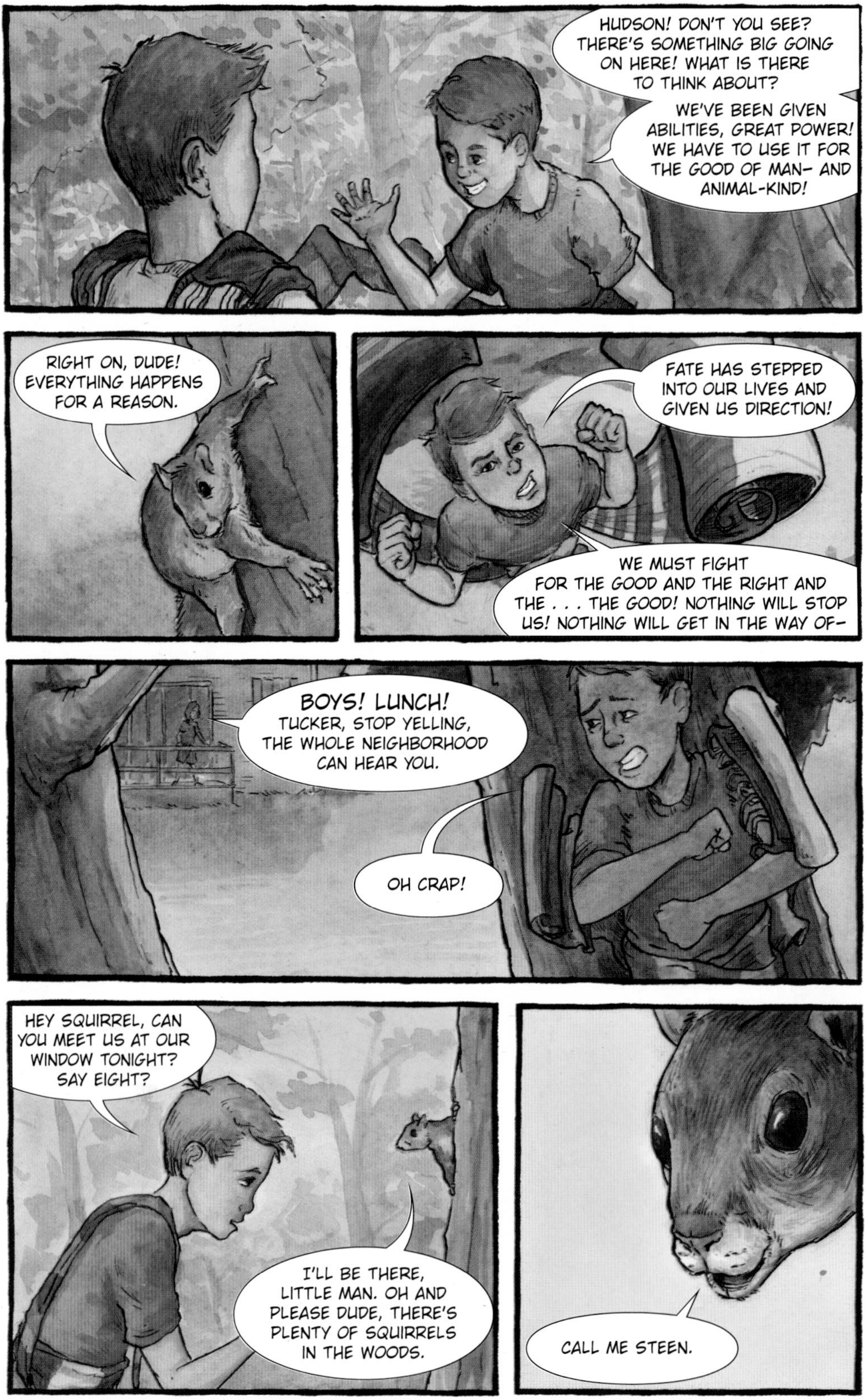
HUDSON! DON'T YOU SEE? THERE'S SOMETHING BIG GOING ON HERE! WHAT IS THERE TO THINK ABOUT?
WE'VE BEEN GIVEN ABILITIES, GREAT POWER! WE HAVE TO USE IT FOR THE GOOD OF MAN– AND ANIMAL-KIND!
RIGHT ON, DUDE! EVERYTHING HAPPENS FOR A REASON.
FATE HAS STEPPED INTO OUR LIVES AND GIVEN US DIRECTION!
WE MUST FIGHT FOR THE GOOD AND THE RIGHT AND THE . . . THE GOOD! NOTHING WILL STOP US! NOTHING WILL GET IN THE WAY OF–
BOYS! LUNCH! TUCKER, STOP YELLING, THE WHOLE NEIGHBORHOOD CAN HEAR YOU.
OH CRAP!
HEY SQUIRREL, CAN YOU MEET US AT OUR WINDOW TONIGHT? SAY EIGHT?
I'LL BE THERE, LITTLE MAN. OH AND PLEASE DUDE, THERE'S PLENTY OF SQUIRRELS IN THE WOODS.
CALL ME STEEN.

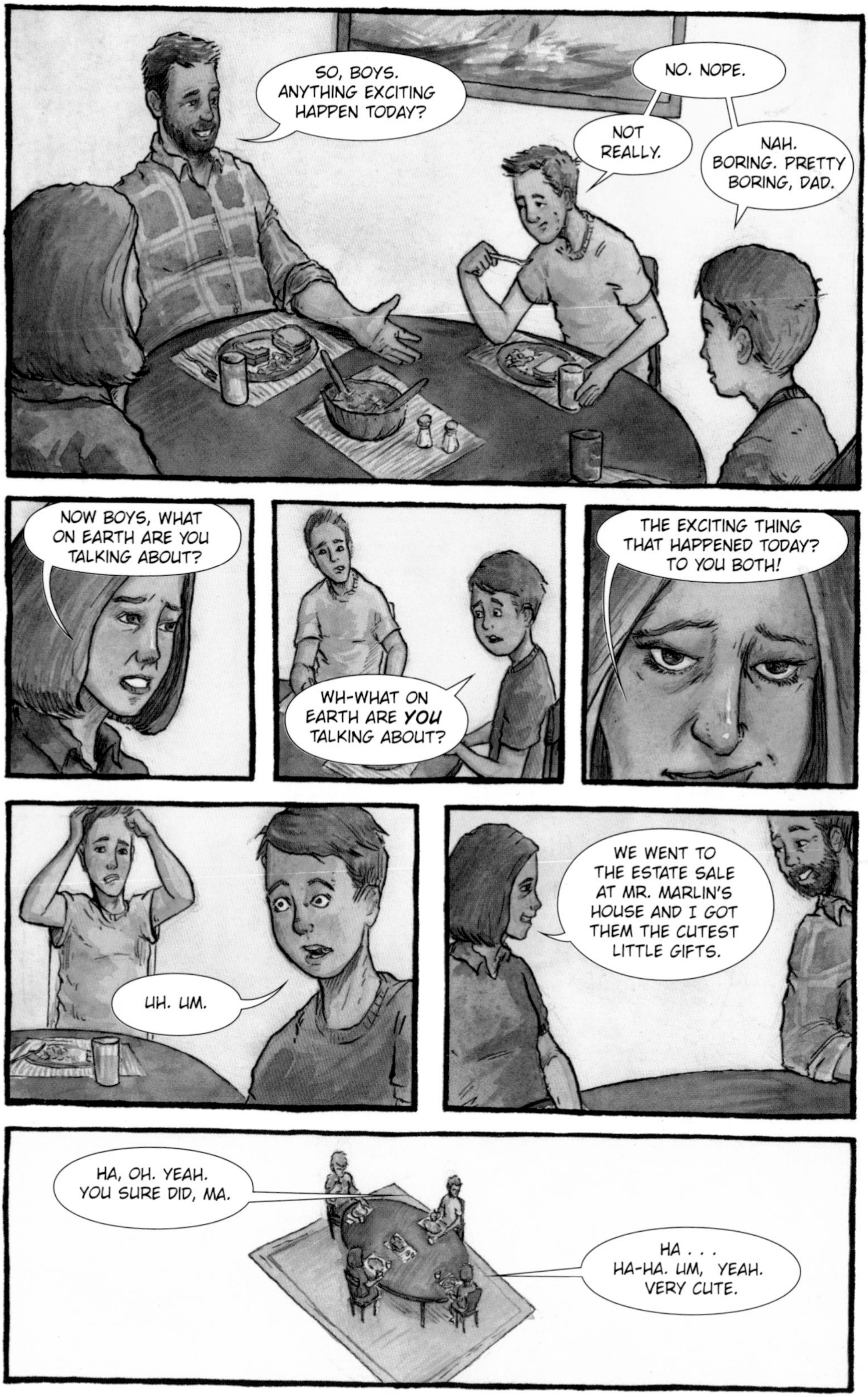
SO, BOYS. ANYTHING EXCITING HAPPEN TODAY?
NO. NOPE.
NOT REALLY.
NAH. BORING. PRETTY BORING, DAD.
NOW BOYS, WHAT ON EARTH ARE YOU TALKING ABOUT?
WH-WHAT ON EARTH ARE *YOU* TALKING ABOUT?
THE EXCITING THING THAT HAPPENED TODAY? TO YOU BOTH!
UH. UM.
WE WENT TO THE ESTATE SALE AT MR. MARLIN'S HOUSE AND I GOT THEM THE CUTEST LITTLE GIFTS.
HA, OH. YEAH. YOU SURE DID, MA.
HA . . . HA-HA. UM, YEAH. VERY CUTE.

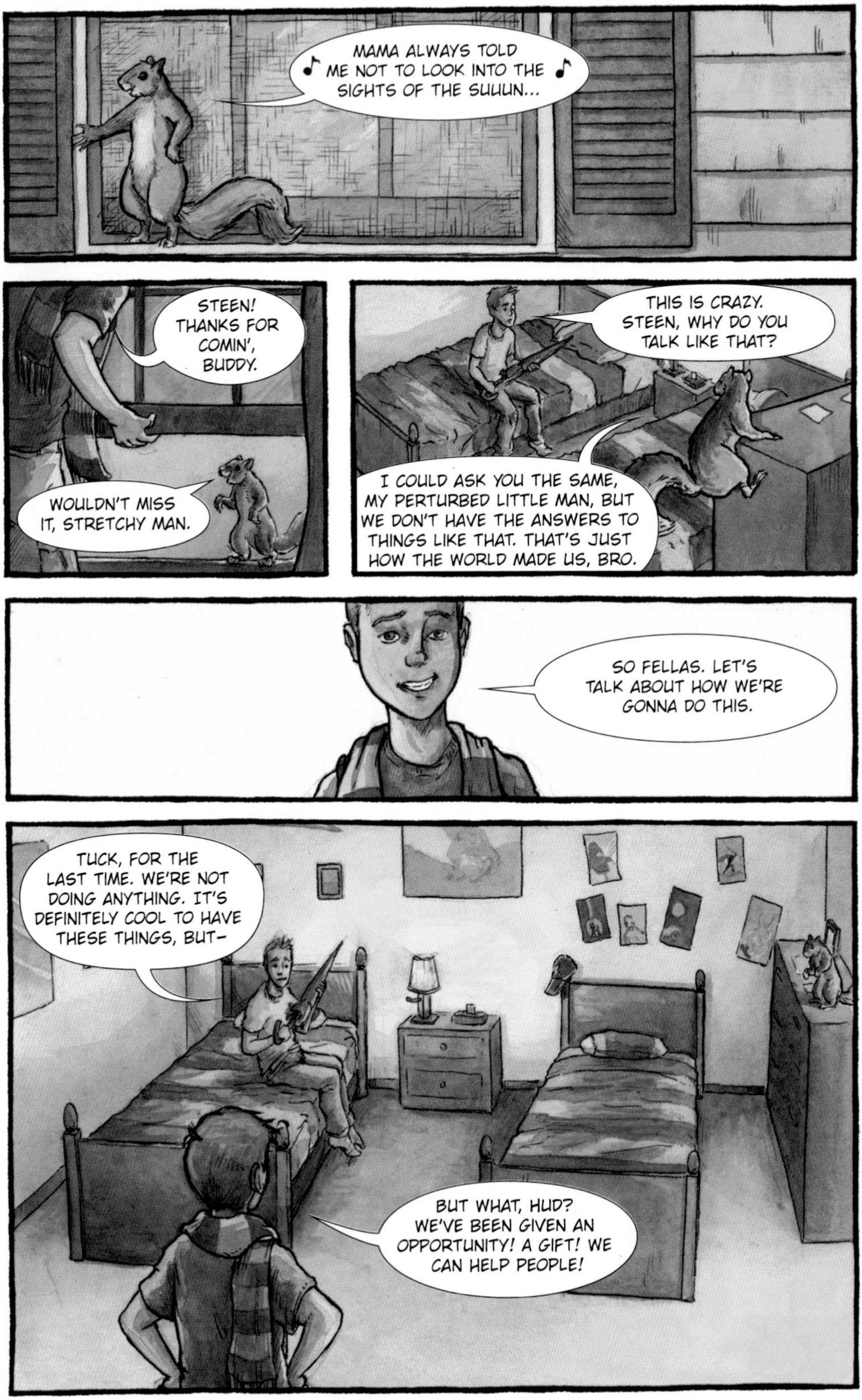
♪ MAMA ALWAYS TOLD ME NOT TO LOOK INTO THE SIGHTS OF THE SUUUN... ♪
STEEN! THANKS FOR COMIN', BUDDY.
WOULDN'T MISS IT, STRETCHY MAN.
THIS IS CRAZY. STEEN, WHY DO YOU TALK LIKE THAT?
I COULD ASK YOU THE SAME, MY PERTURBED LITTLE MAN, BUT WE DON'T HAVE THE ANSWERS TO THINGS LIKE THAT. THAT'S JUST HOW THE WORLD MADE US, BRO.
SO FELLAS. LET'S TALK ABOUT HOW WE'RE GONNA DO THIS.
TUCK, FOR THE LAST TIME. WE'RE NOT DOING ANYTHING. IT'S DEFINITELY COOL TO HAVE THESE THINGS, BUT-
BUT WHAT, HUD? WE'VE BEEN GIVEN AN OPPORTUNITY! A GIFT! WE CAN HELP PEOPLE!

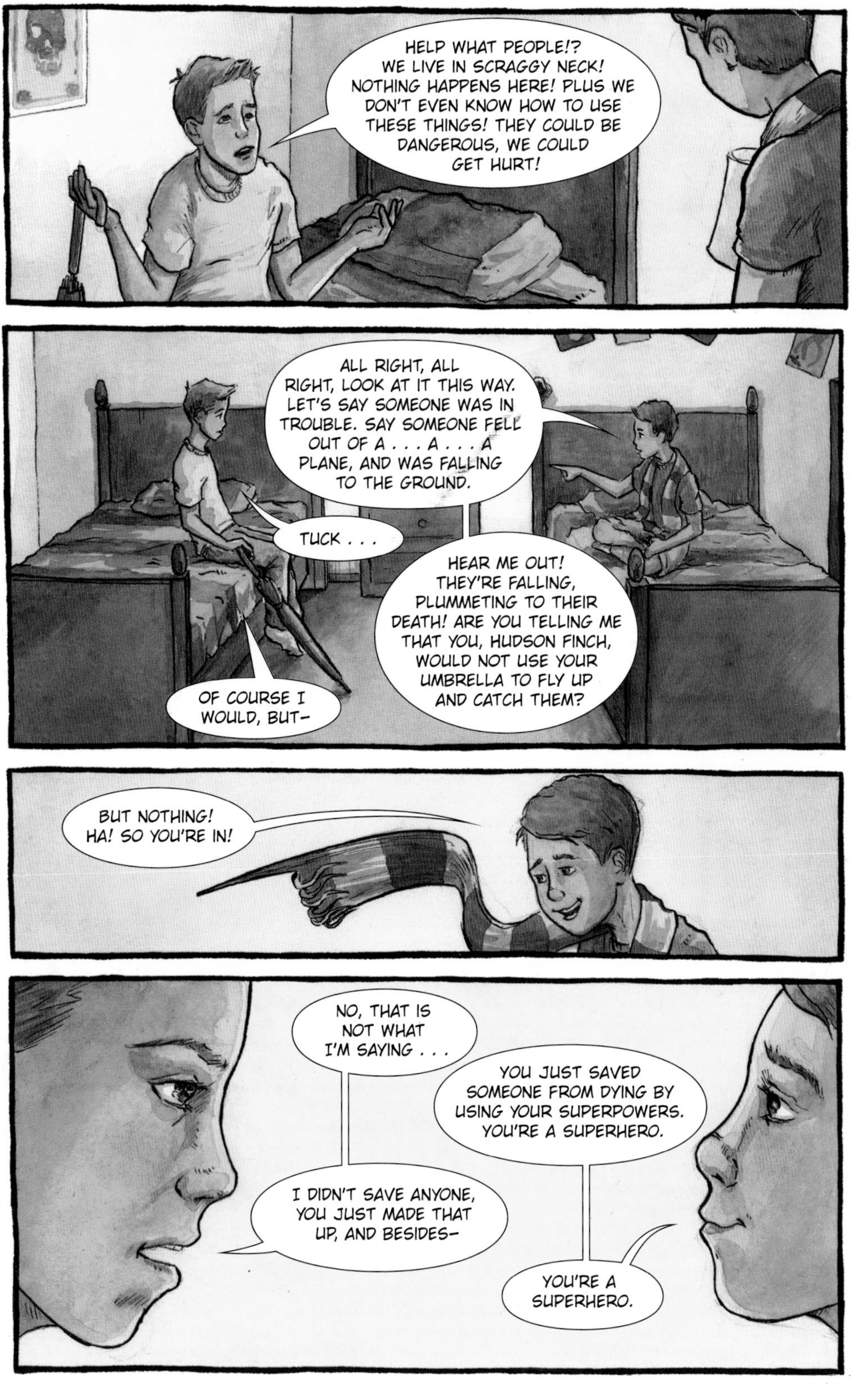
HELP WHAT PEOPLE!? WE LIVE IN SCRAGGY NECK! NOTHING HAPPENS HERE! PLUS WE DON'T EVEN KNOW HOW TO USE THESE THINGS! THEY COULD BE DANGEROUS, WE COULD GET HURT!
ALL RIGHT, ALL RIGHT, LOOK AT IT THIS WAY. LET'S SAY SOMEONE WAS IN TROUBLE. SAY SOMEONE FELL OUT OF A . . . A . . . A PLANE, AND WAS FALLING TO THE GROUND.
TUCK . . .
HEAR ME OUT! THEY'RE FALLING, PLUMMETING TO THEIR DEATH! ARE YOU TELLING ME THAT YOU, HUDSON FINCH, WOULD NOT USE YOUR UMBRELLA TO FLY UP AND CATCH THEM?
OF COURSE I WOULD, BUT–
BUT NOTHING! HA! SO YOU'RE IN!
NO, THAT IS NOT WHAT I'M SAYING . . .
YOU JUST SAVED SOMEONE FROM DYING BY USING YOUR SUPERPOWERS. YOU'RE A SUPERHERO.
I DIDN'T SAVE ANYONE, YOU JUST MADE THAT UP, AND BESIDES–
YOU'RE A SUPERHERO.

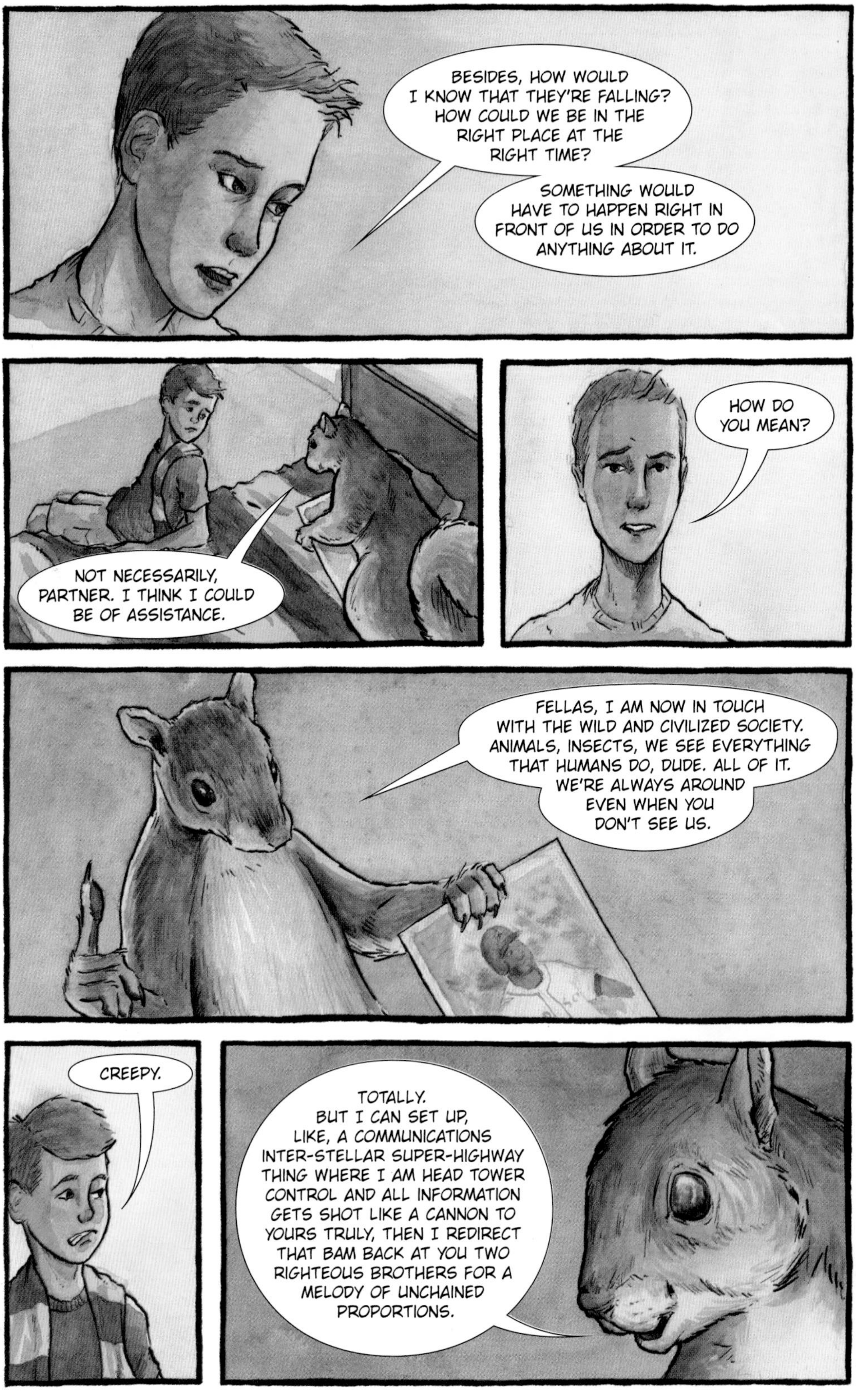
BESIDES, HOW WOULD I KNOW THAT THEY'RE FALLING? HOW COULD WE BE IN THE RIGHT PLACE AT THE RIGHT TIME?
SOMETHING WOULD HAVE TO HAPPEN RIGHT IN FRONT OF US IN ORDER TO DO ANYTHING ABOUT IT.
NOT NECESSARILY, PARTNER. I THINK I COULD BE OF ASSISTANCE.
HOW DO YOU MEAN?
FELLAS, I AM NOW IN TOUCH WITH THE WILD AND CIVILIZED SOCIETY. ANIMALS, INSECTS, WE SEE EVERYTHING THAT HUMANS DO, DUDE. ALL OF IT. WE'RE ALWAYS AROUND EVEN WHEN YOU DON'T SEE US.
CREEPY.
TOTALLY. BUT I CAN SET UP, LIKE, A COMMUNICATIONS INTER-STELLAR SUPER-HIGHWAY THING WHERE I AM HEAD TOWER CONTROL AND ALL INFORMATION GETS SHOT LIKE A CANNON TO YOURS TRULY, THEN I REDIRECT THAT BAM BACK AT YOU TWO RIGHTEOUS BROTHERS FOR A MELODY OF UNCHAINED PROPORTIONS.

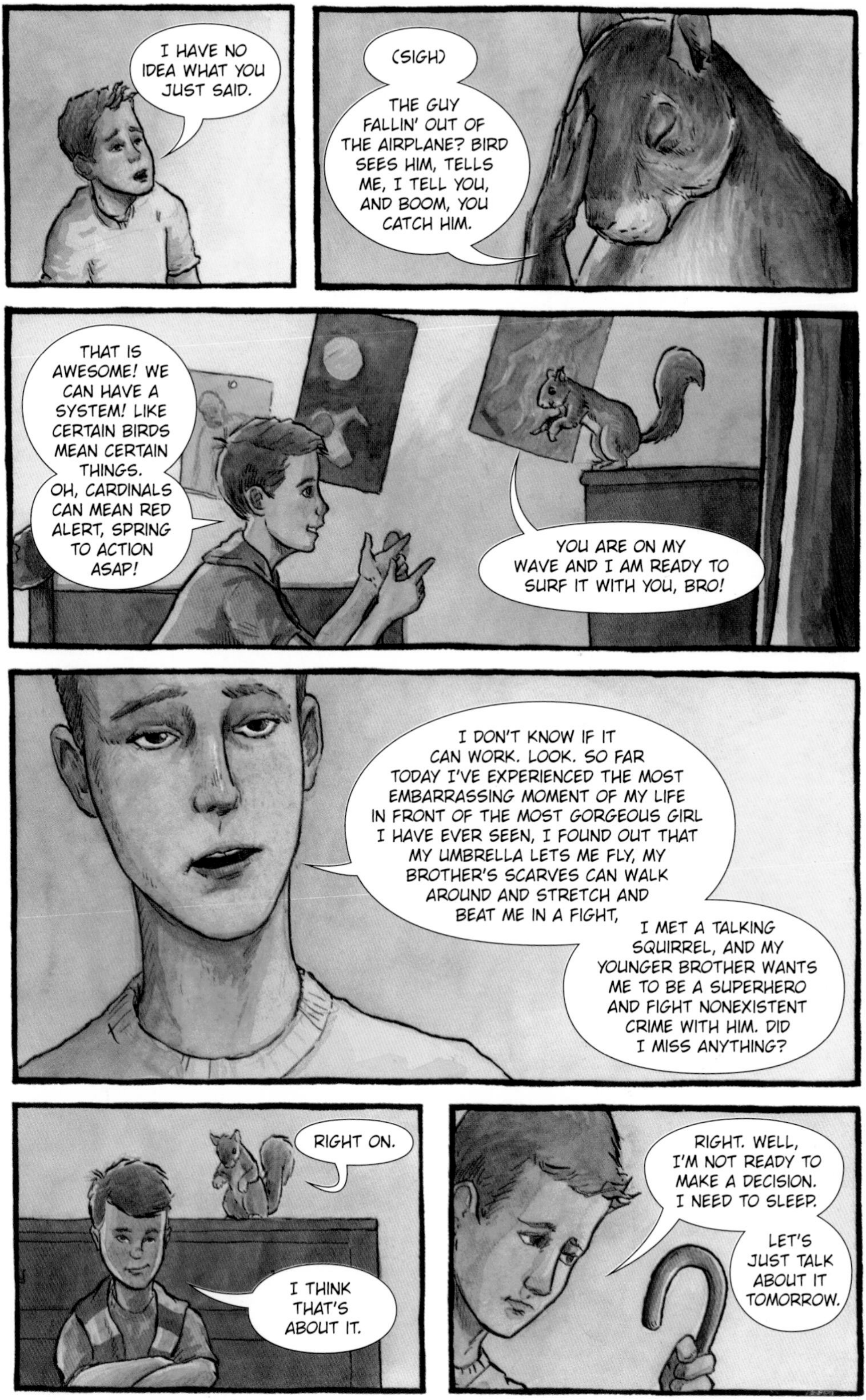
I HAVE NO IDEA WHAT YOU JUST SAID.
(SIGH)
THE GUY FALLIN' OUT OF THE AIRPLANE? BIRD SEES HIM, TELLS ME, I TELL YOU, AND BOOM, YOU CATCH HIM.
THAT IS AWESOME! WE CAN HAVE A SYSTEM! LIKE CERTAIN BIRDS MEAN CERTAIN THINGS. OH, CARDINALS CAN MEAN RED ALERT, SPRING TO ACTION ASAP!
YOU ARE ON MY WAVE AND I AM READY TO SURF IT WITH YOU, BRO!
I DON'T KNOW IF IT CAN WORK. LOOK. SO FAR TODAY I'VE EXPERIENCED THE MOST EMBARRASSING MOMENT OF MY LIFE IN FRONT OF THE MOST GORGEOUS GIRL I HAVE EVER SEEN, I FOUND OUT THAT MY UMBRELLA LETS ME FLY, MY BROTHER'S SCARVES CAN WALK AROUND AND STRETCH AND BEAT ME IN A FIGHT,
I MET A TALKING SQUIRREL, AND MY YOUNGER BROTHER WANTS ME TO BE A SUPERHERO AND FIGHT NONEXISTENT CRIME WITH HIM. DID I MISS ANYTHING?
RIGHT ON.
I THINK THAT'S ABOUT IT.
RIGHT. WELL, I'M NOT READY TO MAKE A DECISION. I NEED TO SLEEP.
LET'S JUST TALK ABOUT IT TOMORROW.

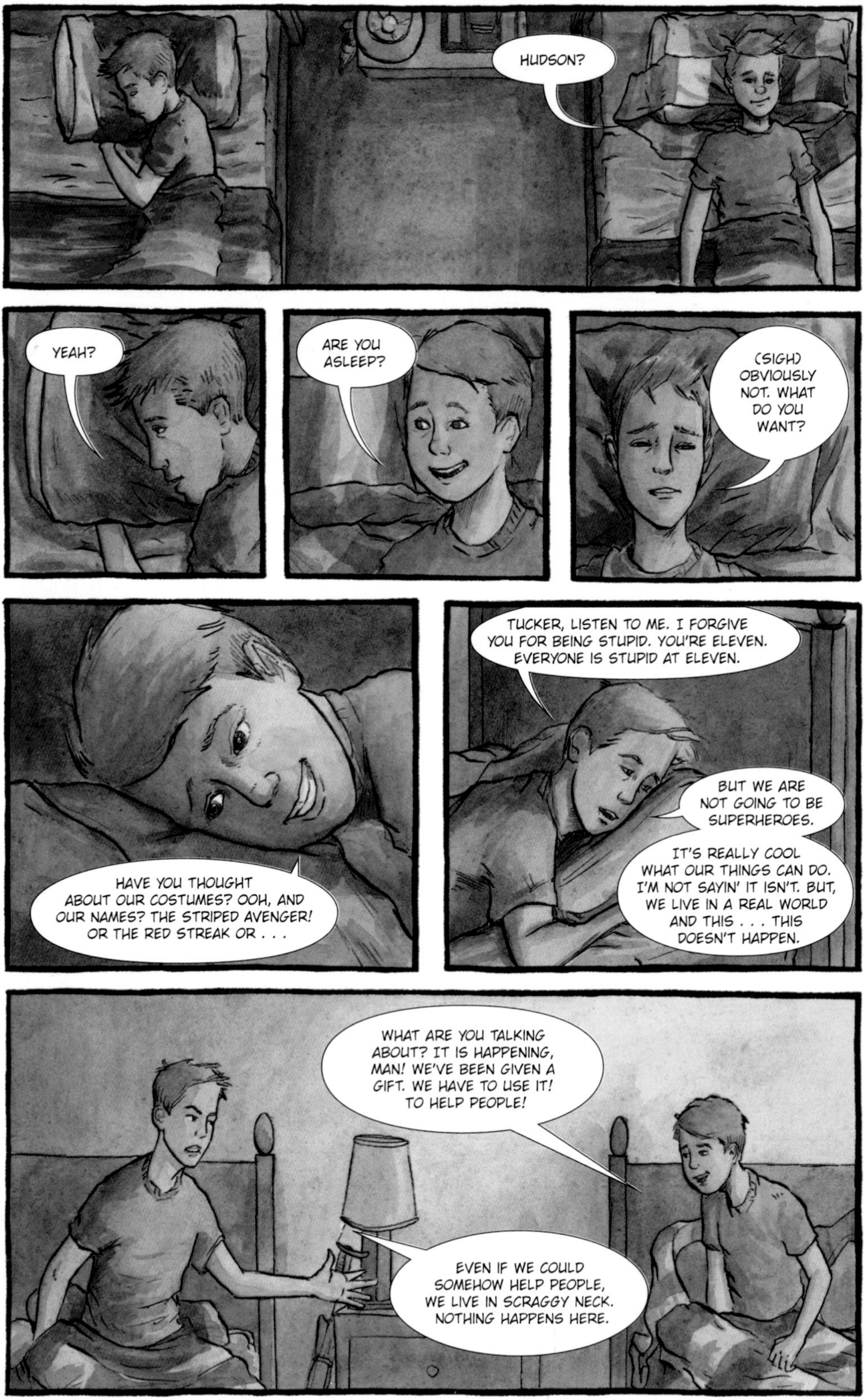
HUDSON?
YEAH?
ARE YOU ASLEEP?
(SIGH) OBVIOUSLY NOT. WHAT DO YOU WANT?
HAVE YOU THOUGHT ABOUT OUR COSTUMES? OOH, AND OUR NAMES? THE STRIPED AVENGER! OR THE RED STREAK OR . . .
TUCKER, LISTEN TO ME. I FORGIVE YOU FOR BEING STUPID. YOU'RE ELEVEN. EVERYONE IS STUPID AT ELEVEN.
BUT WE ARE NOT GOING TO BE SUPERHEROES.
IT'S REALLY COOL WHAT OUR THINGS CAN DO. I'M NOT SAYIN' IT ISN'T. BUT, WE LIVE IN A REAL WORLD AND THIS . . . THIS DOESN'T HAPPEN.
WHAT ARE YOU TALKING ABOUT? IT IS HAPPENING, MAN! WE'VE BEEN GIVEN A GIFT. WE HAVE TO USE IT! TO HELP PEOPLE!
EVEN IF WE COULD SOMEHOW HELP PEOPLE, WE LIVE IN SCRAGGY NECK. NOTHING HAPPENS HERE.

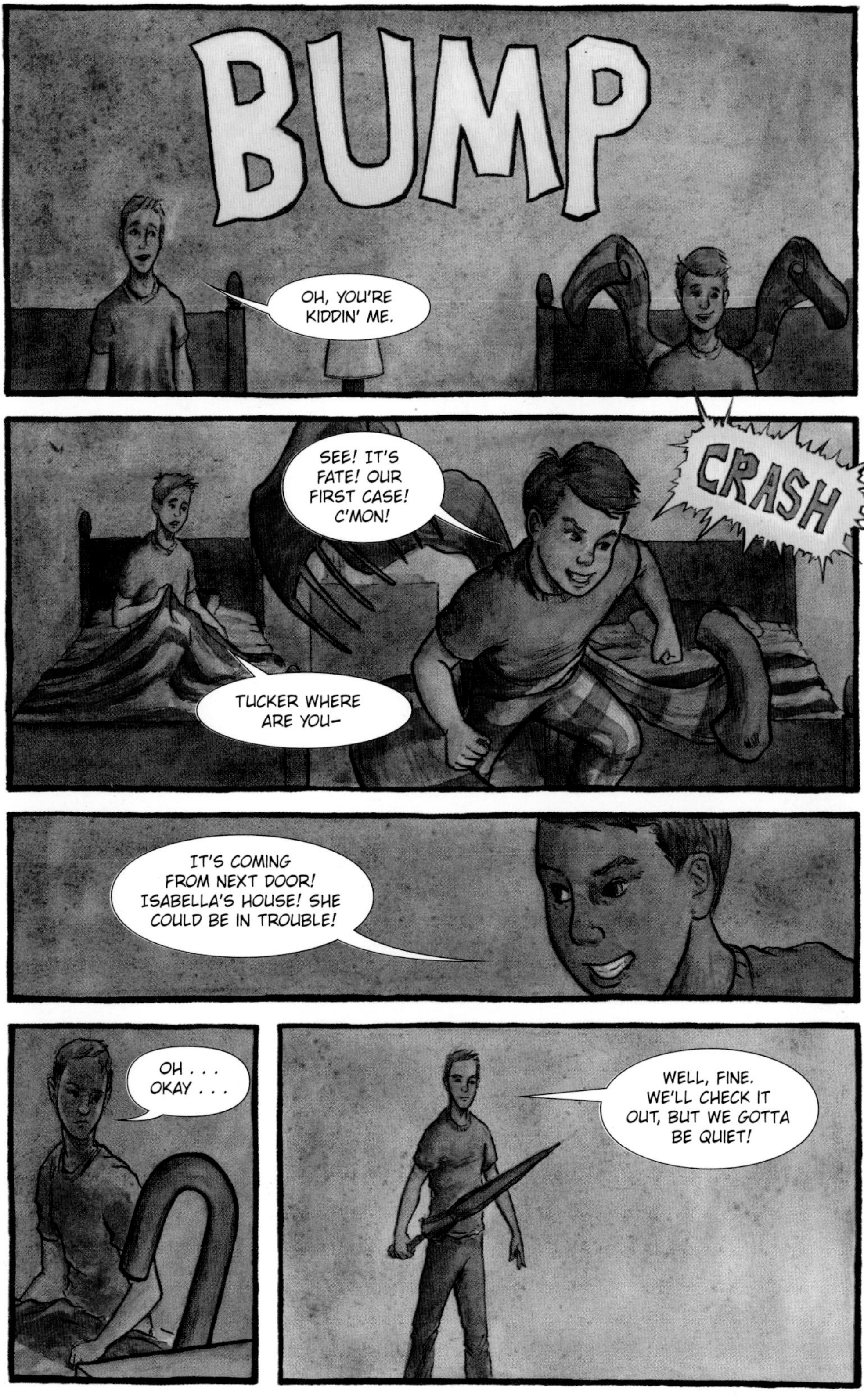
BUMP
OH, YOU'RE KIDDIN' ME.
SEE! IT'S FATE! OUR FIRST CASE! C'MON!
CRASH
TUCKER WHERE ARE YOU-
IT'S COMING FROM NEXT DOOR! ISABELLA'S HOUSE! SHE COULD BE IN TROUBLE!
OH . . . OKAY . . .
WELL, FINE. WE'LL CHECK IT OUT, BUT WE GOTTA BE QUIET!

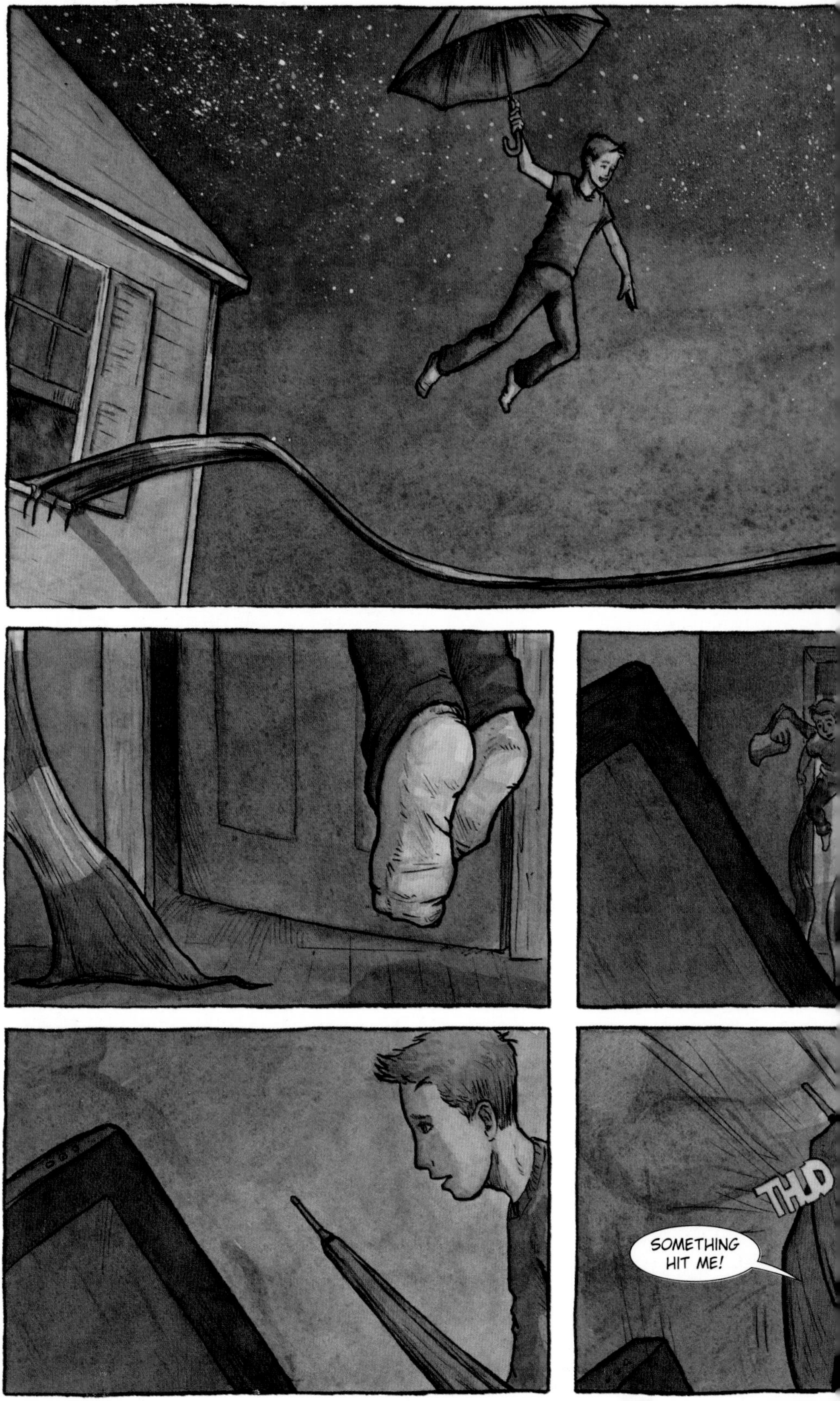
THUD
SOMETHING HIT ME!

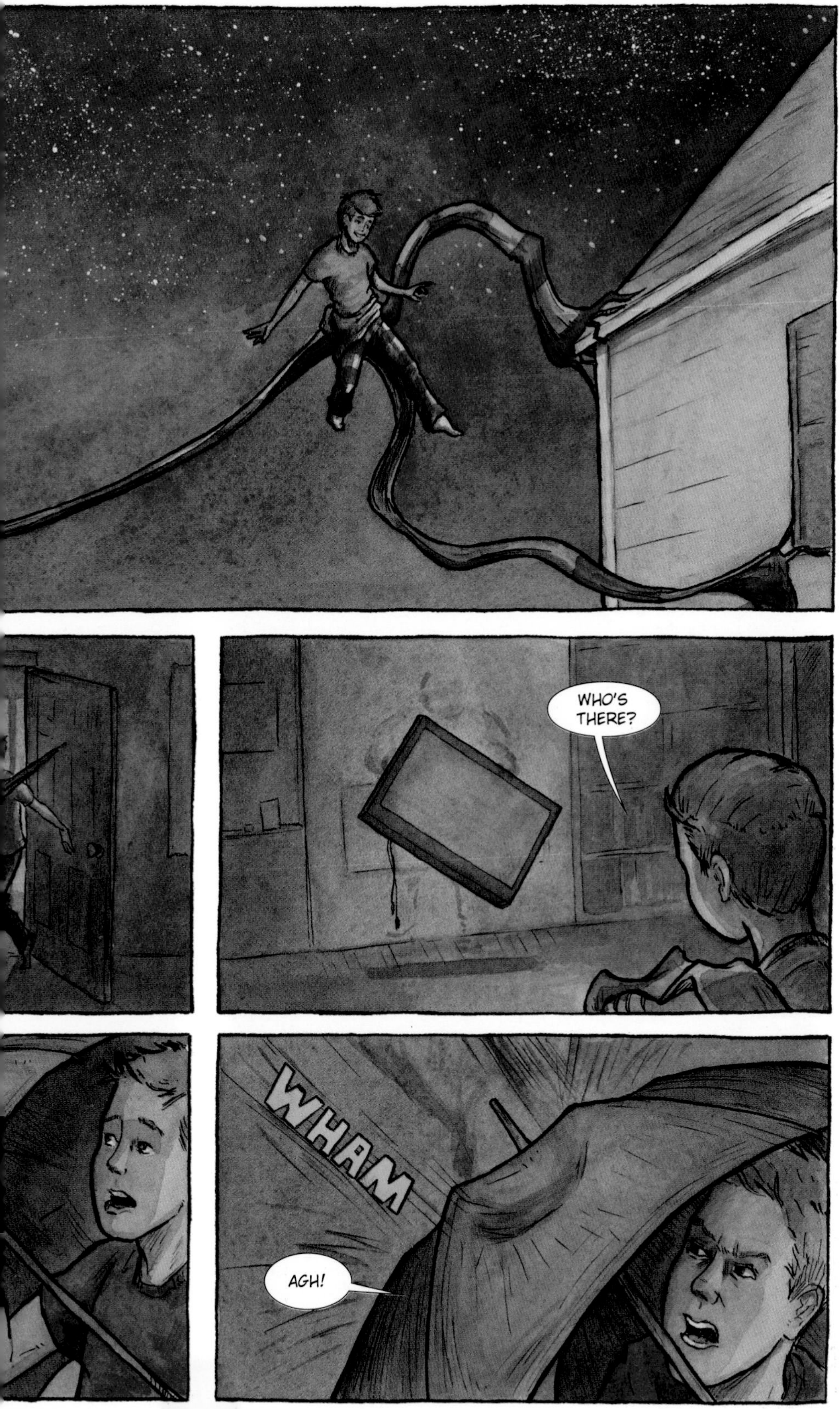
WHO'S THERE?
WHAM
AGH!

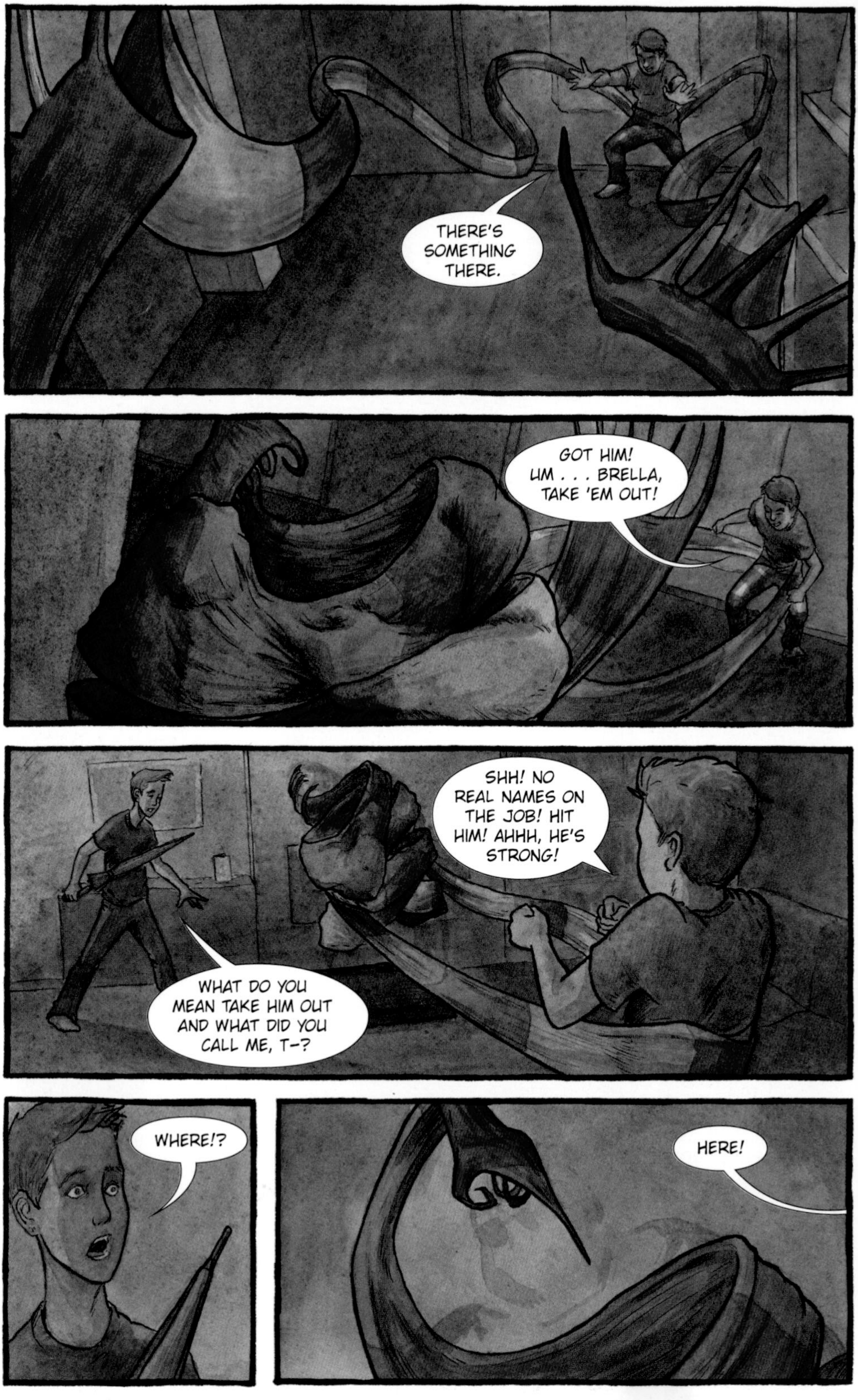
THERE'S SOMETHING THERE.
GOT HIM! UM . . . BRELLA, TAKE 'EM OUT!
SHH! NO REAL NAMES ON THE JOB! HIT HIM! AHHH, HE'S STRONG!
WHAT DO YOU MEAN TAKE HIM OUT AND WHAT DID YOU CALL ME, T–?
WHERE!?
HERE!

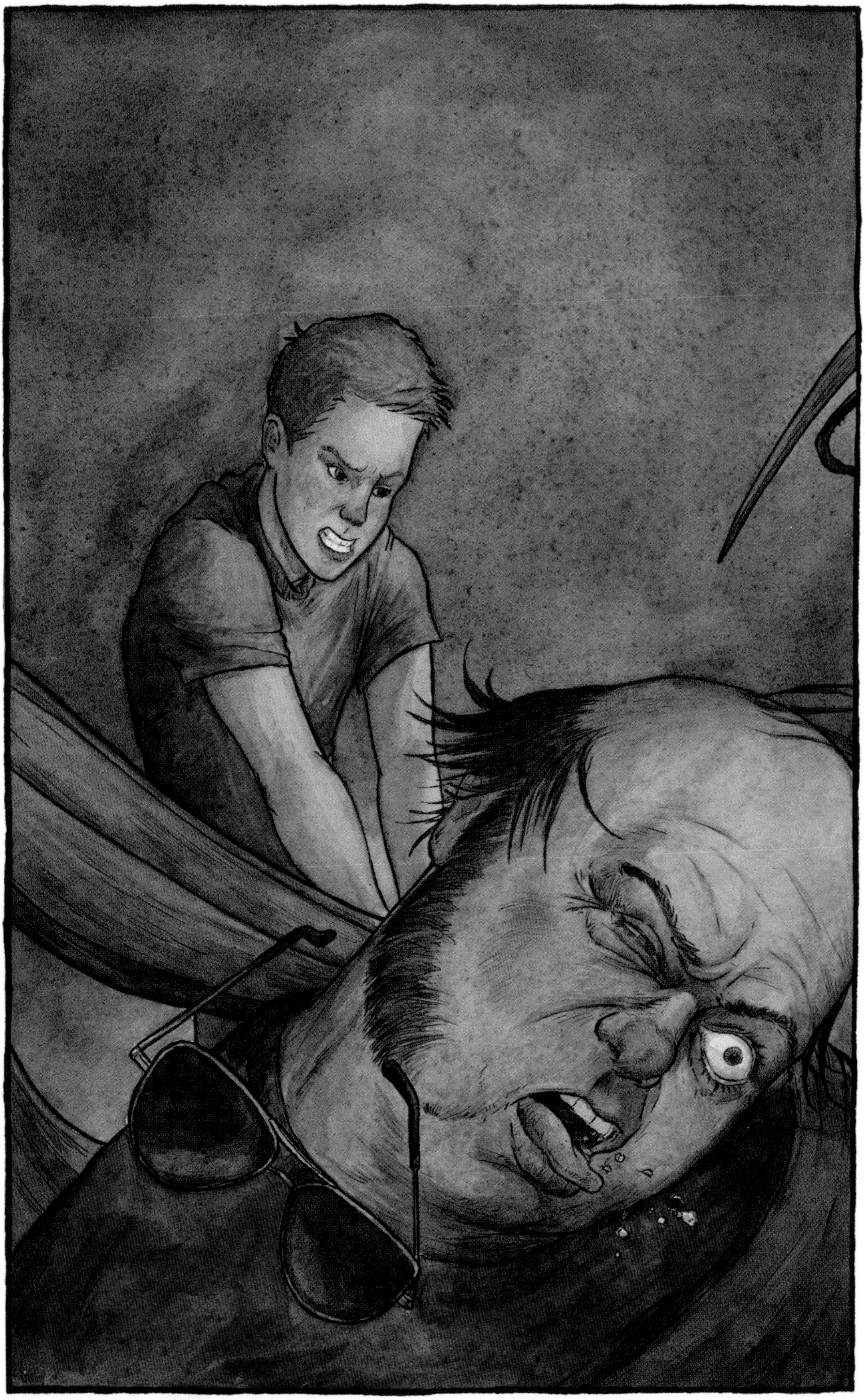

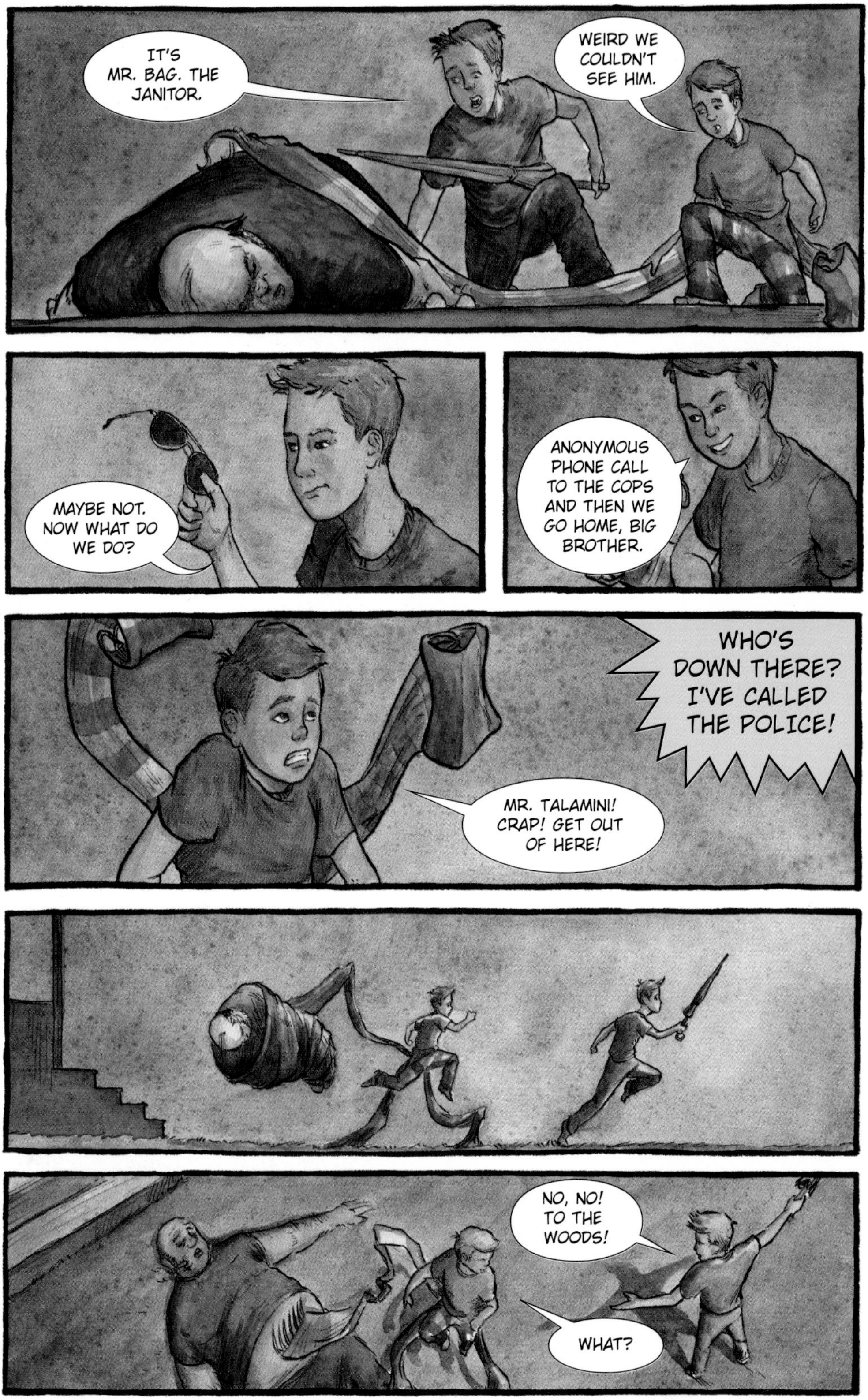
IT'S MR. BAG. THE JANITOR.
WEIRD WE COULDN'T SEE HIM.
MAYBE NOT. NOW WHAT DO WE DO?
ANONYMOUS PHONE CALL TO THE COPS AND THEN WE GO HOME, BIG BROTHER.
WHO'S DOWN THERE? I'VE CALLED THE POLICE!
MR. TALAMINI! CRAP! GET OUT OF HERE!
NO, NO! TO THE WOODS!
WHAT?

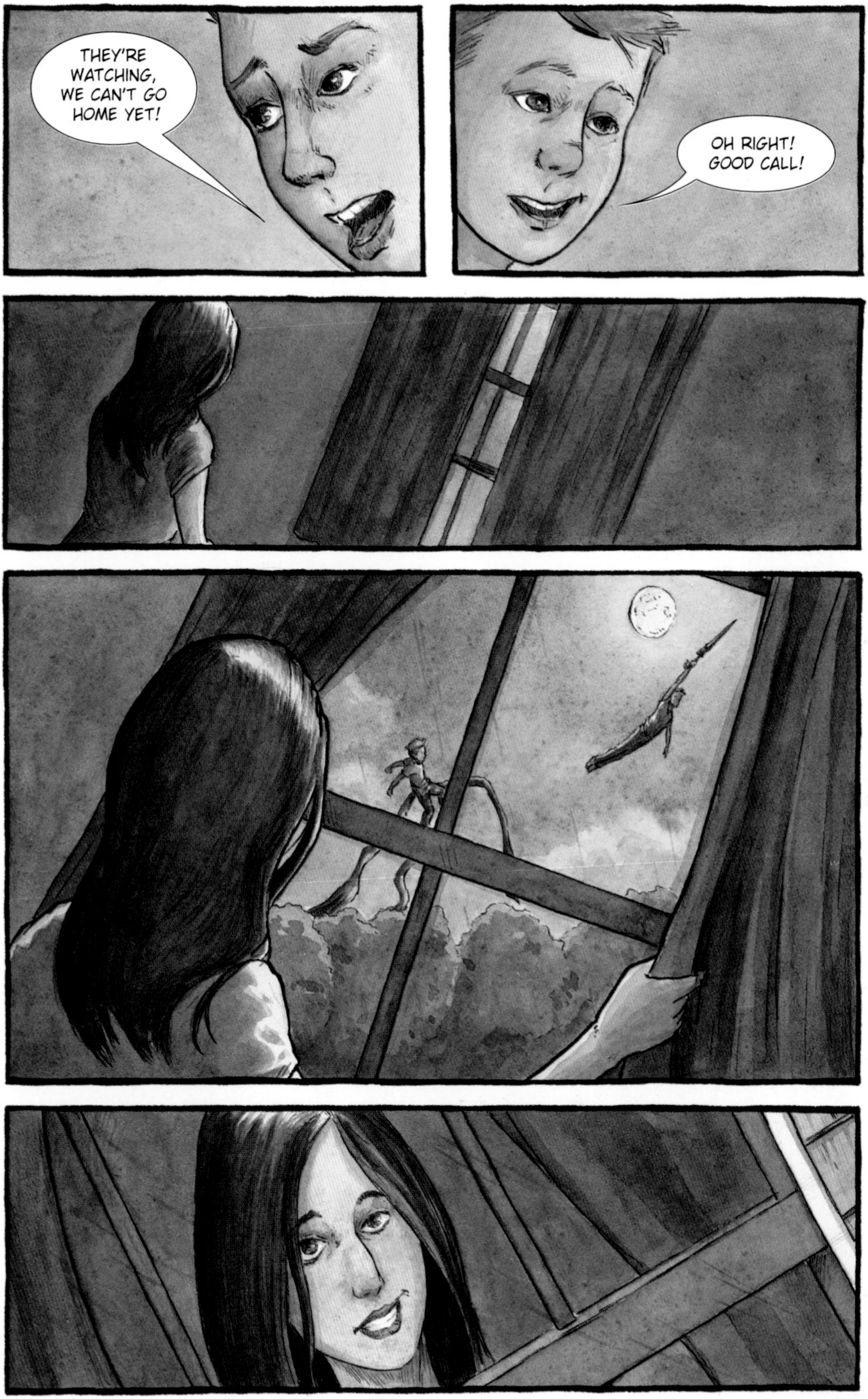
THEY'RE WATCHING, WE CAN'T GO HOME YET!
OH RIGHT! GOOD CALL!

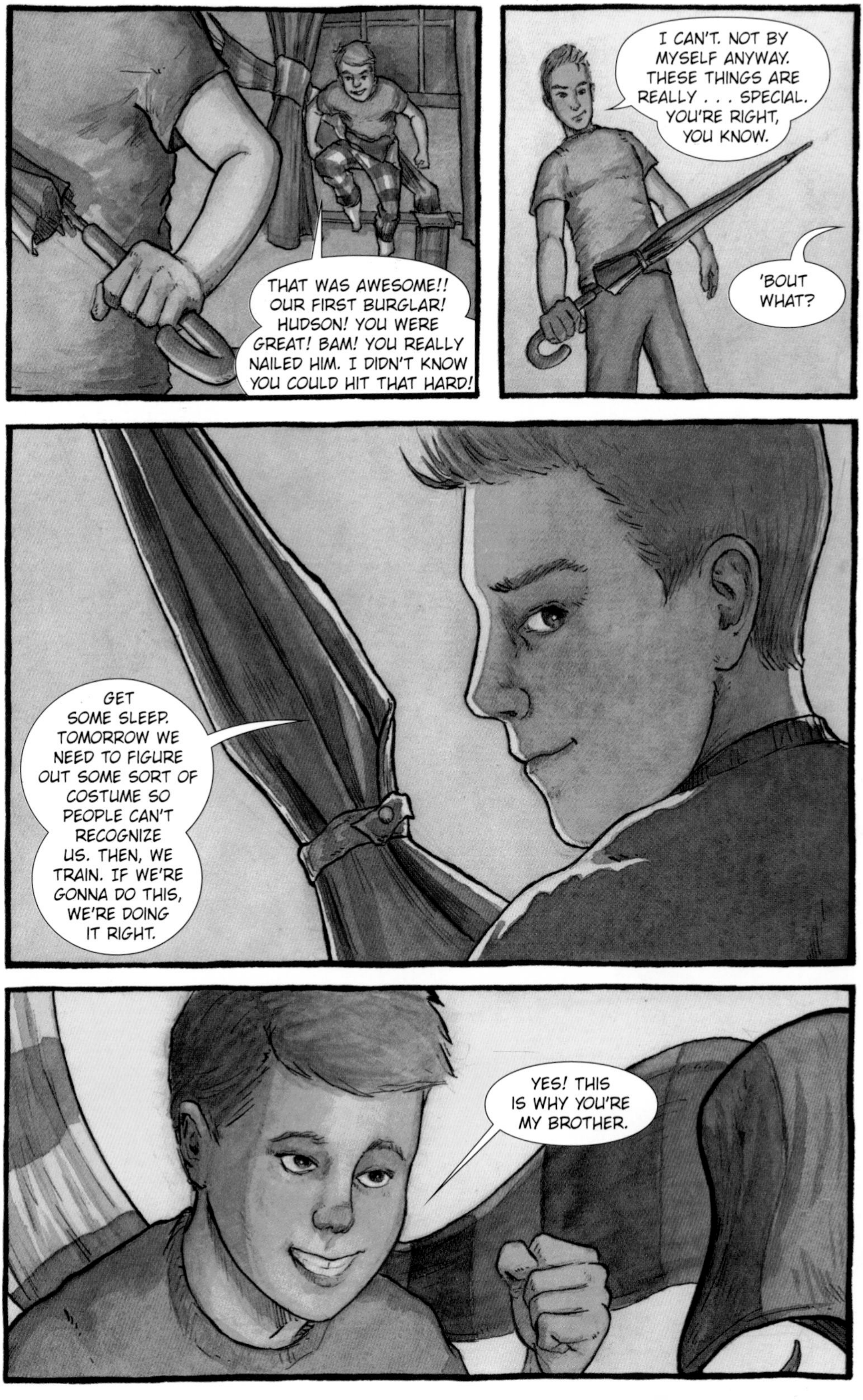
THAT WAS AWESOME!! OUR FIRST BURGLAR! HUDSON! YOU WERE GREAT! BAM! YOU REALLY NAILED HIM. I DIDN'T KNOW YOU COULD HIT THAT HARD!
I CAN'T. NOT BY MYSELF ANYWAY. THESE THINGS ARE REALLY . . . SPECIAL. YOU'RE RIGHT, YOU KNOW.
'BOUT WHAT?
GET SOME SLEEP. TOMORROW WE NEED TO FIGURE OUT SOME SORT OF COSTUME SO PEOPLE CAN'T RECOGNIZE US. THEN, WE TRAIN. IF WE'RE GONNA DO THIS, WE'RE DOING IT RIGHT.
YES! THIS IS WHY YOU'RE MY BROTHER.

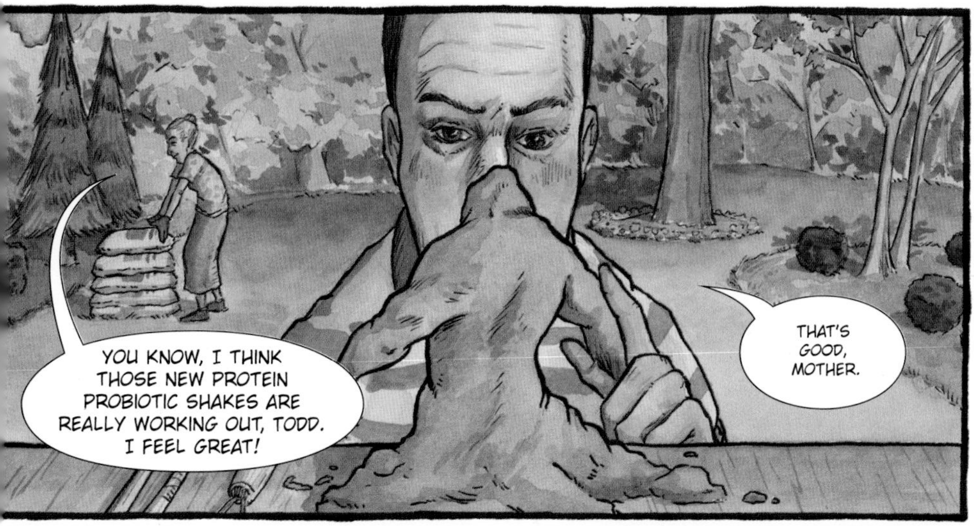
YOU KNOW, I THINK THOSE NEW PROTEIN PROBIOTIC SHAKES ARE REALLY WORKING OUT, TODD. I FEEL GREAT!
THAT'S GOOD, MOTHER.

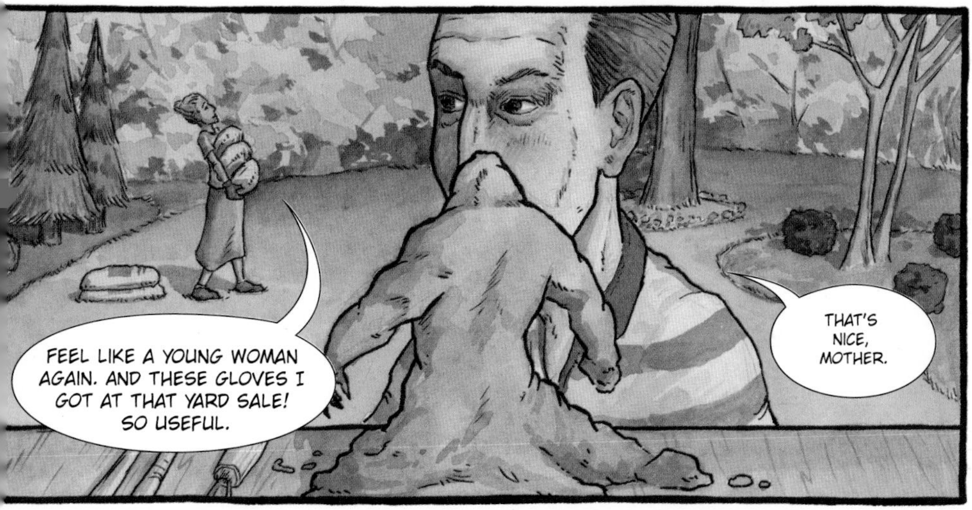
FEEL LIKE A YOUNG WOMAN AGAIN. AND THESE GLOVES I GOT AT THAT YARD SALE! SO USEFUL.
THAT'S NICE, MOTHER.

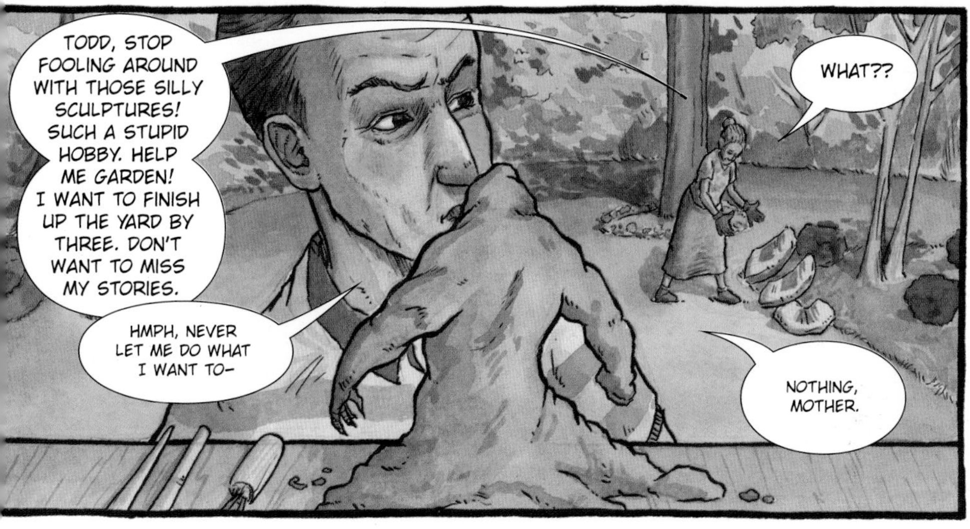
TODD, STOP FOOLING AROUND WITH THOSE SILLY SCULPTURES! SUCH A STUPID HOBBY. HELP ME GARDEN! I WANT TO FINISH UP THE YARD BY THREE. DON'T WANT TO MISS MY STORIES.
HMPH, NEVER LET ME DO WHAT I WANT TO-
WHAT??
NOTHING, MOTHER.

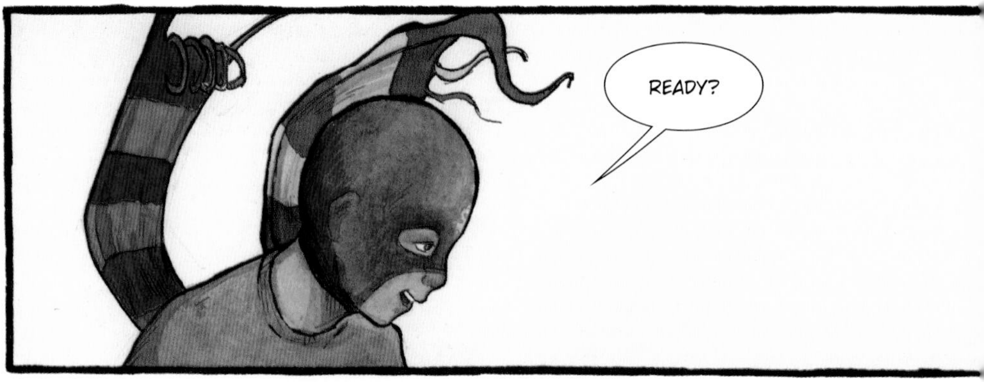
READY?

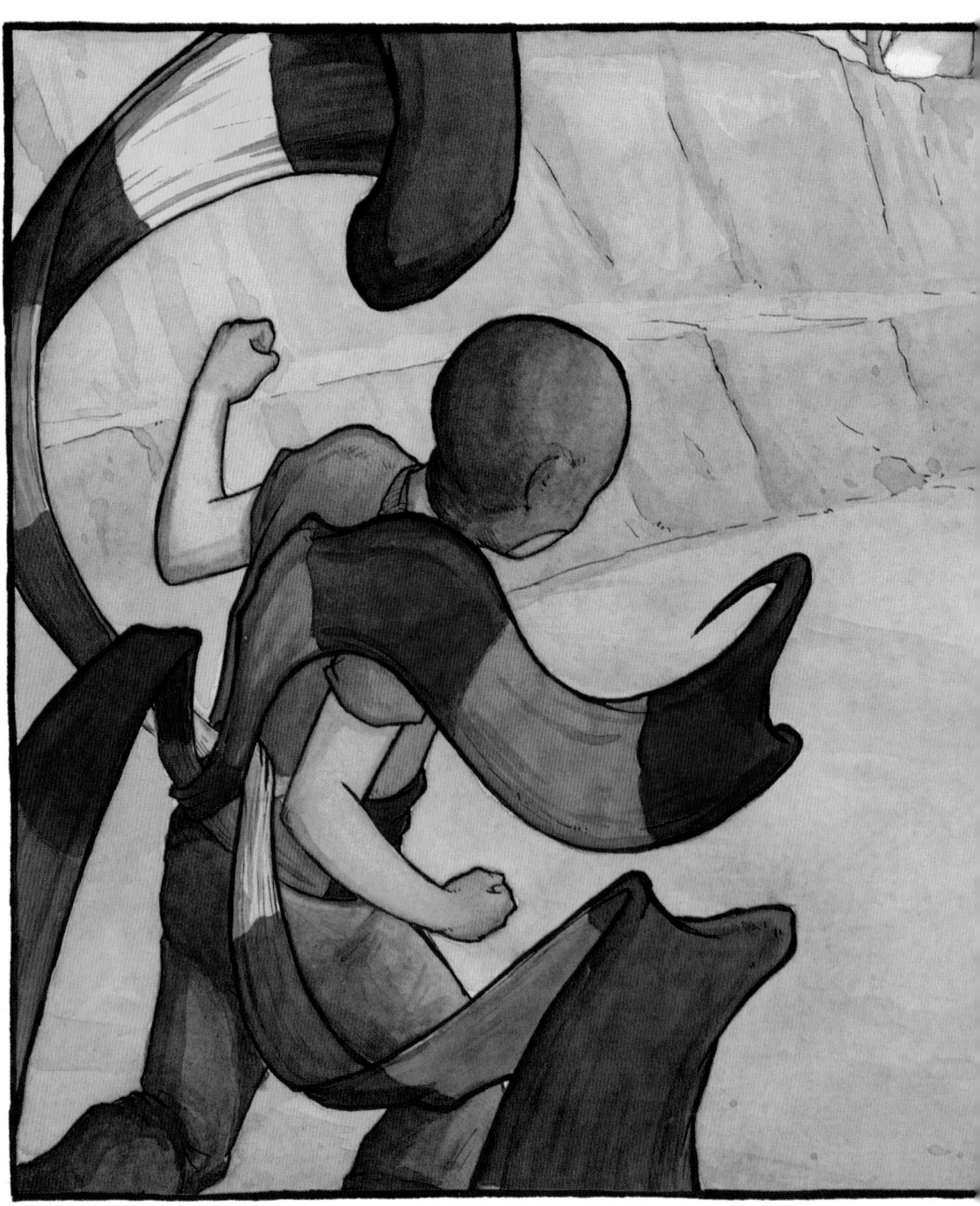

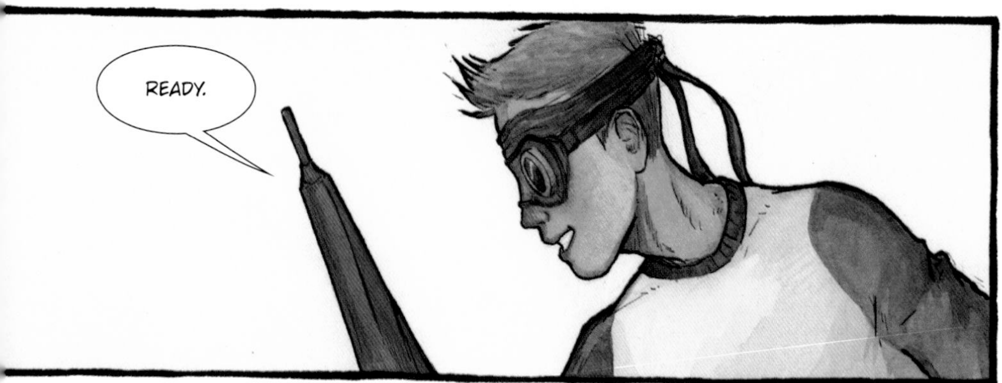
READY.

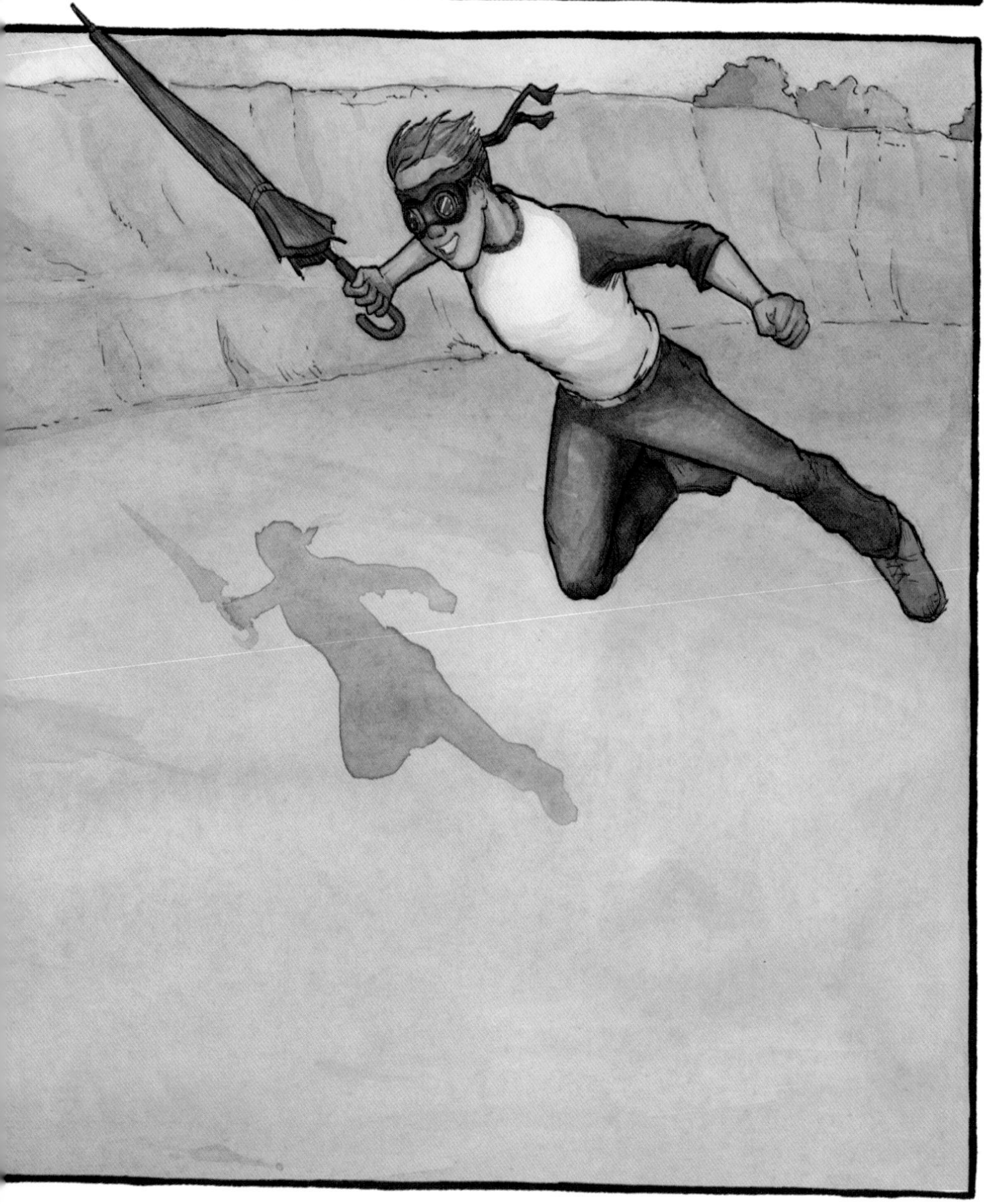

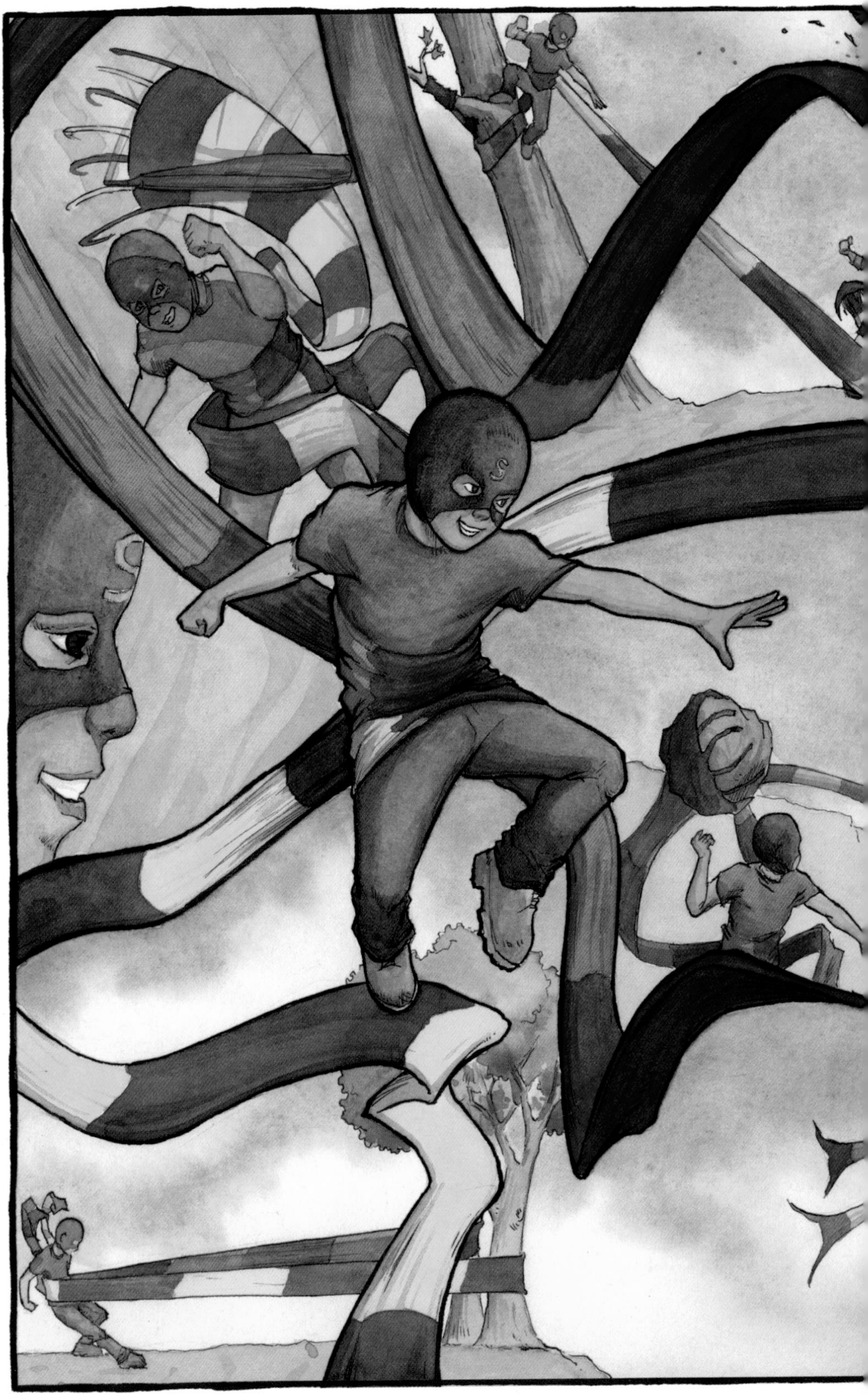

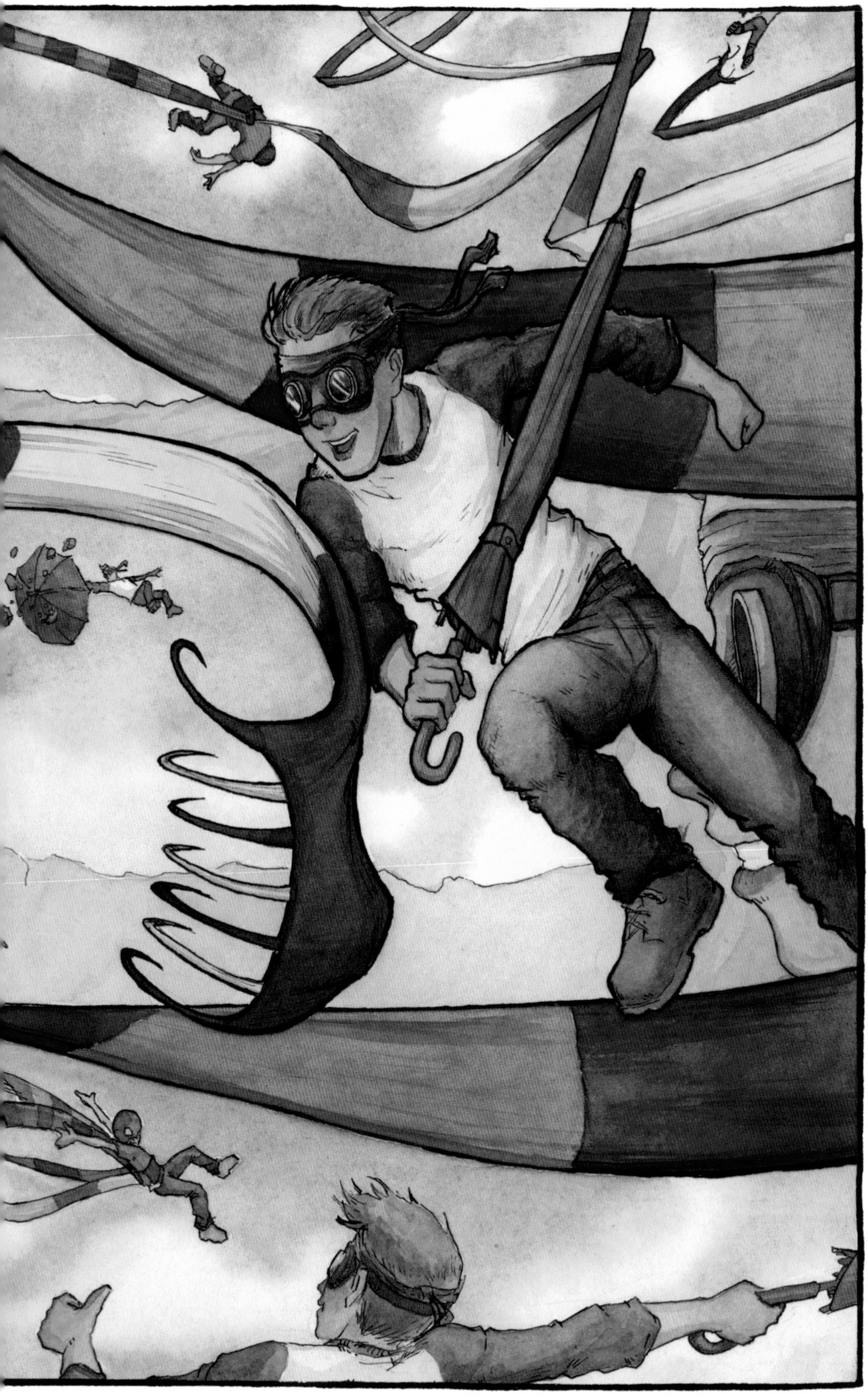

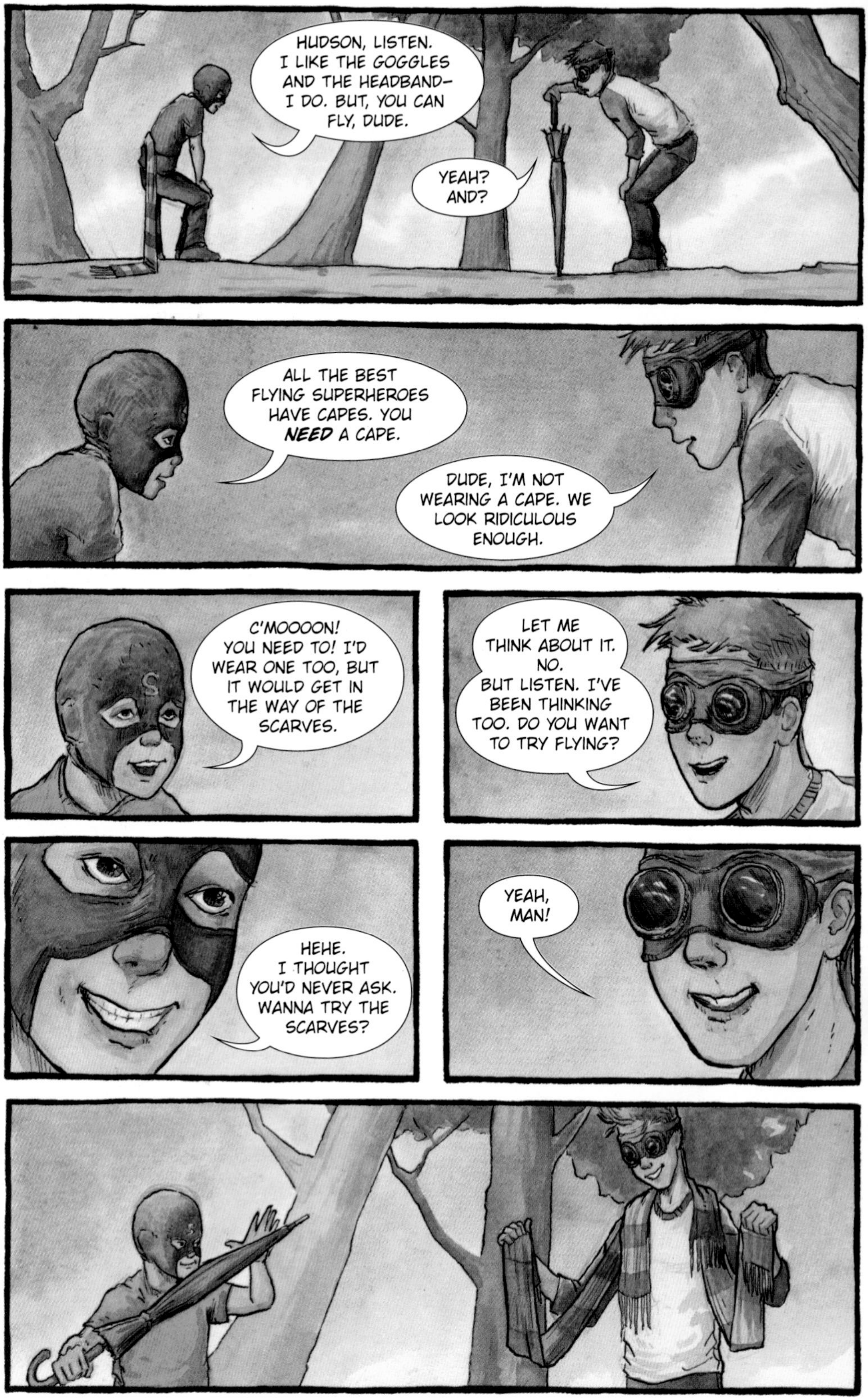
HUDSON, LISTEN. I LIKE THE GOGGLES AND THE HEADBAND— I DO. BUT, YOU CAN FLY, DUDE.
YEAH? AND?
ALL THE BEST FLYING SUPERHEROES HAVE CAPES. YOU ***NEED*** A CAPE.
DUDE, I'M NOT WEARING A CAPE. WE LOOK RIDICULOUS ENOUGH.
C'MOOOON! YOU NEED TO! I'D WEAR ONE TOO, BUT IT WOULD GET IN THE WAY OF THE SCARVES.
LET ME THINK ABOUT IT. NO. BUT LISTEN. I'VE BEEN THINKING TOO. DO YOU WANT TO TRY FLYING?
HEHE. I THOUGHT YOU'D NEVER ASK. WANNA TRY THE SCARVES?
YEAH, MAN!

HMM. THEY AREN'T WORKING. WEIRD. I GUESS THEY ONLY WORK WITH US.

HUH. WELL, ON THE BRIGHT SIDE, WE DON'T HAVE TO WORRY ABOUT ANYONE TAKING THEM AND USING THEM AGAINST US. HEY, I WANNA TRY SOMETHING. I CALL IT THE DOME OF DOOM. READY?

HA. OKAY?

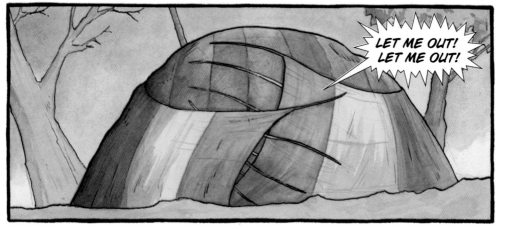
LET ME OUT! LET ME OUT!

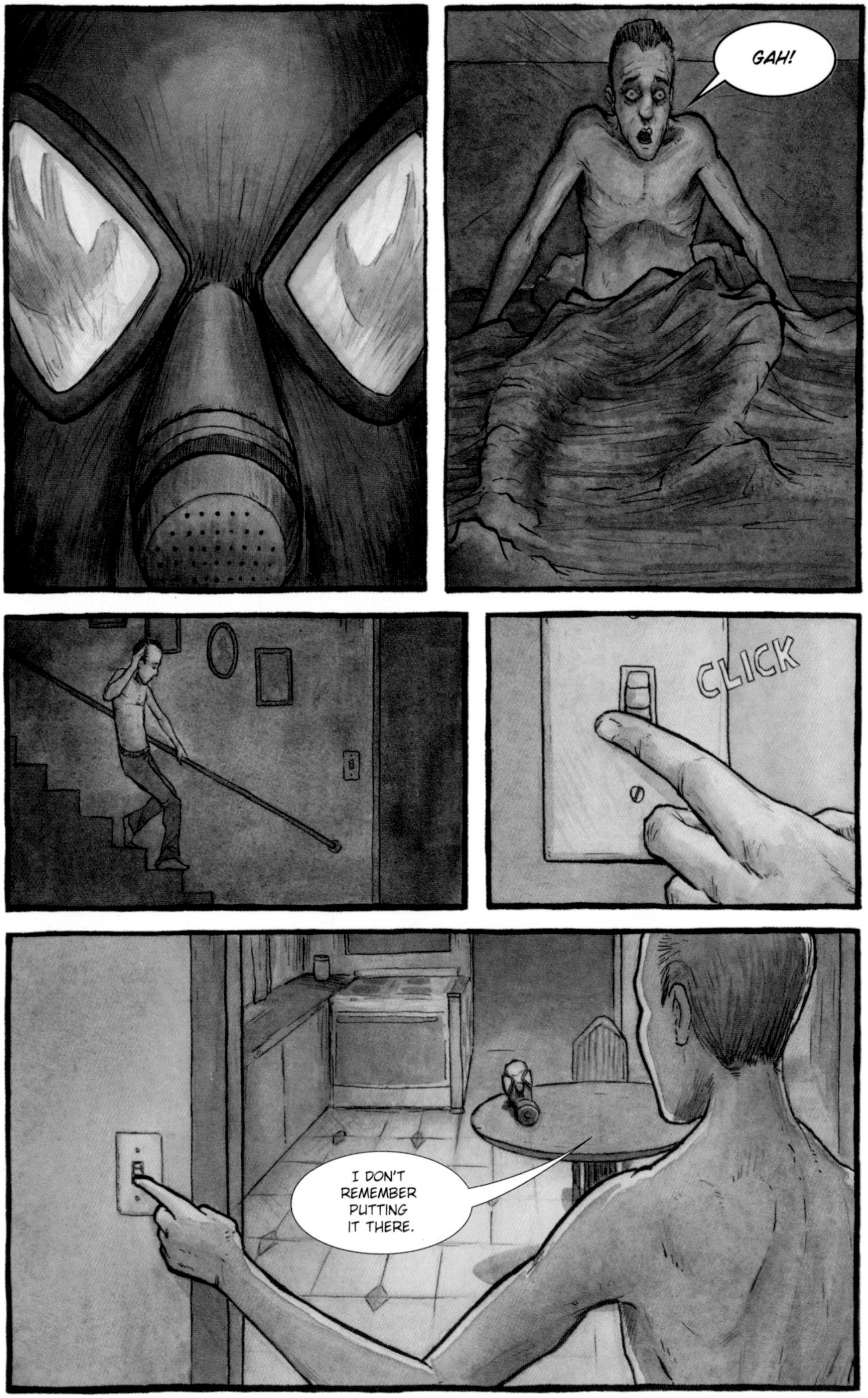
GAH!
CLICK
I DON'T REMEMBER PUTTING IT THERE.

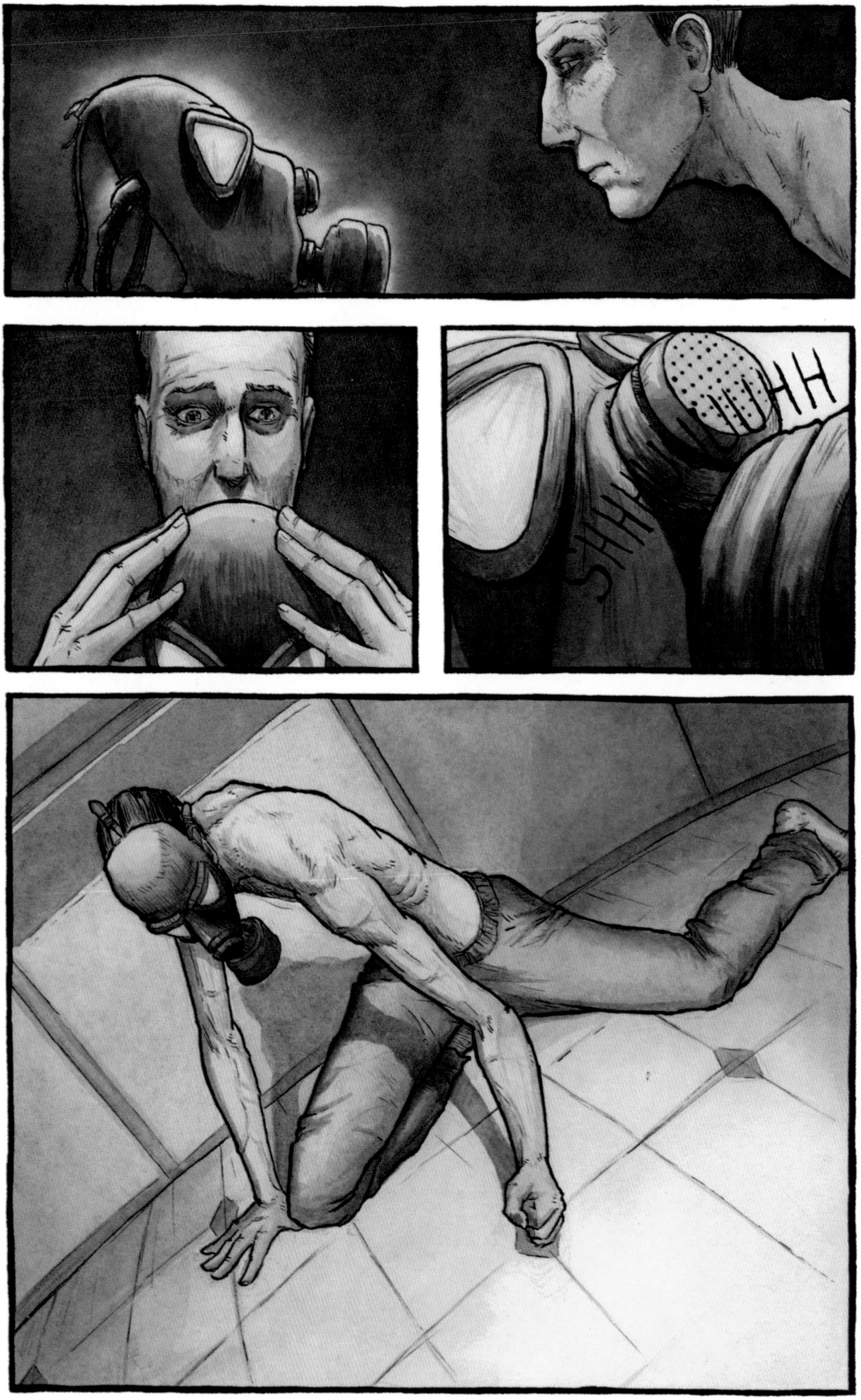
SHHH
HH

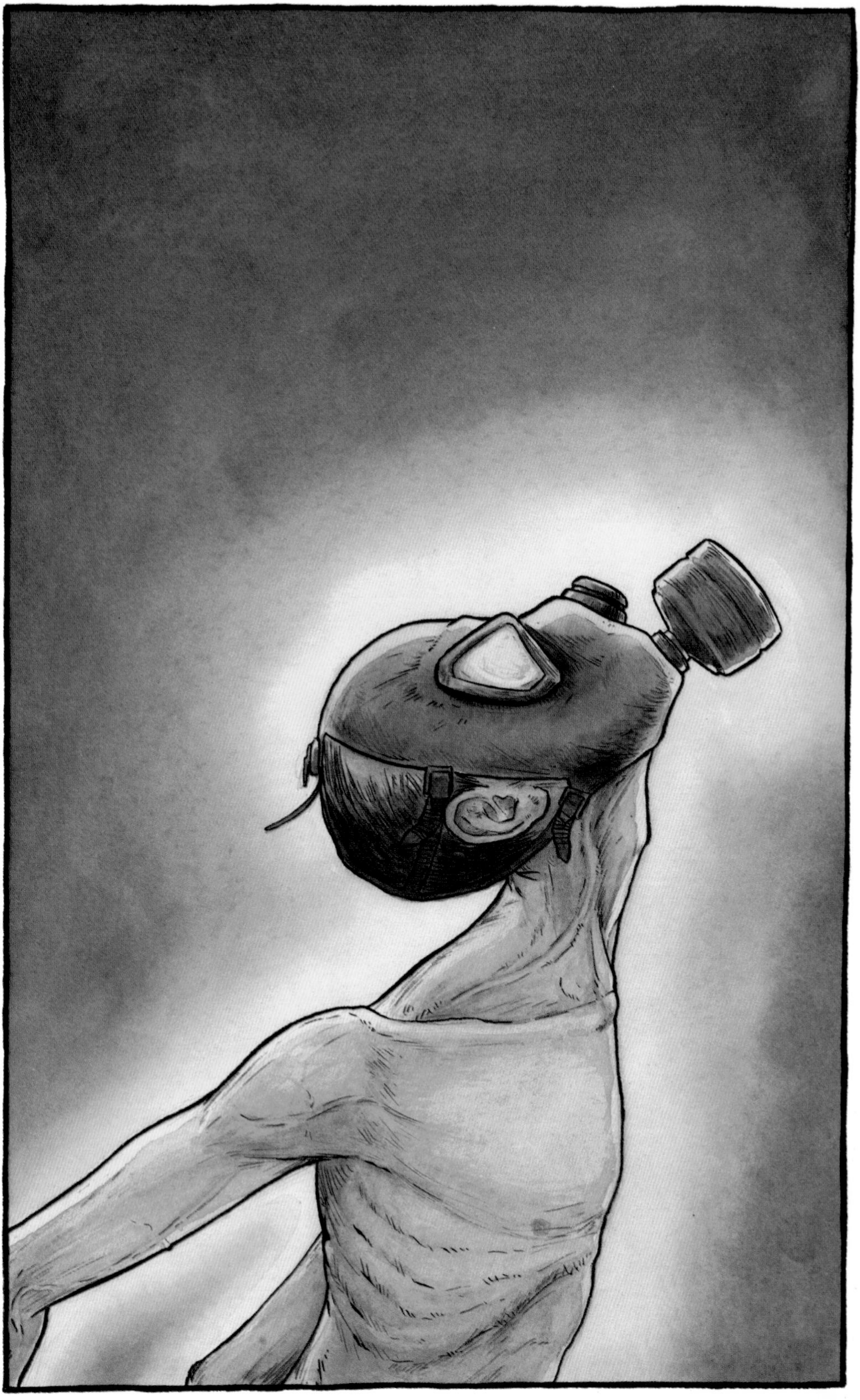

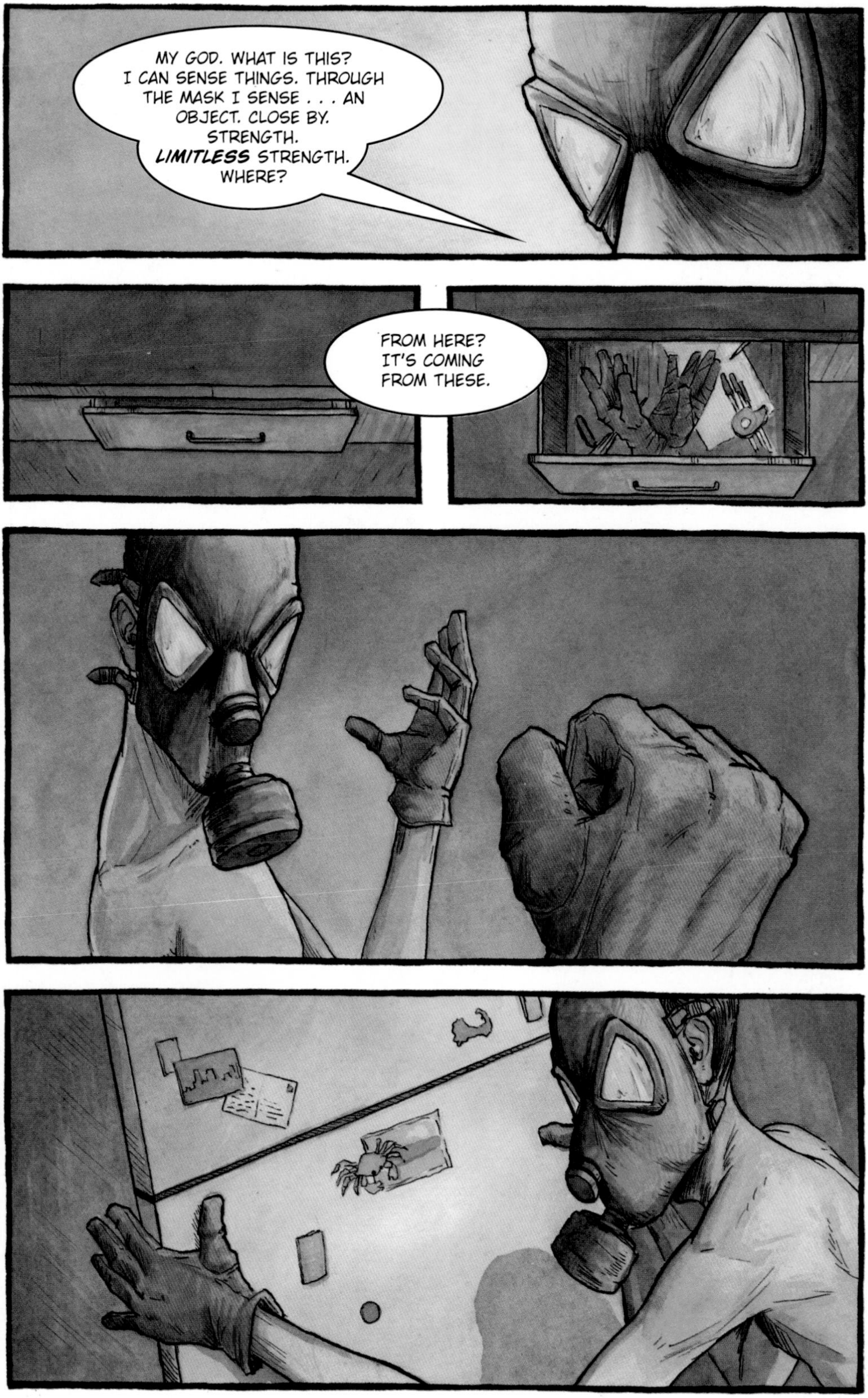
MY GOD. WHAT IS THIS? I CAN SENSE THINGS. THROUGH THE MASK I SENSE . . . AN OBJECT. CLOSE BY. STRENGTH. *LIMITLESS* STRENGTH. WHERE?
FROM HERE? IT'S COMING FROM THESE.

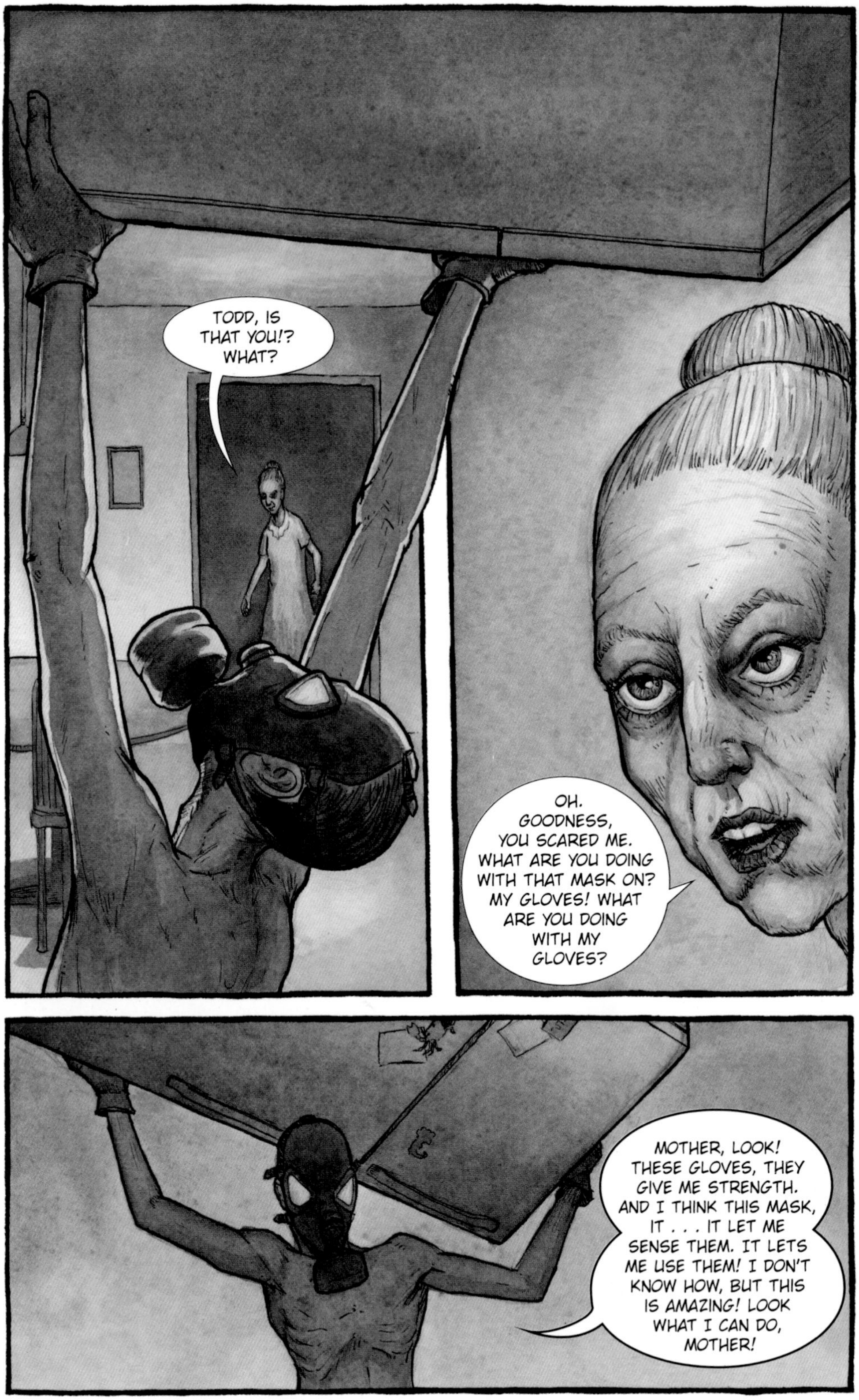
TODD, IS THAT YOU!? WHAT?
OH. GOODNESS, YOU SCARED ME. WHAT ARE YOU DOING WITH THAT MASK ON? MY GLOVES! WHAT ARE YOU DOING WITH MY GLOVES?
MOTHER, LOOK! THESE GLOVES, THEY GIVE ME STRENGTH. AND I THINK THIS MASK, IT . . . IT LET ME SENSE THEM. IT LETS ME USE THEM! I DON'T KNOW HOW, BUT THIS IS AMAZING! LOOK WHAT I CAN DO, MOTHER!

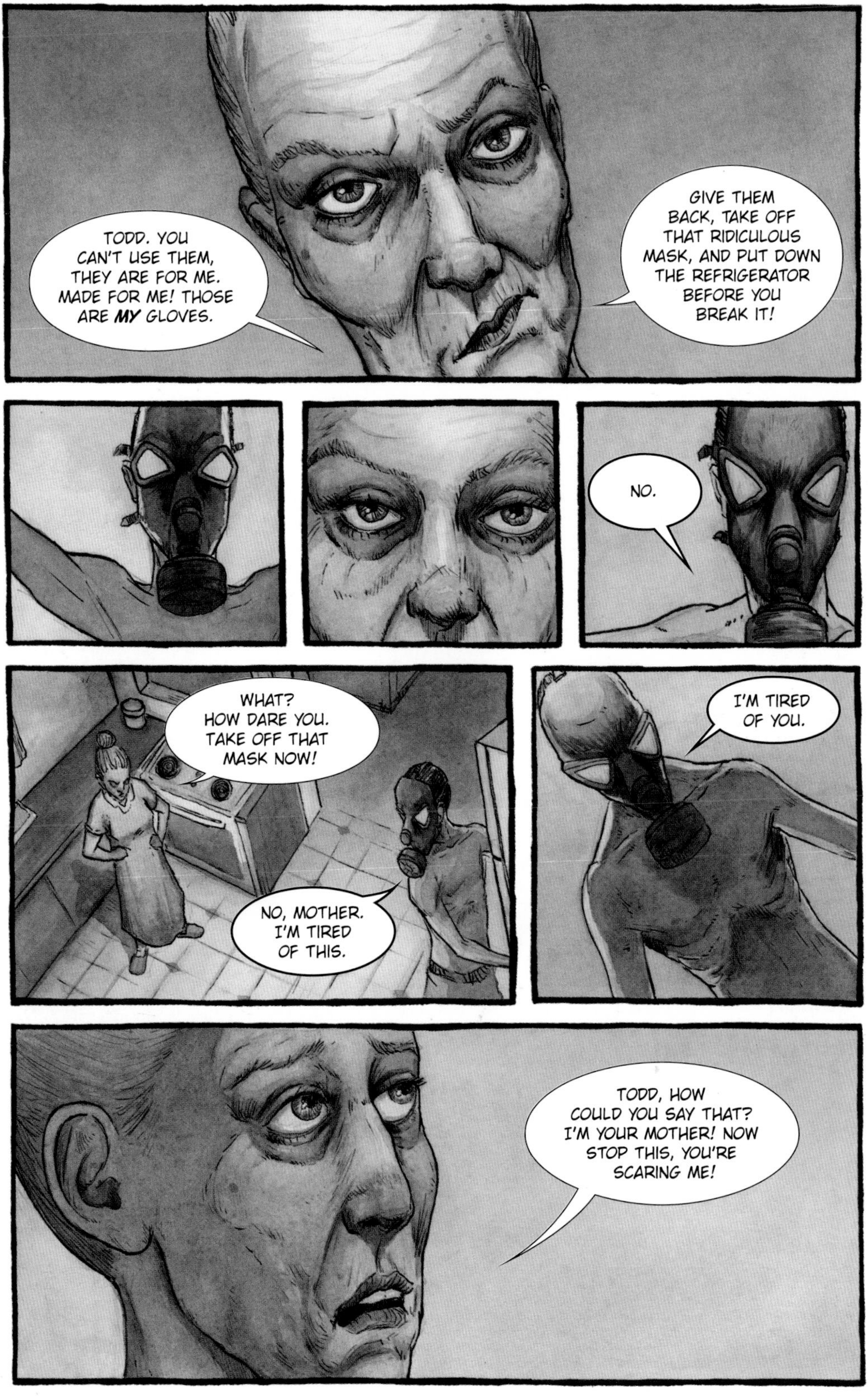
TODD. YOU CAN'T USE THEM, THEY ARE FOR ME. MADE FOR ME! THOSE ARE *MY* GLOVES.
GIVE THEM BACK, TAKE OFF THAT RIDICULOUS MASK, AND PUT DOWN THE REFRIGERATOR BEFORE YOU BREAK IT!
NO.
WHAT? HOW DARE YOU. TAKE OFF THAT MASK NOW!
NO, MOTHER. I'M TIRED OF THIS.
I'M TIRED OF YOU.
TODD, HOW COULD YOU SAY THAT? I'M YOUR MOTHER! NOW STOP THIS, YOU'RE SCARING ME!

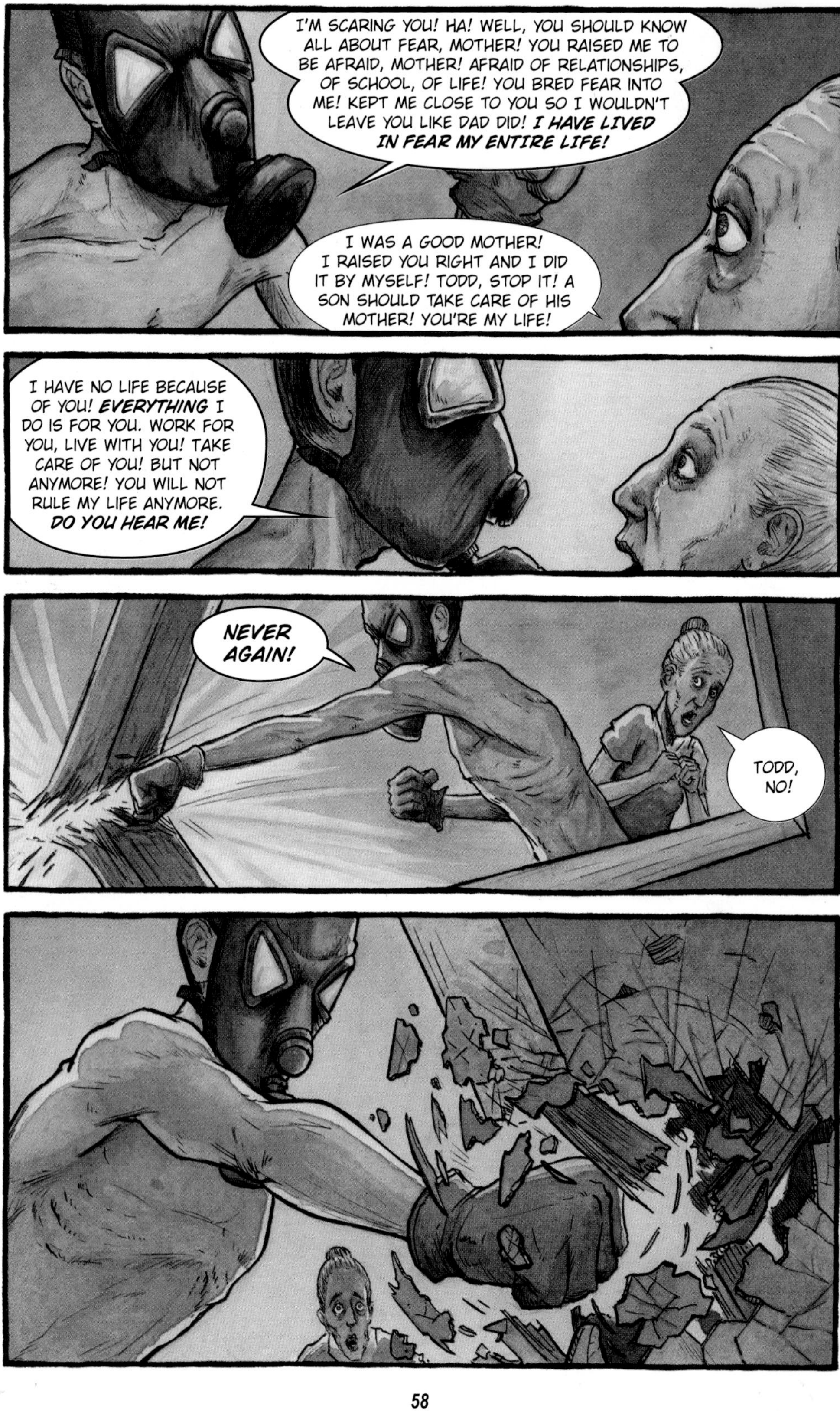
I'M SCARING YOU! HA! WELL, YOU SHOULD KNOW ALL ABOUT FEAR, MOTHER! YOU RAISED ME TO BE AFRAID, MOTHER! AFRAID OF RELATIONSHIPS, OF SCHOOL, OF LIFE! YOU BRED FEAR INTO ME! KEPT ME CLOSE TO YOU SO I WOULDN'T LEAVE YOU LIKE DAD DID! ***I HAVE LIVED IN FEAR MY ENTIRE LIFE!***
I WAS A GOOD MOTHER! I RAISED YOU RIGHT AND I DID IT BY MYSELF! TODD, STOP IT! A SON SHOULD TAKE CARE OF HIS MOTHER! YOU'RE MY LIFE!
I HAVE NO LIFE BECAUSE OF YOU! ***EVERYTHING*** I DO IS FOR YOU. WORK FOR YOU, LIVE WITH YOU! TAKE CARE OF YOU! BUT NOT ANYMORE! YOU WILL NOT RULE MY LIFE ANYMORE. ***DO YOU HEAR ME!***
NEVER AGAIN!
TODD, NO!

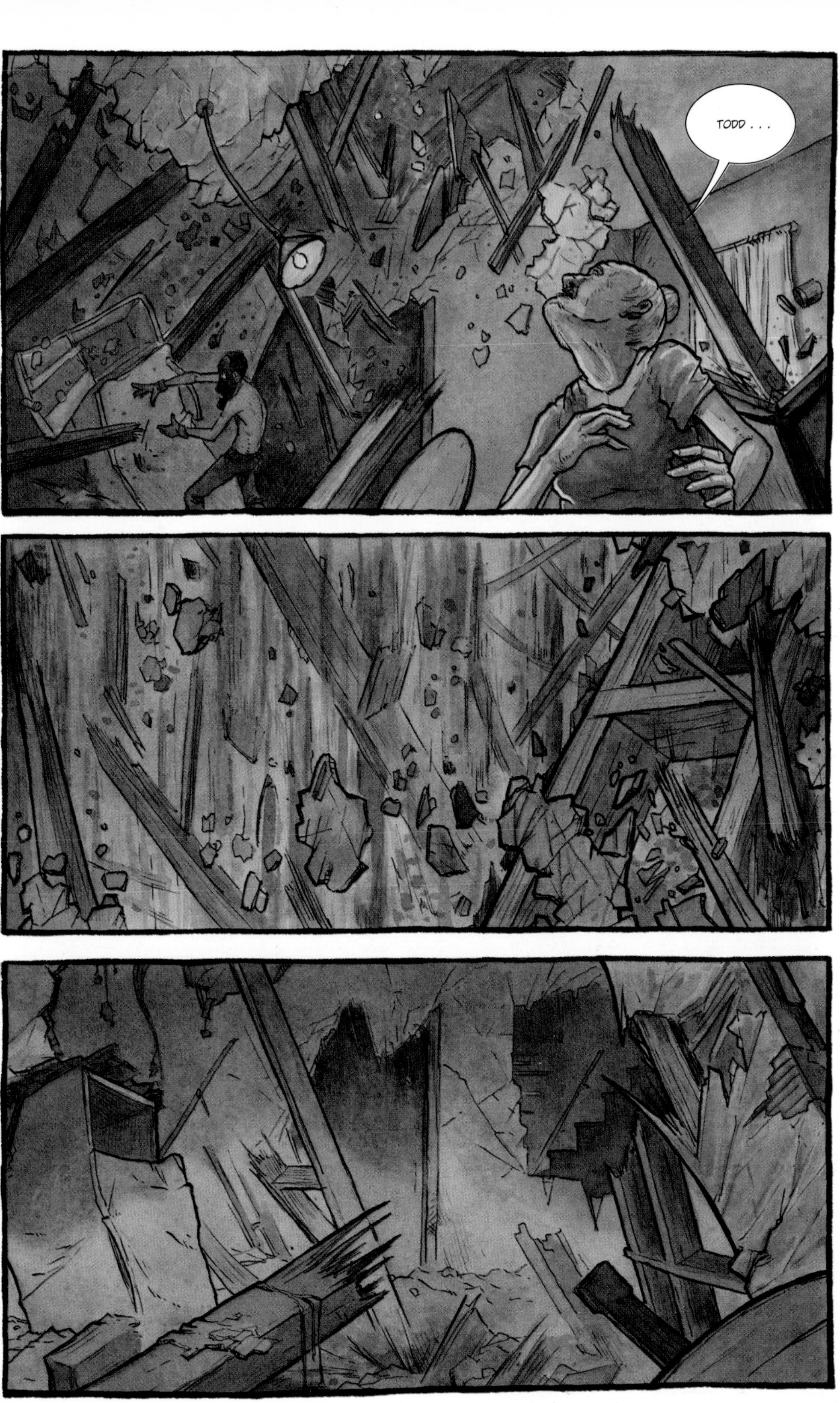
TODD . . .

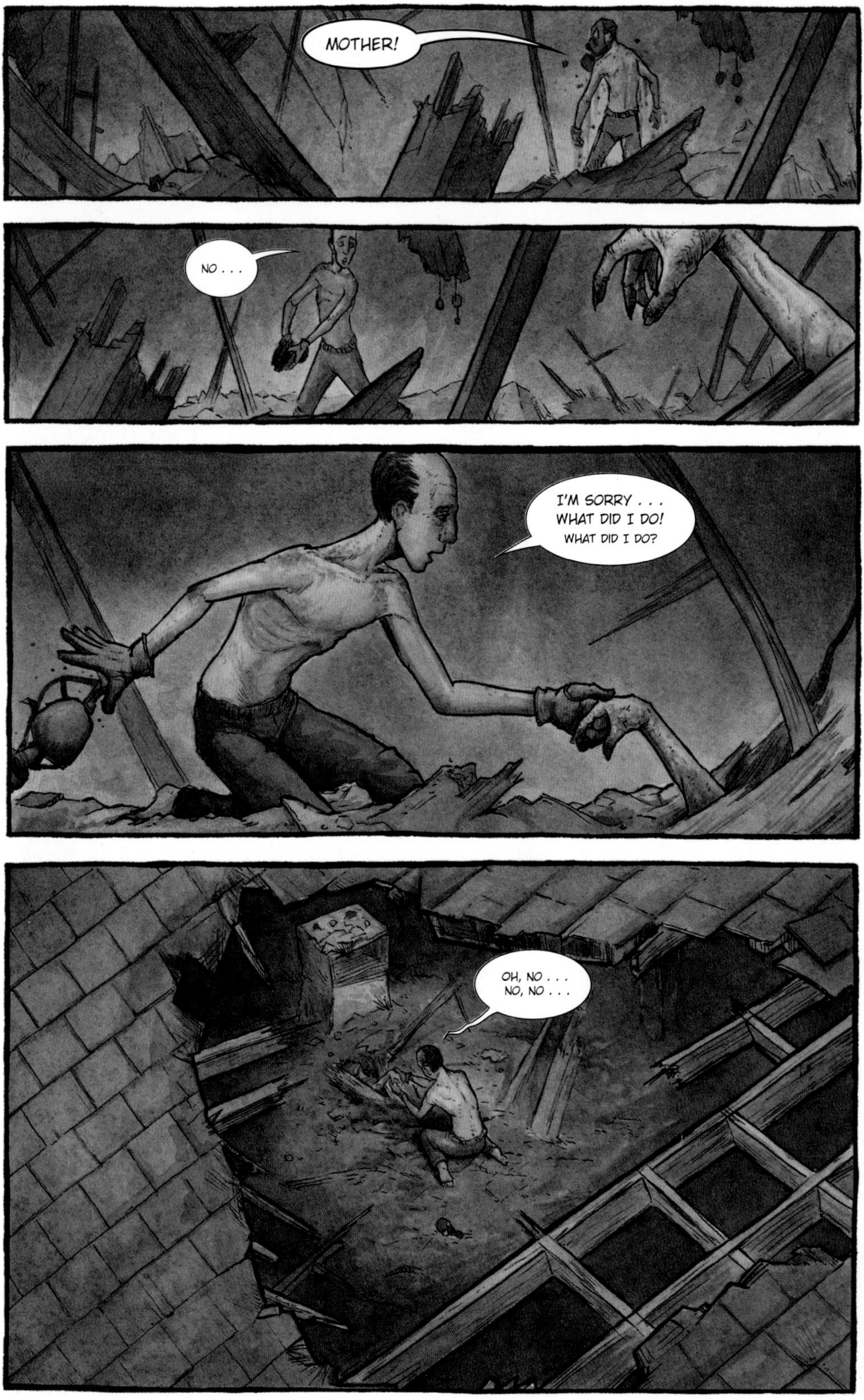
MOTHER!
NO . . .
I'M SORRY . . .
WHAT DID I DO!
WHAT DID I DO?
OH, NO . . .
NO, NO . . .

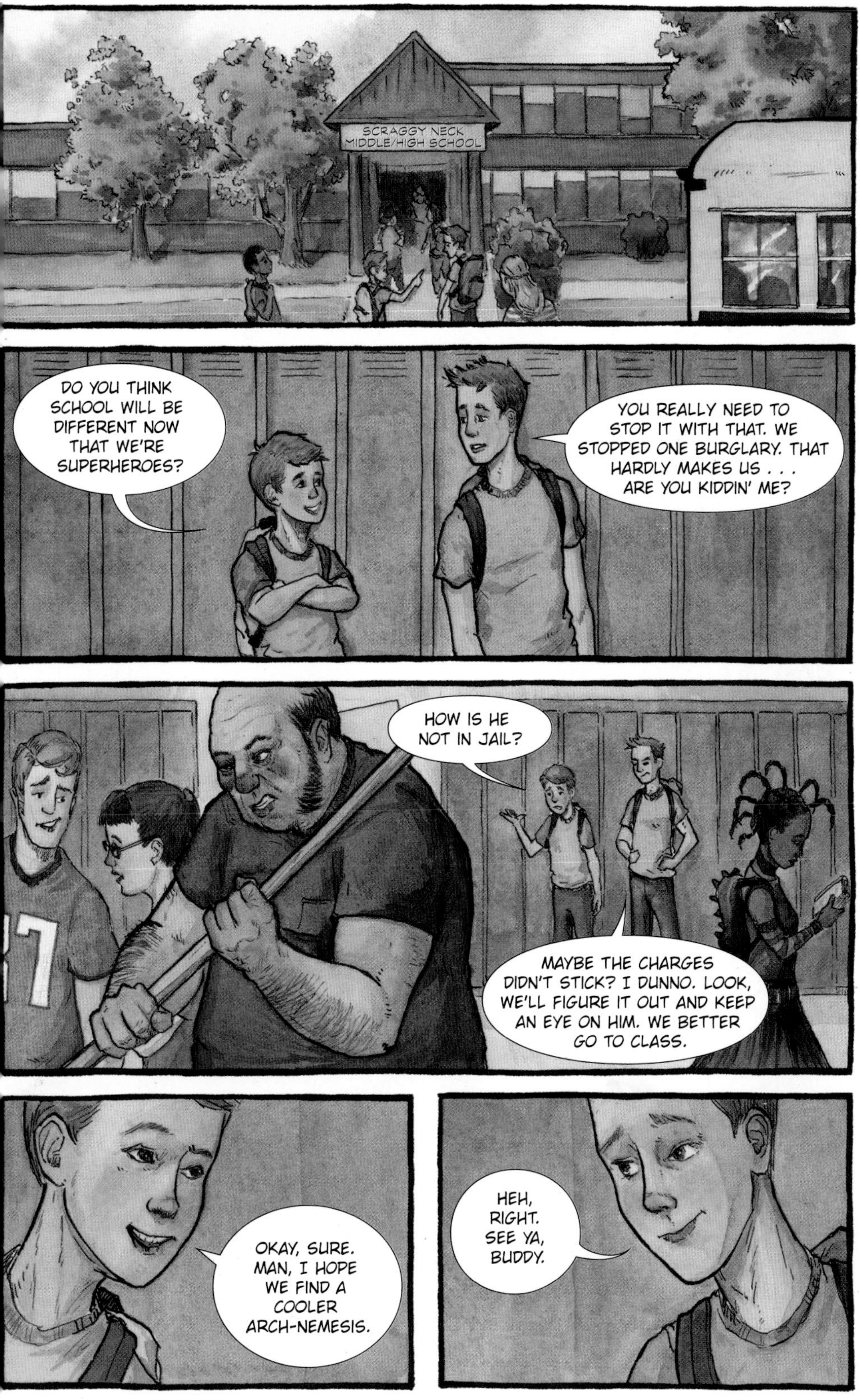
SCRAGGY NECK MIDDLE/HIGH SCHOOL
DO YOU THINK SCHOOL WILL BE DIFFERENT NOW THAT WE'RE SUPERHEROES?
YOU REALLY NEED TO STOP IT WITH THAT. WE STOPPED ONE BURGLARY. THAT HARDLY MAKES US . . . ARE YOU KIDDIN' ME?
HOW IS HE NOT IN JAIL?
MAYBE THE CHARGES DIDN'T STICK? I DUNNO. LOOK, WE'LL FIGURE IT OUT AND KEEP AN EYE ON HIM. WE BETTER GO TO CLASS.
OKAY, SURE. MAN, I HOPE WE FIND A COOLER ARCH-NEMESIS.
HEH, RIGHT. SEE YA, BUDDY.

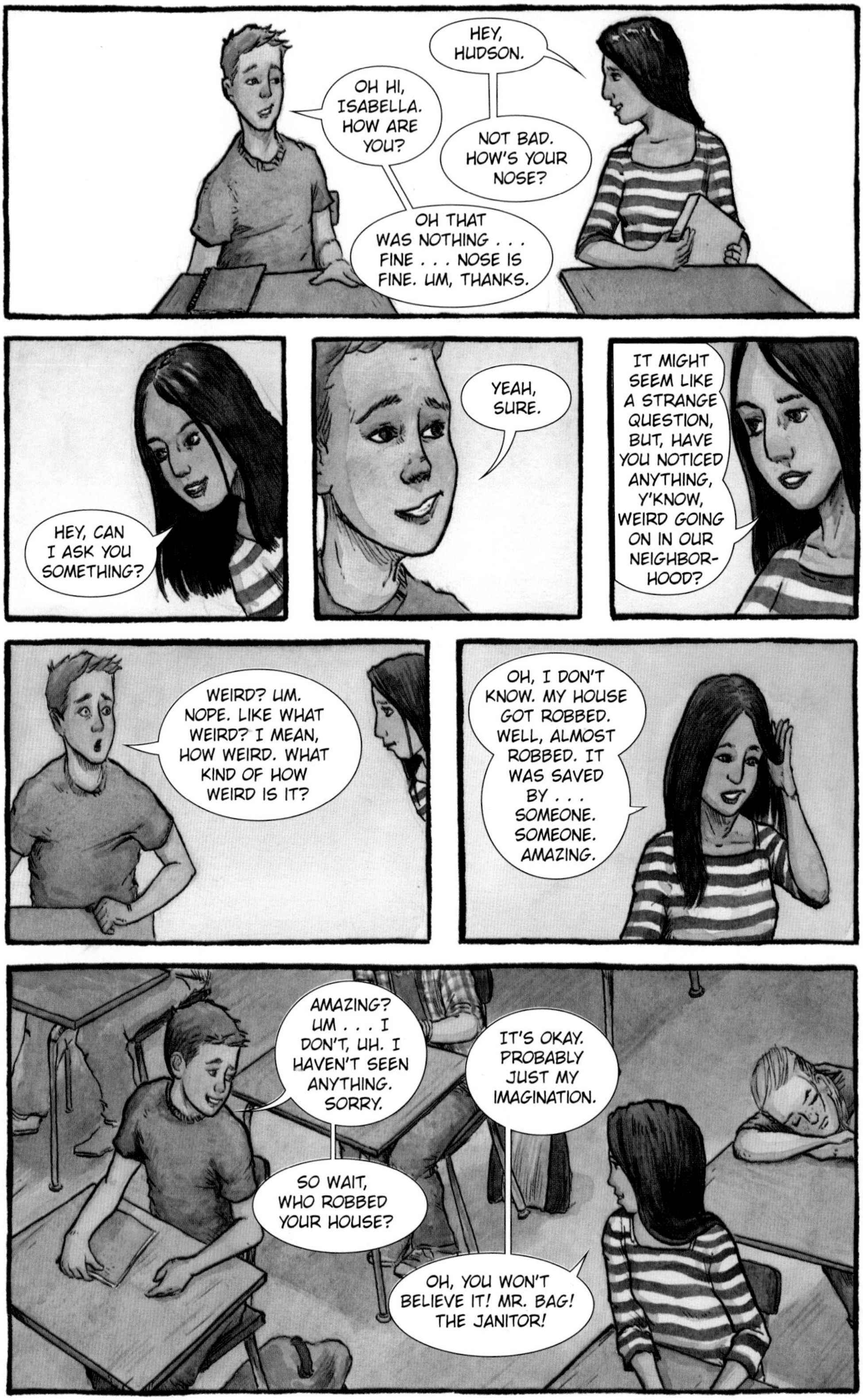
HEY, HUDSON.
OH HI, ISABELLA. HOW ARE YOU?
NOT BAD. HOW'S YOUR NOSE?
OH THAT WAS NOTHING . . . FINE . . . NOSE IS FINE. UM, THANKS.
HEY, CAN I ASK YOU SOMETHING?
YEAH, SURE.
IT MIGHT SEEM LIKE A STRANGE QUESTION, BUT, HAVE YOU NOTICED ANYTHING, Y'KNOW, WEIRD GOING ON IN OUR NEIGHBOR-HOOD?
WEIRD? UM. NOPE. LIKE WHAT WEIRD? I MEAN, HOW WEIRD. WHAT KIND OF HOW WEIRD IS IT?
OH, I DON'T KNOW. MY HOUSE GOT ROBBED. WELL, ALMOST ROBBED. IT WAS SAVED BY . . . SOMEONE. SOMEONE. AMAZING.
AMAZING? UM . . . I DON'T, UH. I HAVEN'T SEEN ANYTHING. SORRY.
IT'S OKAY. PROBABLY JUST MY IMAGINATION.
SO WAIT, WHO ROBBED YOUR HOUSE?
OH, YOU WON'T BELIEVE IT! MR. BAG! THE JANITOR!

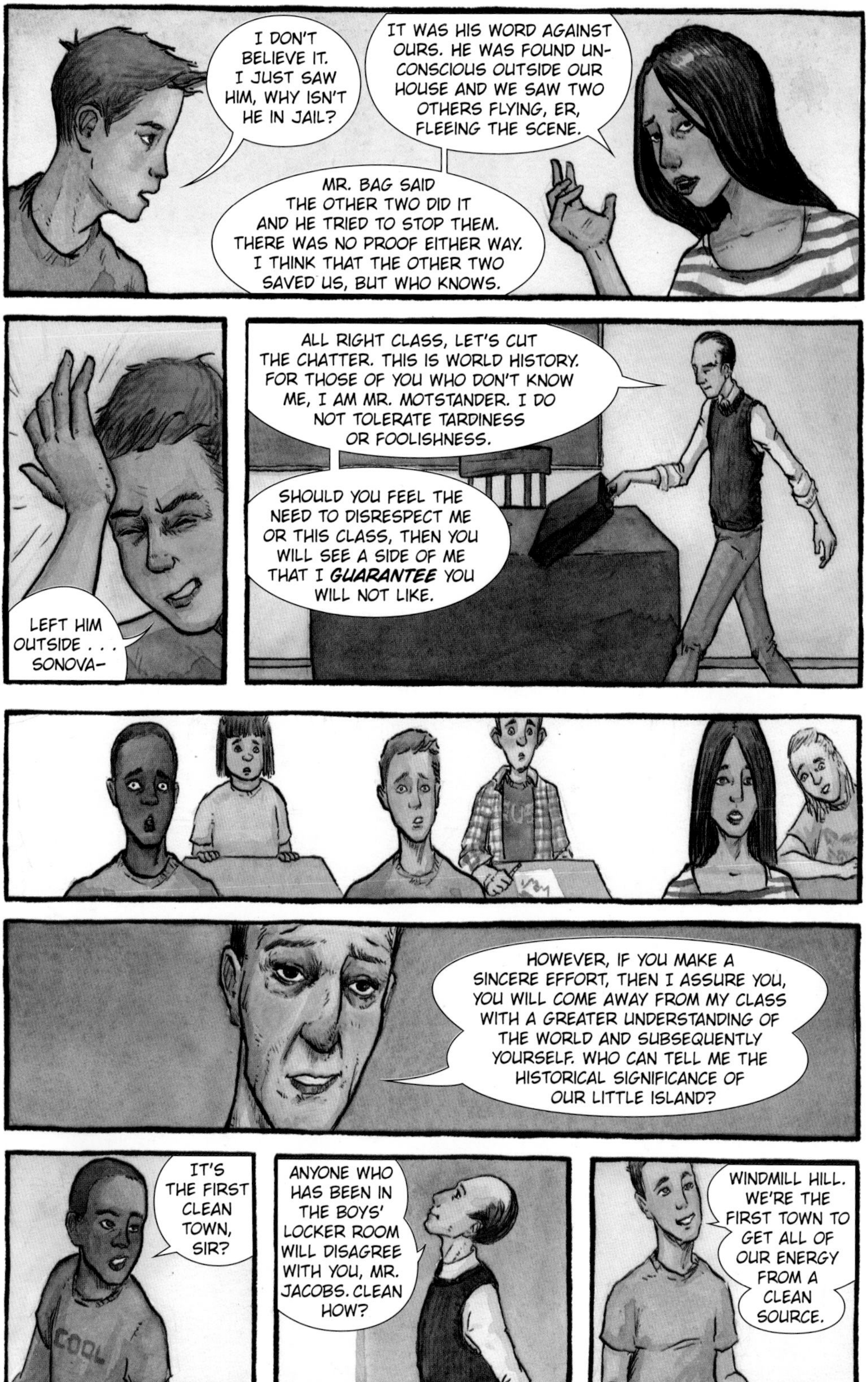
I DON'T BELIEVE IT. I JUST SAW HIM, WHY ISN'T HE IN JAIL?
IT WAS HIS WORD AGAINST OURS. HE WAS FOUND UN-CONSCIOUS OUTSIDE OUR HOUSE AND WE SAW TWO OTHERS FLYING, ER, FLEEING THE SCENE.
MR. BAG SAID THE OTHER TWO DID IT AND HE TRIED TO STOP THEM. THERE WAS NO PROOF EITHER WAY. I THINK THAT THE OTHER TWO SAVED US, BUT WHO KNOWS.
LEFT HIM OUTSIDE . . . SONOVA-
ALL RIGHT CLASS, LET'S CUT THE CHATTER. THIS IS WORLD HISTORY. FOR THOSE OF YOU WHO DON'T KNOW ME, I AM MR. MOTSTANDER. I DO NOT TOLERATE TARDINESS OR FOOLISHNESS.
SHOULD YOU FEEL THE NEED TO DISRESPECT ME OR THIS CLASS, THEN YOU WILL SEE A SIDE OF ME THAT I ***GUARANTEE*** YOU WILL NOT LIKE.
HOWEVER, IF YOU MAKE A SINCERE EFFORT, THEN I ASSURE YOU, YOU WILL COME AWAY FROM MY CLASS WITH A GREATER UNDERSTANDING OF THE WORLD AND SUBSEQUENTLY YOURSELF. WHO CAN TELL ME THE HISTORICAL SIGNIFICANCE OF OUR LITTLE ISLAND?
IT'S THE FIRST CLEAN TOWN, SIR?
ANYONE WHO HAS BEEN IN THE BOYS' LOCKER ROOM WILL DISAGREE WITH YOU, MR. JACOBS. CLEAN HOW?
WINDMILL HILL. WE'RE THE FIRST TOWN TO GET ALL OF OUR ENERGY FROM A CLEAN SOURCE.

VERY GOOD. NOW EVERYONE, TAKE A DEEP BREATH. OUR AIR IS SOME OF THE CLEANEST IN THE COUNTRY. NOW COMPARE THAT WITH FRENCH SOLDIERS IN THE SECOND BATTLE OF YPRES.

THE HORROR THEY MUST HAVE EXPERIENCED AS A THICK GREEN CLOUD OF POISON GAS DRIFTED TOWARD THEM AND SETTLED IN THEIR TRENCHES, BURNING THEIR EYES AND STEALING THEIR BREATH.

I BROUGHT SOMETHING IN TO . . .

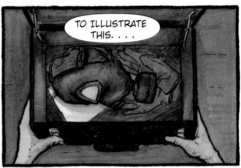

TO ILLUSTRATE THIS. . . .

SNAP

AH, SEEMS I'VE LEFT THE BOOK AT HOME. NOW TO FIGURE OUT HOW WE GOT FROM THERE TO HERE, WE MUST TRAVEL EVEN FURTHER BACK INTO OUR WORLD'S HISTORY.

BRIIINNG

GREAT CLASS, MR. MOTSTANDER

THANKS, MR. MOTSTANDER.

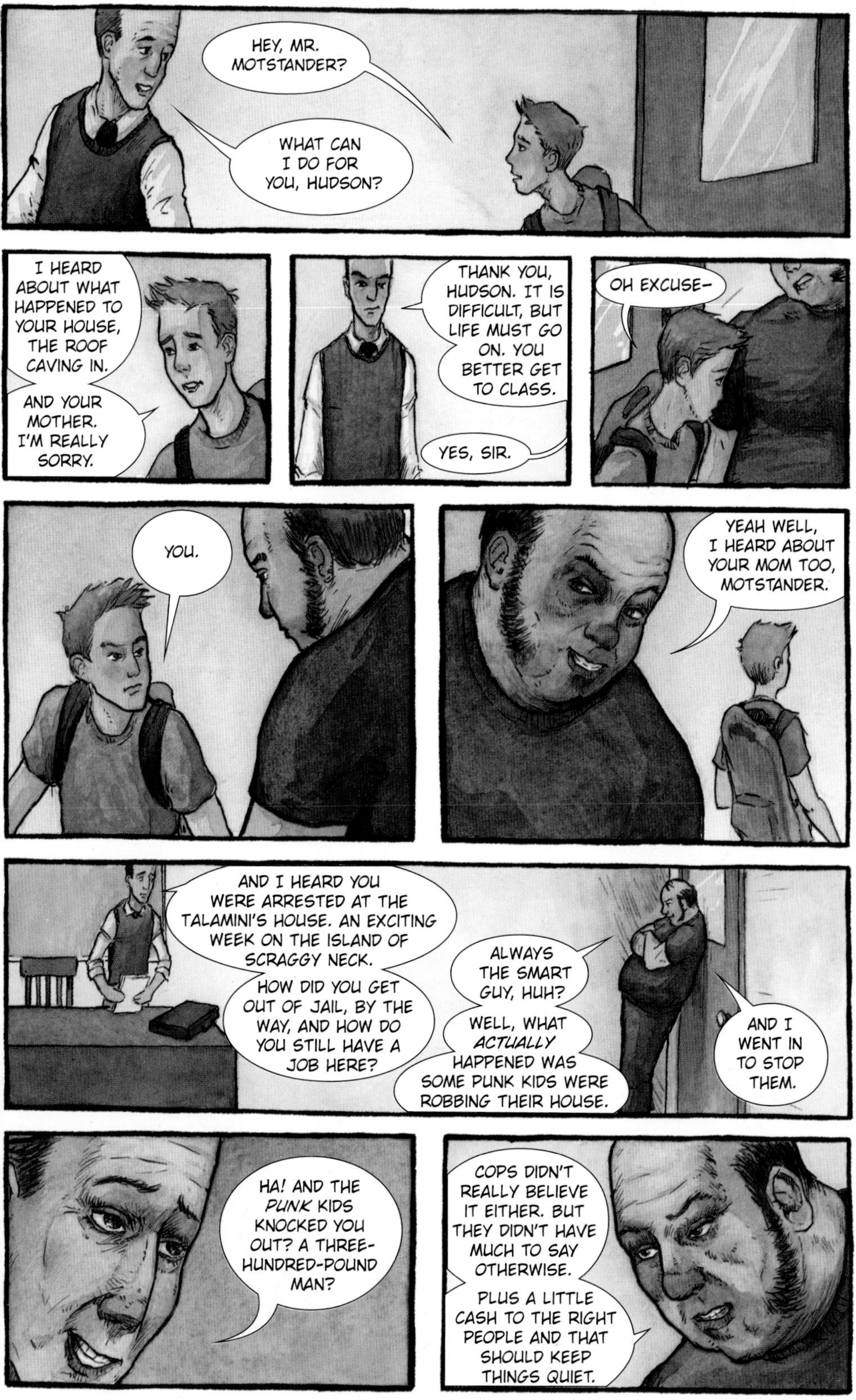
HEY, MR. MOTSTANDER?
WHAT CAN I DO FOR YOU, HUDSON?
I HEARD ABOUT WHAT HAPPENED TO YOUR HOUSE, THE ROOF CAVING IN.
AND YOUR MOTHER. I'M REALLY SORRY.
THANK YOU, HUDSON. IT IS DIFFICULT, BUT LIFE MUST GO ON. YOU BETTER GET TO CLASS.
YES, SIR.
OH EXCUSE-
YOU.
YEAH WELL, I HEARD ABOUT YOUR MOM TOO, MOTSTANDER.
AND I HEARD YOU WERE ARRESTED AT THE TALAMINI'S HOUSE. AN EXCITING WEEK ON THE ISLAND OF SCRAGGY NECK.
HOW DID YOU GET OUT OF JAIL, BY THE WAY, AND HOW DO YOU STILL HAVE A JOB HERE?
ALWAYS THE SMART GUY, HUH?
WELL, WHAT *ACTUALLY* HAPPENED WAS SOME PUNK KIDS WERE ROBBING THEIR HOUSE.
AND I WENT IN TO STOP THEM.
HA! AND THE *PUNK* KIDS KNOCKED YOU OUT? A THREE-HUNDRED-POUND MAN?
COPS DIDN'T REALLY BELIEVE IT EITHER. BUT THEY DIDN'T HAVE MUCH TO SAY OTHERWISE.
PLUS A LITTLE CASH TO THE RIGHT PEOPLE AND THAT SHOULD KEEP THINGS QUIET.

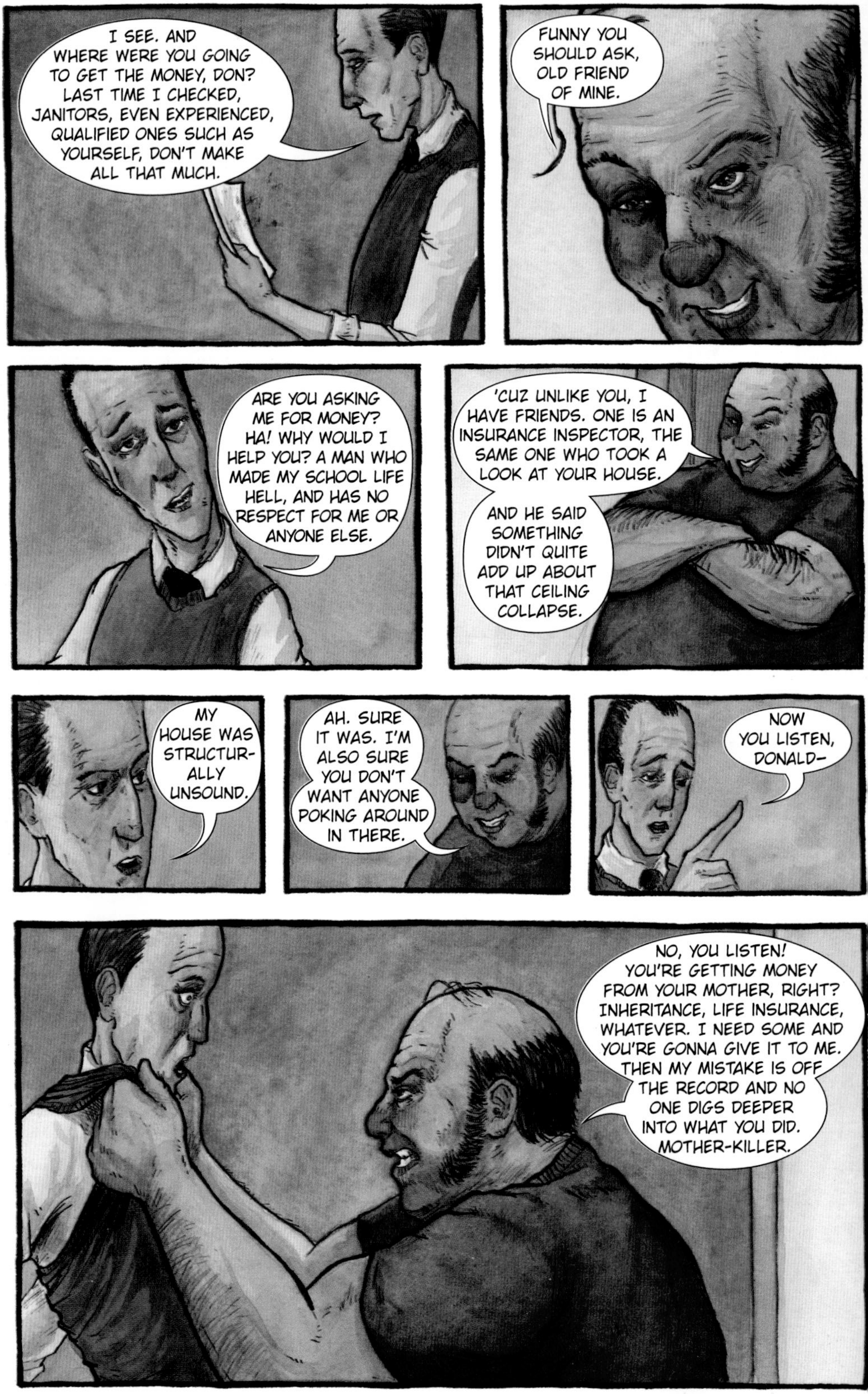
I SEE. AND WHERE WERE YOU GOING TO GET THE MONEY, DON? LAST TIME I CHECKED, JANITORS, EVEN EXPERIENCED, QUALIFIED ONES SUCH AS YOURSELF, DON'T MAKE ALL THAT MUCH.
FUNNY YOU SHOULD ASK, OLD FRIEND OF MINE.
ARE YOU ASKING ME FOR MONEY? HA! WHY WOULD I HELP YOU? A MAN WHO MADE MY SCHOOL LIFE HELL, AND HAS NO RESPECT FOR ME OR ANYONE ELSE.
'CUZ UNLIKE YOU, I HAVE FRIENDS. ONE IS AN INSURANCE INSPECTOR, THE SAME ONE WHO TOOK A LOOK AT YOUR HOUSE.
AND HE SAID SOMETHING DIDN'T QUITE ADD UP ABOUT THAT CEILING COLLAPSE.
MY HOUSE WAS STRUCTURALLY UNSOUND.
AH. SURE IT WAS. I'M ALSO SURE YOU DON'T WANT ANYONE POKING AROUND IN THERE.
NOW YOU LISTEN, DONALD—
NO, YOU LISTEN! YOU'RE GETTING MONEY FROM YOUR MOTHER, RIGHT? INHERITANCE, LIFE INSURANCE, WHATEVER. I NEED SOME AND YOU'RE GONNA GIVE IT TO ME. THEN MY MISTAKE IS OFF THE RECORD AND NO ONE DIGS DEEPER INTO WHAT YOU DID. MOTHER-KILLER.

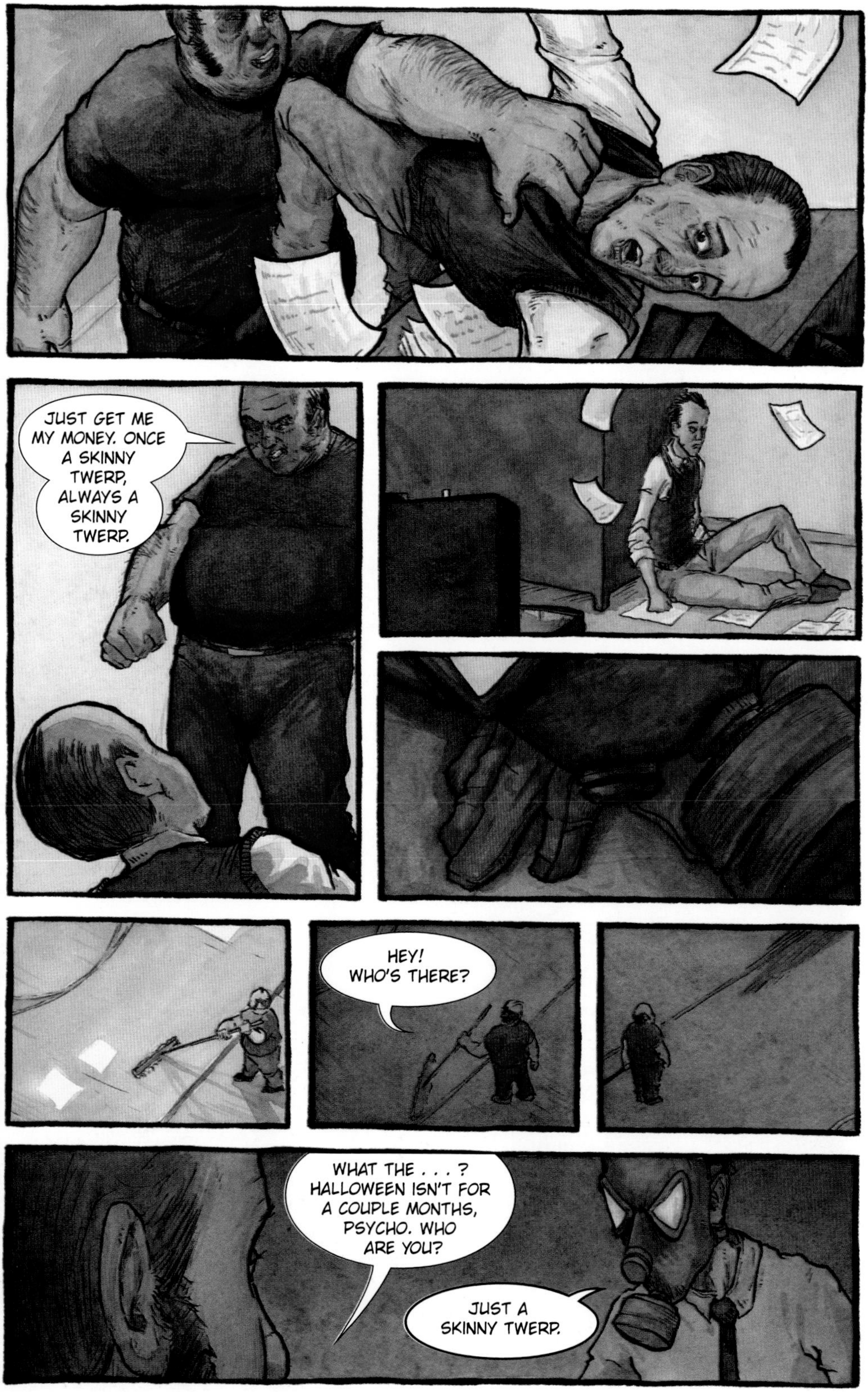
JUST GET ME MY MONEY. ONCE A SKINNY TWERP, ALWAYS A SKINNY TWERP.
HEY! WHO'S THERE?
WHAT THE . . . ? HALLOWEEN ISN'T FOR A COUPLE MONTHS, PSYCHO. WHO ARE YOU?
JUST A SKINNY TWERP.

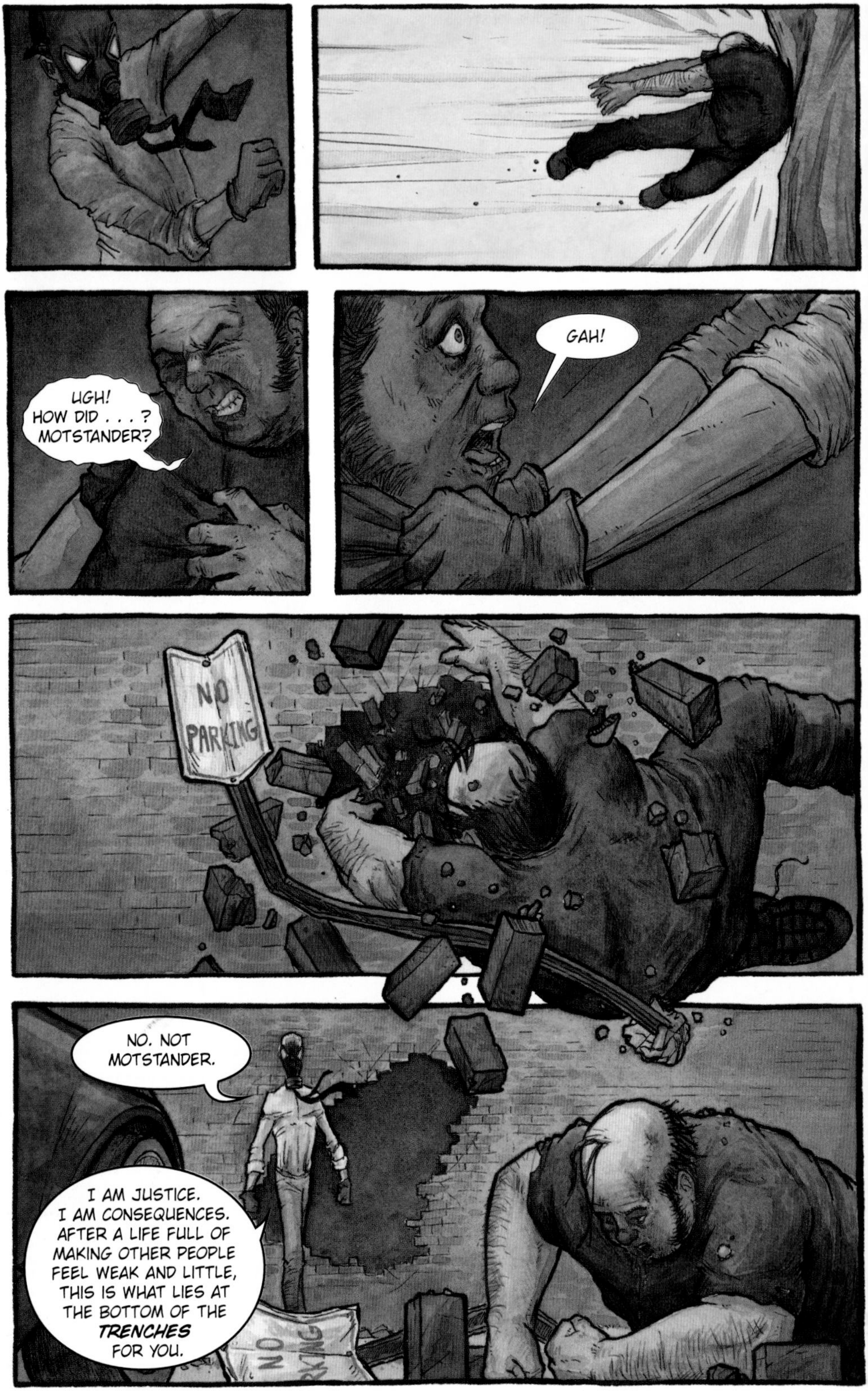
UGH!
HOW DID . . . ?
MOTSTANDER?
GAH!
NO PARKING
NO. NOT MOTSTANDER.
I AM JUSTICE. I AM CONSEQUENCES. AFTER A LIFE FULL OF MAKING OTHER PEOPLE FEEL WEAK AND LITTLE, THIS IS WHAT LIES AT THE BOTTOM OF THE ***TRENCHES*** FOR YOU.

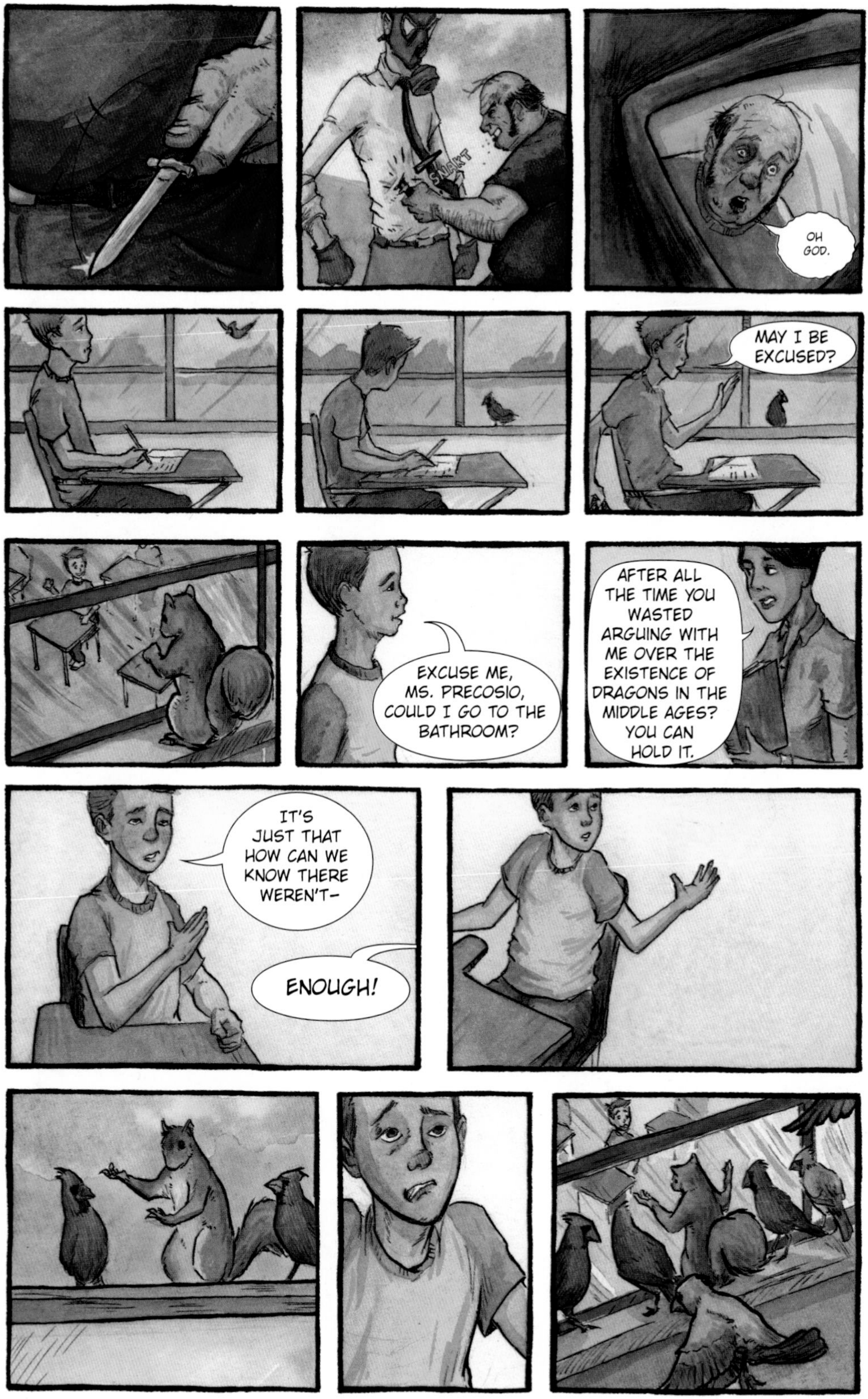
SNAKT
OH GOD.
MAY I BE EXCUSED?
EXCUSE ME, MS. PRECOSIO, COULD I GO TO THE BATHROOM?
AFTER ALL THE TIME YOU WASTED ARGUING WITH ME OVER THE EXISTENCE OF DRAGONS IN THE MIDDLE AGES? YOU CAN HOLD IT.
IT'S JUST THAT HOW CAN WE KNOW THERE WEREN'T–
ENOUGH!

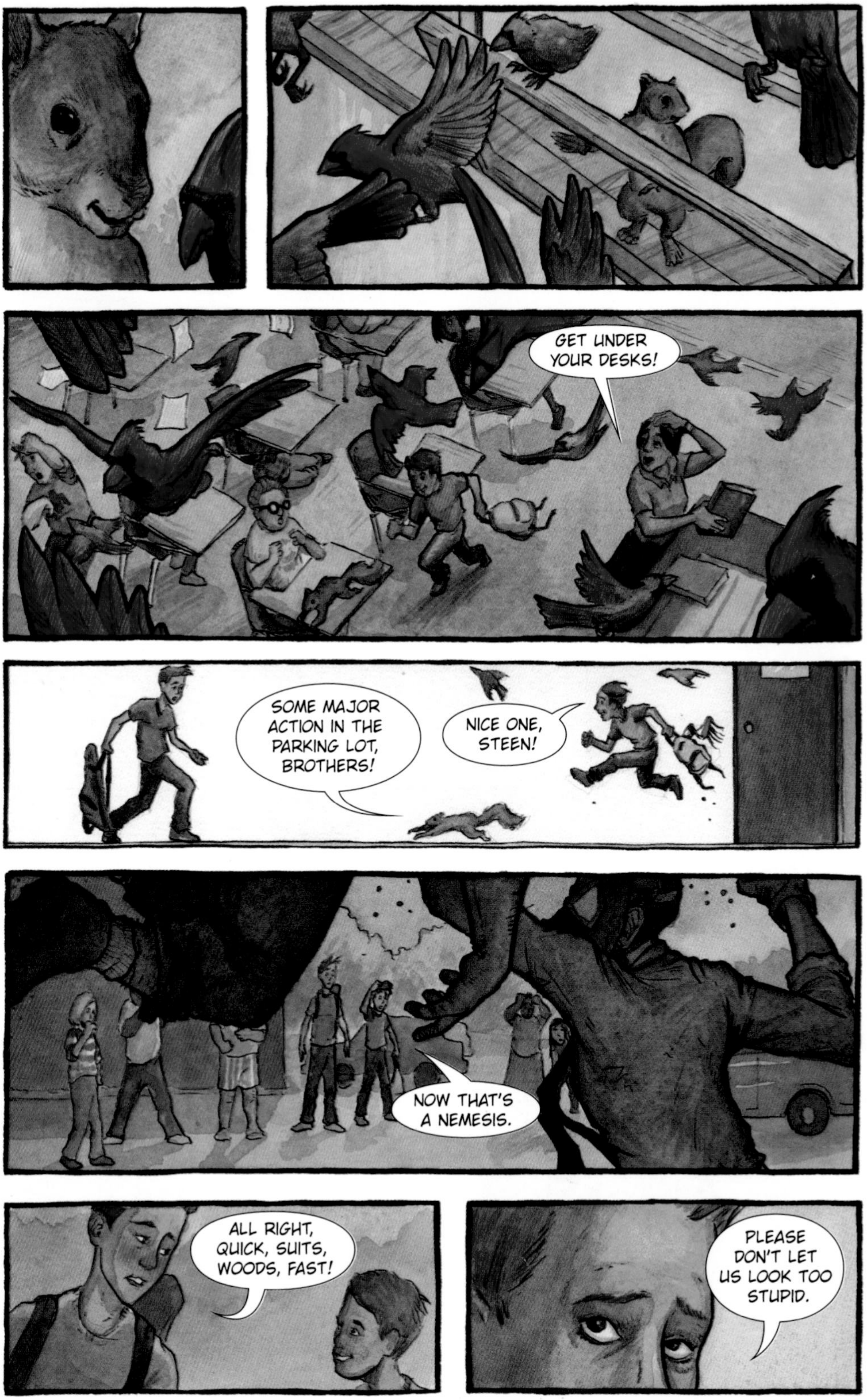
GET UNDER YOUR DESKS!
SOME MAJOR ACTION IN THE PARKING LOT, BROTHERS!
NICE ONE, STEEN!
NOW THAT'S A NEMESIS.
ALL RIGHT, QUICK, SUITS, WOODS, FAST!
PLEASE DON'T LET US LOOK TOO STUPID.

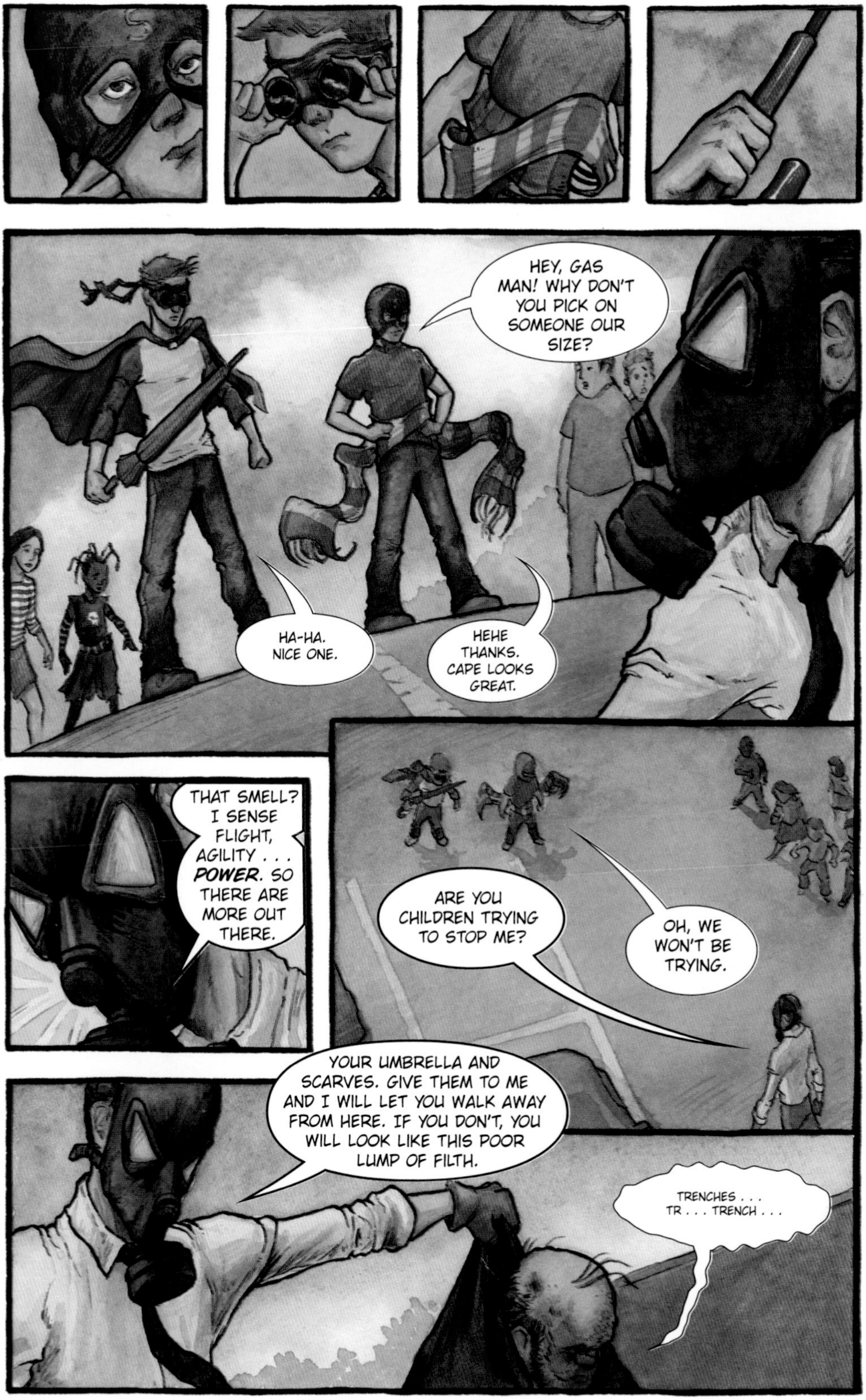
HEY, GAS MAN! WHY DON'T YOU PICK ON SOMEONE OUR SIZE?
HA-HA. NICE ONE.
HEHE THANKS. CAPE LOOKS GREAT.
THAT SMELL? I SENSE FLIGHT, AGILITY . . . POWER. SO THERE ARE MORE OUT THERE.
ARE YOU CHILDREN TRYING TO STOP ME?
OH, WE WON'T BE TRYING.
YOUR UMBRELLA AND SCARVES. GIVE THEM TO ME AND I WILL LET YOU WALK AWAY FROM HERE. IF YOU DON'T, YOU WILL LOOK LIKE THIS POOR LUMP OF FILTH.
TRENCHES . . . TR . . . TRENCH . . .

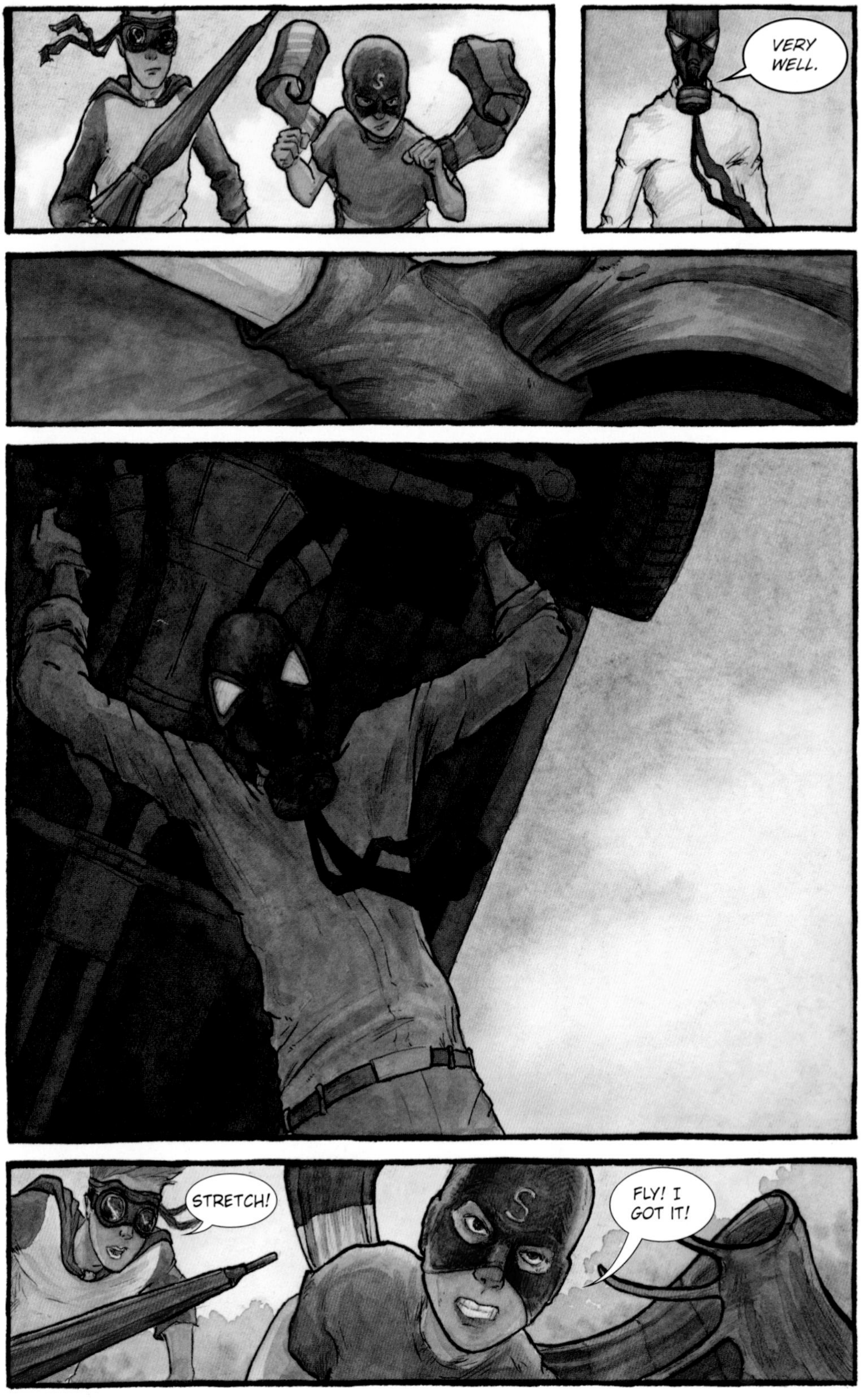
VERY WELL.
STRETCH!
FLY! I GOT IT!

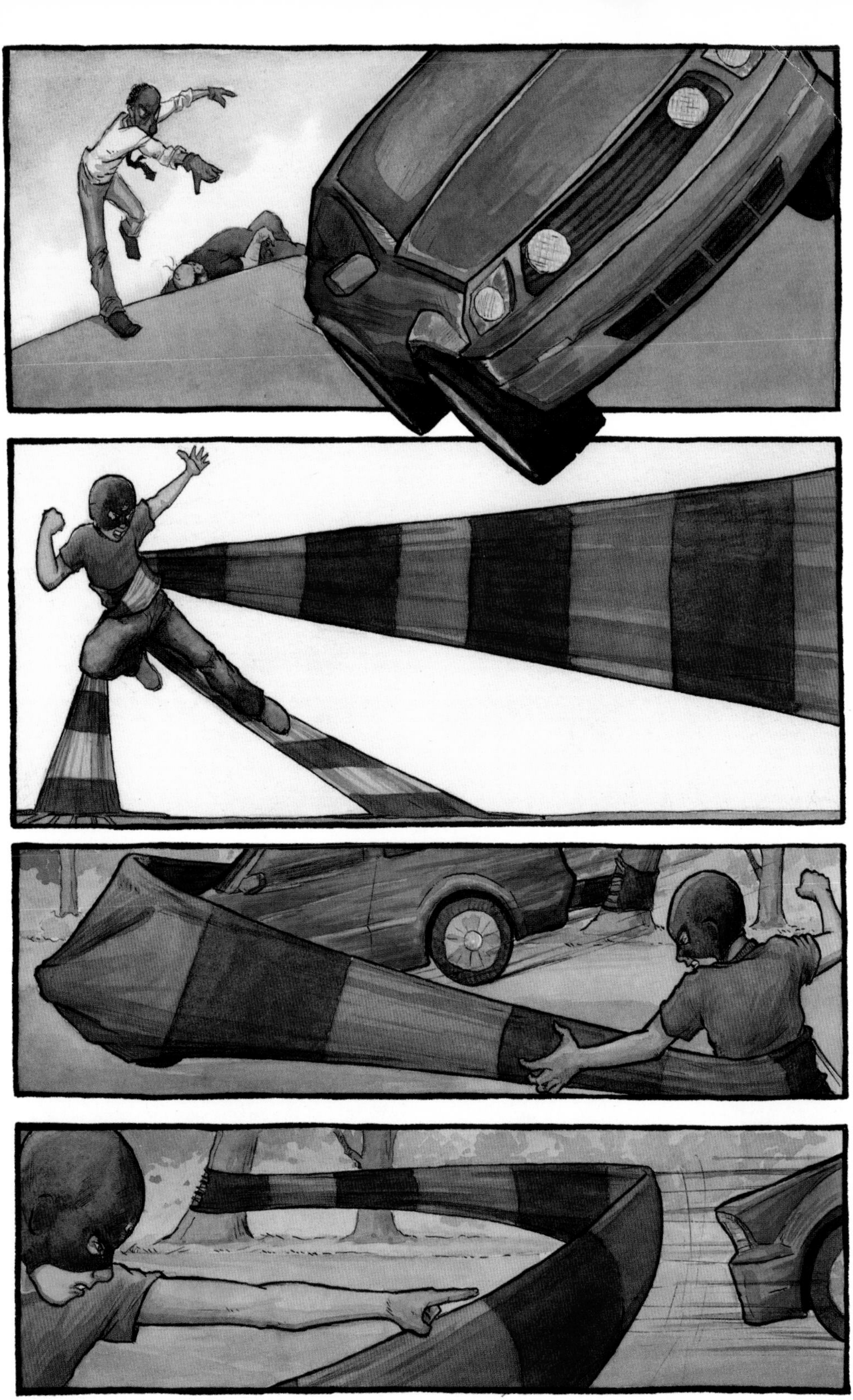

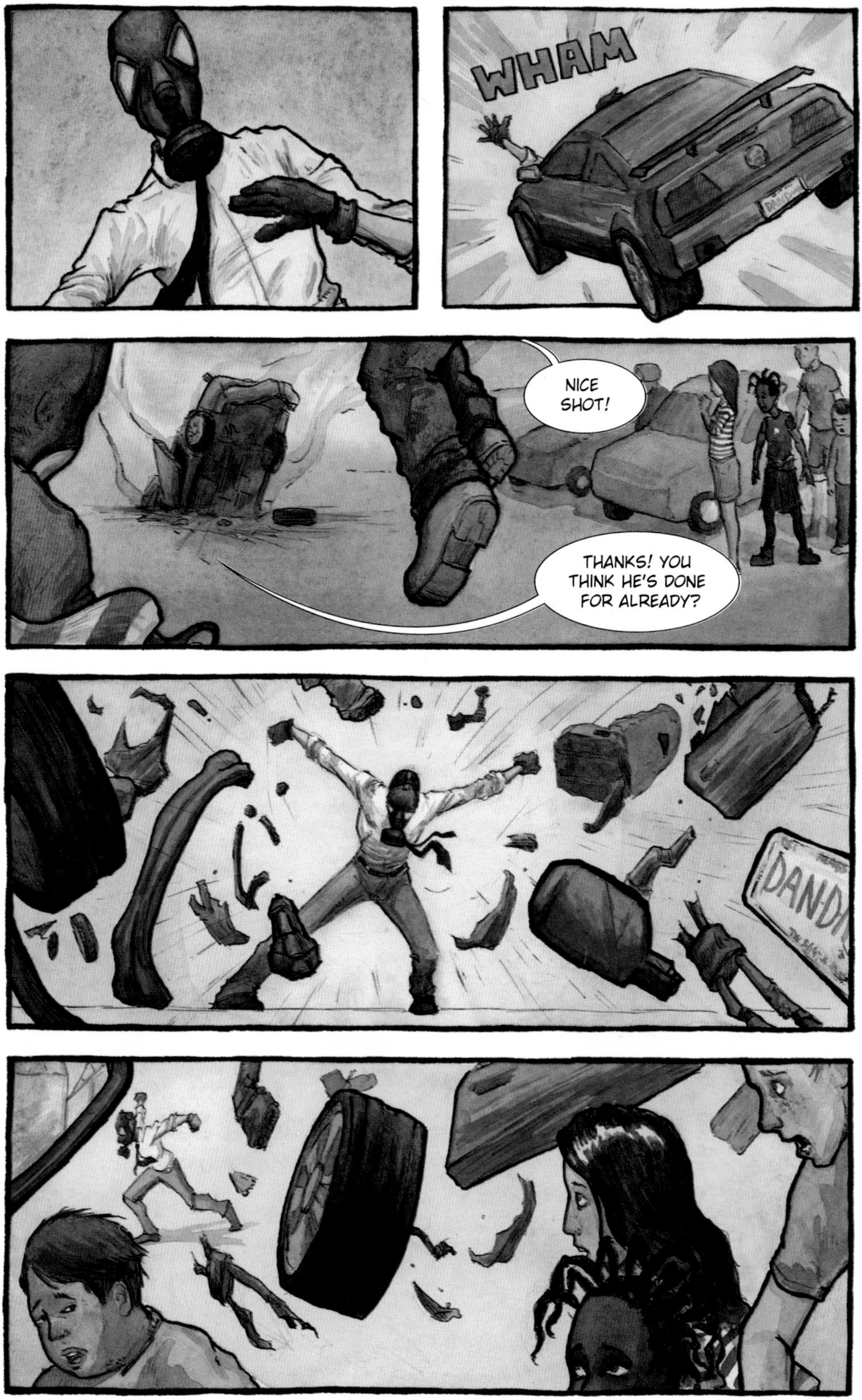
WHAM
NICE SHOT!
THANKS! YOU THINK HE'S DONE FOR ALREADY?

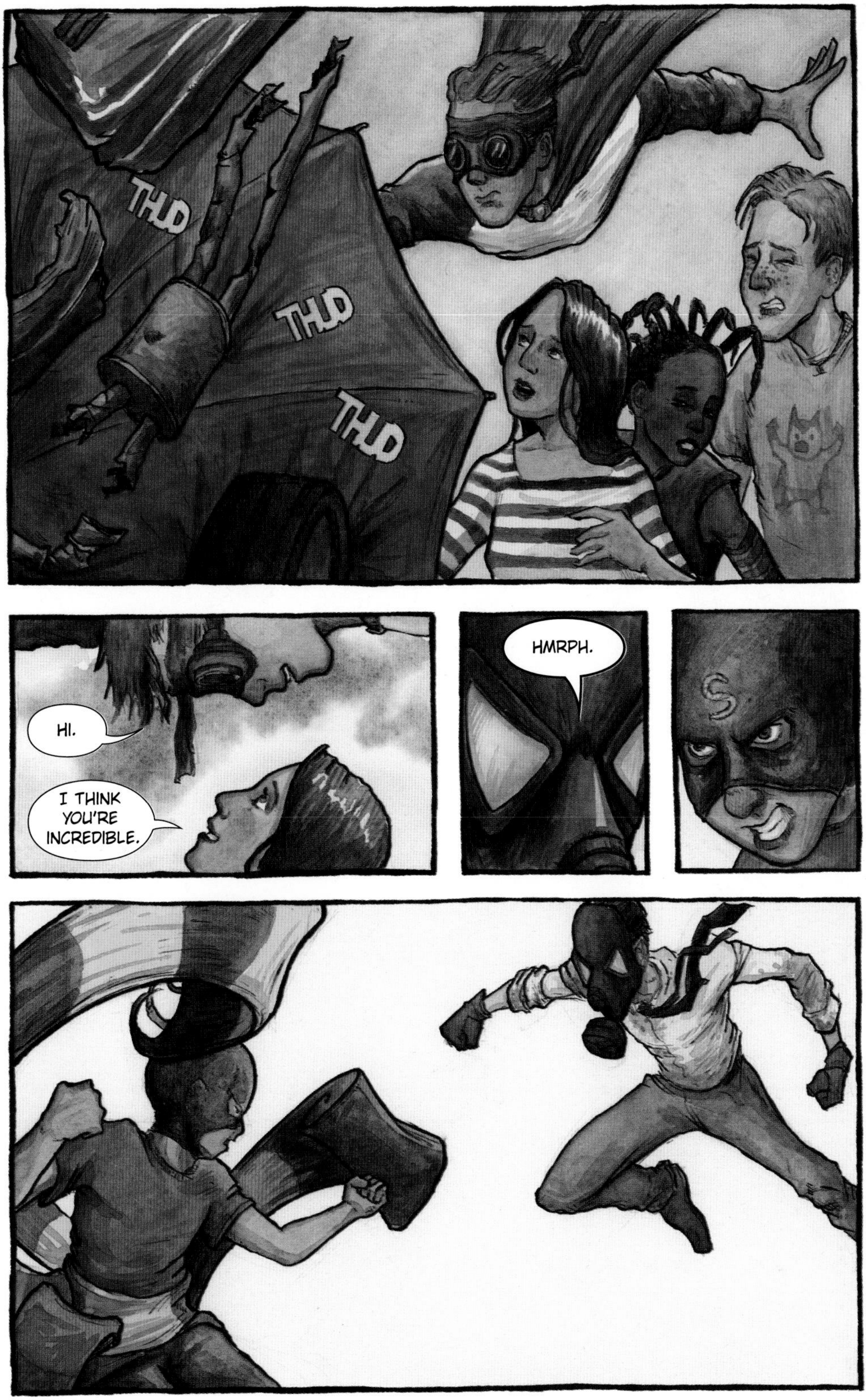
THUD
THUD
THUD
HI.
I THINK YOU'RE INCREDIBLE.
HMRPH.

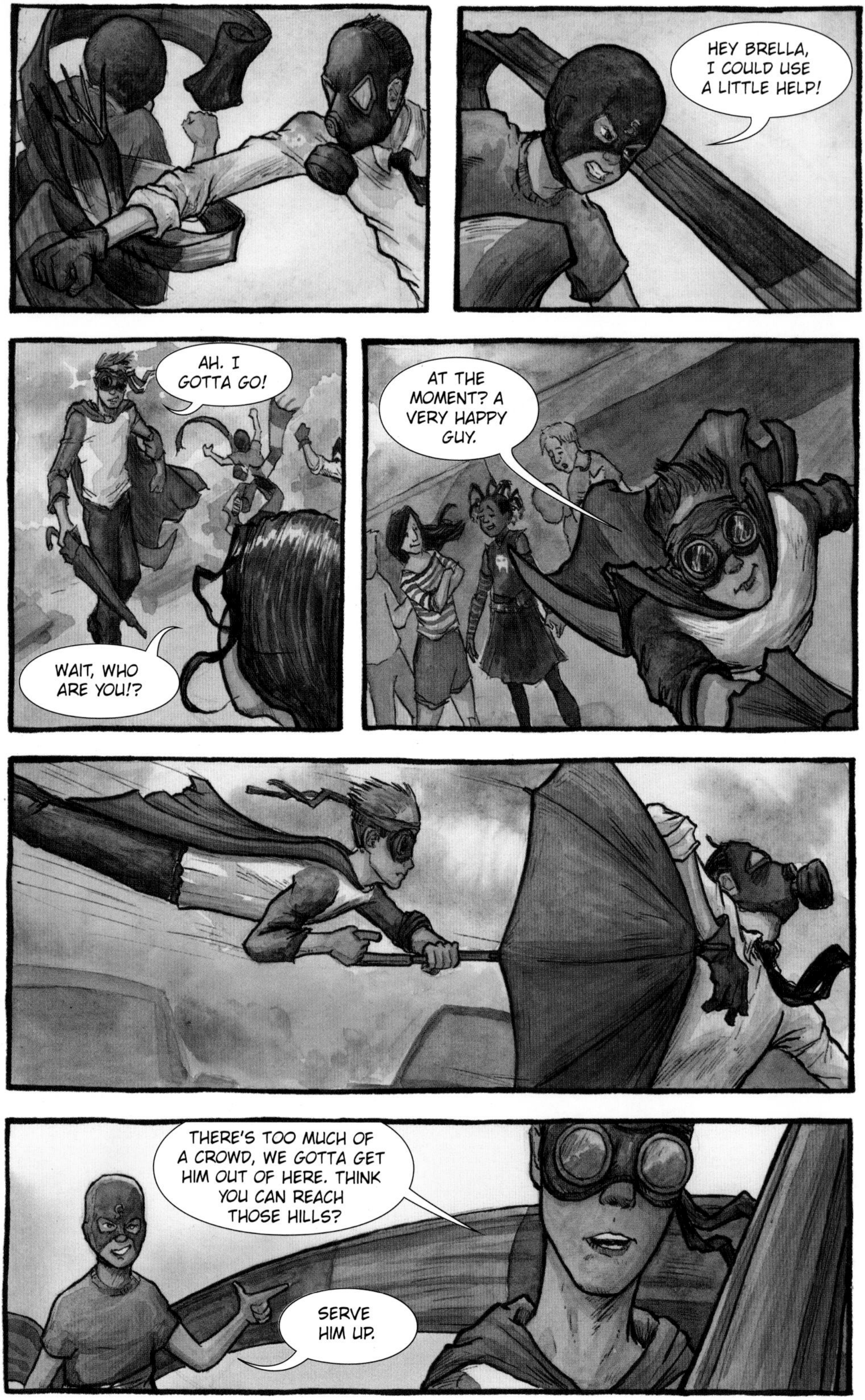
HEY BRELLA, I COULD USE A LITTLE HELP!
AH. I GOTTA GO!
WAIT, WHO ARE YOU!?
AT THE MOMENT? A VERY HAPPY GUY.
THERE'S TOO MUCH OF A CROWD, WE GOTTA GET HIM OUT OF HERE. THINK YOU CAN REACH THOSE HILLS?
SERVE HIM UP.

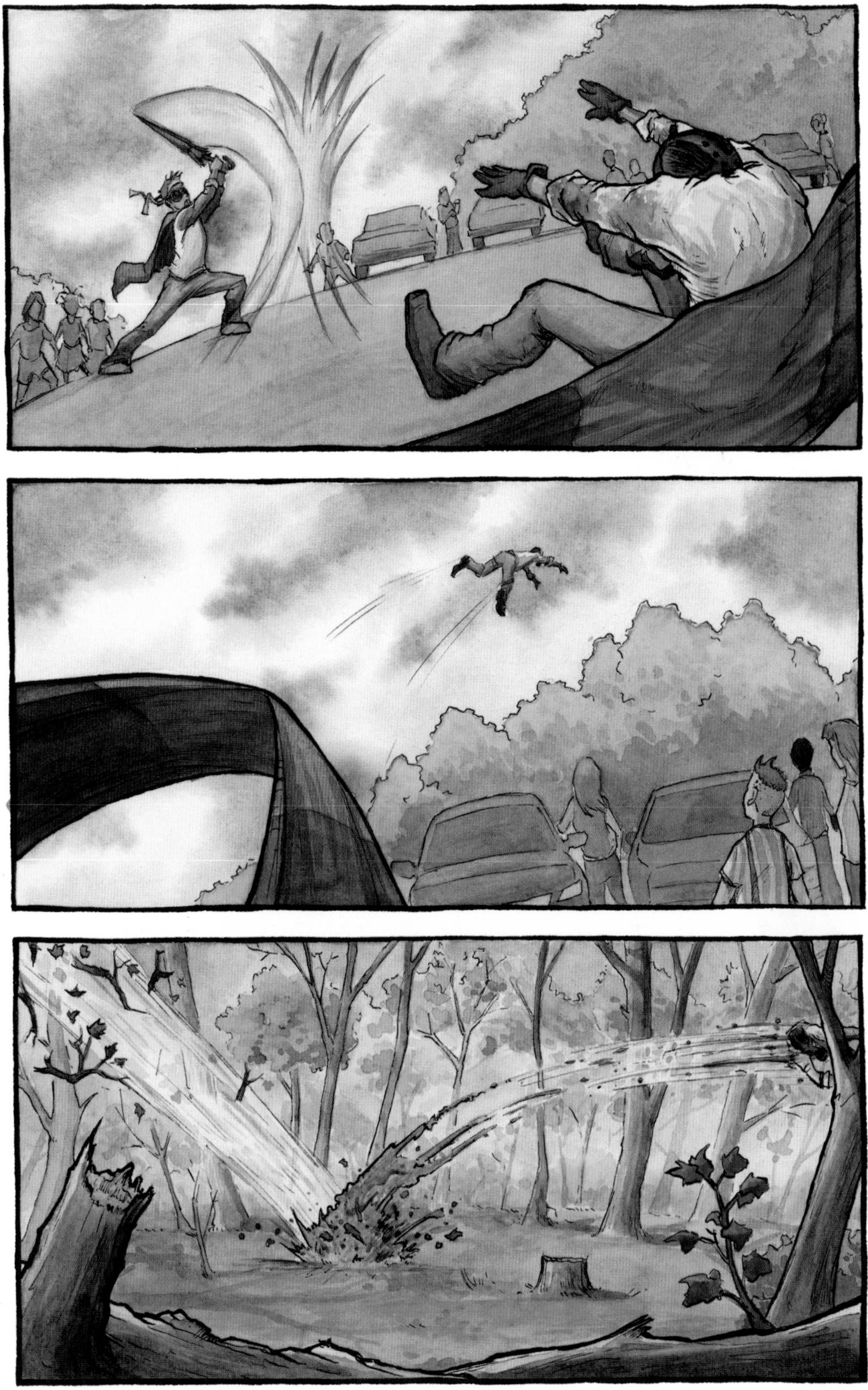

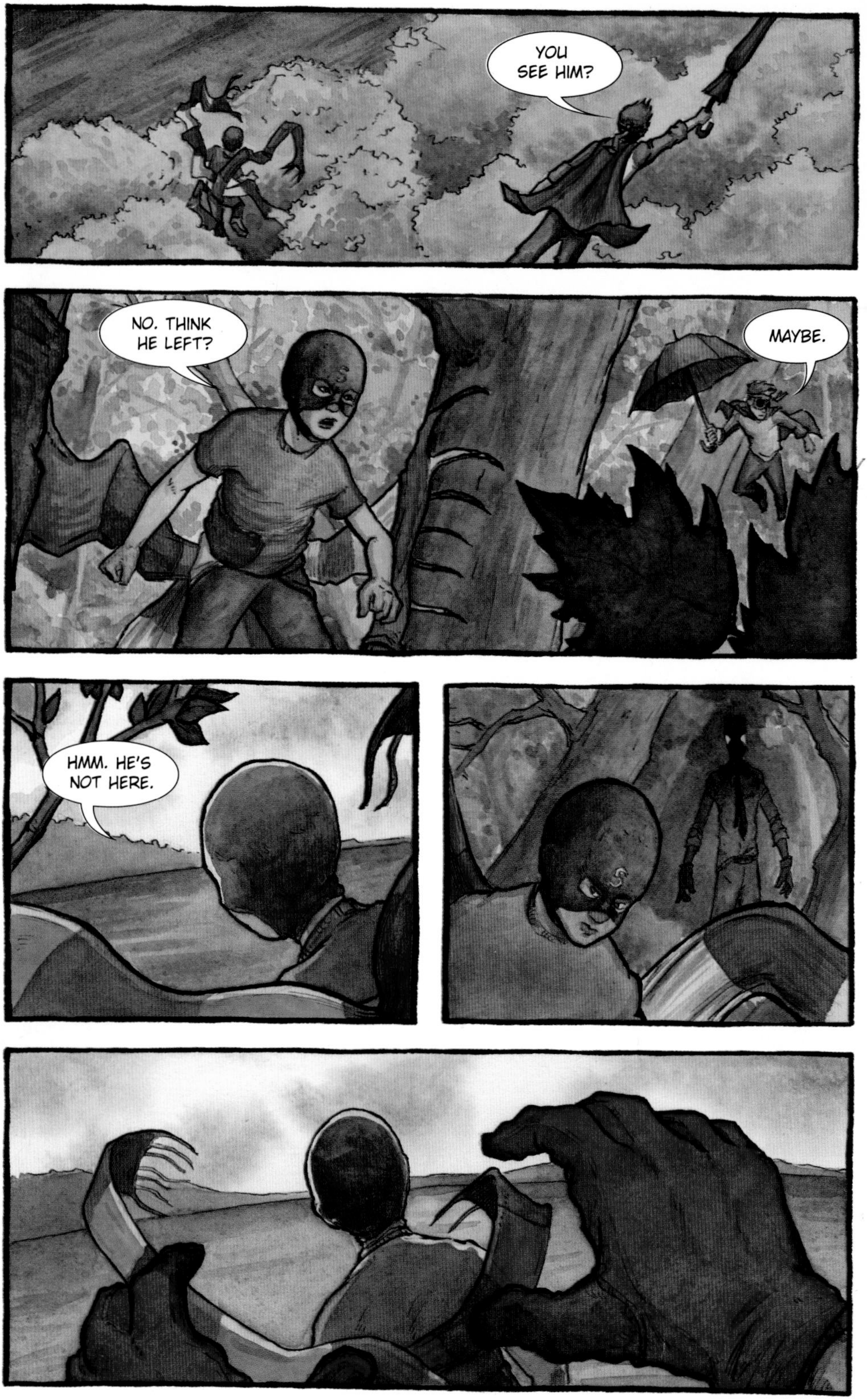
YOU SEE HIM?
NO. THINK HE LEFT?
MAYBE.
HMM. HE'S NOT HERE.

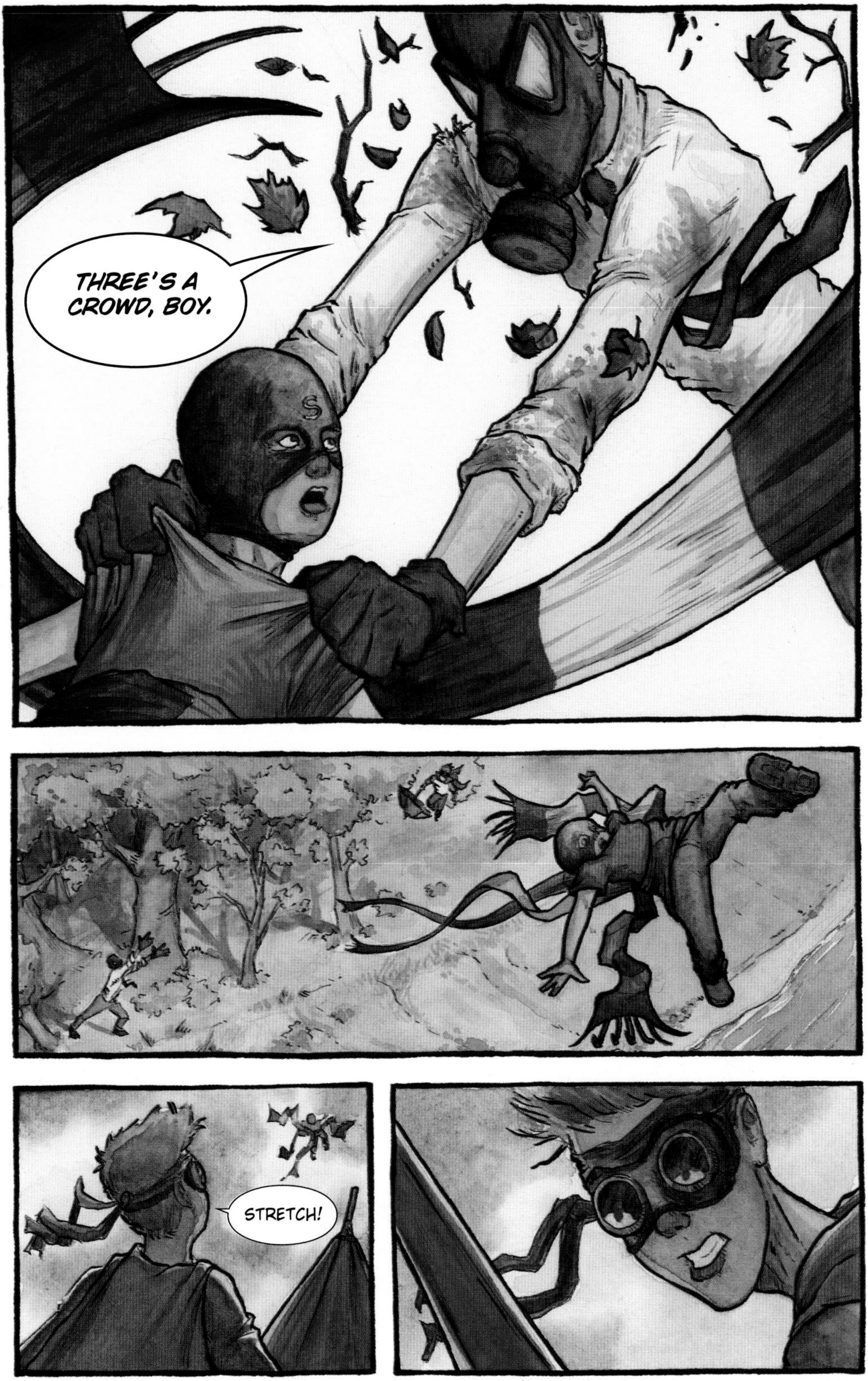
THREE'S A CROWD, BOY.
STRETCH!

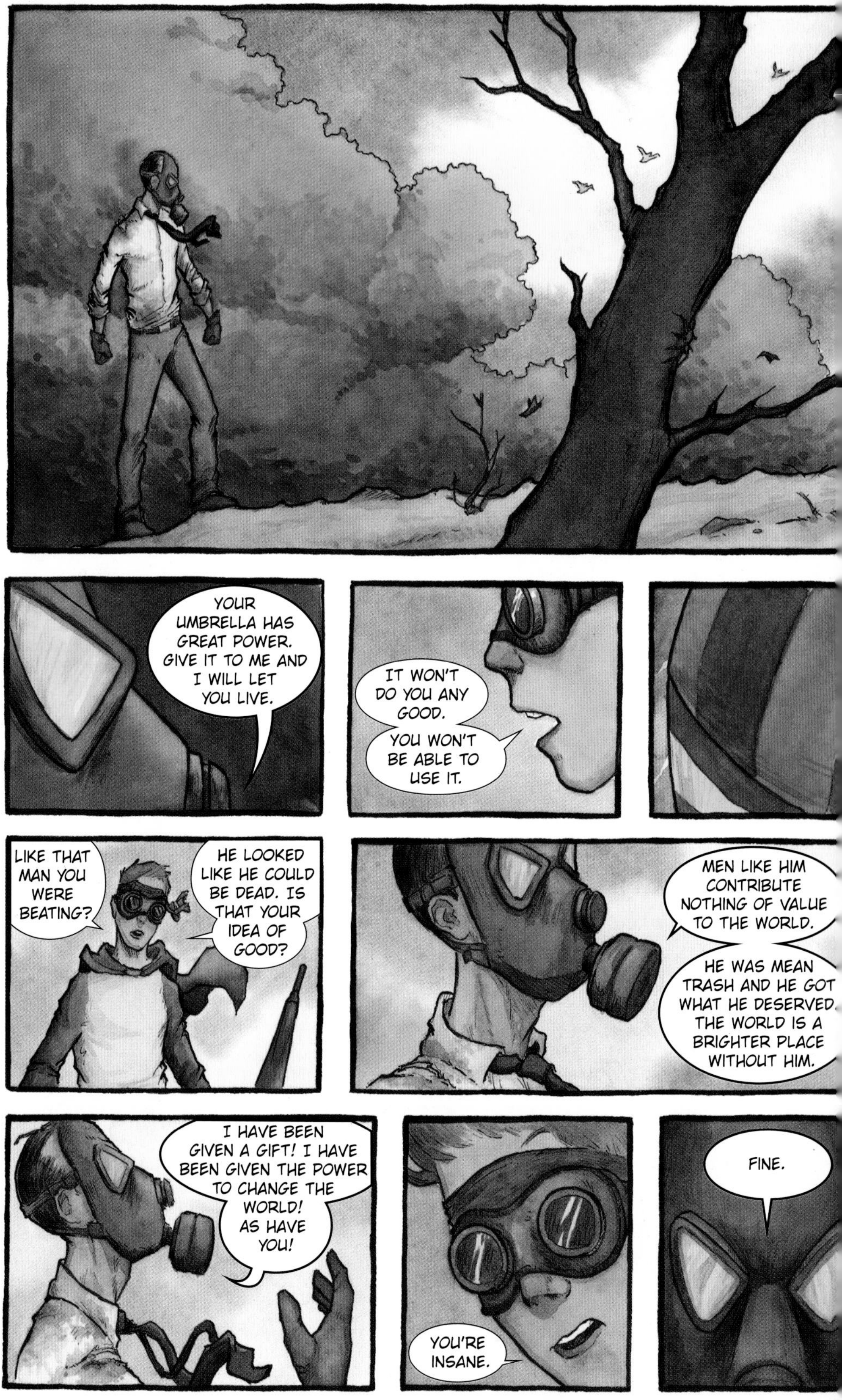
YOUR UMBRELLA HAS GREAT POWER. GIVE IT TO ME AND I WILL LET YOU LIVE.
IT WON'T DO YOU ANY GOOD.
YOU WON'T BE ABLE TO USE IT.
LIKE THAT MAN YOU WERE BEATING?
HE LOOKED LIKE HE COULD BE DEAD. IS THAT YOUR IDEA OF GOOD?
MEN LIKE HIM CONTRIBUTE NOTHING OF VALUE TO THE WORLD.
HE WAS MEAN TRASH AND HE GOT WHAT HE DESERVED. THE WORLD IS A BRIGHTER PLACE WITHOUT HIM.
I HAVE BEEN GIVEN A GIFT! I HAVE BEEN GIVEN THE POWER TO CHANGE THE WORLD! AS HAVE YOU!
YOU'RE INSANE.
FINE.

OH, BUT I CAN. I'M SPECIAL. I *CAN* USE THEM. I CAN SENSE THAT YOU HAVE YET TO UNLOCK THE TRUE POWER OF YOUR UMBRELLA.

LOOK AT YOU. DRESSING UP AND PLAYING HERO. I WILL USE THEM FOR GOOD. MAKE A REAL DIFFERENCE IN THE WORLD.

WHO ARE YOU TO JUDGE THAT?

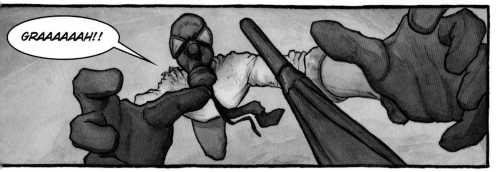

GRAAAAAAH!!

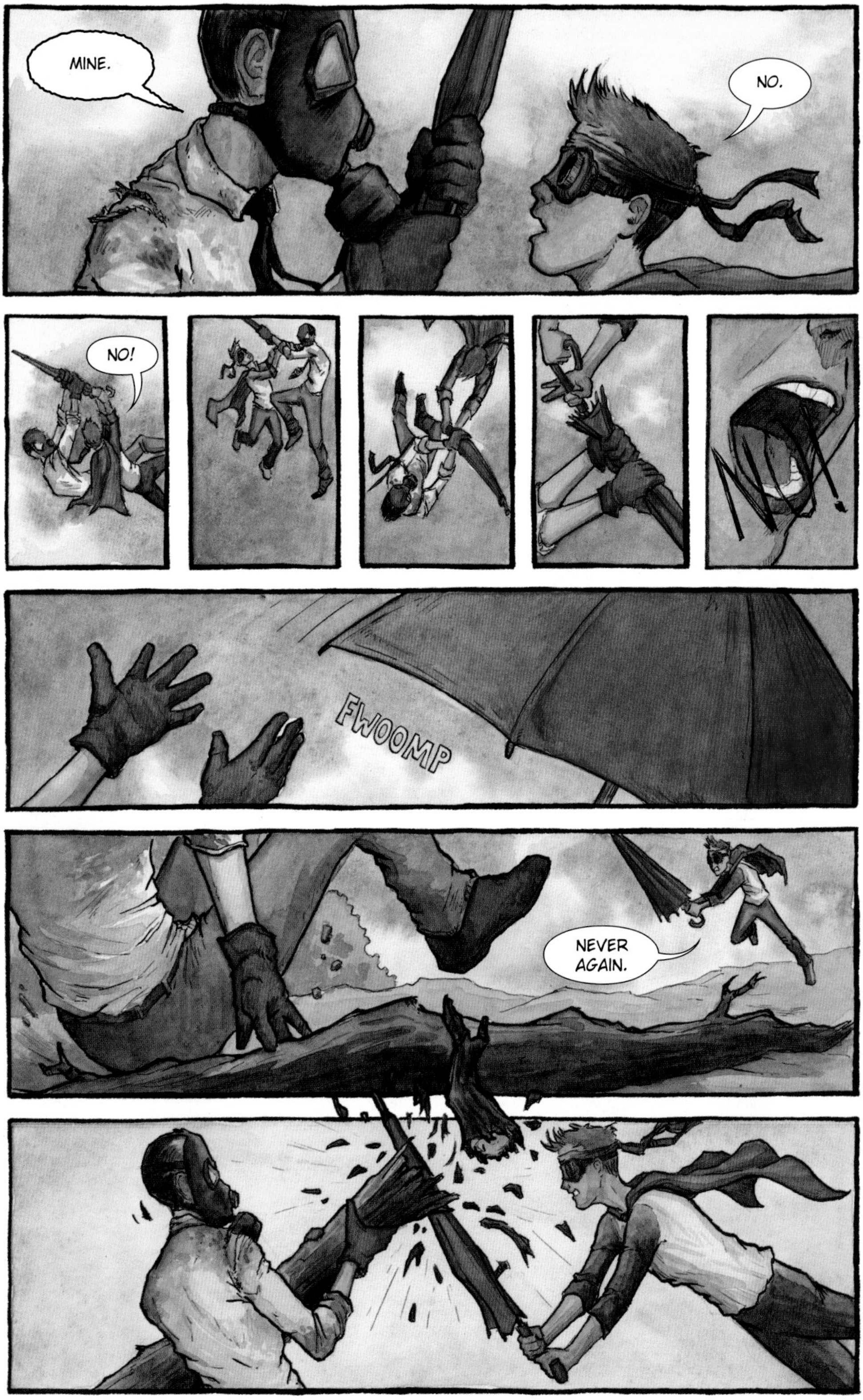
MINE.
NO.
NO!
FWOOMP
NEVER AGAIN.

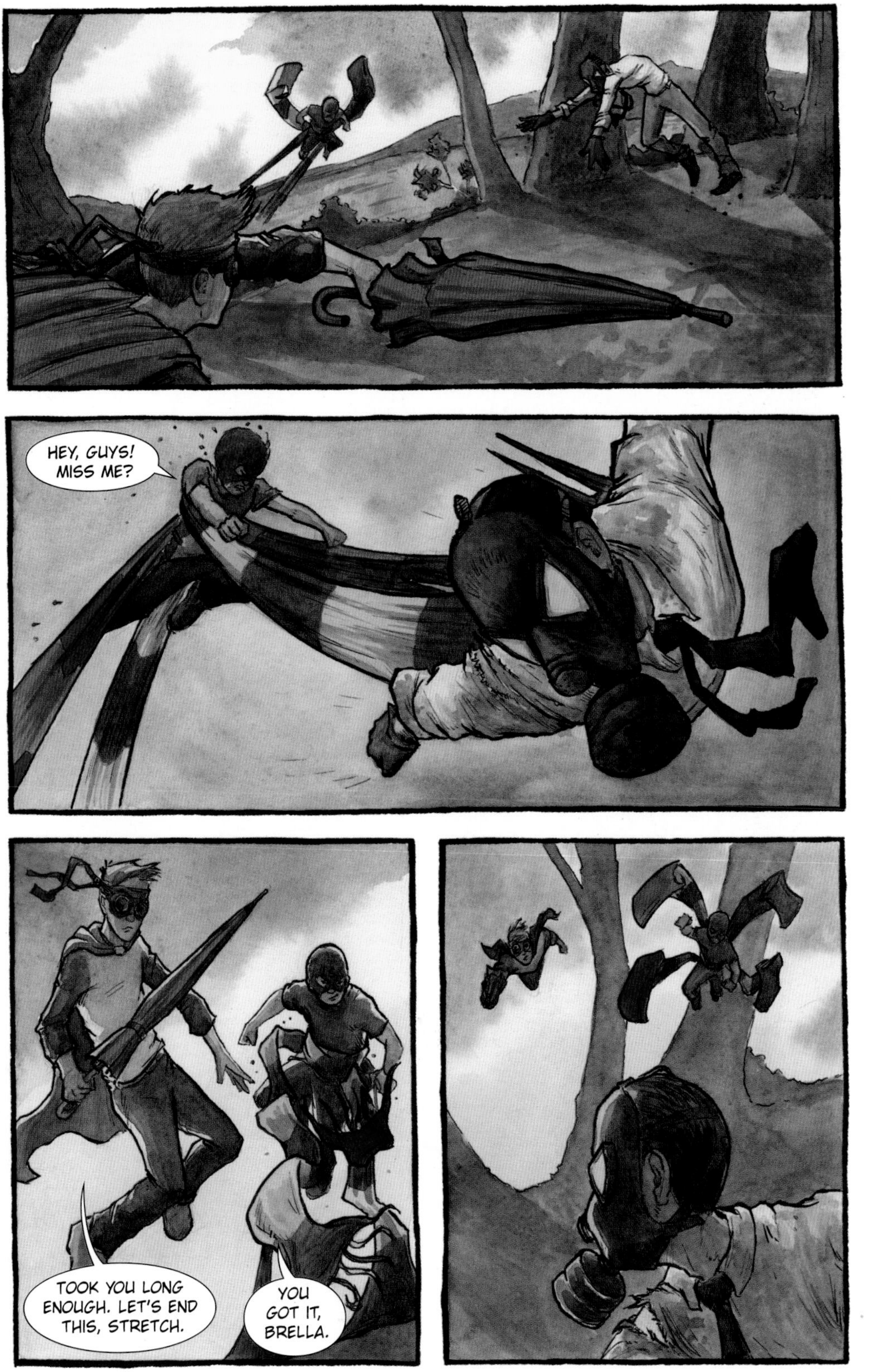
HEY, GUYS! MISS ME?
TOOK YOU LONG ENOUGH. LET'S END THIS, STRETCH.
YOU GOT IT, BRELLA.

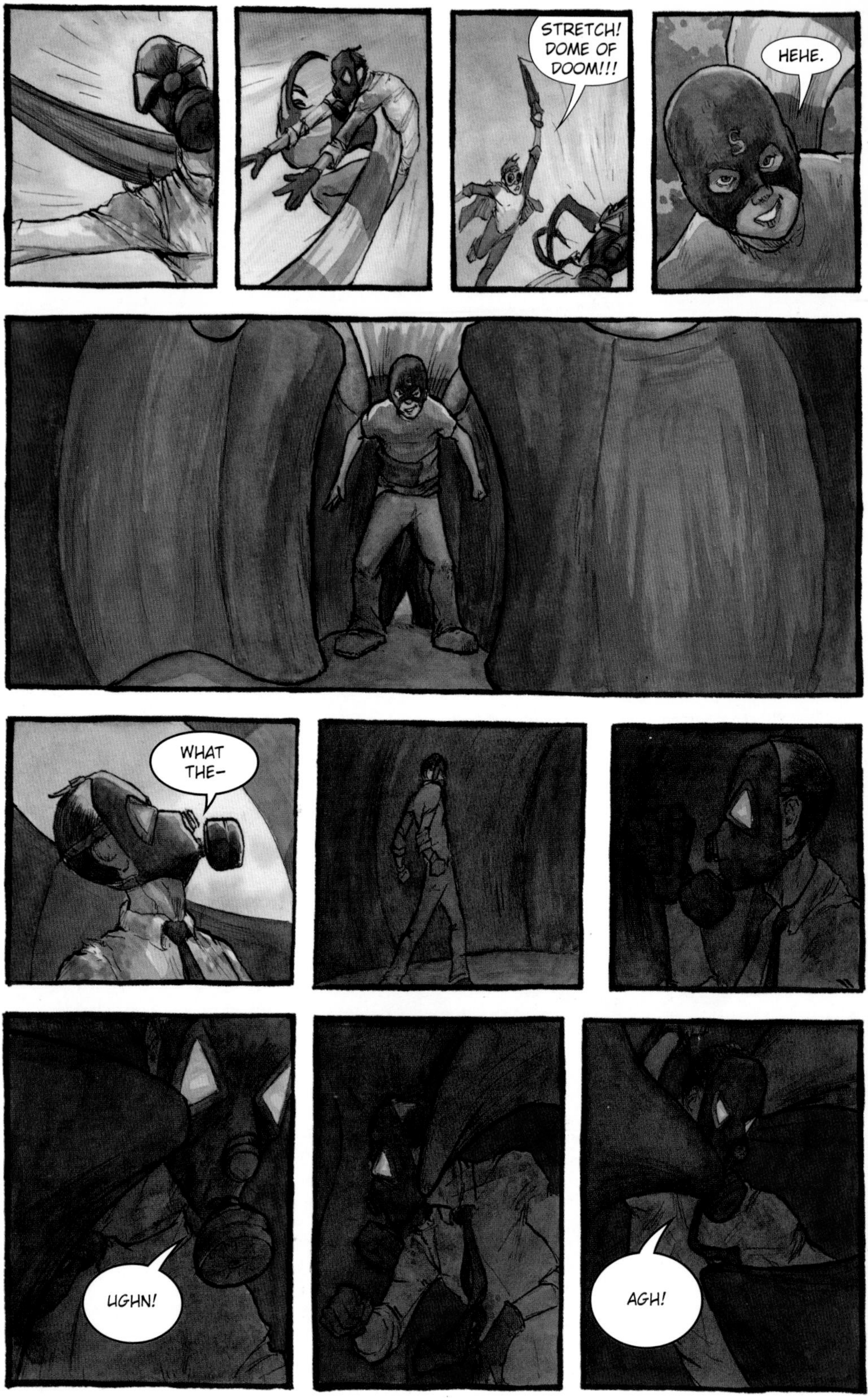
STRETCH! DOME OF DOOM!!!
HEHE.
WHAT THE-
UGHN!
AGH!

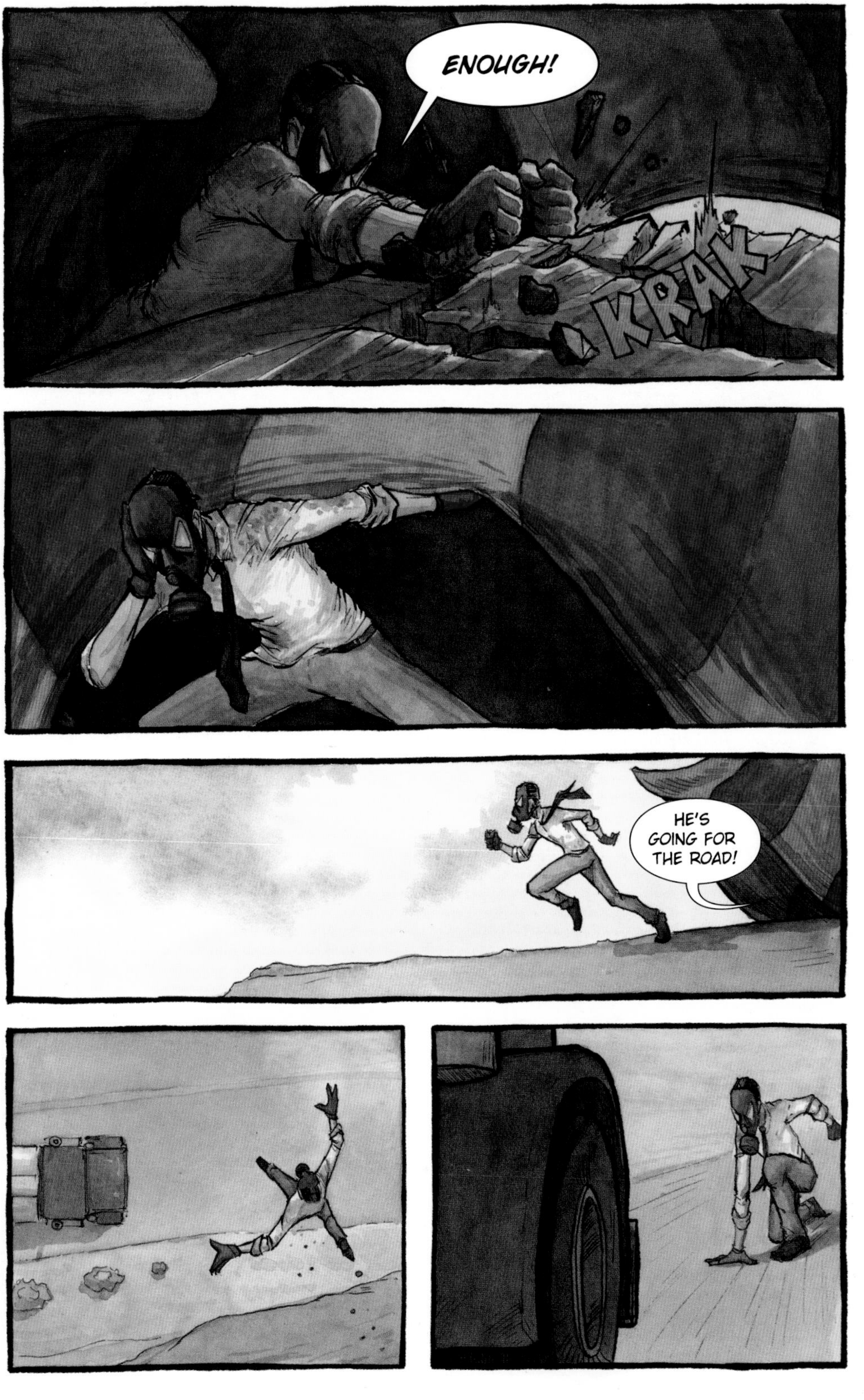
ENOUGH!
KRAK
HE'S GOING FOR THE ROAD!

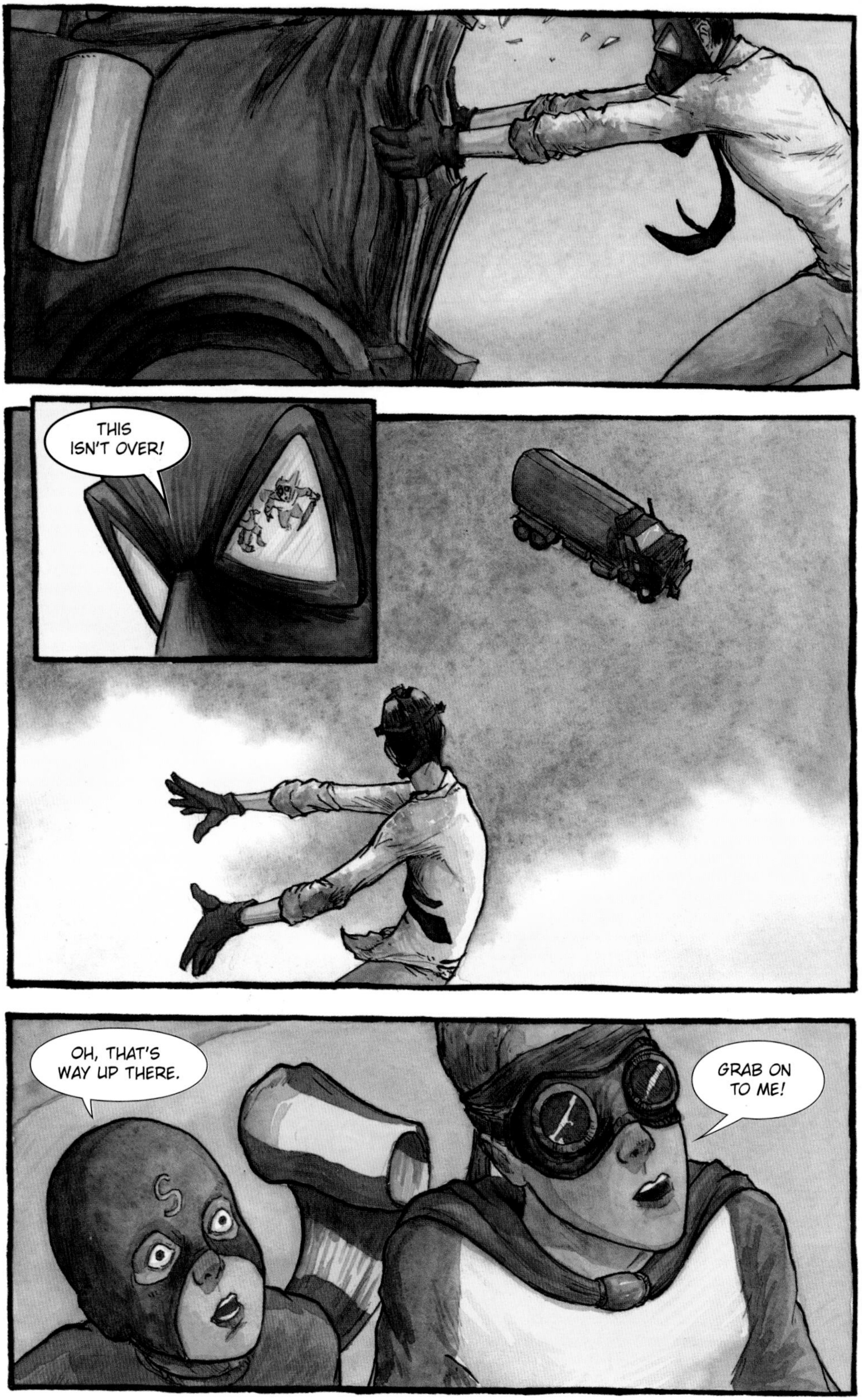
THIS ISN'T OVER!
OH, THAT'S WAY UP THERE.
GRAB ON TO ME!

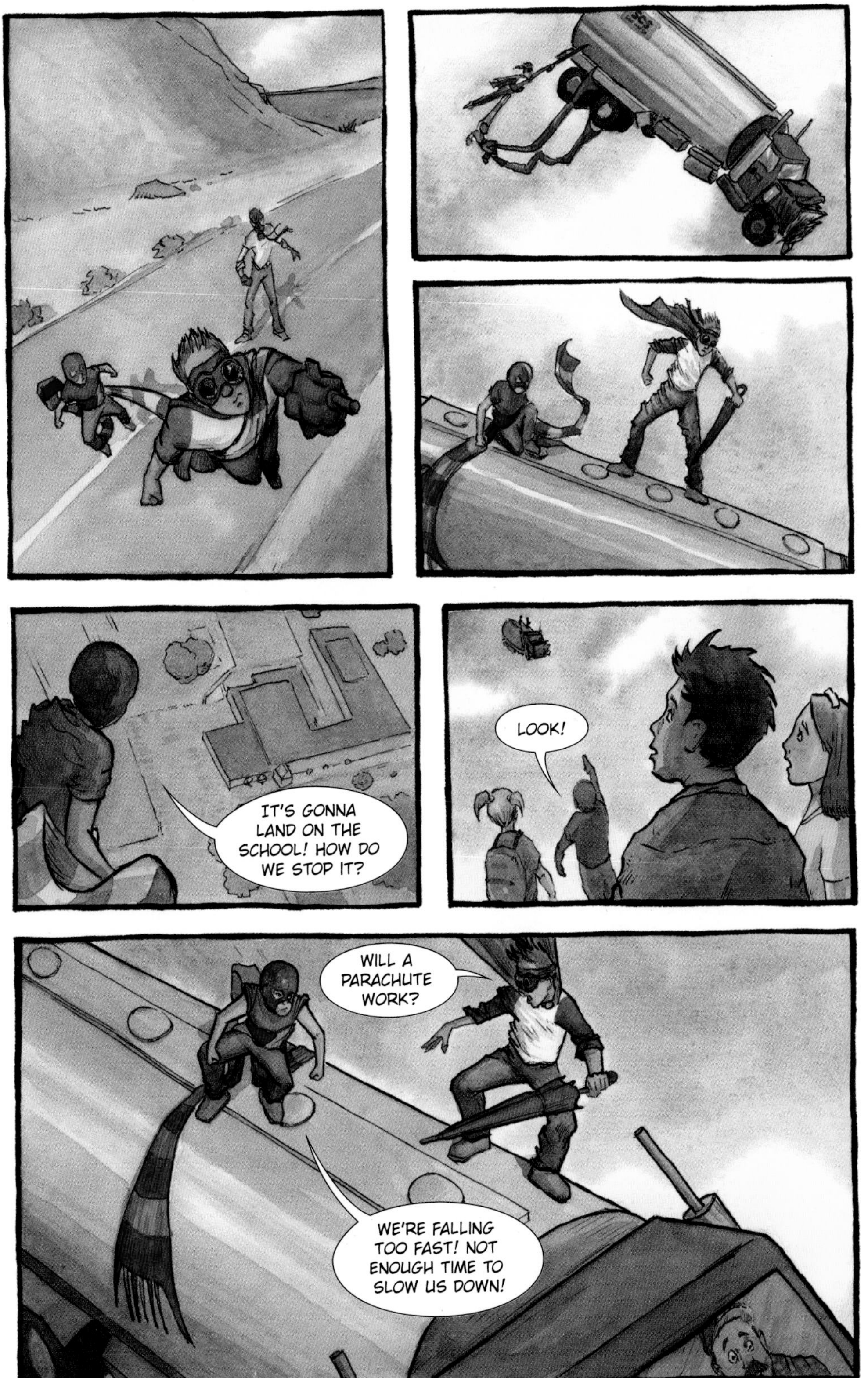
IT'S GONNA LAND ON THE SCHOOL! HOW DO WE STOP IT?
LOOK!
WILL A PARACHUTE WORK?
WE'RE FALLING TOO FAST! NOT ENOUGH TIME TO SLOW US DOWN!

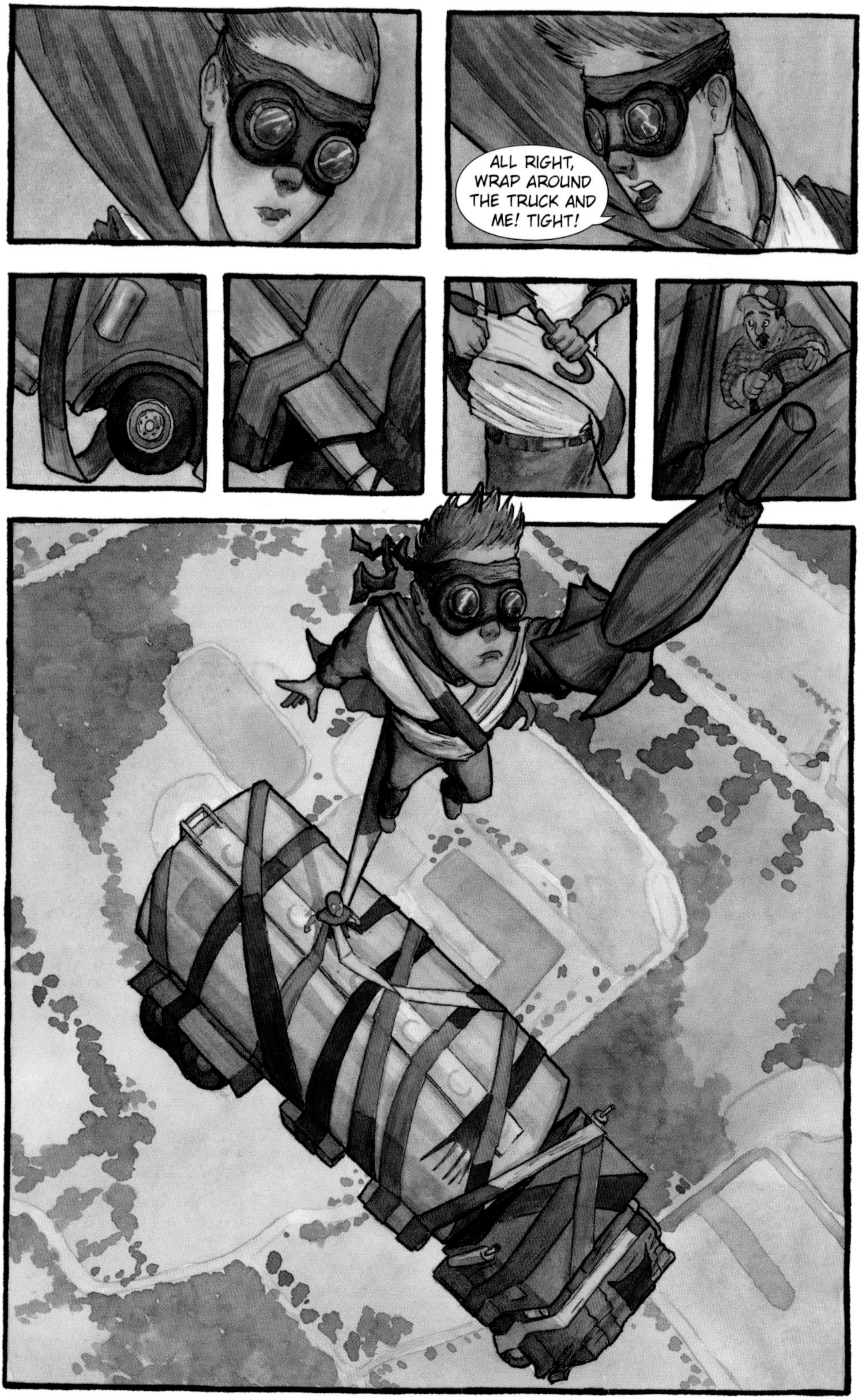
ALL RIGHT, WRAP AROUND THE TRUCK AND ME! TIGHT!

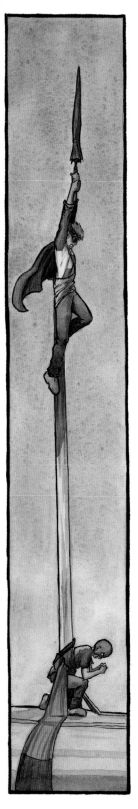

ISABELLA, MOVE!

HE'LL STOP IT. I KNOW HE'LL STOP IT.

RRRGGHH!

AARGH!

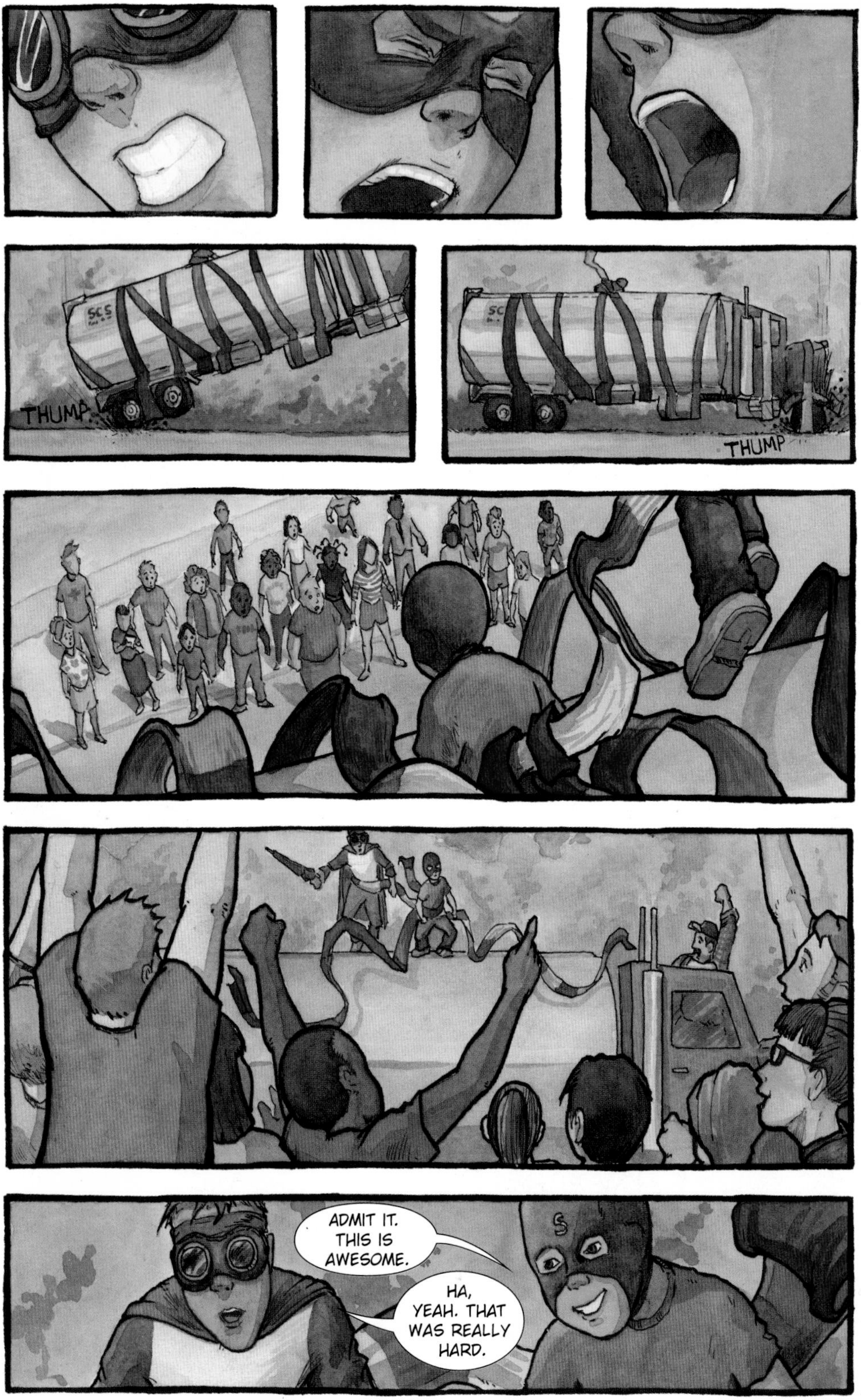
THUMP
THUMP
ADMIT IT. THIS IS AWESOME.
HA, YEAH. THAT WAS REALLY HARD.

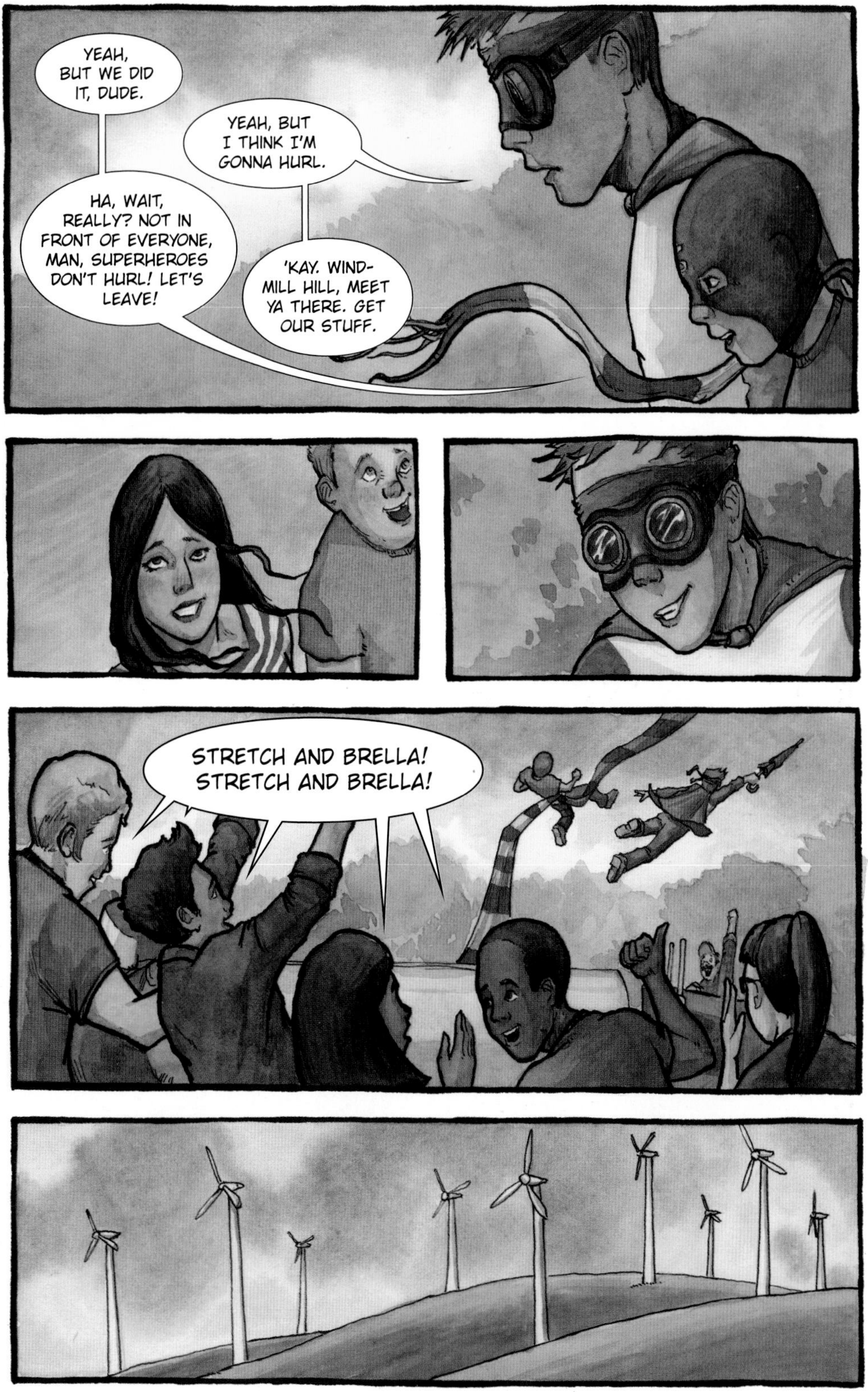
YEAH, BUT WE DID IT, DUDE.
YEAH, BUT I THINK I'M GONNA HURL.
HA, WAIT, REALLY? NOT IN FRONT OF EVERYONE, MAN, SUPERHEROES DON'T HURL! LET'S LEAVE!
'KAY. WIND-MILL HILL, MEET YA THERE. GET OUR STUFF.
STRETCH AND BRELLA! STRETCH AND BRELLA!

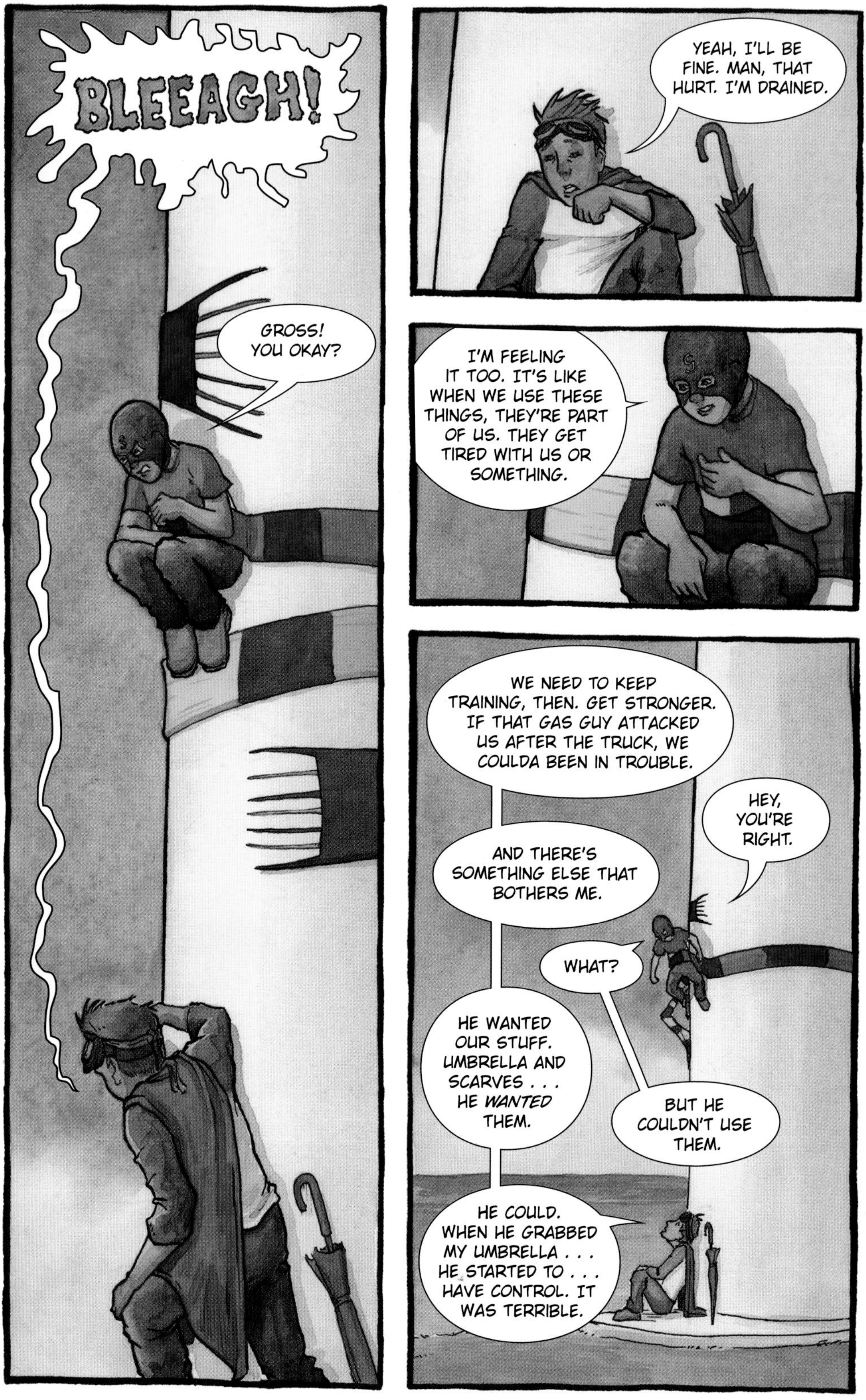
BLEEAGH!
GROSS! YOU OKAY?
YEAH, I'LL BE FINE. MAN, THAT HURT. I'M DRAINED.
I'M FEELING IT TOO. IT'S LIKE WHEN WE USE THESE THINGS, THEY'RE PART OF US. THEY GET TIRED WITH US OR SOMETHING.
WE NEED TO KEEP TRAINING, THEN. GET STRONGER. IF THAT GAS GUY ATTACKED US AFTER THE TRUCK, WE COULDA BEEN IN TROUBLE.
HEY, YOU'RE RIGHT.
AND THERE'S SOMETHING ELSE THAT BOTHERS ME.
WHAT?
HE WANTED OUR STUFF. UMBRELLA AND SCARVES . . . HE *WANTED* THEM.
BUT HE COULDN'T USE THEM.
HE COULD. WHEN HE GRABBED MY UMBRELLA . . . HE STARTED TO . . . HAVE CONTROL. IT WAS TERRIBLE.

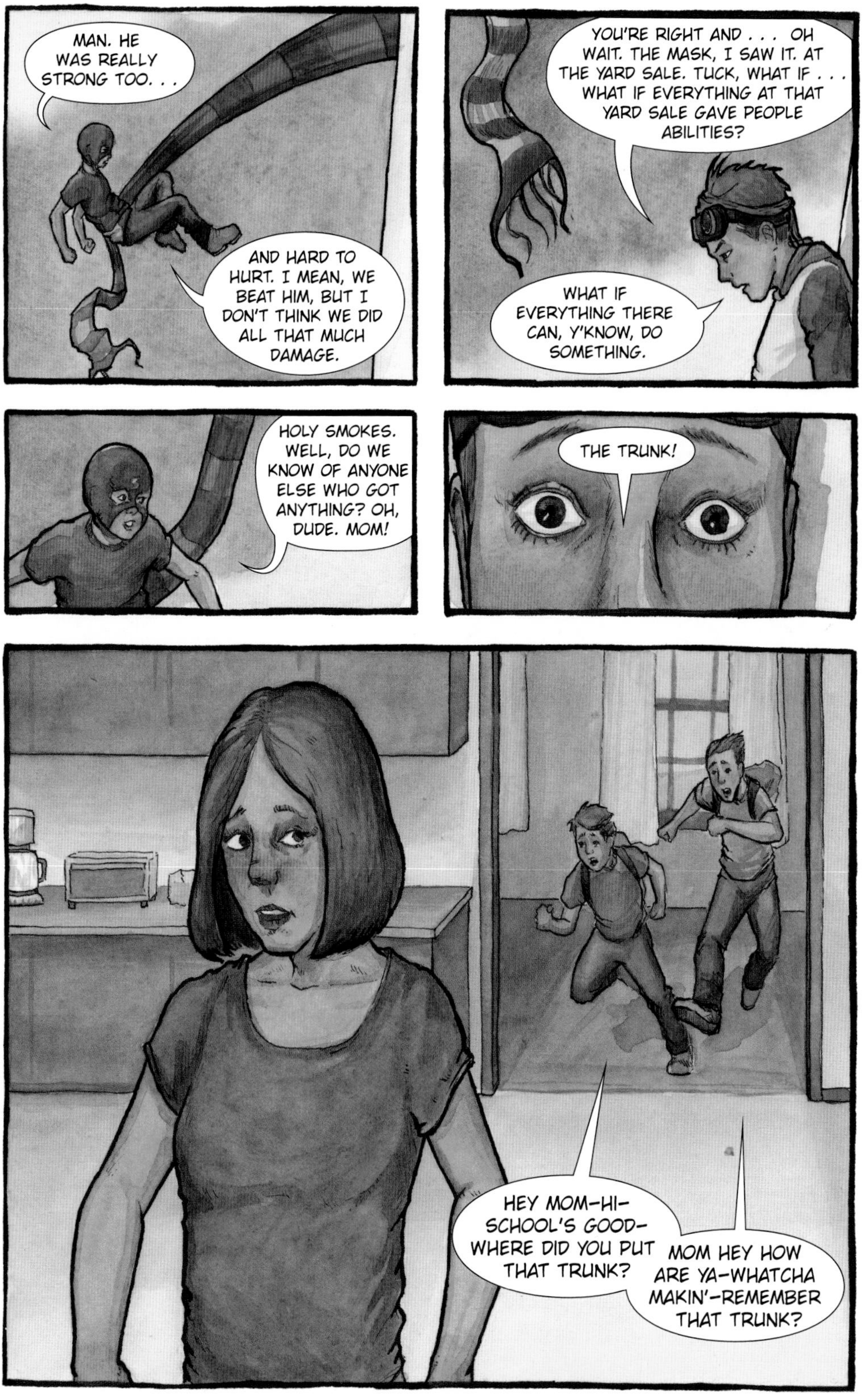
MAN. HE WAS REALLY STRONG TOO. . .
AND HARD TO HURT. I MEAN, WE BEAT HIM, BUT I DON'T THINK WE DID ALL THAT MUCH DAMAGE.
YOU'RE RIGHT AND . . . OH WAIT. THE MASK, I SAW IT. AT THE YARD SALE. TUCK, WHAT IF . . . WHAT IF EVERYTHING AT THAT YARD SALE GAVE PEOPLE ABILITIES?
WHAT IF EVERYTHING THERE CAN, Y'KNOW, DO SOMETHING.
HOLY SMOKES. WELL, DO WE KNOW OF ANYONE ELSE WHO GOT ANYTHING? OH, DUDE. MOM!
THE TRUNK!
HEY MOM–HI–SCHOOL'S GOOD–WHERE DID YOU PUT THAT TRUNK?
MOM HEY HOW ARE YA–WHATCHA MAKIN'–REMEMBER THAT TRUNK?

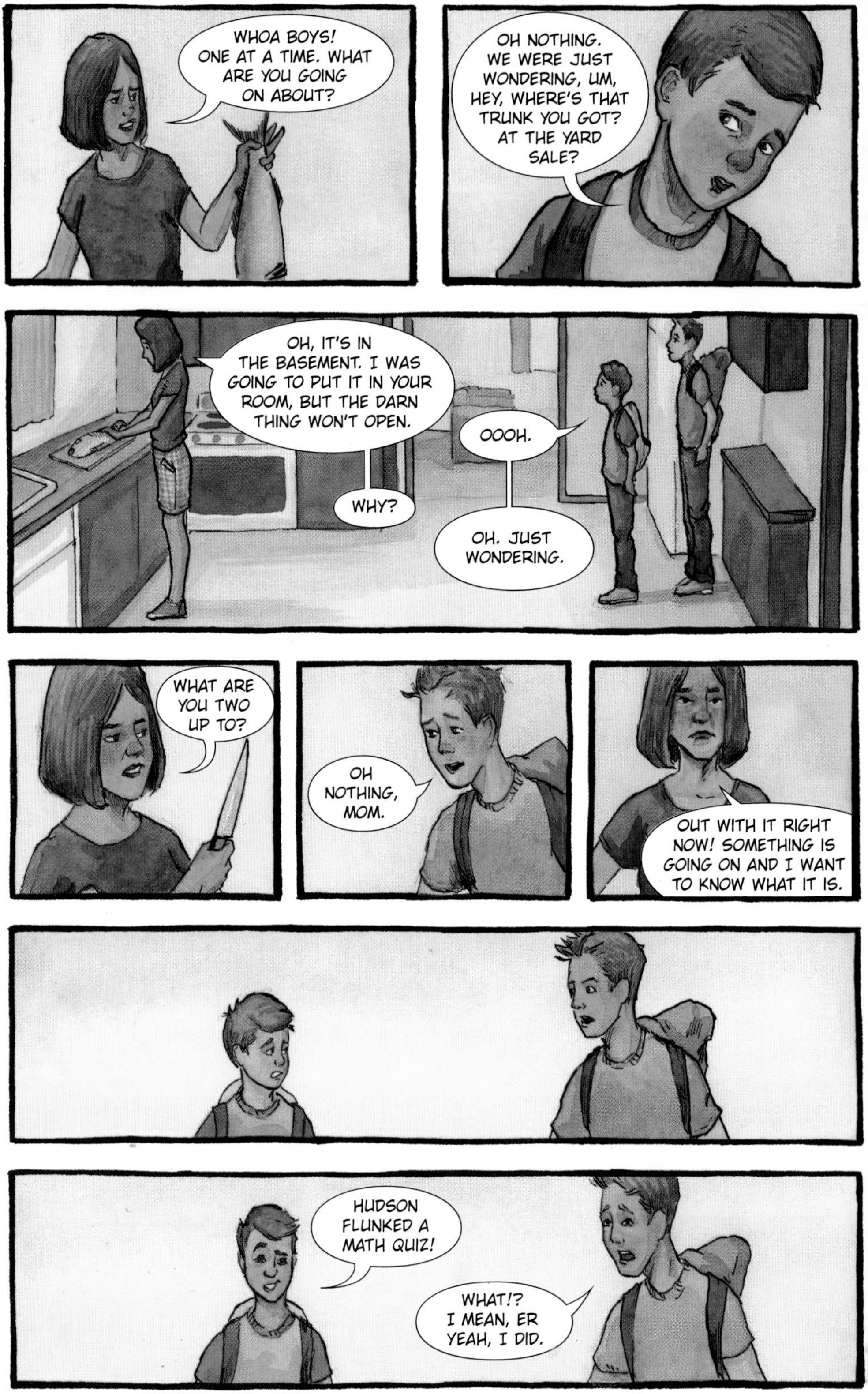
WHOA BOYS! ONE AT A TIME. WHAT ARE YOU GOING ON ABOUT?
OH NOTHING. WE WERE JUST WONDERING, UM, HEY, WHERE'S THAT TRUNK YOU GOT? AT THE YARD SALE?
OH, IT'S IN THE BASEMENT. I WAS GOING TO PUT IT IN YOUR ROOM, BUT THE DARN THING WON'T OPEN.
WHY?
OOOH.
OH. JUST WONDERING.
WHAT ARE YOU TWO UP TO?
OH NOTHING, MOM.
OUT WITH IT RIGHT NOW! SOMETHING IS GOING ON AND I WANT TO KNOW WHAT IT IS.
HUDSON FLUNKED A MATH QUIZ!
WHAT!? I MEAN, ER YEAH, I DID.

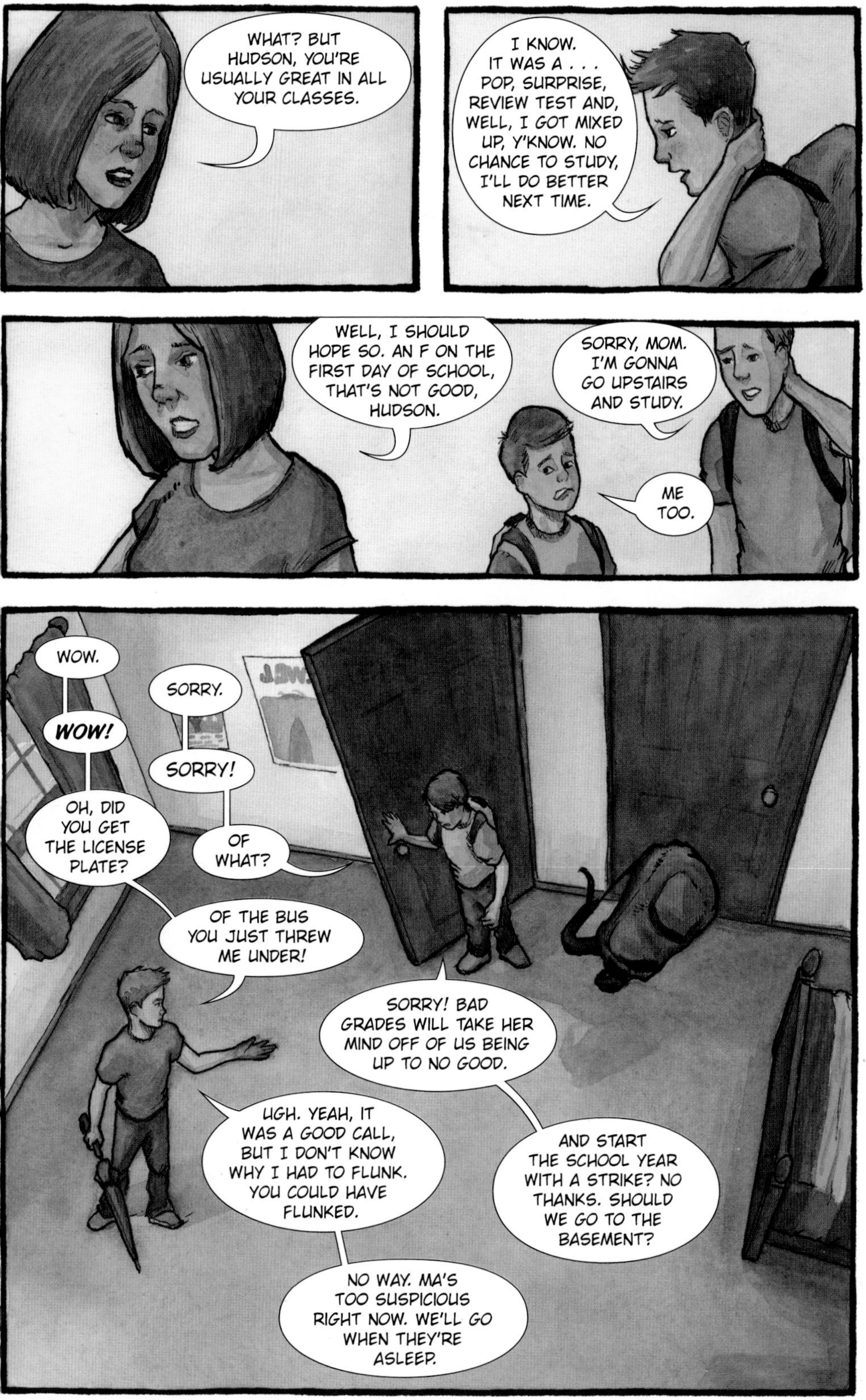
WHAT? BUT HUDSON, YOU'RE USUALLY GREAT IN ALL YOUR CLASSES.
I KNOW. IT WAS A . . . POP, SURPRISE, REVIEW TEST AND, WELL, I GOT MIXED UP, Y'KNOW. NO CHANCE TO STUDY, I'LL DO BETTER NEXT TIME.
WELL, I SHOULD HOPE SO. AN F ON THE FIRST DAY OF SCHOOL, THAT'S NOT GOOD, HUDSON.
SORRY, MOM. I'M GONNA GO UPSTAIRS AND STUDY.
ME TOO.
WOW.
SORRY.
WOW!
SORRY!
OH, DID YOU GET THE LICENSE PLATE?
OF WHAT?
OF THE BUS YOU JUST THREW ME UNDER!
SORRY! BAD GRADES WILL TAKE HER MIND OFF OF US BEING UP TO NO GOOD.
UGH. YEAH, IT WAS A GOOD CALL, BUT I DON'T KNOW WHY I HAD TO FLUNK. YOU COULD HAVE FLUNKED.
AND START THE SCHOOL YEAR WITH A STRIKE? NO THANKS. SHOULD WE GO TO THE BASEMENT?
NO WAY. MA'S TOO SUSPICIOUS RIGHT NOW. WE'LL GO WHEN THEY'RE ASLEEP.

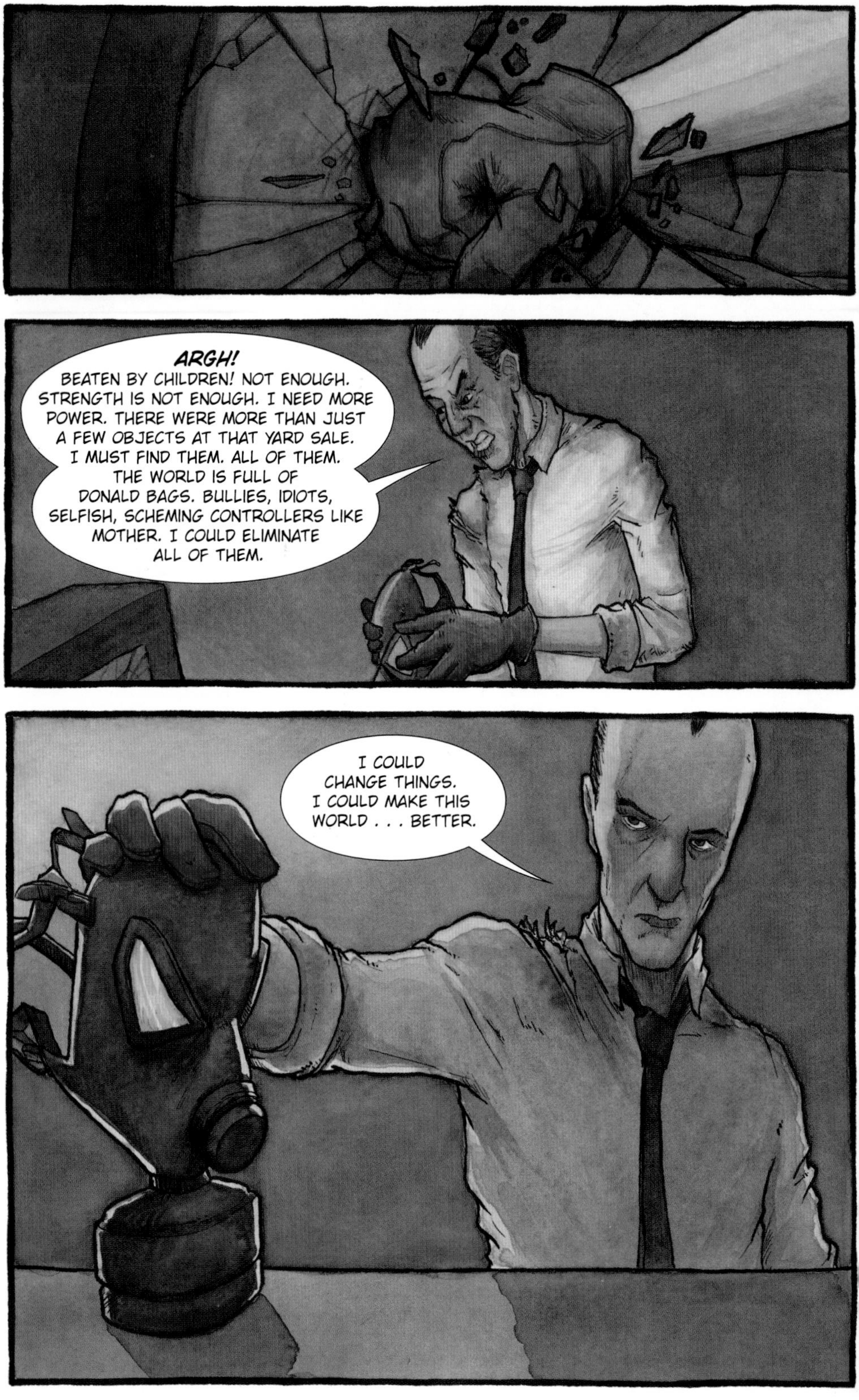
ARGH!
BEATEN BY CHILDREN! NOT ENOUGH. STRENGTH IS NOT ENOUGH. I NEED MORE POWER. THERE WERE MORE THAN JUST A FEW OBJECTS AT THAT YARD SALE. I MUST FIND THEM. ALL OF THEM. THE WORLD IS FULL OF DONALD BAGS. BULLIES, IDIOTS, SELFISH, SCHEMING CONTROLLERS LIKE MOTHER. I COULD ELIMINATE ALL OF THEM.
I COULD CHANGE THINGS. I COULD MAKE THIS WORLD . . . BETTER.

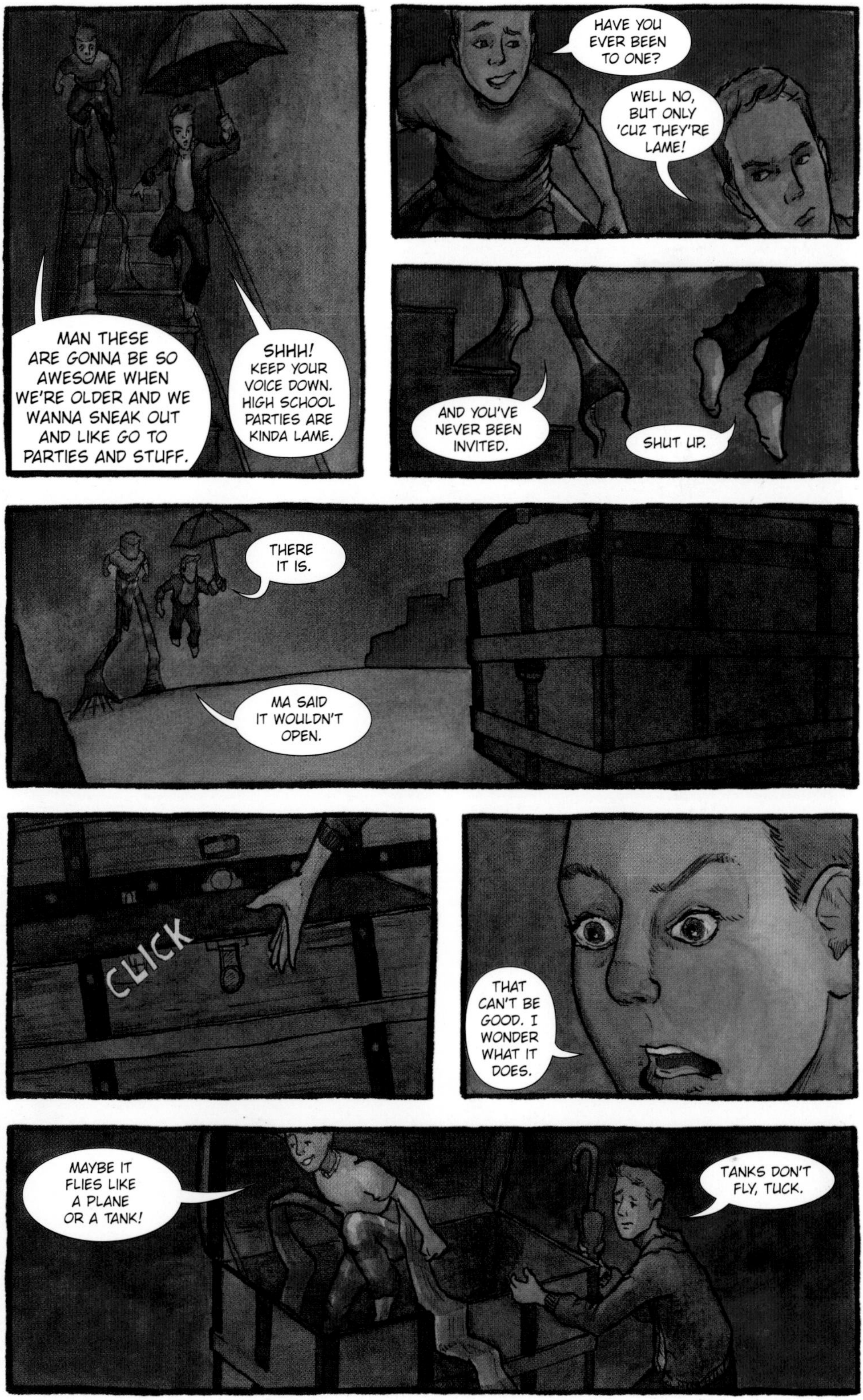
MAN THESE ARE GONNA BE SO AWESOME WHEN WE'RE OLDER AND WE WANNA SNEAK OUT AND LIKE GO TO PARTIES AND STUFF.
SHHH! KEEP YOUR VOICE DOWN. HIGH SCHOOL PARTIES ARE KINDA LAME.
HAVE YOU EVER BEEN TO ONE?
WELL NO, BUT ONLY 'CUZ THEY'RE LAME!
AND YOU'VE NEVER BEEN INVITED.
SHUT UP.
THERE IT IS.
MA SAID IT WOULDN'T OPEN.
CLICK
THAT CAN'T BE GOOD. I WONDER WHAT IT DOES.
MAYBE IT FLIES LIKE A PLANE OR A TANK!
TANKS DON'T FLY, TUCK.

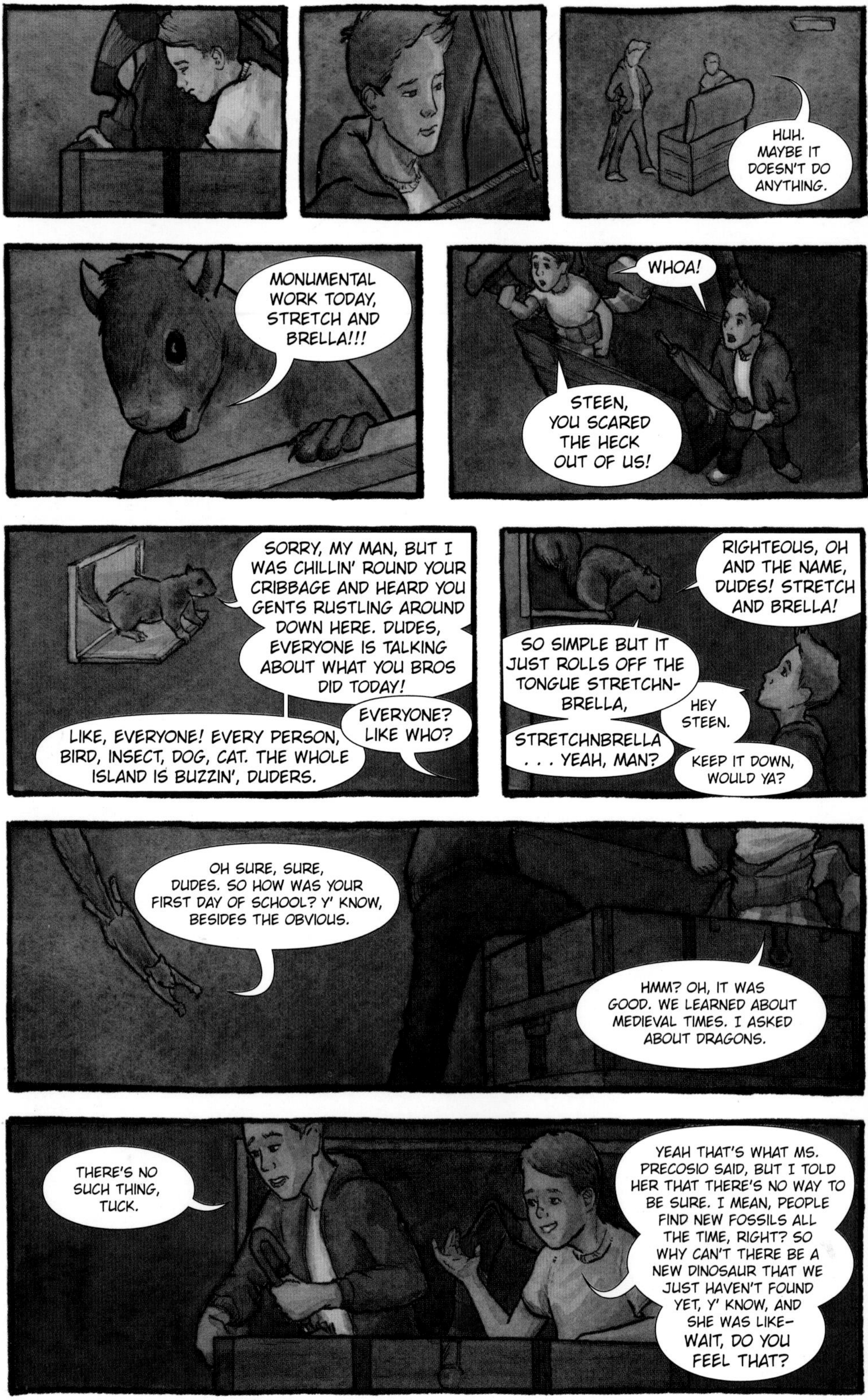
HUH. MAYBE IT DOESN'T DO ANYTHING.
MONUMENTAL WORK TODAY, STRETCH AND BRELLA!!!
WHOA!
STEEN, YOU SCARED THE HECK OUT OF US!
SORRY, MY MAN, BUT I WAS CHILLIN' ROUND YOUR CRIBBAGE AND HEARD YOU GENTS RUSTLING AROUND DOWN HERE. DUDES, EVERYONE IS TALKING ABOUT WHAT YOU BROS DID TODAY!
EVERYONE? LIKE WHO?
LIKE, EVERYONE! EVERY PERSON, BIRD, INSECT, DOG, CAT. THE WHOLE ISLAND IS BUZZIN', DUDERS.
RIGHTEOUS, OH AND THE NAME, DUDES! STRETCH AND BRELLA!
SO SIMPLE BUT IT JUST ROLLS OFF THE TONGUE STRETCHN-BRELLA,
HEY STEEN.
STRETCHNBRELLA . . . YEAH, MAN?
KEEP IT DOWN, WOULD YA?
OH SURE, SURE, DUDES. SO HOW WAS YOUR FIRST DAY OF SCHOOL? Y' KNOW, BESIDES THE OBVIOUS.
HMM? OH, IT WAS GOOD. WE LEARNED ABOUT MEDIEVAL TIMES. I ASKED ABOUT DRAGONS.
THERE'S NO SUCH THING, TUCK.
YEAH THAT'S WHAT MS. PRECOSIO SAID, BUT I TOLD HER THAT THERE'S NO WAY TO BE SURE. I MEAN, PEOPLE FIND NEW FOSSILS ALL THE TIME, RIGHT? SO WHY CAN'T THERE BE A NEW DINOSAUR THAT WE JUST HAVEN'T FOUND YET, Y' KNOW, AND SHE WAS LIKE- WAIT, DO YOU FEEL THAT?

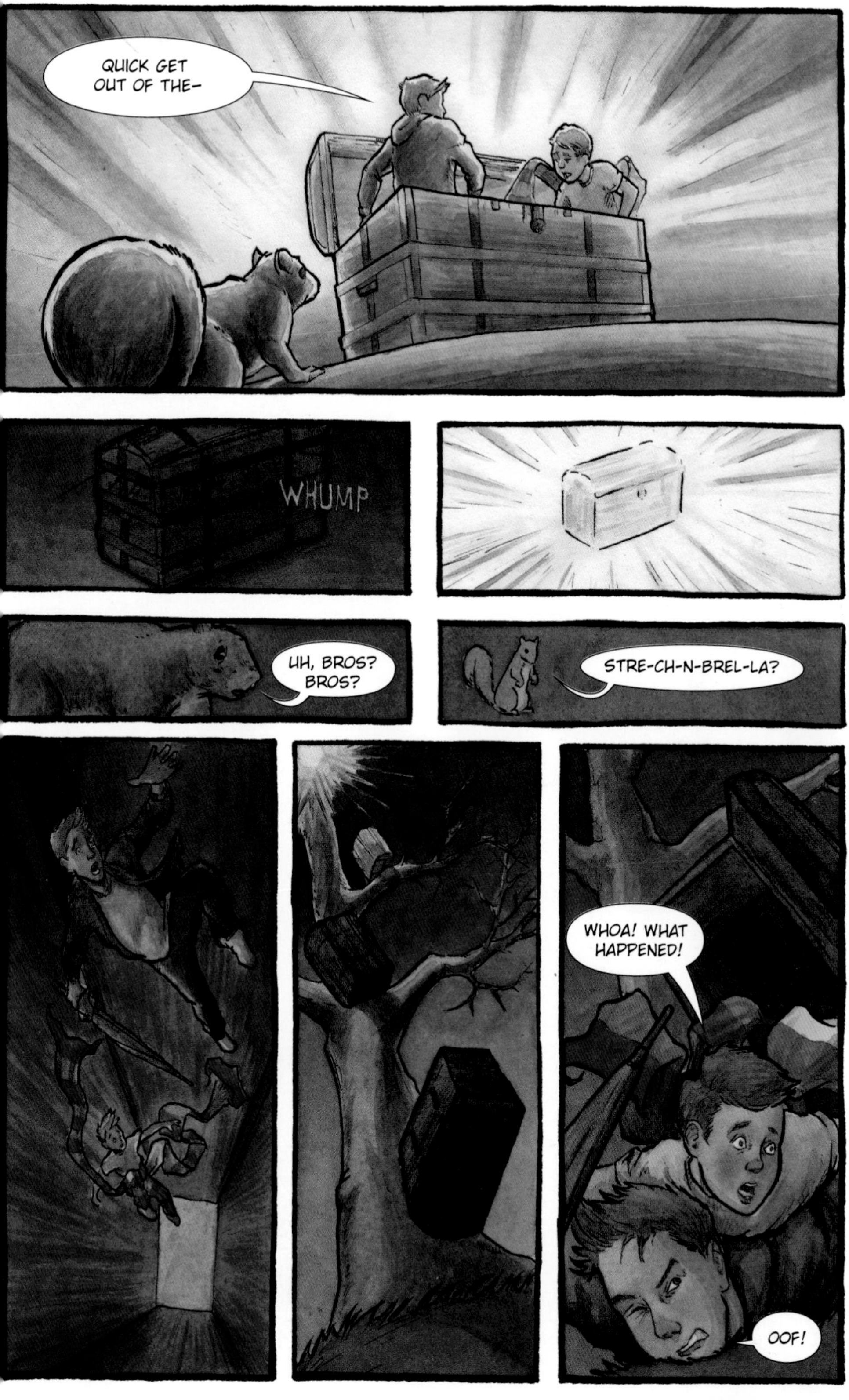
QUICK GET OUT OF THE-
WHUMP
UH, BROS? BROS?
STRE-CH-N-BREL-LA?
WHOA! WHAT HAPPENED!
OOF!

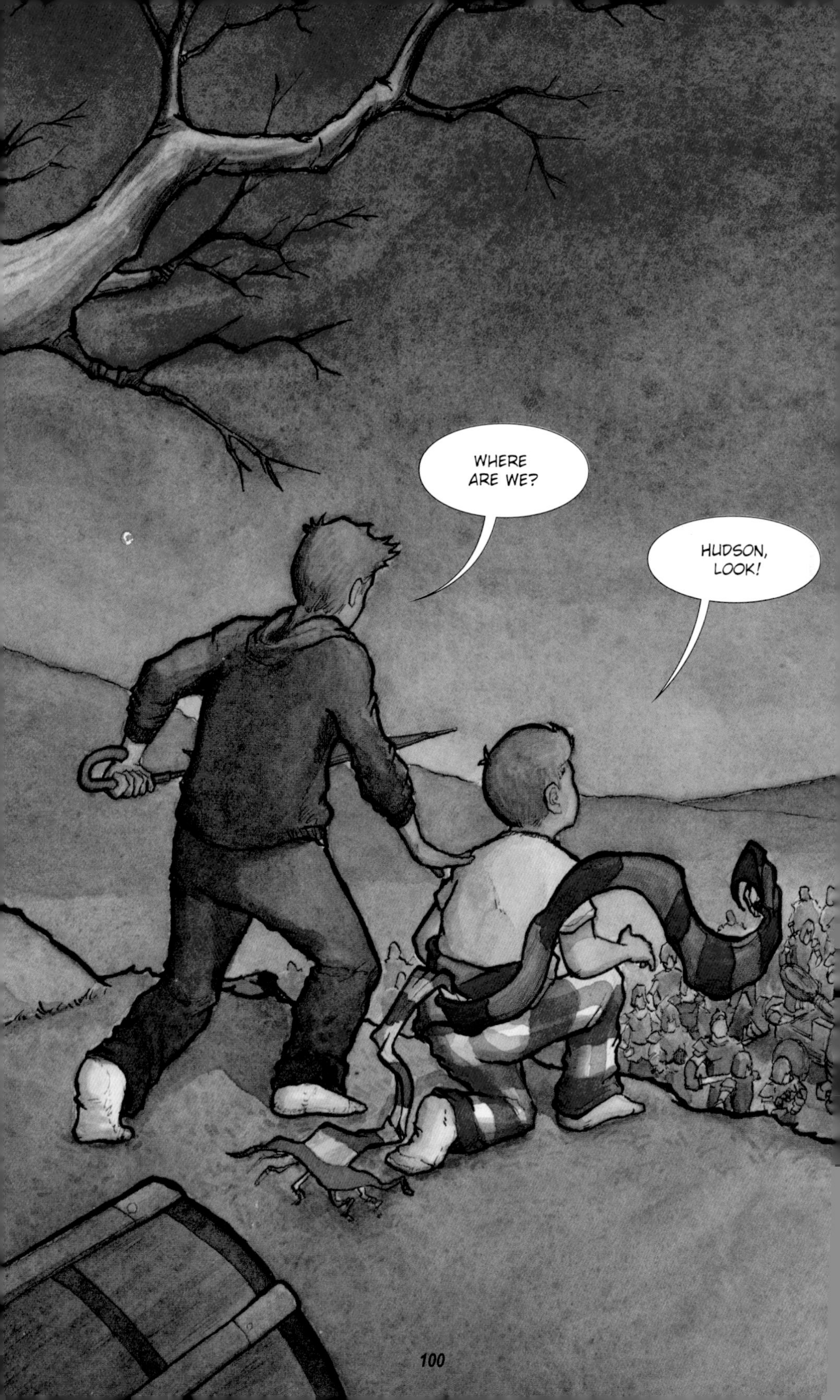
WHERE ARE WE?
HUDSON, LOOK!

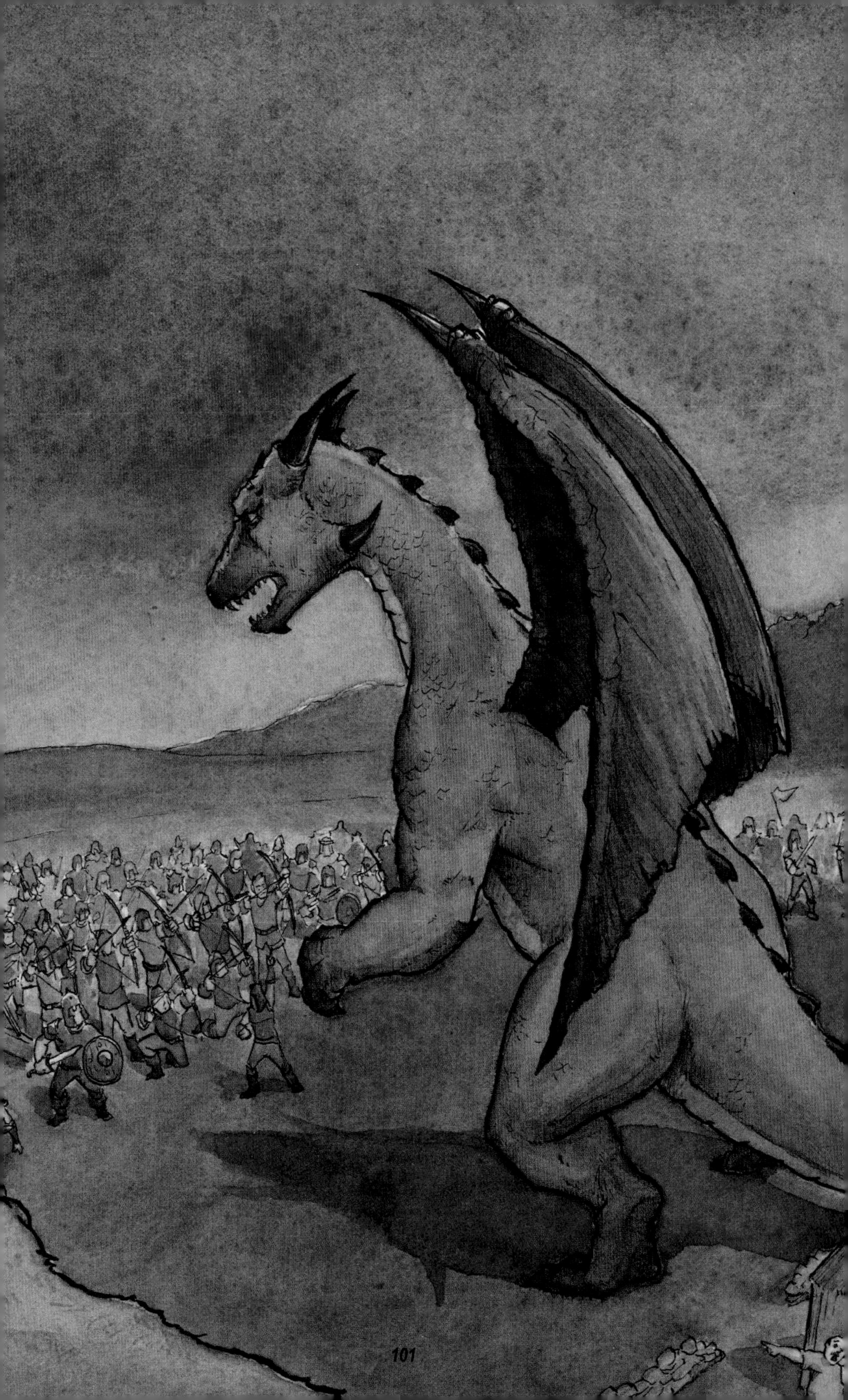

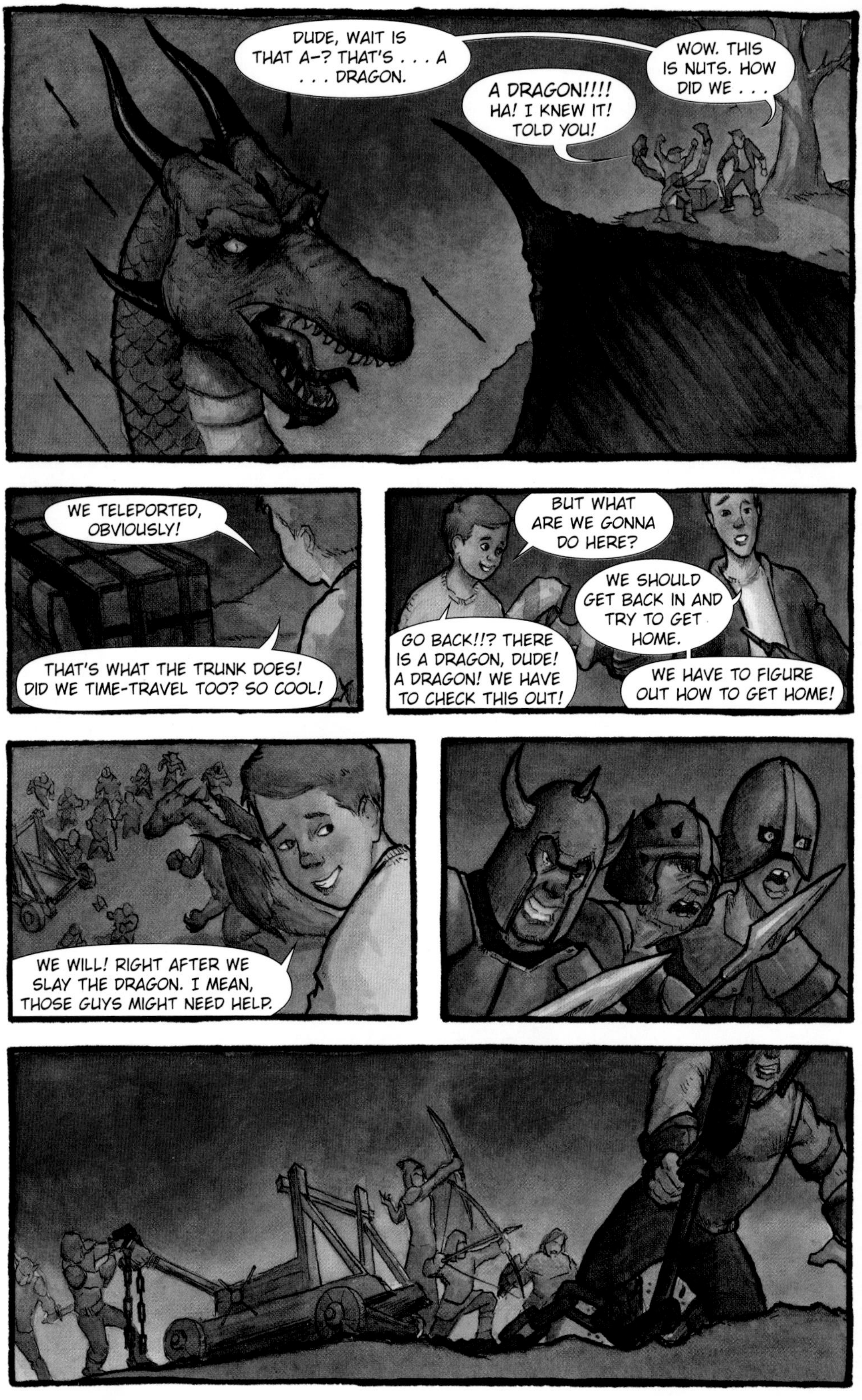
DUDE, WAIT IS THAT A–? THAT'S . . . A . . . DRAGON.
A DRAGON!!!! HA! I KNEW IT! TOLD YOU!
WOW. THIS IS NUTS. HOW DID WE . . .
WE TELEPORTED, OBVIOUSLY!
THAT'S WHAT THE TRUNK DOES! DID WE TIME-TRAVEL TOO? SO COOL!
BUT WHAT ARE WE GONNA DO HERE?
WE SHOULD GET BACK IN AND TRY TO GET HOME.
GO BACK!!? THERE IS A DRAGON, DUDE! A DRAGON! WE HAVE TO CHECK THIS OUT!
WE HAVE TO FIGURE OUT HOW TO GET HOME!
WE WILL! RIGHT AFTER WE SLAY THE DRAGON. I MEAN, THOSE GUYS MIGHT NEED HELP.

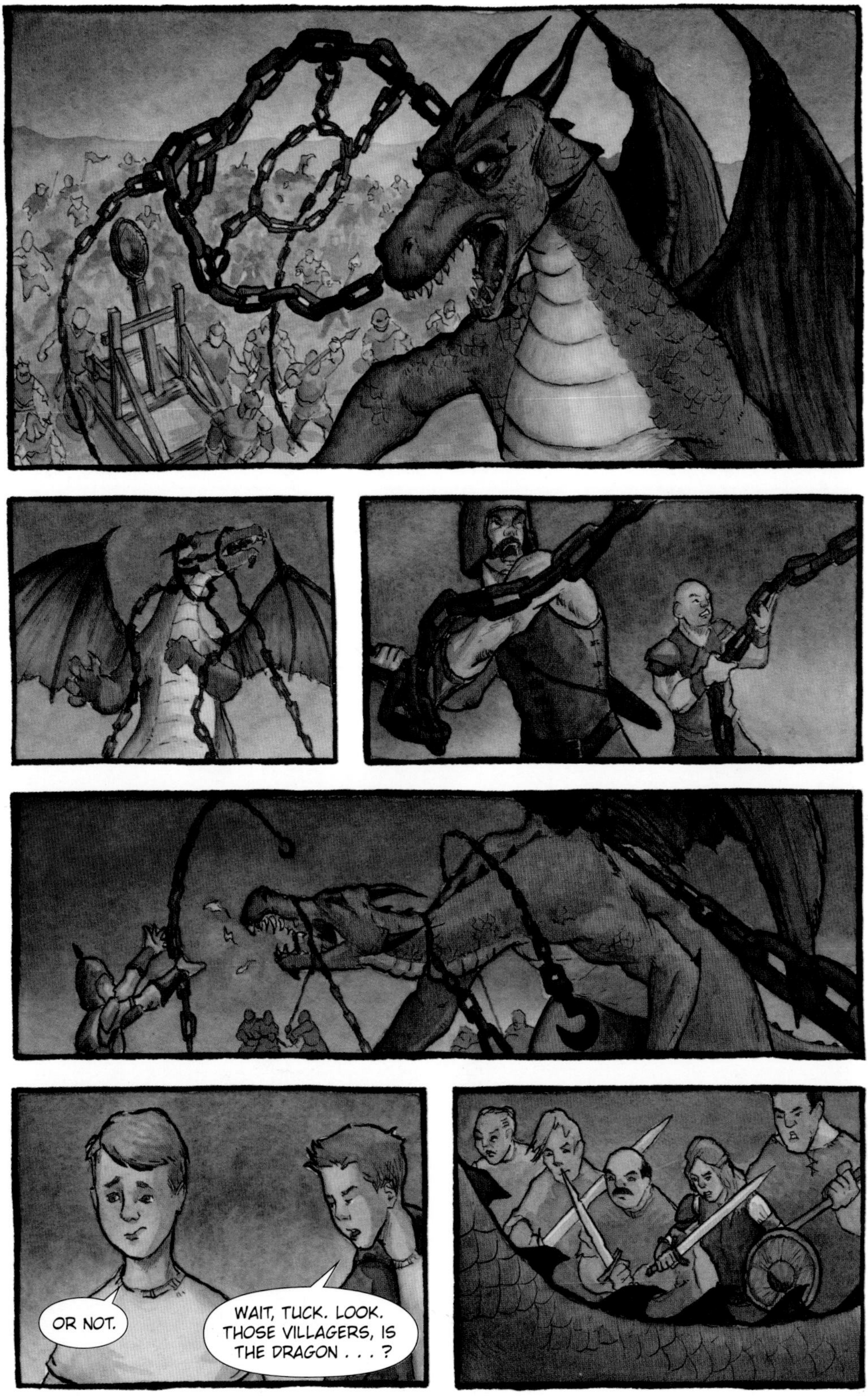
OR NOT.
WAIT, TUCK. LOOK. THOSE VILLAGERS, IS THE DRAGON . . . ?

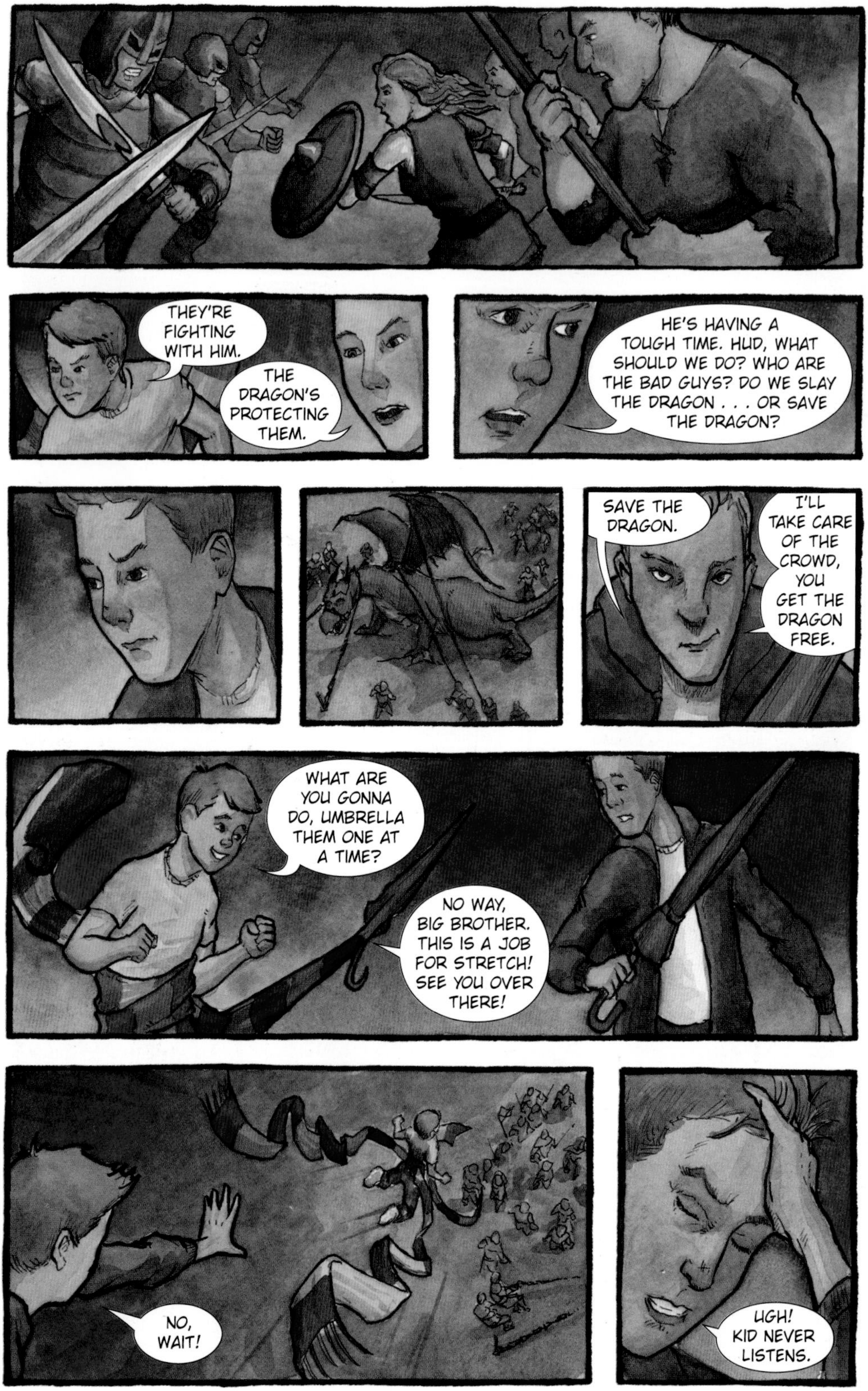
THEY'RE FIGHTING WITH HIM.
THE DRAGON'S PROTECTING THEM.
HE'S HAVING A TOUGH TIME. HUD, WHAT SHOULD WE DO? WHO ARE THE BAD GUYS? DO WE SLAY THE DRAGON . . . OR SAVE THE DRAGON?
SAVE THE DRAGON.
I'LL TAKE CARE OF THE CROWD, YOU GET THE DRAGON FREE.
WHAT ARE YOU GONNA DO, UMBRELLA THEM ONE AT A TIME?
NO WAY, BIG BROTHER. THIS IS A JOB FOR STRETCH! SEE YOU OVER THERE!
NO, WAIT!
UGH! KID NEVER LISTENS.

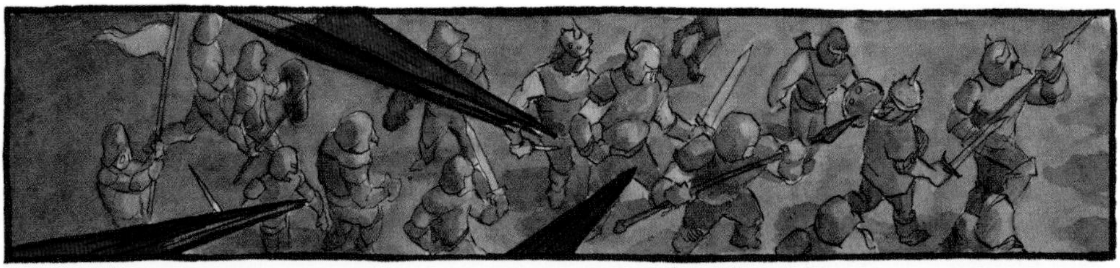

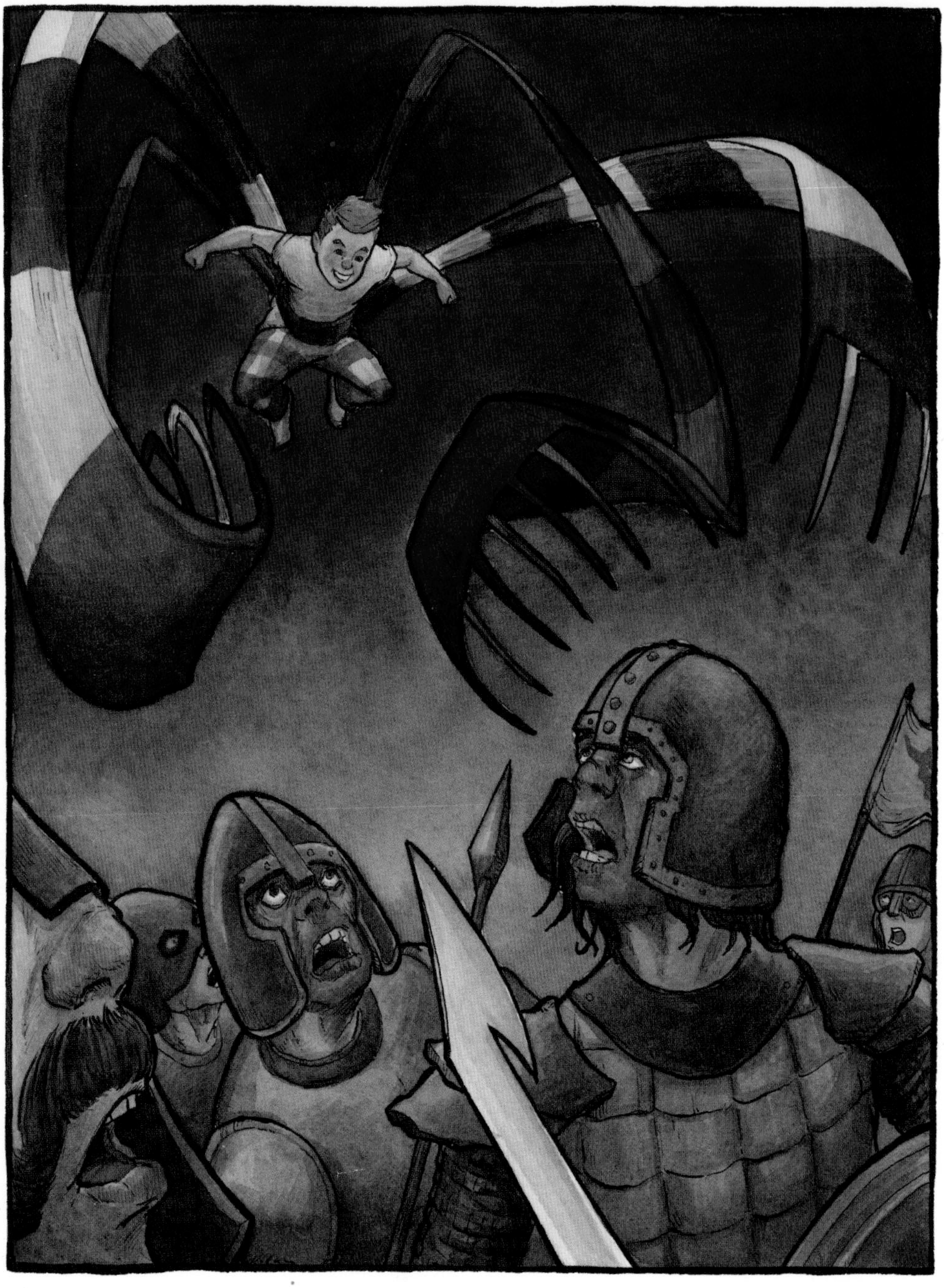

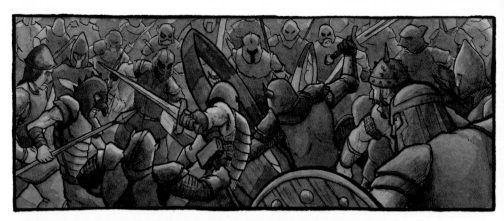

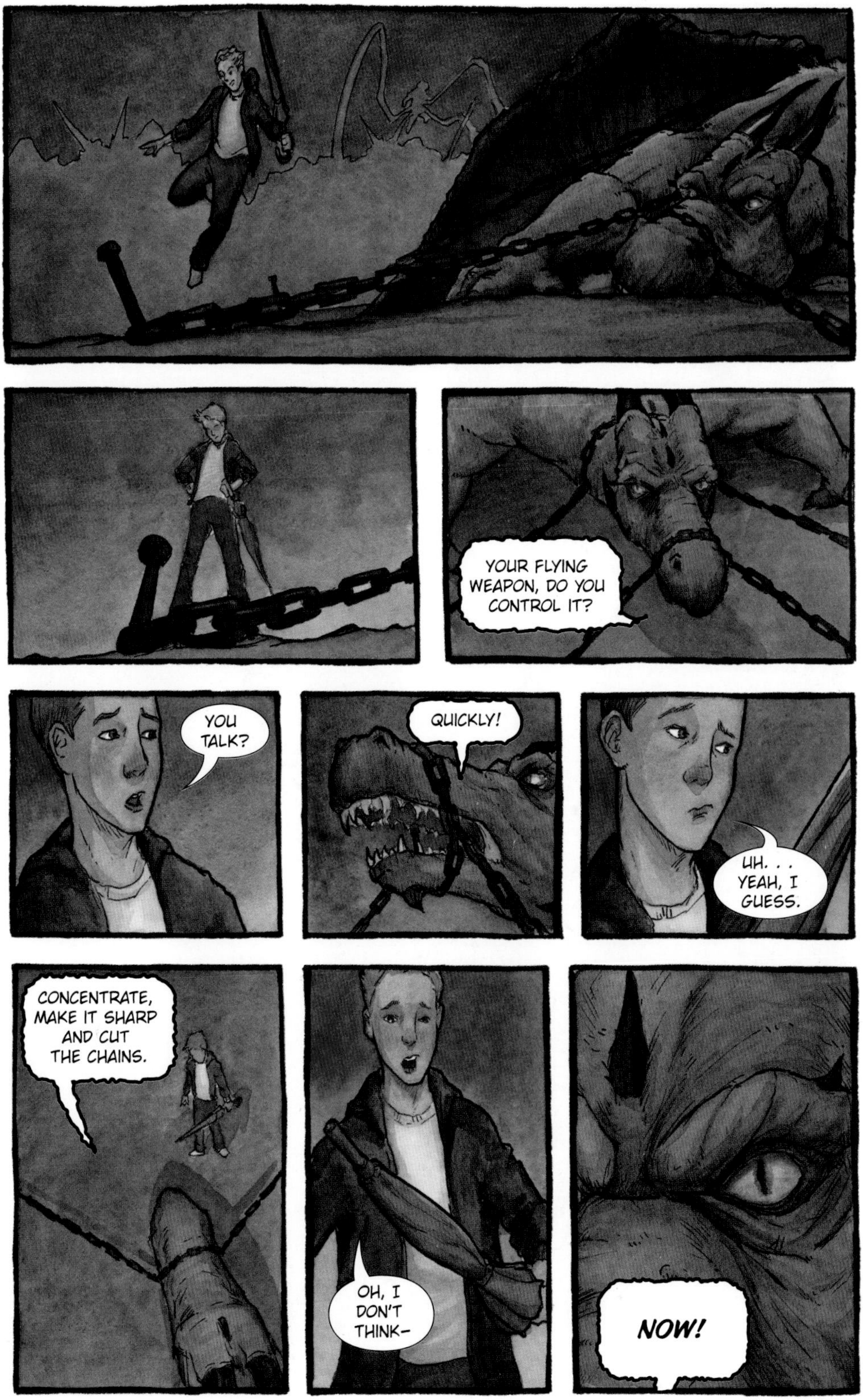
YOUR FLYING WEAPON, DO YOU CONTROL IT?
YOU TALK?
QUICKLY!
UH. . . YEAH, I GUESS.
CONCENTRATE, MAKE IT SHARP AND CUT THE CHAINS.
OH, I DON'T THINK-
NOW!

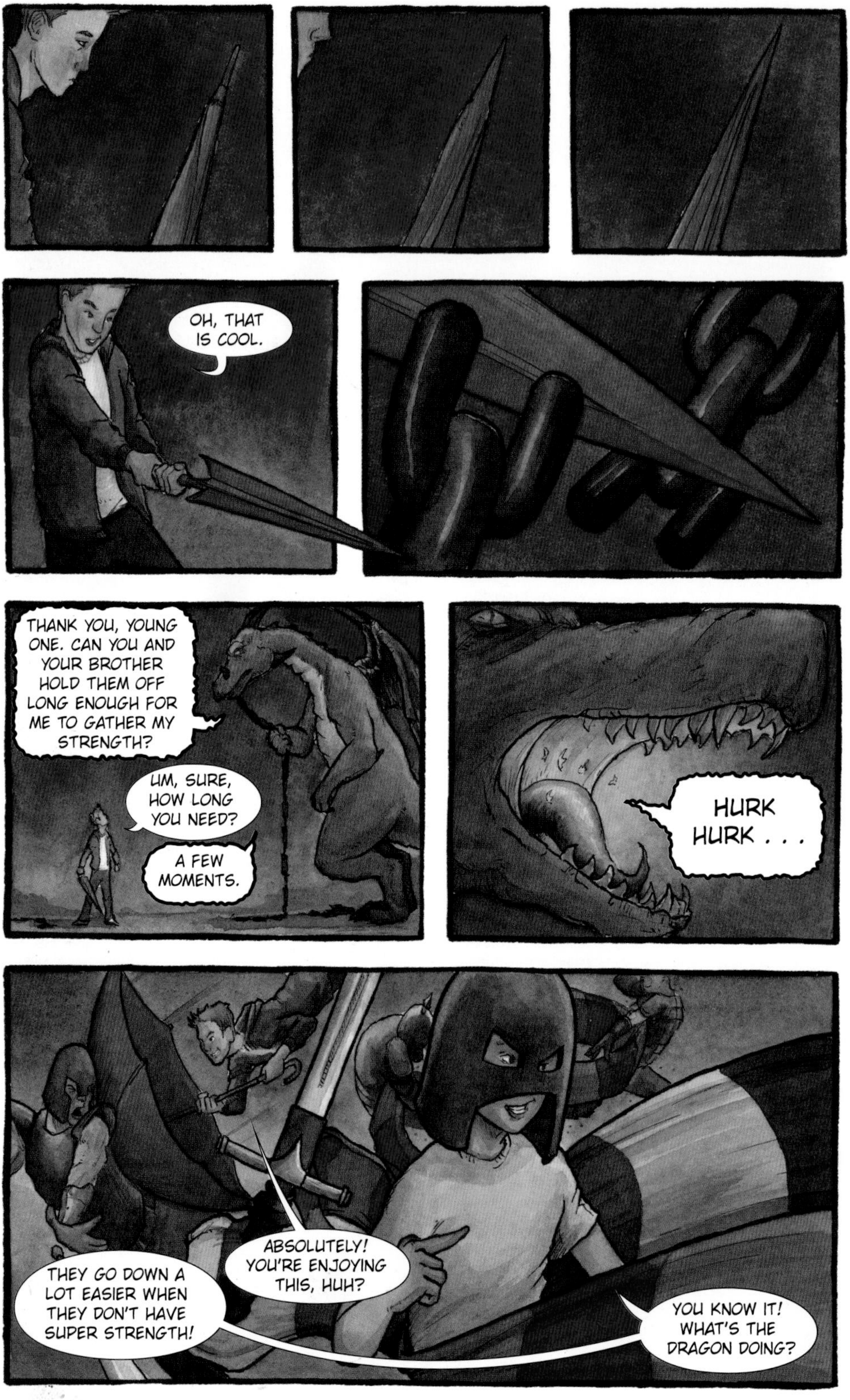
OH, THAT IS COOL.
THANK YOU, YOUNG ONE. CAN YOU AND YOUR BROTHER HOLD THEM OFF LONG ENOUGH FOR ME TO GATHER MY STRENGTH?
UM, SURE, HOW LONG YOU NEED?
A FEW MOMENTS.
HURK HURK . . .
THEY GO DOWN A LOT EASIER WHEN THEY DON'T HAVE SUPER STRENGTH!
ABSOLUTELY! YOU'RE ENJOYING THIS, HUH?
YOU KNOW IT! WHAT'S THE DRAGON DOING?

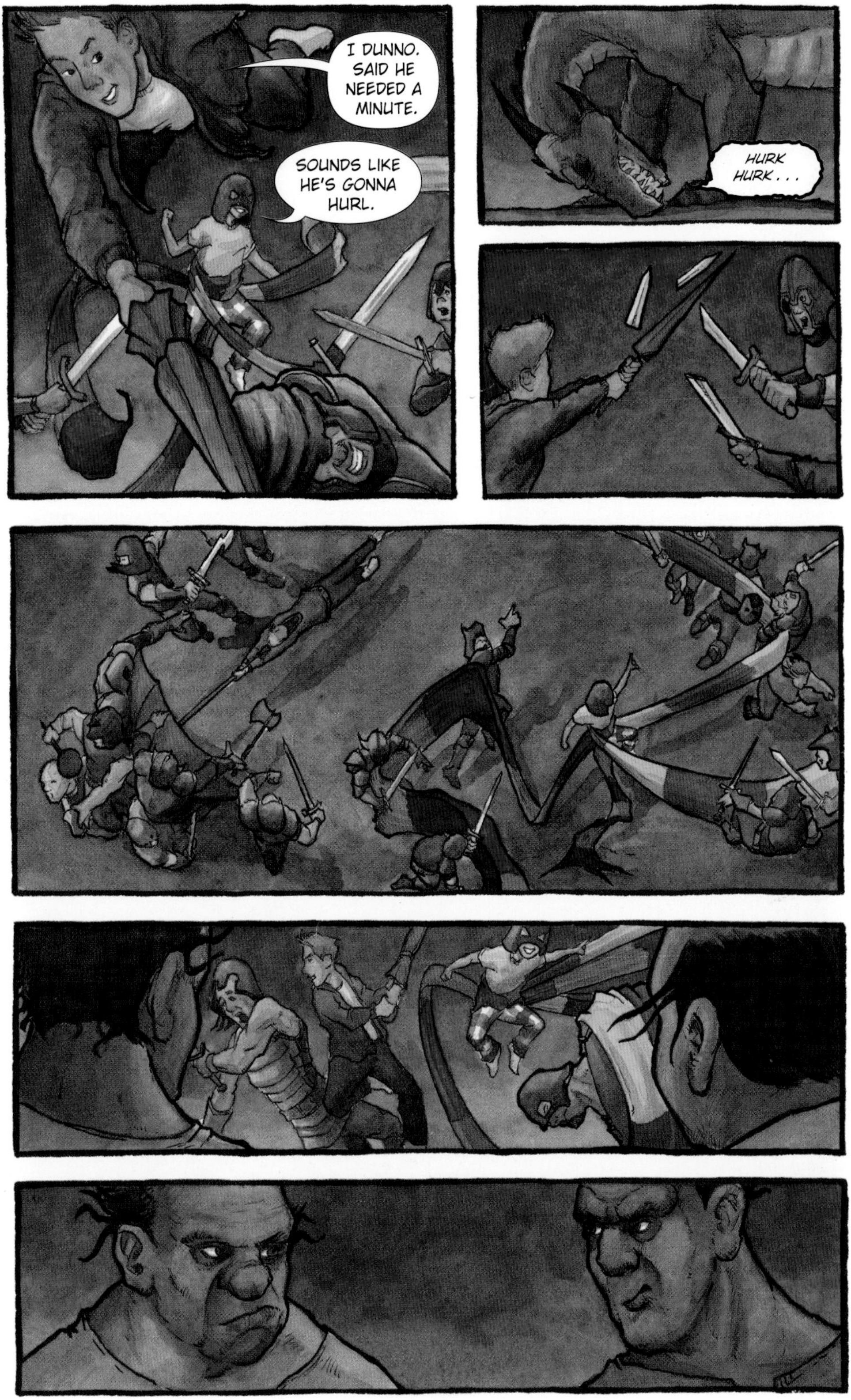
I DUNNO. SAID HE NEEDED A MINUTE.
SOUNDS LIKE HE'S GONNA HURL.
HURK HURK . . .

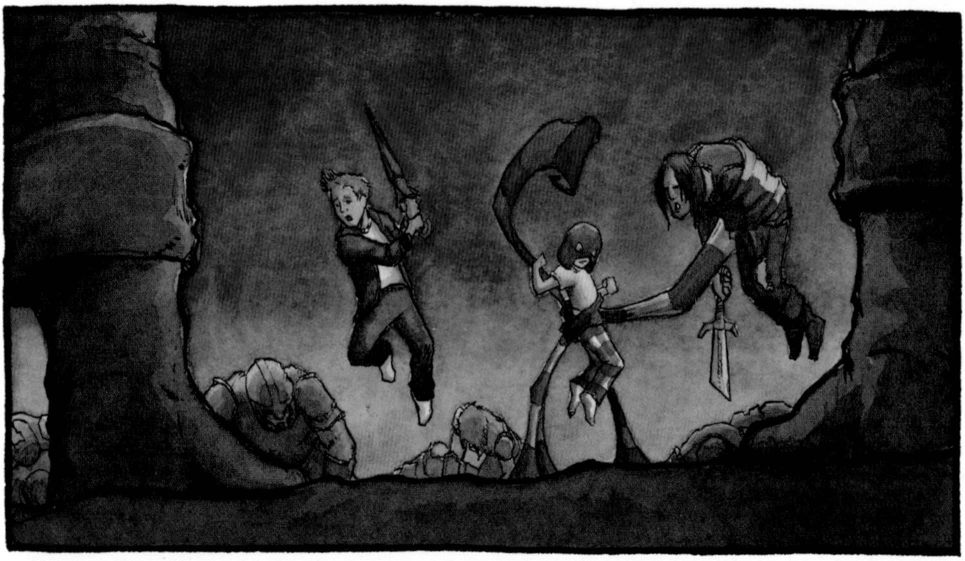

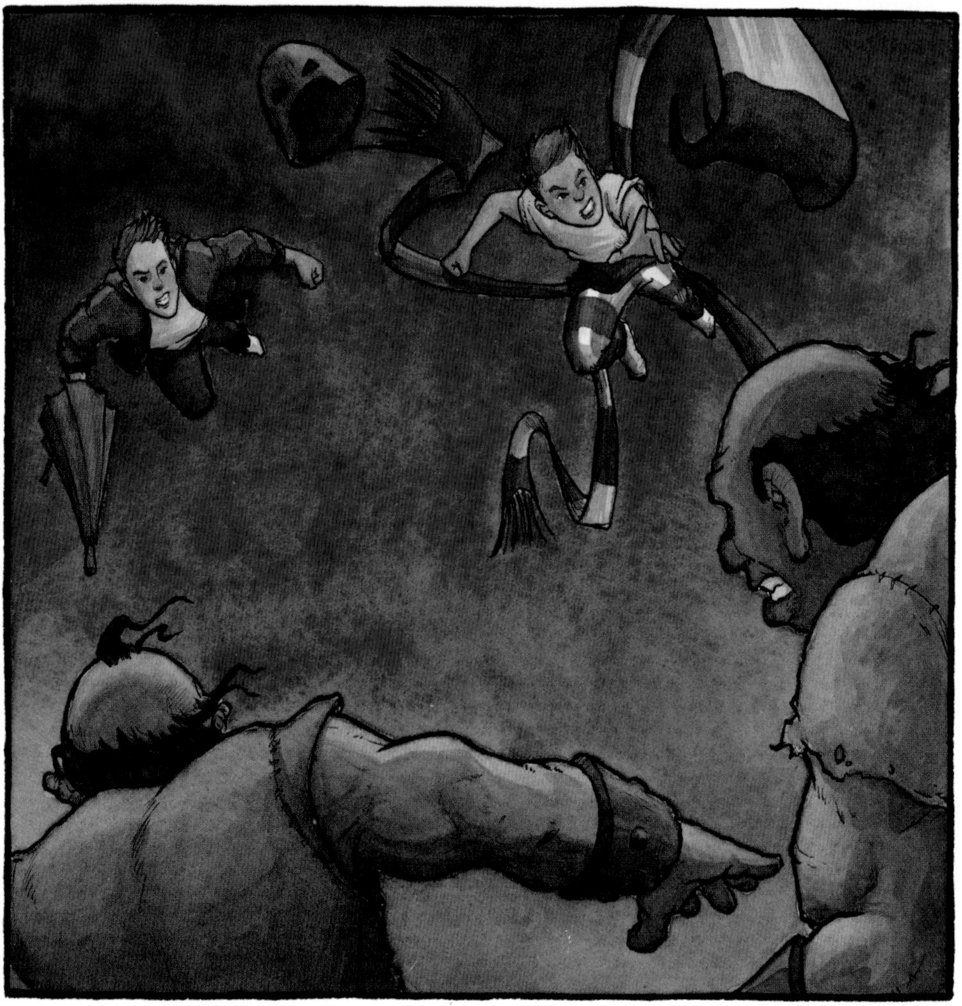

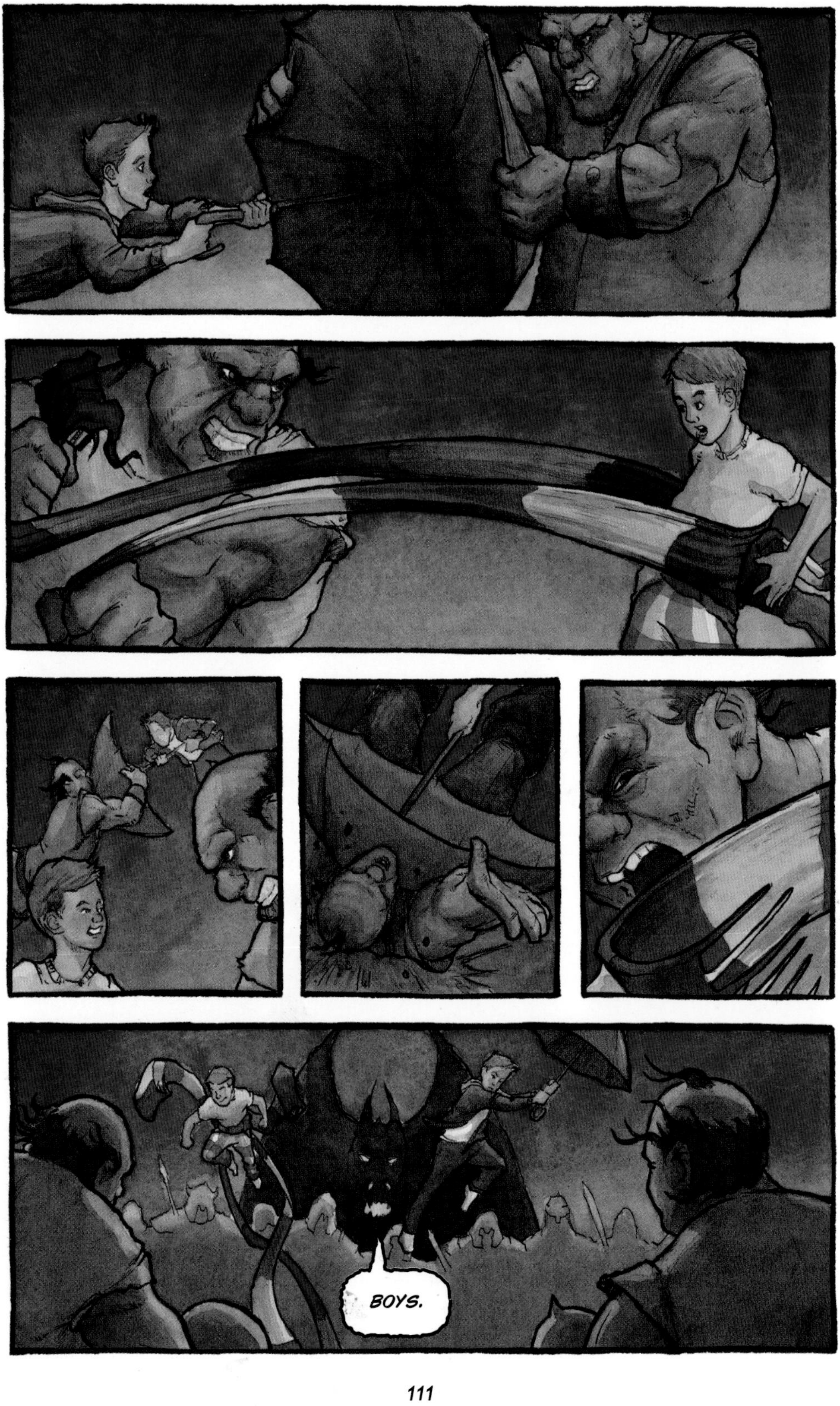
BOYS.

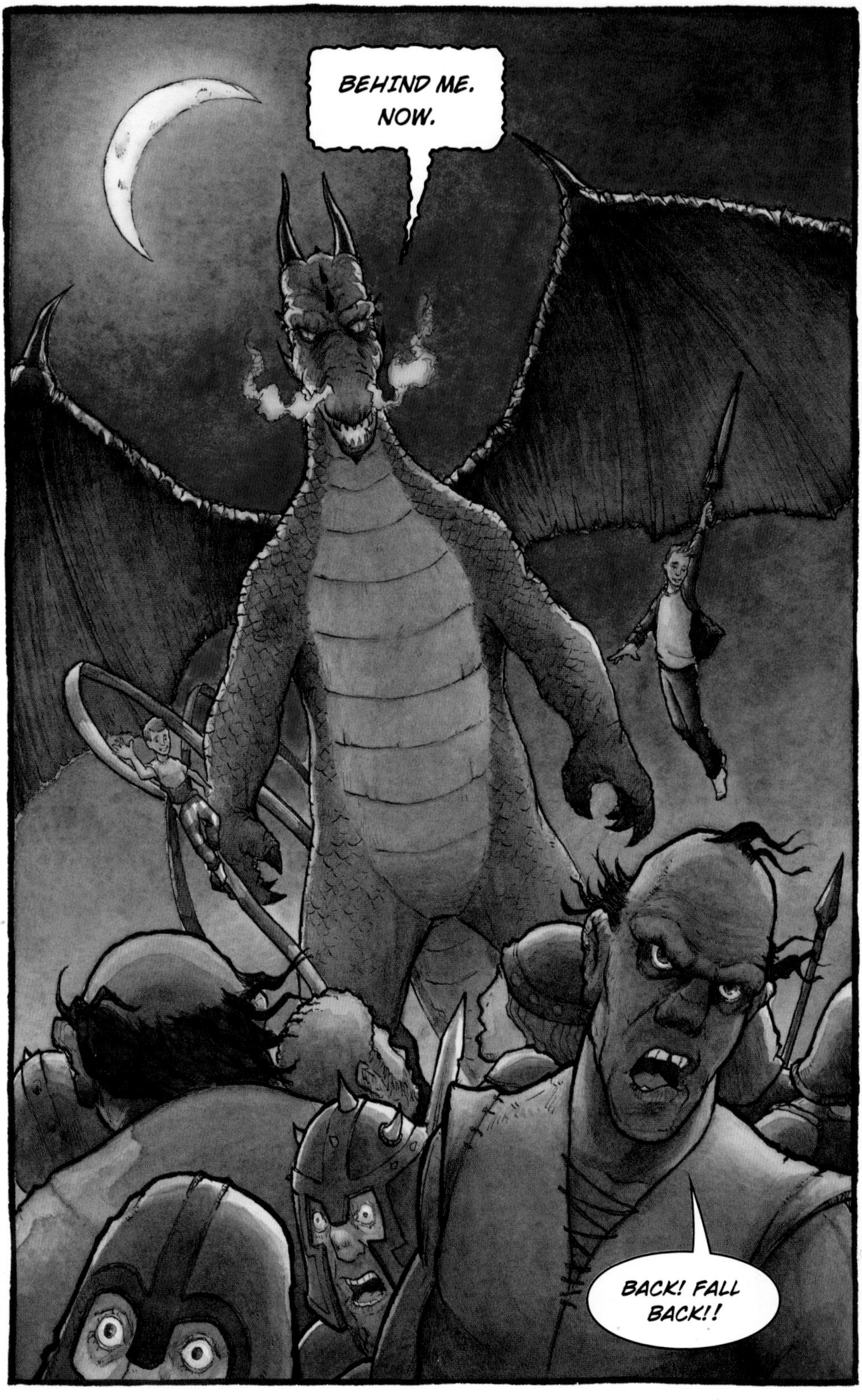
BEHIND ME. NOW.
BACK! FALL BACK!!

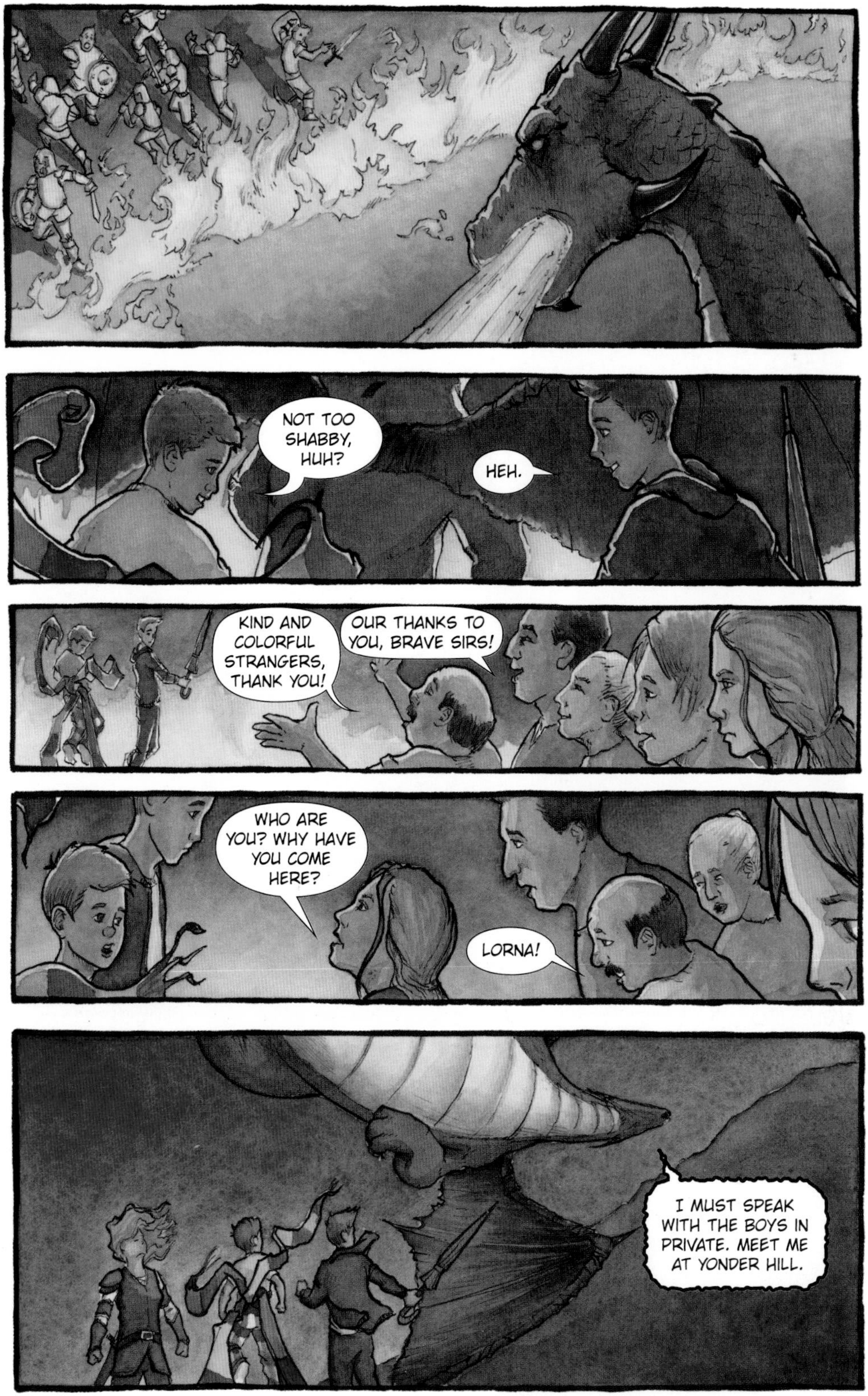
NOT TOO SHABBY, HUH?
HEH.
KIND AND COLORFUL STRANGERS, THANK YOU!
OUR THANKS TO YOU, BRAVE SIRS!
WHO ARE YOU? WHY HAVE YOU COME HERE?
LORNA!
I MUST SPEAK WITH THE BOYS IN PRIVATE. MEET ME AT YONDER HILL.

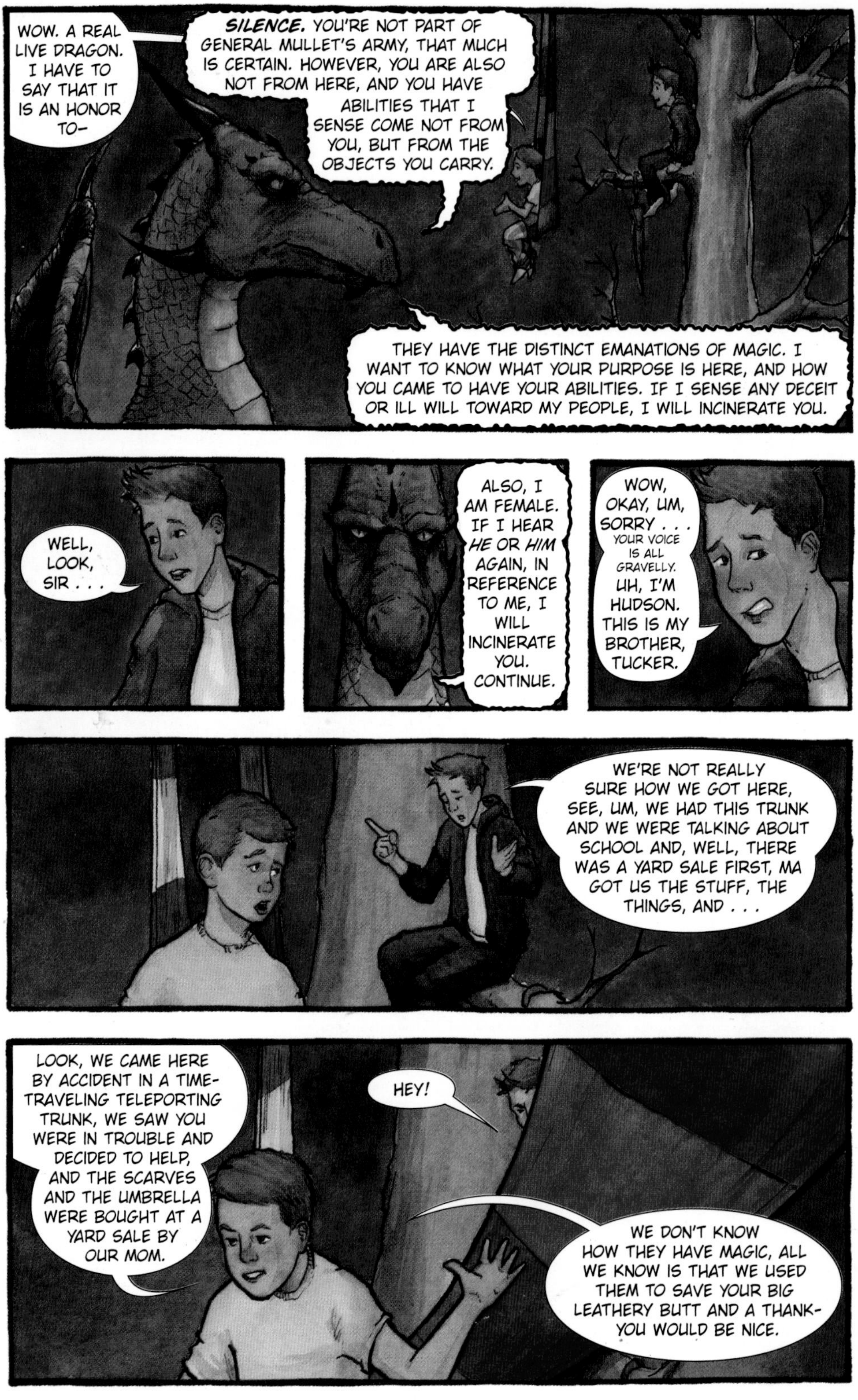
WOW. A REAL LIVE DRAGON. I HAVE TO SAY THAT IT IS AN HONOR TO—
SILENCE. YOU'RE NOT PART OF GENERAL MULLET'S ARMY, THAT MUCH IS CERTAIN. HOWEVER, YOU ARE ALSO NOT FROM HERE, AND YOU HAVE ABILITIES THAT I SENSE COME NOT FROM YOU, BUT FROM THE OBJECTS YOU CARRY.
THEY HAVE THE DISTINCT EMANATIONS OF MAGIC. I WANT TO KNOW WHAT YOUR PURPOSE IS HERE, AND HOW YOU CAME TO HAVE YOUR ABILITIES. IF I SENSE ANY DECEIT OR ILL WILL TOWARD MY PEOPLE, I WILL INCINERATE YOU.
WELL, LOOK, SIR . . .
ALSO, I AM FEMALE. IF I HEAR *HE* OR *HIM* AGAIN, IN REFERENCE TO ME, I WILL INCINERATE YOU. CONTINUE.
WOW, OKAY, UM, SORRY . . . YOUR VOICE IS ALL GRAVELLY. UH, I'M HUDSON. THIS IS MY BROTHER, TUCKER.
WE'RE NOT REALLY SURE HOW WE GOT HERE, SEE, UM, WE HAD THIS TRUNK AND WE WERE TALKING ABOUT SCHOOL AND, WELL, THERE WAS A YARD SALE FIRST, MA GOT US THE STUFF, THE THINGS, AND . . .
LOOK, WE CAME HERE BY ACCIDENT IN A TIME-TRAVELING TELEPORTING TRUNK, WE SAW YOU WERE IN TROUBLE AND DECIDED TO HELP, AND THE SCARVES AND THE UMBRELLA WERE BOUGHT AT A YARD SALE BY OUR MOM.
HEY!
WE DON'T KNOW HOW THEY HAVE MAGIC, ALL WE KNOW IS THAT WE USED THEM TO SAVE YOUR BIG LEATHERY BUTT AND A THANK-YOU WOULD BE NICE.

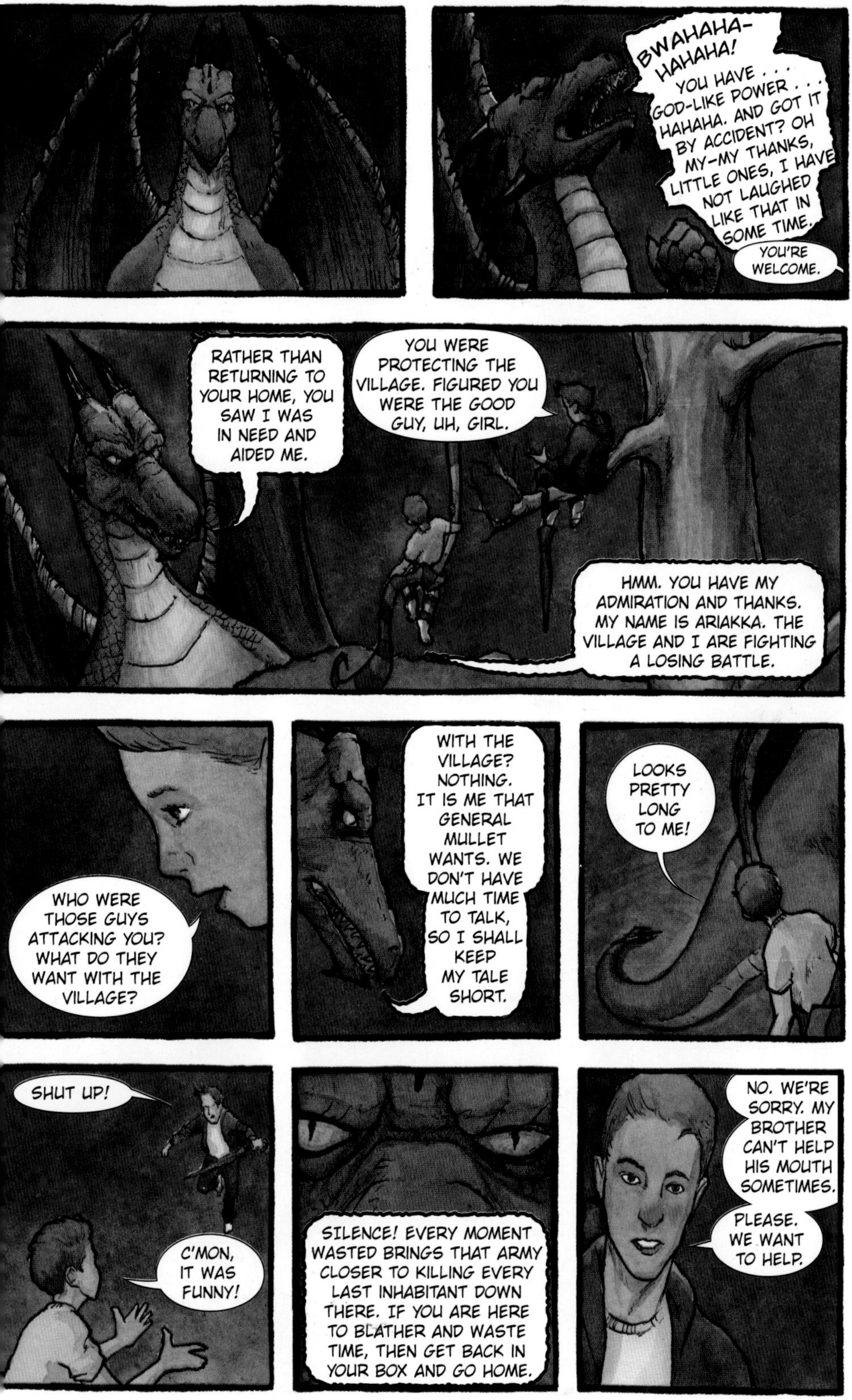
BWAHAHA-HAHAHA! YOU HAVE . . . GOD-LIKE POWER . . . HAHAHA. AND GOT IT BY ACCIDENT? OH MY-MY THANKS, LITTLE ONES, I HAVE NOT LAUGHED LIKE THAT IN SOME TIME.
YOU'RE WELCOME.
RATHER THAN RETURNING TO YOUR HOME, YOU SAW I WAS IN NEED AND AIDED ME.
YOU WERE PROTECTING THE VILLAGE. FIGURED YOU WERE THE GOOD GUY, UH, GIRL.
HMM. YOU HAVE MY ADMIRATION AND THANKS. MY NAME IS ARIAKKA. THE VILLAGE AND I ARE FIGHTING A LOSING BATTLE.
WHO WERE THOSE GUYS ATTACKING YOU? WHAT DO THEY WANT WITH THE VILLAGE?
WITH THE VILLAGE? NOTHING. IT IS ME THAT GENERAL MULLET WANTS. WE DON'T HAVE MUCH TIME TO TALK, SO I SHALL KEEP MY TALE SHORT.
LOOKS PRETTY LONG TO ME!
SHUT UP!
C'MON, IT WAS FUNNY!
SILENCE! EVERY MOMENT WASTED BRINGS THAT ARMY CLOSER TO KILLING EVERY LAST INHABITANT DOWN THERE. IF YOU ARE HERE TO BLATHER AND WASTE TIME, THEN GET BACK IN YOUR BOX AND GO HOME.
NO. WE'RE SORRY. MY BROTHER CAN'T HELP HIS MOUTH SOMETIMES.
PLEASE. WE WANT TO HELP.

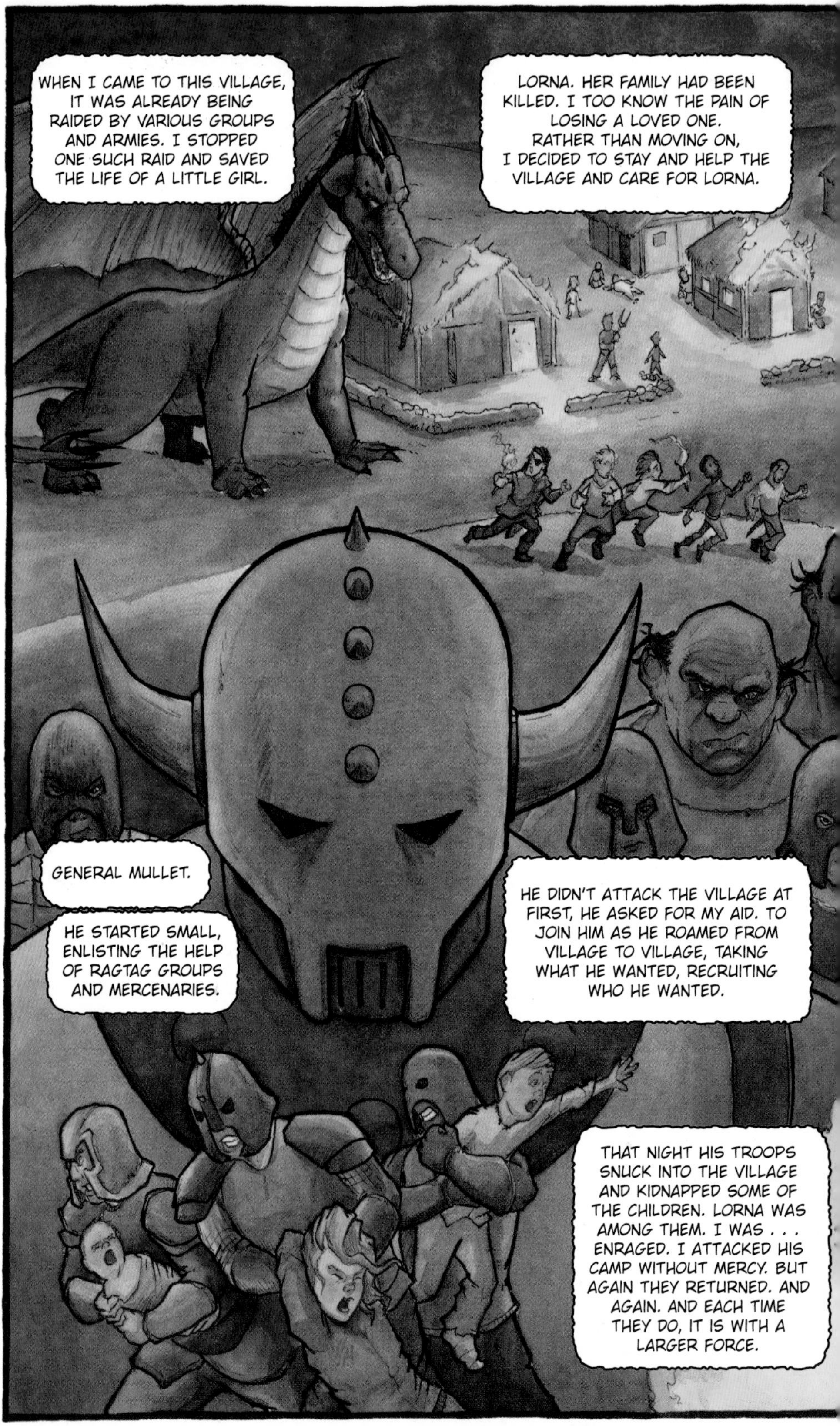
WHEN I CAME TO THIS VILLAGE, IT WAS ALREADY BEING RAIDED BY VARIOUS GROUPS AND ARMIES. I STOPPED ONE SUCH RAID AND SAVED THE LIFE OF A LITTLE GIRL.
LORNA. HER FAMILY HAD BEEN KILLED. I TOO KNOW THE PAIN OF LOSING A LOVED ONE. RATHER THAN MOVING ON, I DECIDED TO STAY AND HELP THE VILLAGE AND CARE FOR LORNA.
GENERAL MULLET.
HE STARTED SMALL, ENLISTING THE HELP OF RAGTAG GROUPS AND MERCENARIES.
HE DIDN'T ATTACK THE VILLAGE AT FIRST, HE ASKED FOR MY AID. TO JOIN HIM AS HE ROAMED FROM VILLAGE TO VILLAGE, TAKING WHAT HE WANTED, RECRUITING WHO HE WANTED.
THAT NIGHT HIS TROOPS SNUCK INTO THE VILLAGE AND KIDNAPPED SOME OF THE CHILDREN. LORNA WAS AMONG THEM. I WAS . . . ENRAGED. I ATTACKED HIS CAMP WITHOUT MERCY. BUT AGAIN THEY RETURNED. AND AGAIN. AND EACH TIME THEY DO, IT IS WITH A LARGER FORCE.

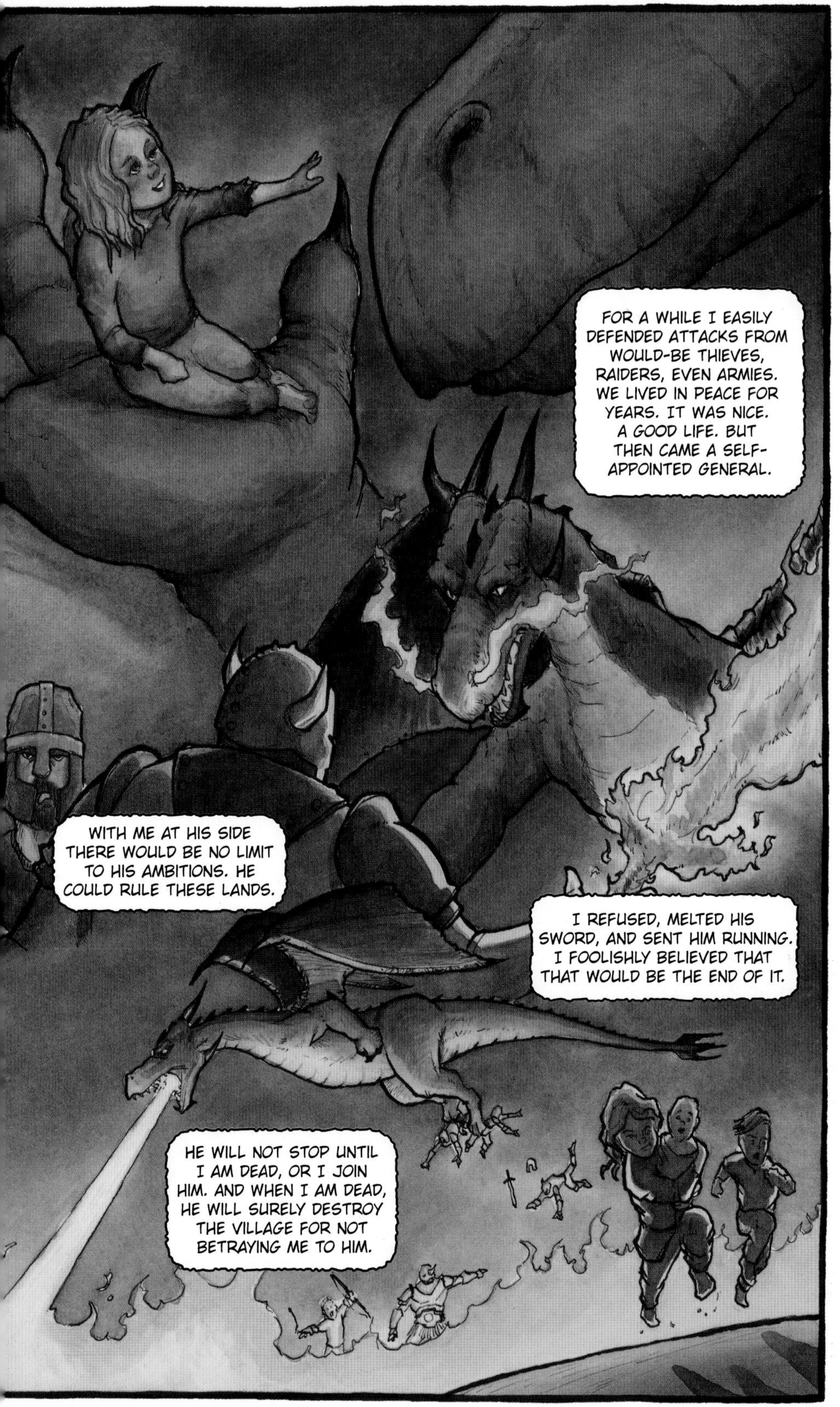
FOR A WHILE I EASILY DEFENDED ATTACKS FROM WOULD-BE THIEVES, RAIDERS, EVEN ARMIES. WE LIVED IN PEACE FOR YEARS. IT WAS NICE. A GOOD LIFE. BUT THEN CAME A SELF-APPOINTED GENERAL.
WITH ME AT HIS SIDE THERE WOULD BE NO LIMIT TO HIS AMBITIONS. HE COULD RULE THESE LANDS.
I REFUSED, MELTED HIS SWORD, AND SENT HIM RUNNING. I FOOLISHLY BELIEVED THAT THAT WOULD BE THE END OF IT.
HE WILL NOT STOP UNTIL I AM DEAD, OR I JOIN HIM. AND WHEN I AM DEAD, HE WILL SURELY DESTROY THE VILLAGE FOR NOT BETRAYING ME TO HIM.

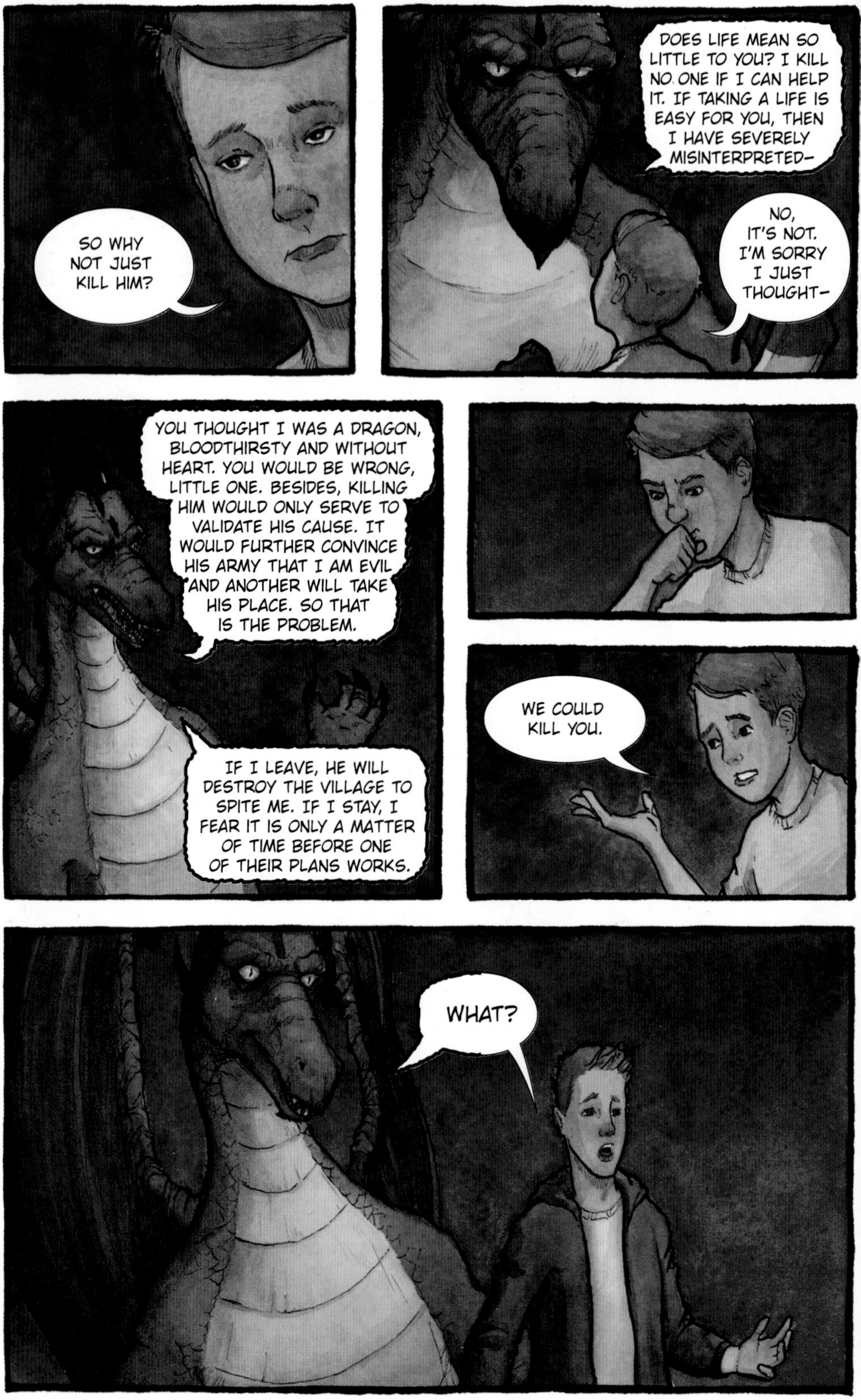
SO WHY NOT JUST KILL HIM?
DOES LIFE MEAN SO LITTLE TO YOU? I KILL NO ONE IF I CAN HELP IT. IF TAKING A LIFE IS EASY FOR YOU, THEN I HAVE SEVERELY MISINTERPRETED–
NO, IT'S NOT. I'M SORRY I JUST THOUGHT–
YOU THOUGHT I WAS A DRAGON, BLOODTHIRSTY AND WITHOUT HEART. YOU WOULD BE WRONG, LITTLE ONE. BESIDES, KILLING HIM WOULD ONLY SERVE TO VALIDATE HIS CAUSE. IT WOULD FURTHER CONVINCE HIS ARMY THAT I AM EVIL AND ANOTHER WILL TAKE HIS PLACE. SO THAT IS THE PROBLEM.
IF I LEAVE, HE WILL DESTROY THE VILLAGE TO SPITE ME. IF I STAY, I FEAR IT IS ONLY A MATTER OF TIME BEFORE ONE OF THEIR PLANS WORKS.
WE COULD KILL YOU.
WHAT?

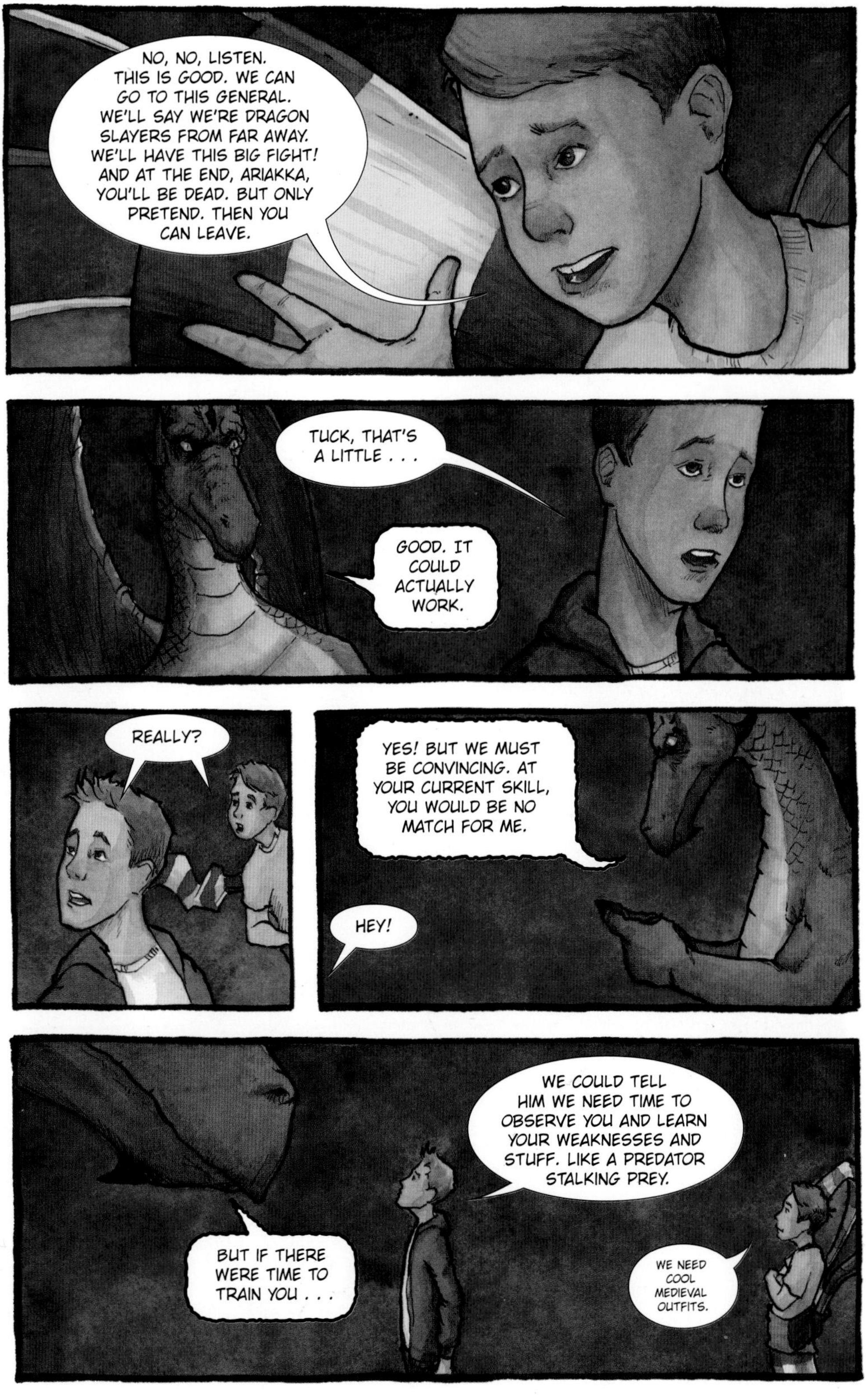
NO, NO, LISTEN. THIS IS GOOD. WE CAN GO TO THIS GENERAL. WE'LL SAY WE'RE DRAGON SLAYERS FROM FAR AWAY. WE'LL HAVE THIS BIG FIGHT! AND AT THE END, ARIAKKA, YOU'LL BE DEAD. BUT ONLY PRETEND. THEN YOU CAN LEAVE.
TUCK, THAT'S A LITTLE . . .
GOOD. IT COULD ACTUALLY WORK.
REALLY?
YES! BUT WE MUST BE CONVINCING. AT YOUR CURRENT SKILL, YOU WOULD BE NO MATCH FOR ME.
HEY!
BUT IF THERE WERE TIME TO TRAIN YOU . . .
WE COULD TELL HIM WE NEED TIME TO OBSERVE YOU AND LEARN YOUR WEAKNESSES AND STUFF. LIKE A PREDATOR STALKING PREY.
WE NEED COOL MEDIEVAL OUTFITS.

EXCELLENT. AND MEANWHILE I WILL TEACH YOU TO UNLOCK THE SECRETS OF YOUR GIFTS. YOU BOTH HAVE GREAT POWER, BUT NO KNOWLEDGE OF HOW TO WIELD IT.

BUT BOYS, I MUST WARN YOU. IF WE START DOWN THIS PATH, IT WILL BE ARDUOUS. I WILL PUSH YOU HARDER THAN YOU HAVE EVER BEEN PUSHED. OUR FIGHT MUST BE BELIEVED.

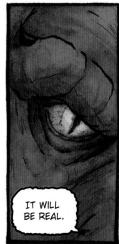

IT WILL BE REAL.

AWKWAAAARD. HEY LOOK. IT'S THOSE TWO TROLLS WE FOUGHT LAST NIGHT.

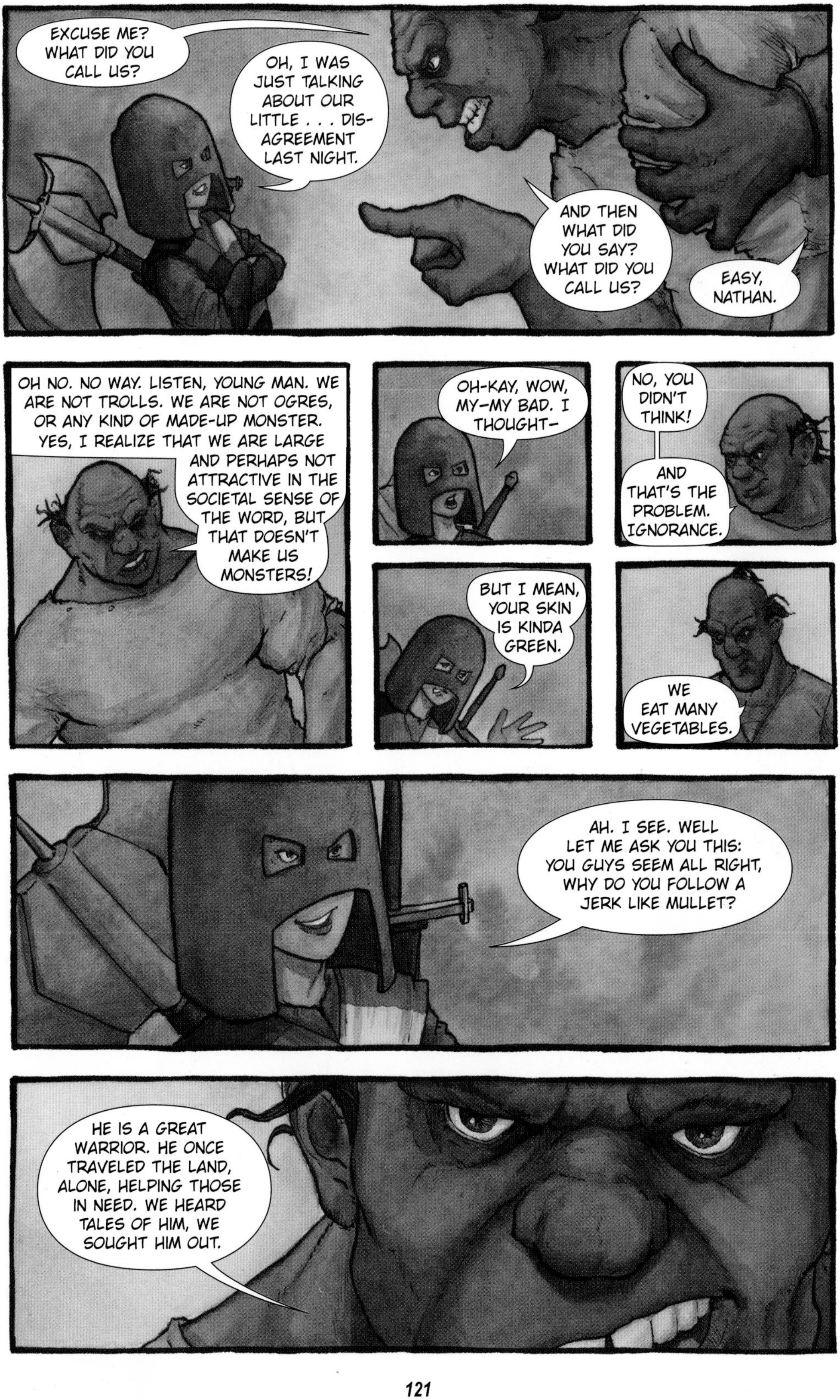
EXCUSE ME? WHAT DID YOU CALL US?
OH, I WAS JUST TALKING ABOUT OUR LITTLE . . . DIS-AGREEMENT LAST NIGHT.
AND THEN WHAT DID YOU SAY? WHAT DID YOU CALL US?
EASY, NATHAN.
OH NO. NO WAY. LISTEN, YOUNG MAN. WE ARE NOT TROLLS. WE ARE NOT OGRES, OR ANY KIND OF MADE-UP MONSTER. YES, I REALIZE THAT WE ARE LARGE AND PERHAPS NOT ATTRACTIVE IN THE SOCIETAL SENSE OF THE WORD, BUT THAT DOESN'T MAKE US MONSTERS!
OH-KAY, WOW, MY—MY BAD. I THOUGHT—
NO, YOU DIDN'T THINK!
AND THAT'S THE PROBLEM. IGNORANCE.
BUT I MEAN, YOUR SKIN IS KINDA GREEN.
WE EAT MANY VEGETABLES.
AH. I SEE. WELL LET ME ASK YOU THIS: YOU GUYS SEEM ALL RIGHT, WHY DO YOU FOLLOW A JERK LIKE MULLET?
HE IS A GREAT WARRIOR. HE ONCE TRAVELED THE LAND, ALONE, HELPING THOSE IN NEED. WE HEARD TALES OF HIM, WE SOUGHT HIM OUT.

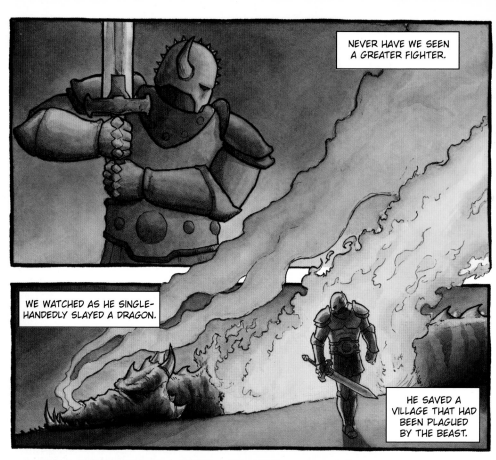

NEVER HAVE WE SEEN A GREATER FIGHTER.

WE WATCHED AS HE SINGLE-HANDEDLY SLAYED A DRAGON.

HE SAVED A VILLAGE THAT HAD BEEN PLAGUED BY THE BEAST.

WE ASKED TO JOIN HIM, AND HE DENIED US.

BUT THE NEXT MORNING, HE HAD A CHANGE OF HEART. HE WANTED TO CREATE AN ARMY, AND ERADICATE DRAGONS FROM THE EARTH.

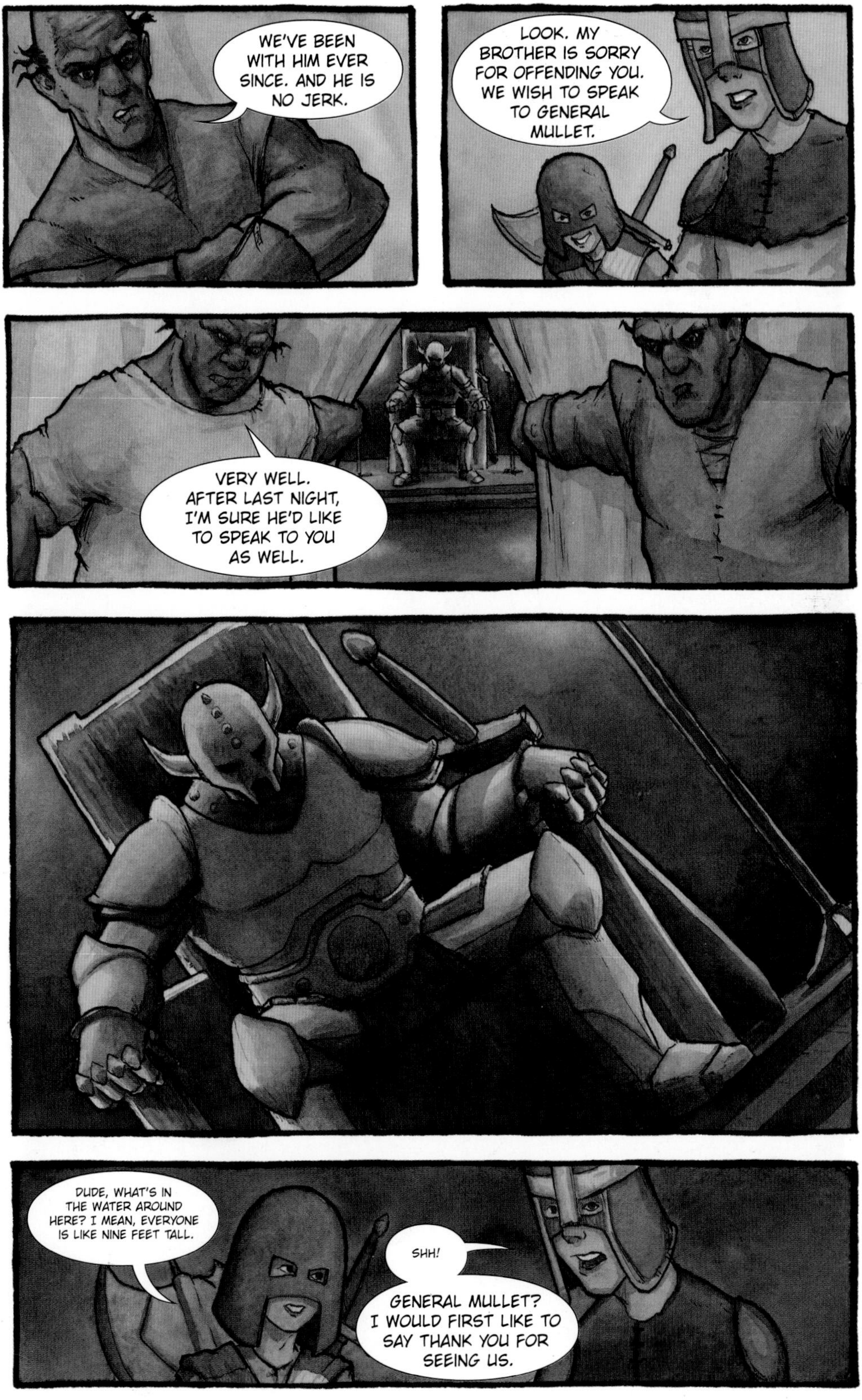
WE'VE BEEN WITH HIM EVER SINCE. AND HE IS NO JERK.
LOOK. MY BROTHER IS SORRY FOR OFFENDING YOU. WE WISH TO SPEAK TO GENERAL MULLET.
VERY WELL. AFTER LAST NIGHT, I'M SURE HE'D LIKE TO SPEAK TO YOU AS WELL.
DUDE, WHAT'S IN THE WATER AROUND HERE? I MEAN, EVERYONE IS LIKE NINE FEET TALL.
SHH!
GENERAL MULLET? I WOULD FIRST LIKE TO SAY THANK YOU FOR SEEING US.

MY FORCES TELL ME YOU ARE GREAT WARRIORS. REGRETTABLY, I DID NOT WITNESS THIS MYSELF.

YOUR WEAPONS AND MANNER OF DRESS ARE STRANGE TO ME. WHERE ARE YOU FROM?

LET'S JUST SAY WE'RE FROM VERY, VERY FAR AWAY. A LAND MUCH DIFFERENT FROM THIS ONE.

I SEE. I WORKED VERY HARD PLOTTING THAT FILTHY BEAST'S DESTRUCTION. A PLOT THAT YOU TWO INTERFERED WITH. TELL ME, WHY SHOULD I NOT KILL YOU BOTH RIGHT NOW?

WE HAVE A COMMON PURPOSE. WE STOPPED YOU FROM KILLING THE DRAGON, SO THAT WE MAY DO IT.

WHAT?

YOU SEE, GENERAL, MY BROTHER AND I ARE DRAGON SLAYERS. WE'VE TRAVELED THE WORLD KILLING DRAGONS. SURELY YOU'VE HEARD OF US? THE, ER, DRAGON-SLAYING FINCH SLAYER BROTHERS?

WORLD-RENOWNED TEN-YEAR-OLD DRAGON SLAYERS? I TIRE OF THIS. KILL THEM.

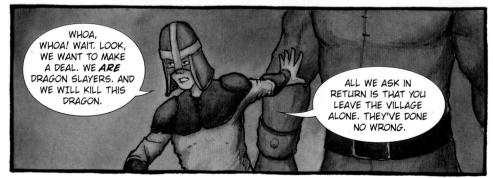

WHOA, WHOA! WAIT. LOOK, WE WANT TO MAKE A DEAL. WE *ARE* DRAGON SLAYERS. AND WE WILL KILL THIS DRAGON.

ALL WE ASK IN RETURN IS THAT YOU LEAVE THE VILLAGE ALONE. THEY'VE DONE NO WRONG.

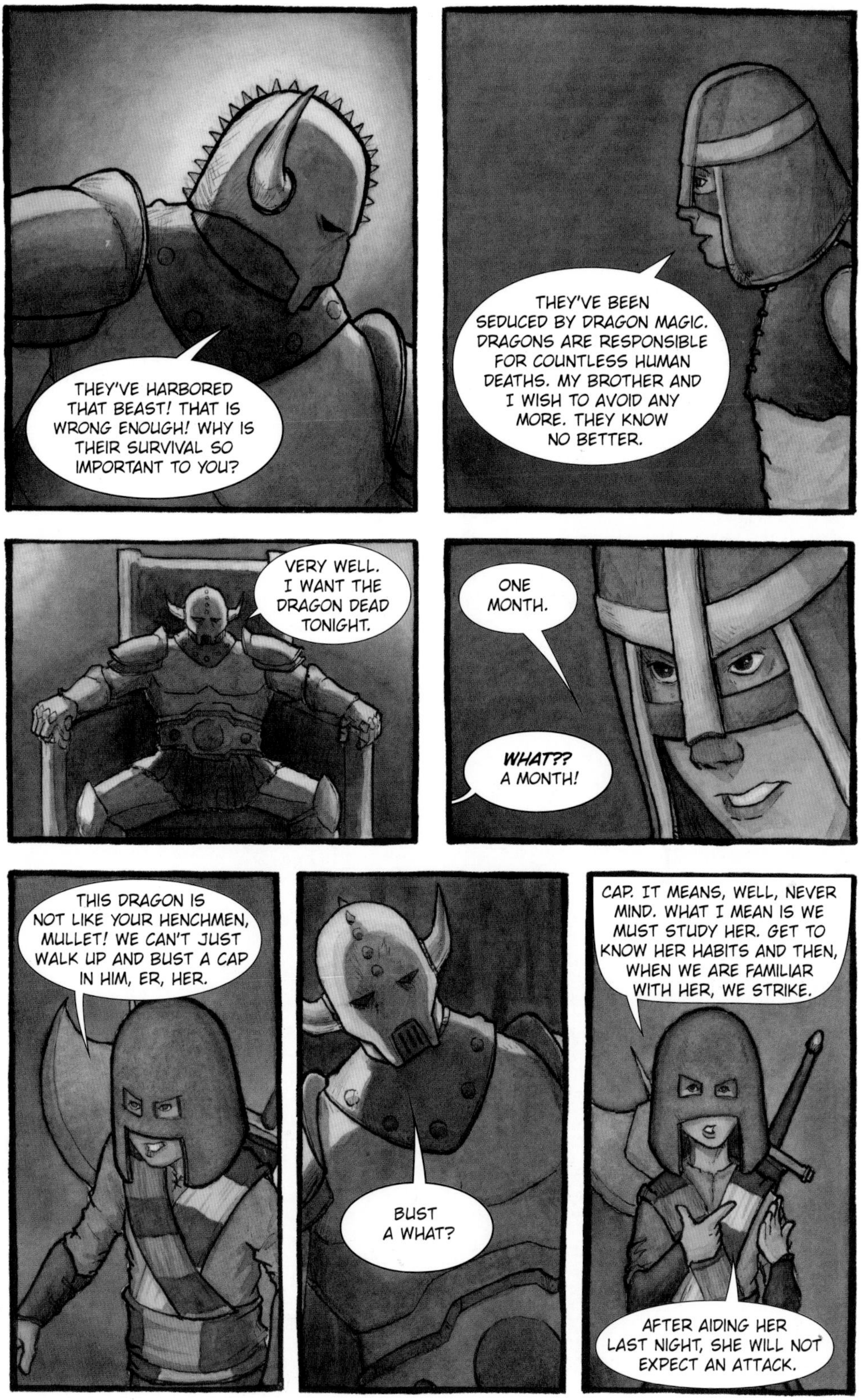
THEY'VE HARBORED THAT BEAST! THAT IS WRONG ENOUGH! WHY IS THEIR SURVIVAL SO IMPORTANT TO YOU?
THEY'VE BEEN SEDUCED BY DRAGON MAGIC. DRAGONS ARE RESPONSIBLE FOR COUNTLESS HUMAN DEATHS. MY BROTHER AND I WISH TO AVOID ANY MORE. THEY KNOW NO BETTER.
VERY WELL. I WANT THE DRAGON DEAD TONIGHT.
ONE MONTH.
WHAT?? A MONTH!
THIS DRAGON IS NOT LIKE YOUR HENCHMEN, MULLET! WE CAN'T JUST WALK UP AND BUST A CAP IN HIM, ER, HER.
BUST A WHAT?
CAP. IT MEANS, WELL, NEVER MIND. WHAT I MEAN IS WE MUST STUDY HER. GET TO KNOW HER HABITS AND THEN, WHEN WE ARE FAMILIAR WITH HER, WE STRIKE.
AFTER AIDING HER LAST NIGHT, SHE WILL NOT EXPECT AN ATTACK.

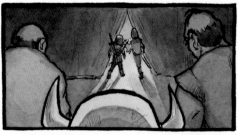

STALKING YOUR PREY. I LIKE THAT. VERY WELL. I WILL ACCEPT YOUR PROPOSAL, BUT KNOW THIS.

IF YOU EVEN THINK ABOUT BETRAYING ME, I WILL HAVE YOUR HEADS ON MY SWORD AND I WILL BURN EVERY LAST VILLAGER ALIVE; IS THAT UNDERSTOOD? NOW, AWAY WITH YOU.

I DO NOT TRUST THEM. I WANT TO KNOW EVERYTHING THEY DO. SHADOW THEM BUT DO NOT BE SEEN.

YES SIR, BUT THEY . . .

THEY FOUGHT BRAVELY LAST NIGHT, SIR. THEY SEEM, HONORABLE.

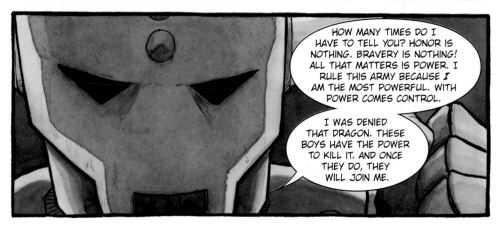

HOW MANY TIMES DO I HAVE TO TELL YOU? HONOR IS NOTHING. BRAVERY IS NOTHING! ALL THAT MATTERS IS POWER. I RULE THIS ARMY BECAUSE *I* AM THE MOST POWERFUL. WITH POWER COMES CONTROL.

I WAS DENIED THAT DRAGON. THESE BOYS HAVE THE POWER TO KILL IT. AND ONCE THEY DO, THEY WILL JOIN ME.

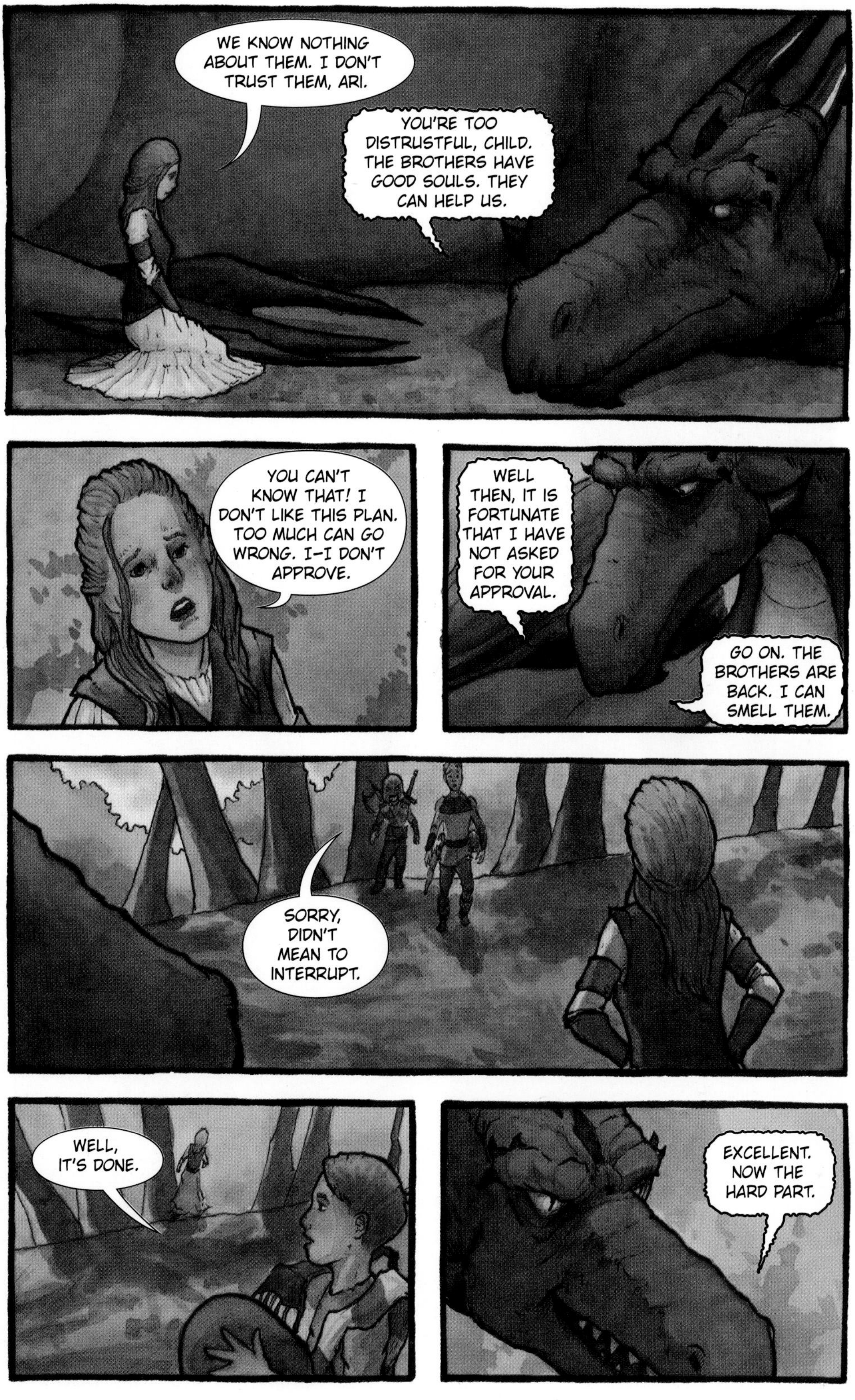
WE KNOW NOTHING ABOUT THEM. I DON'T TRUST THEM, ARI.
YOU'RE TOO DISTRUSTFUL, CHILD. THE BROTHERS HAVE GOOD SOULS. THEY CAN HELP US.
YOU CAN'T KNOW THAT! I DON'T LIKE THIS PLAN. TOO MUCH CAN GO WRONG. I–I DON'T APPROVE.
WELL THEN, IT IS FORTUNATE THAT I HAVE NOT ASKED FOR YOUR APPROVAL.
GO ON. THE BROTHERS ARE BACK. I CAN SMELL THEM.
SORRY, DIDN'T MEAN TO INTERRUPT.
WELL, IT'S DONE.
EXCELLENT. NOW THE HARD PART.

BOTH OF YOU ARE VERY BRAVE AND HAVE GREAT SPIRIT. BUT THIS WILL NOT BE ENOUGH. YOU EACH HAVE A HANDLE ON YOUR OBJECTS, BUT DO NOT YET HAVE MASTERY OVER THEM. FOR ONE THING, YOU THINK OF THEM AS OBJECTS, THINGS TO USE.

SOON YOU WILL COME TO REALIZE THAT THE BOND THAT YOU SHARE WITH THEM IS MUCH GREATER, AND THAT IN ACTUALITY, THEY ARE EXTENSIONS OF YOU. YOU, YOUNG ONE.

TUCKER.

YOU TRULY BELIEVE IN THEIR MAGIC. THIS IS COMMON WITH THE YOUNG. BUT YOU ARE STILL USING THEM IN A VERY LIMITED WAY. YOU MUST THINK OF THEM AS EXTENSIONS, FLUID, MERCILESS EXTENSIONS OF YOU THAT YOU CAN SEND WHEREVER YOUR MIND TELLS THEM TO GO.

TUCKER. YOU HAVE GREATER CONTROL OVER YOUR SCARVES THAN YOUR BROTHER DOES HIS UMBRELLA.

THEY CAN GROW AND STRETCH, YES? YOU CAN PUSH THIS TO THE ABSOLUTE LIMITS OF YOUR IMAGINATION.

LAUNCH YOURSELF INTO THE AIR, I'M GOING TO STRIKE AT YOU, I WANT YOU TO DEFEND YOURSELF.

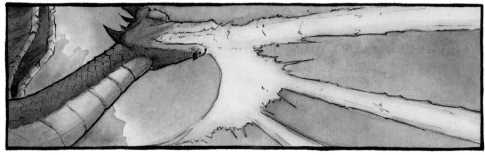

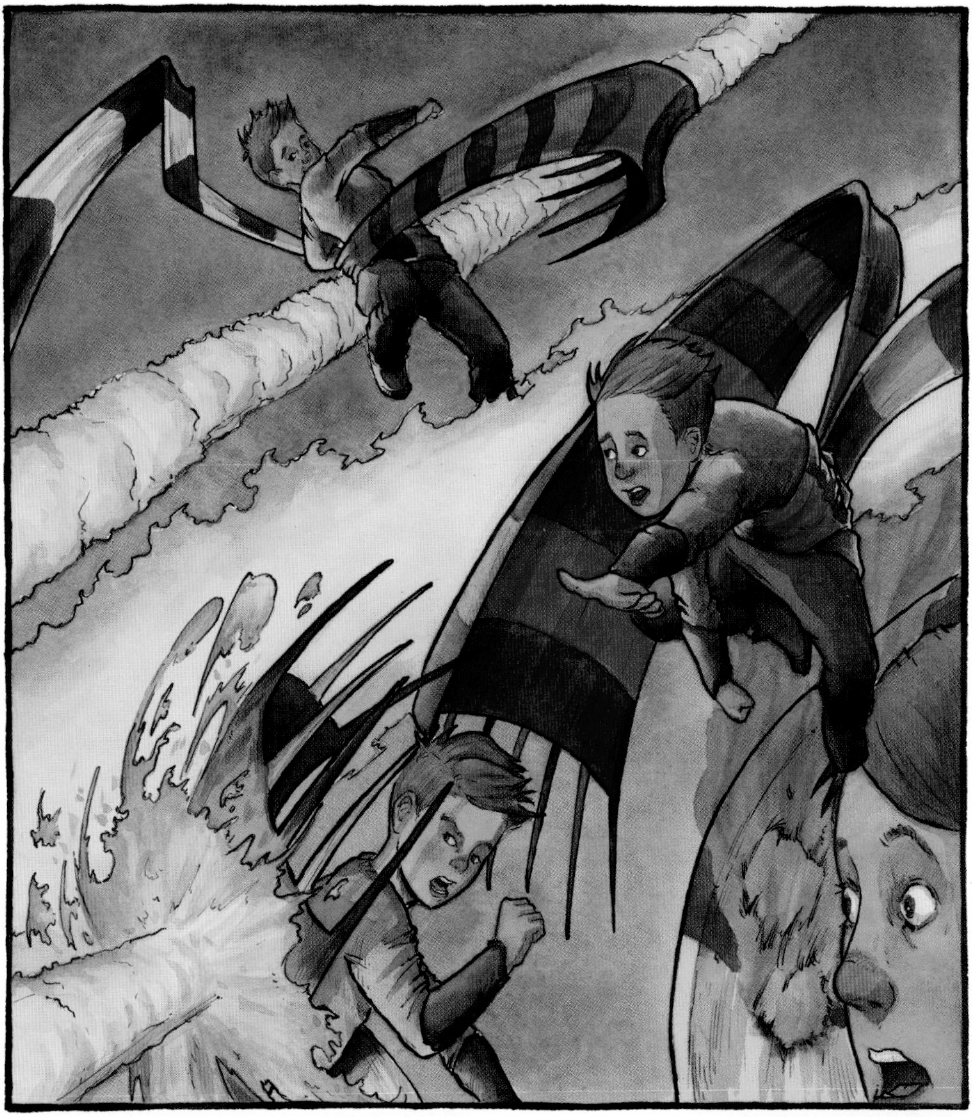

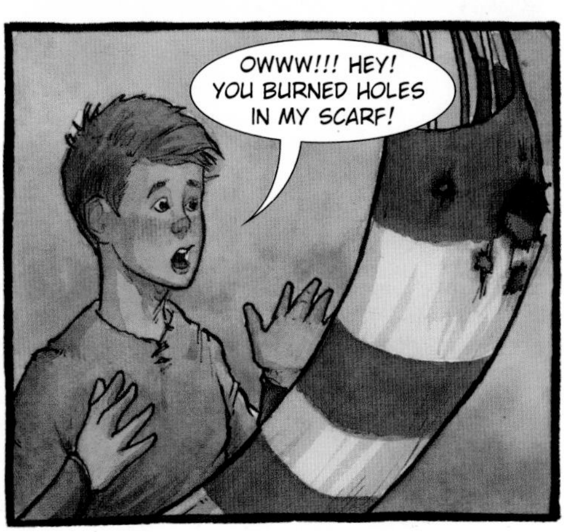
OWWW!!! HEY! YOU BURNED HOLES IN MY SCARF!

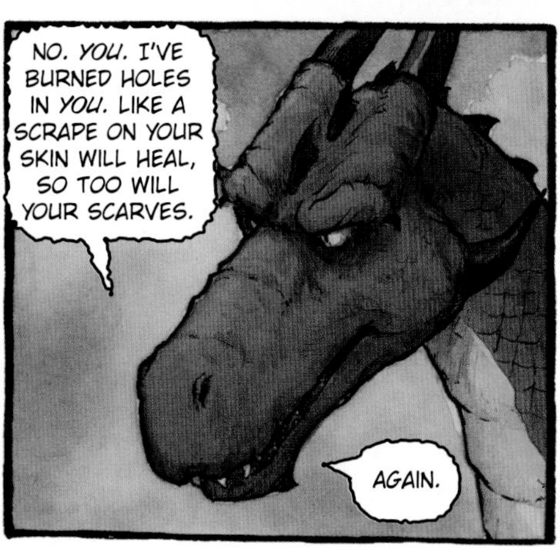
NO. *YOU*. I'VE BURNED HOLES IN *YOU*. LIKE A SCRAPE ON YOUR SKIN WILL HEAL, SO TOO WILL YOUR SCARVES.
AGAIN.

YOU USE IT TO FLY, YOU'VE FOUND YOU CAN HIT THINGS WITH GREAT FORCE, DEFEND. BUT ALL OF THESE YOU ARE DOING AT VERY ORDINARY LEVELS.

YOU HAVE MAGIC AT YOUR COMMAND. THERE ARE RULES WITH MAGIC, BUT NO LIMITS. FOR EXAMPLE, HOW FAST CAN YOU FLY?

HUDSON, YOU HAVE JUST SCRAPED THE SURFACE OF YOUR POWER.

OH, UH . . . I DUNNO.

AS FAST AS THIS?

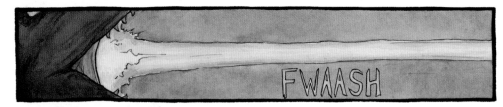

FWAASH

AH. NO. NOT THAT FAST.

HMM. TUCKER, SHOW ME YOUR SPEED, LAUNCH YOURSELF AS FAST AND AS FAR AS YOU CAN.

YOU GOT IT!

ARE YOU SURE YOU CANNOT GO FASTER THAN MY FLAME?

PRETTY SURE, YEAH.

THAT IS VERY UNFORTUNATE . . . FOR YOUR BROTHER.

NO!

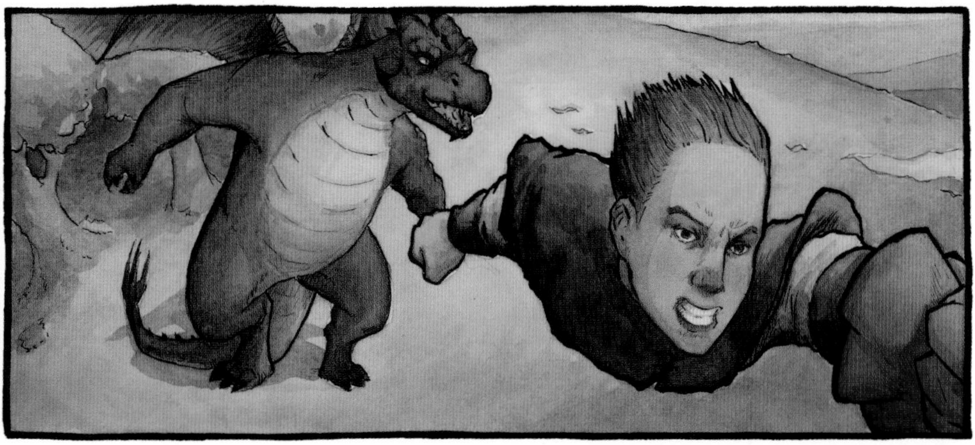

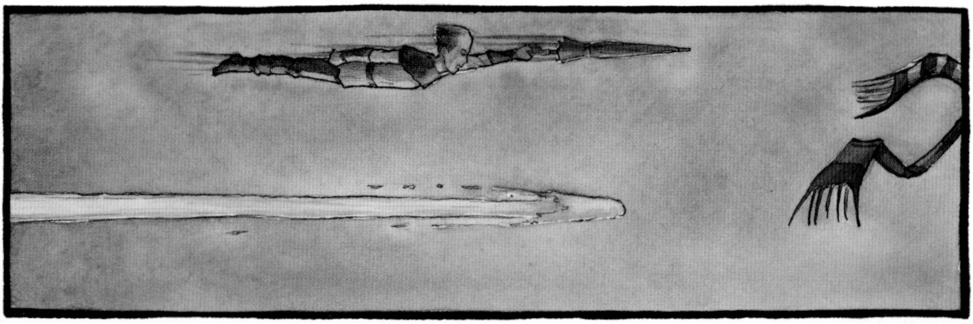

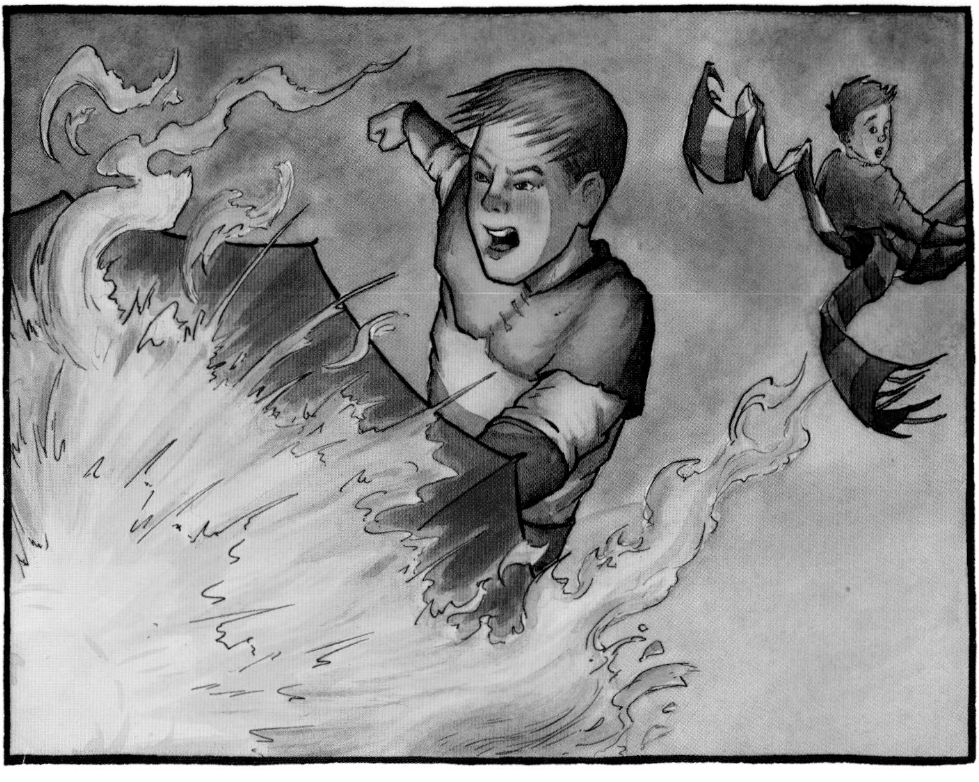

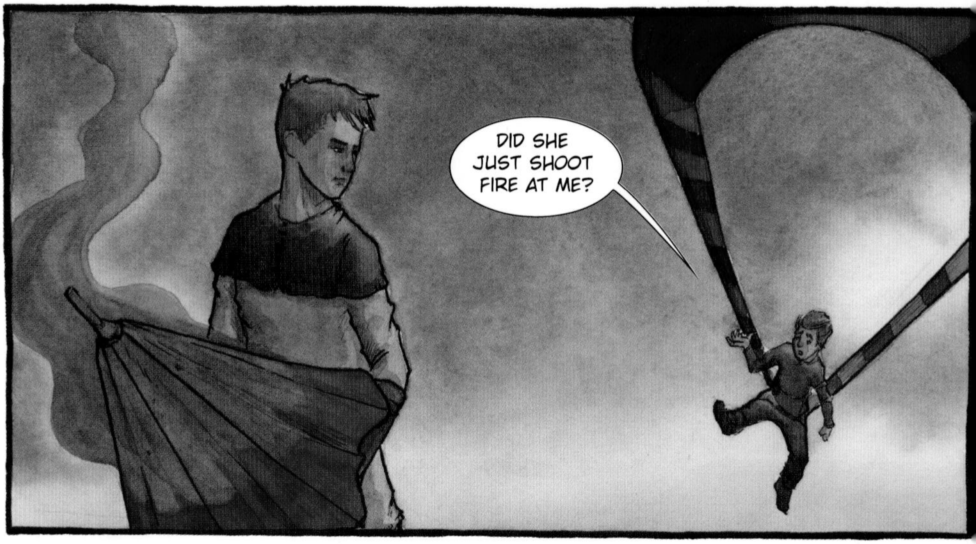
DID SHE JUST SHOOT FIRE AT ME?

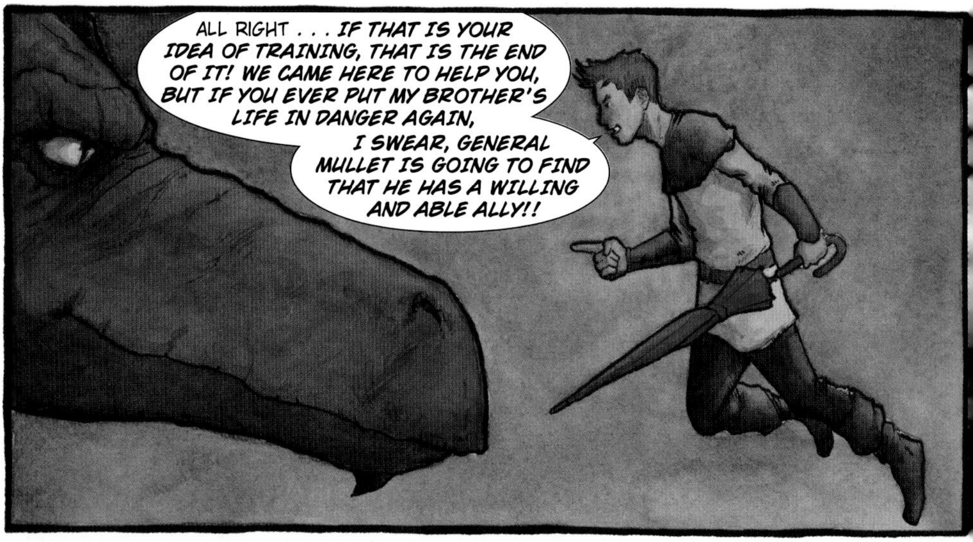
ALL RIGHT . . . IF THAT IS YOUR IDEA OF TRAINING, THAT IS THE END OF IT! WE CAME HERE TO HELP YOU, BUT IF YOU EVER PUT MY BROTHER'S LIFE IN DANGER AGAIN, I SWEAR, GENERAL MULLET IS GOING TO FIND THAT HE HAS A WILLING AND ABLE ALLY!!

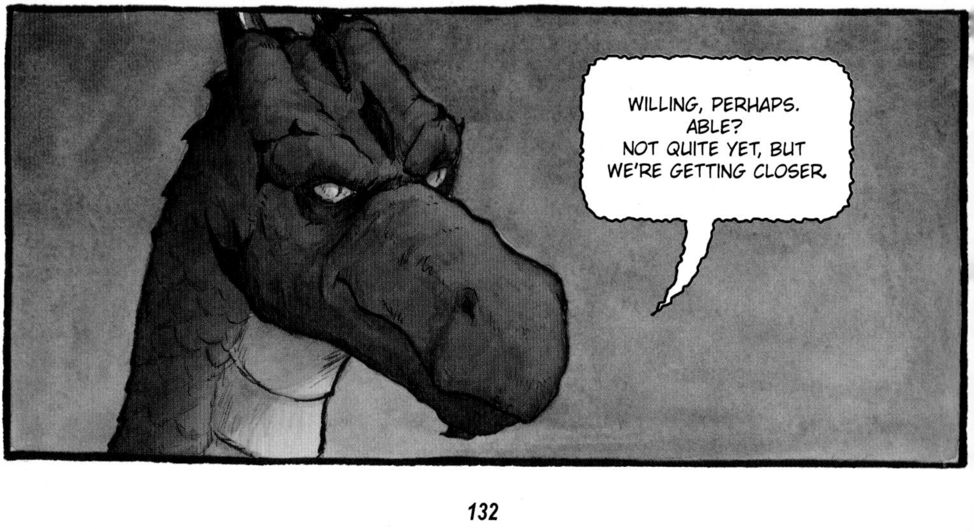
WILLING, PERHAPS. ABLE? NOT QUITE YET, BUT WE'RE GETTING CLOSER.

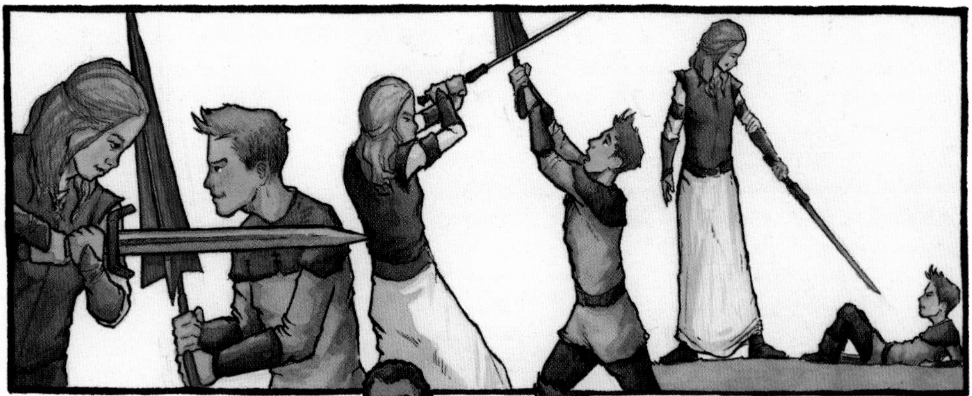

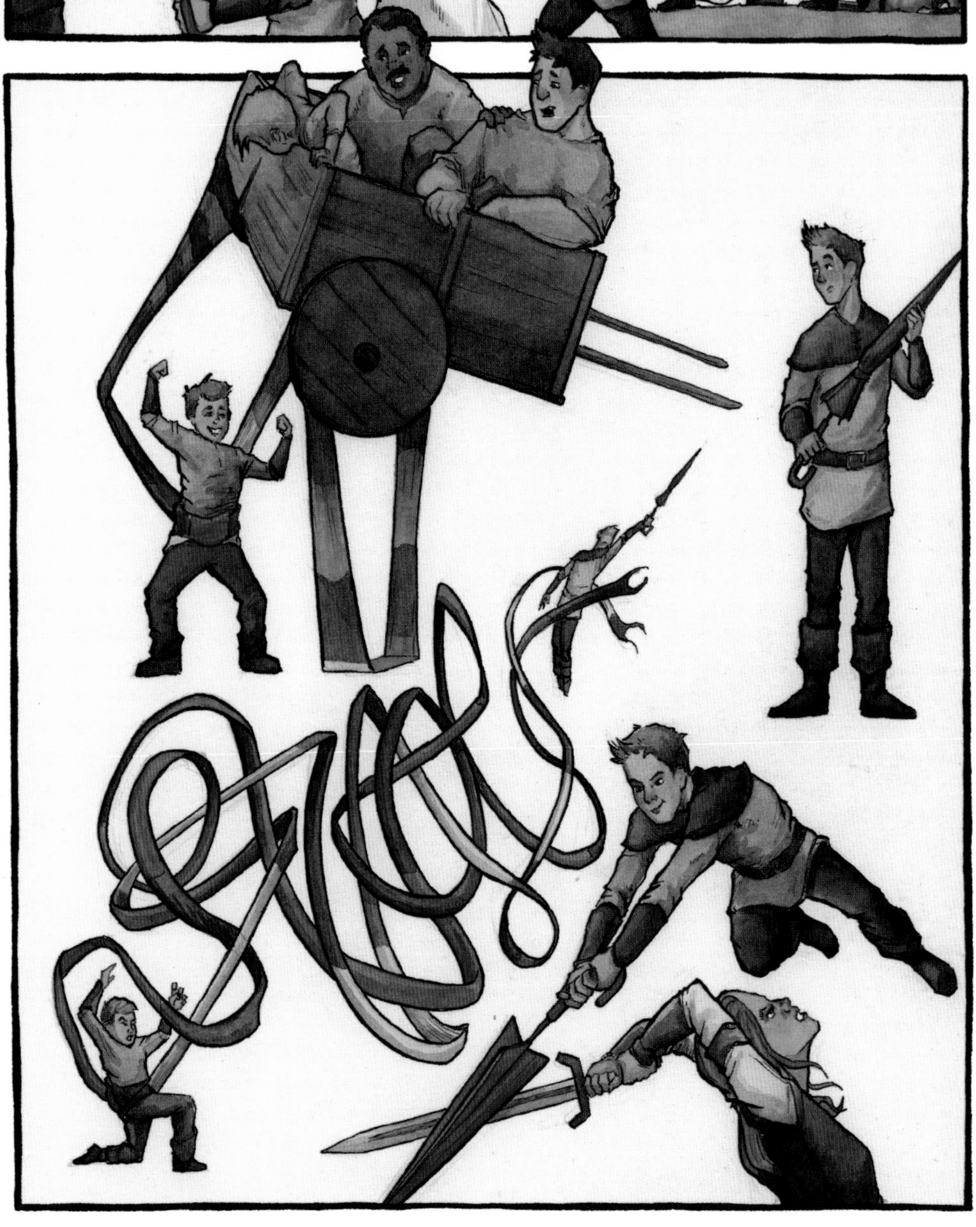

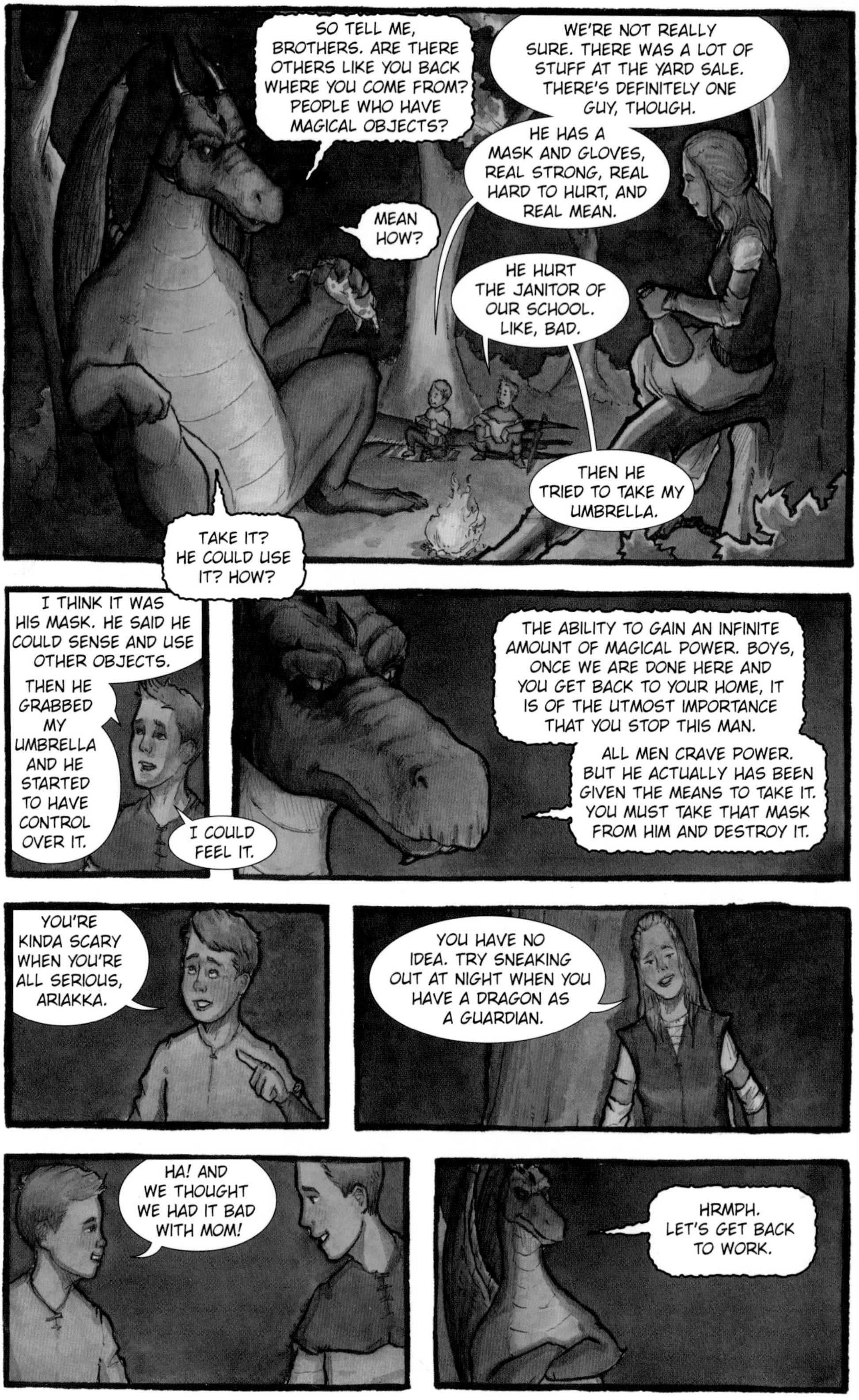
SO TELL ME, BROTHERS. ARE THERE OTHERS LIKE YOU BACK WHERE YOU COME FROM? PEOPLE WHO HAVE MAGICAL OBJECTS?
WE'RE NOT REALLY SURE. THERE WAS A LOT OF STUFF AT THE YARD SALE. THERE'S DEFINITELY ONE GUY, THOUGH.
HE HAS A MASK AND GLOVES, REAL STRONG, REAL HARD TO HURT, AND REAL MEAN.
MEAN HOW?
HE HURT THE JANITOR OF OUR SCHOOL. LIKE, BAD.
THEN HE TRIED TO TAKE MY UMBRELLA.
TAKE IT? HE COULD USE IT? HOW?
I THINK IT WAS HIS MASK. HE SAID HE COULD SENSE AND USE OTHER OBJECTS.
THEN HE GRABBED MY UMBRELLA AND HE STARTED TO HAVE CONTROL OVER IT.
I COULD FEEL IT.
THE ABILITY TO GAIN AN INFINITE AMOUNT OF MAGICAL POWER. BOYS, ONCE WE ARE DONE HERE AND YOU GET BACK TO YOUR HOME, IT IS OF THE UTMOST IMPORTANCE THAT YOU STOP THIS MAN.
ALL MEN CRAVE POWER. BUT HE ACTUALLY HAS BEEN GIVEN THE MEANS TO TAKE IT. YOU MUST TAKE THAT MASK FROM HIM AND DESTROY IT.
YOU'RE KINDA SCARY WHEN YOU'RE ALL SERIOUS, ARIAKKA.
YOU HAVE NO IDEA. TRY SNEAKING OUT AT NIGHT WHEN YOU HAVE A DRAGON AS A GUARDIAN.
HA! AND WE THOUGHT WE HAD IT BAD WITH MOM!
HRMPH. LET'S GET BACK TO WORK.

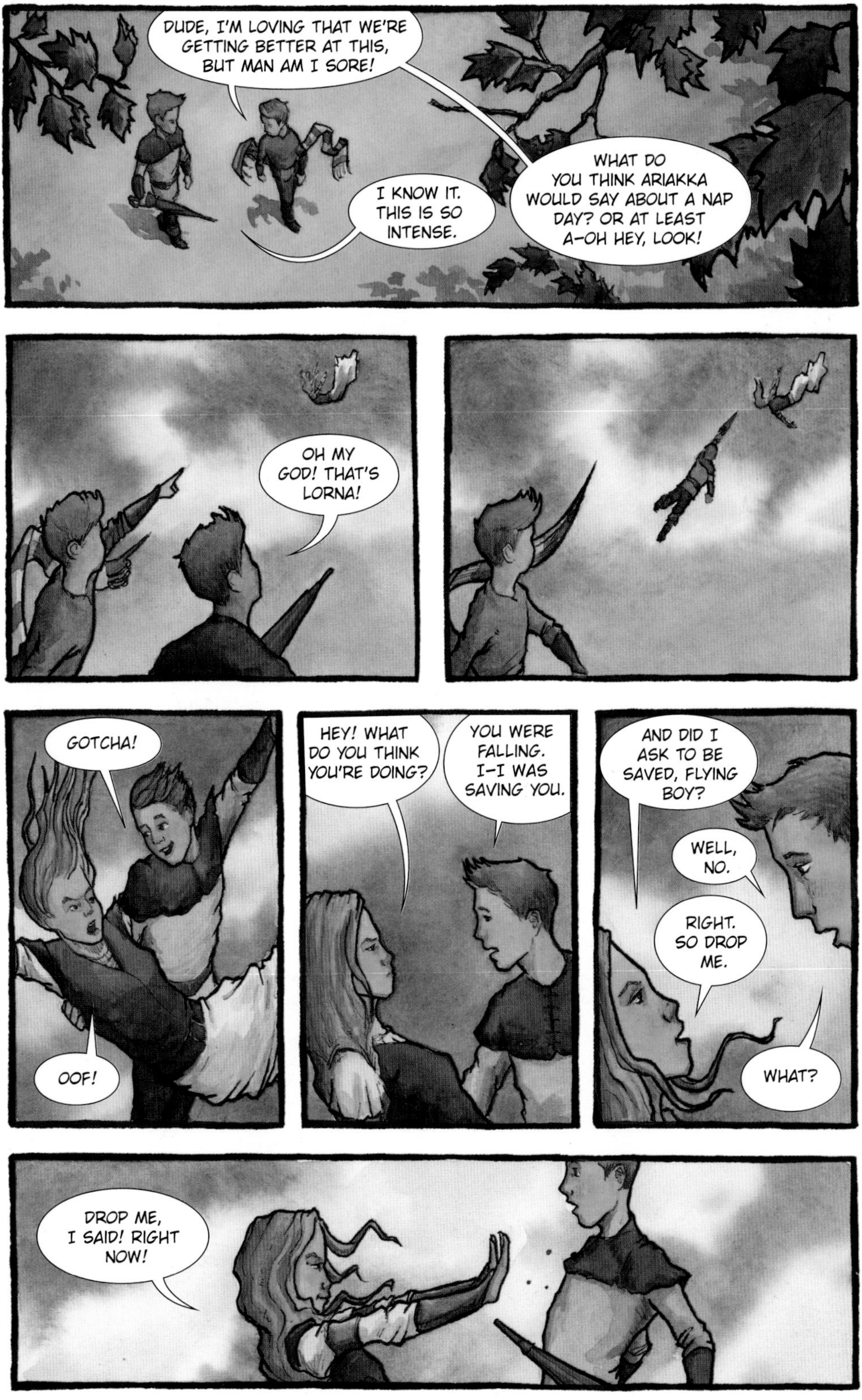
DUDE, I'M LOVING THAT WE'RE GETTING BETTER AT THIS, BUT MAN AM I SORE!
I KNOW IT. THIS IS SO INTENSE.
WHAT DO YOU THINK ARIAKKA WOULD SAY ABOUT A NAP DAY? OR AT LEAST A—OH HEY, LOOK!
OH MY GOD! THAT'S LORNA!
GOTCHA!
OOF!
HEY! WHAT DO YOU THINK YOU'RE DOING?
YOU WERE FALLING. I—I WAS SAVING YOU.
AND DID I ASK TO BE SAVED, FLYING BOY?
WELL, NO.
RIGHT. SO DROP ME.
WHAT?
DROP ME, I SAID! RIGHT NOW!

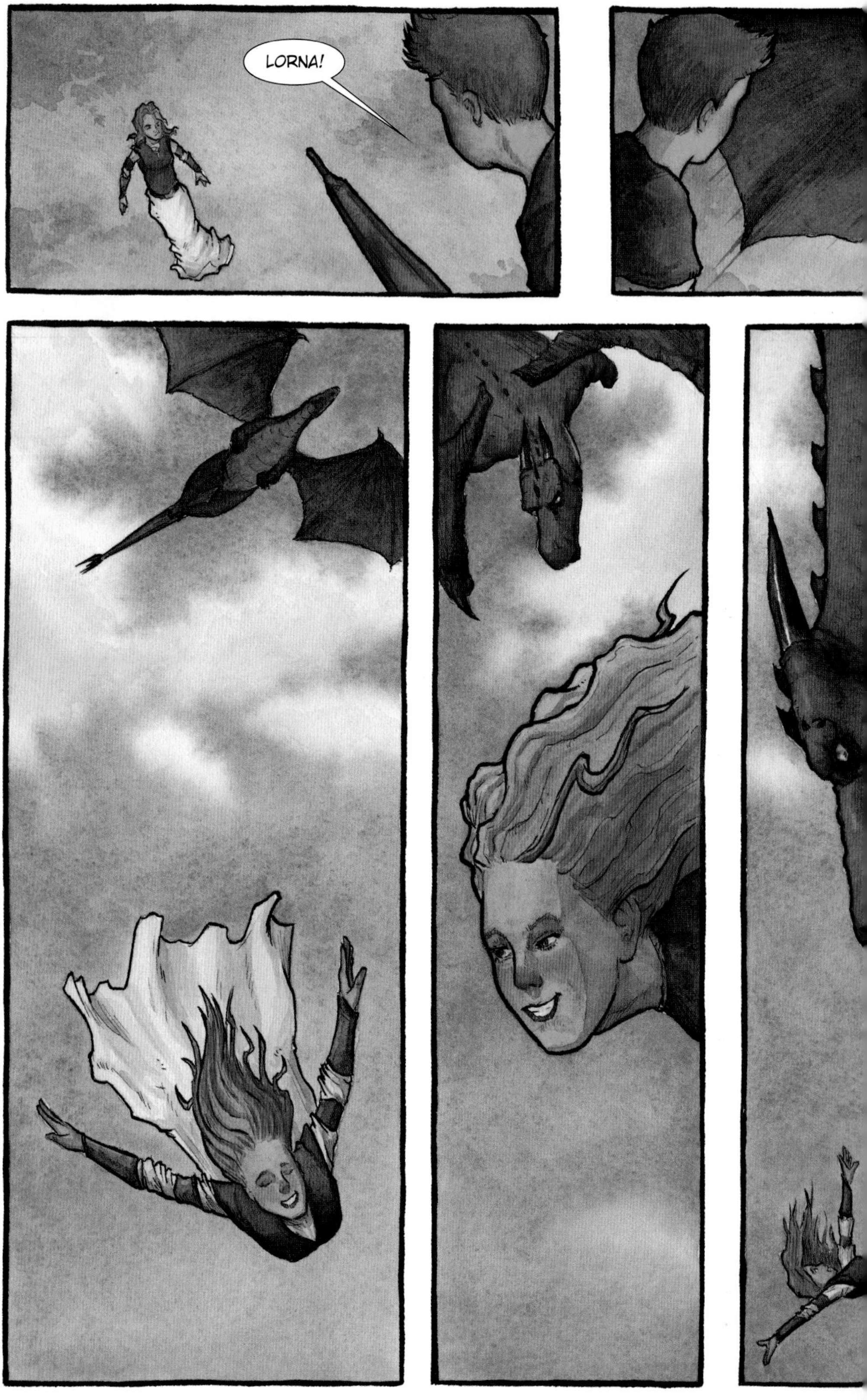
LORNA!

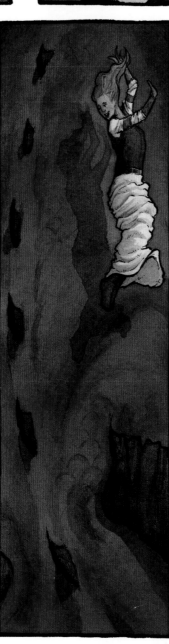

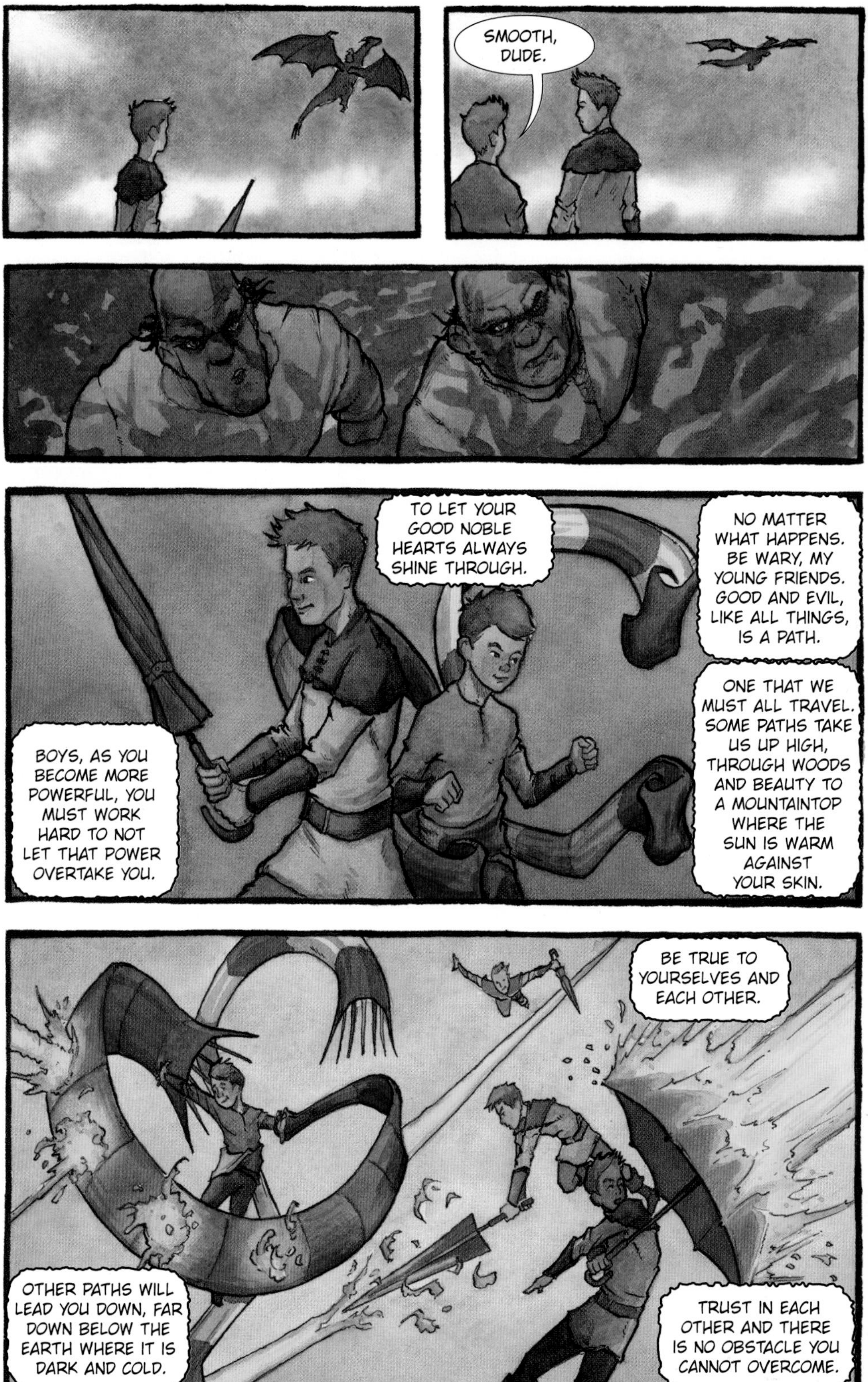
SMOOTH, DUDE.
TO LET YOUR GOOD NOBLE HEARTS ALWAYS SHINE THROUGH.
NO MATTER WHAT HAPPENS. BE WARY, MY YOUNG FRIENDS. GOOD AND EVIL, LIKE ALL THINGS, IS A PATH.
ONE THAT WE MUST ALL TRAVEL. SOME PATHS TAKE US UP HIGH, THROUGH WOODS AND BEAUTY TO A MOUNTAINTOP WHERE THE SUN IS WARM AGAINST YOUR SKIN.
BOYS, AS YOU BECOME MORE POWERFUL, YOU MUST WORK HARD TO NOT LET THAT POWER OVERTAKE YOU.
BE TRUE TO YOURSELVES AND EACH OTHER.
OTHER PATHS WILL LEAD YOU DOWN, FAR DOWN BELOW THE EARTH WHERE IT IS DARK AND COLD.
TRUST IN EACH OTHER AND THERE IS NO OBSTACLE YOU CANNOT OVERCOME.

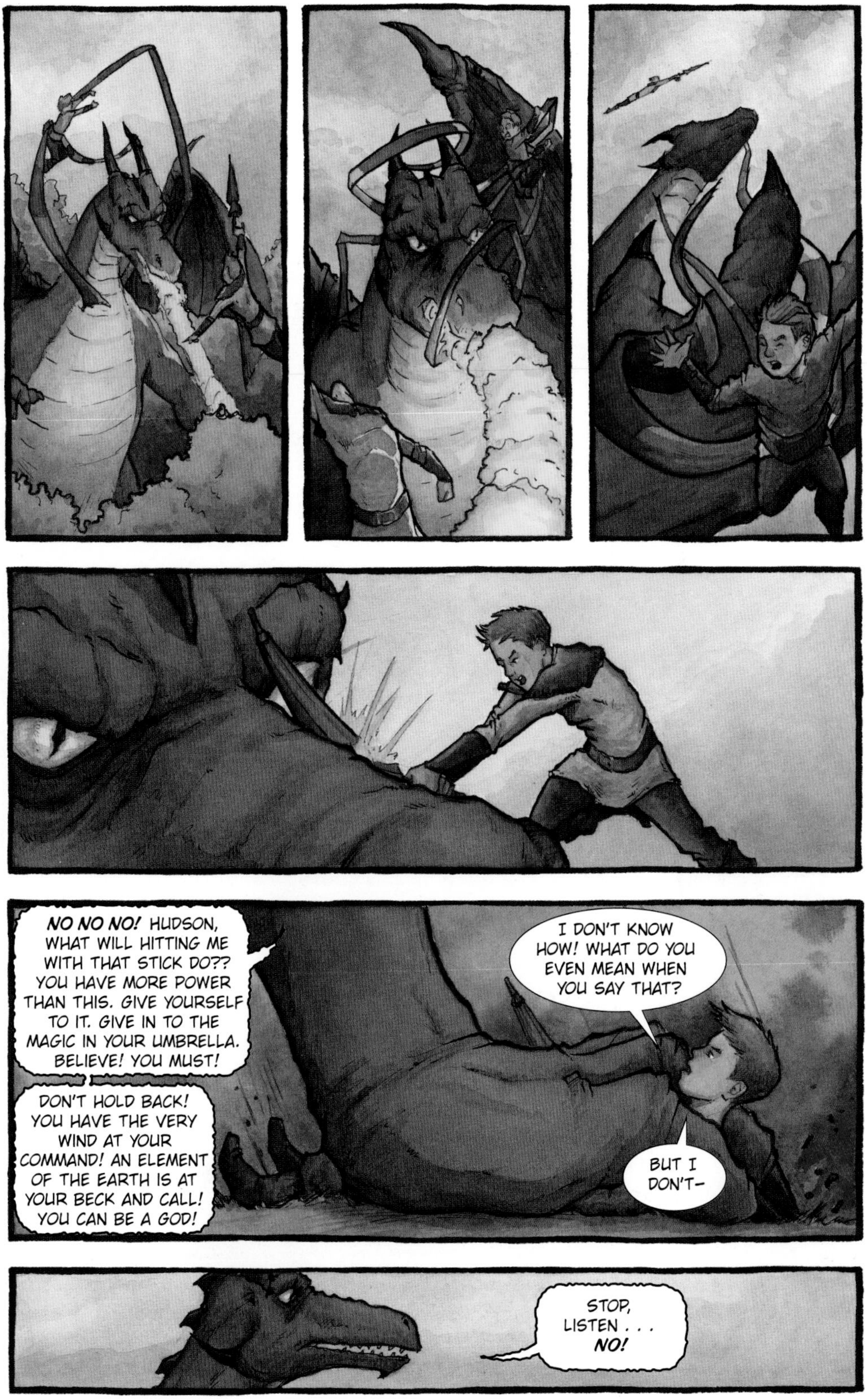
NO NO NO! HUDSON, WHAT WILL HITTING ME WITH THAT STICK DO?? YOU HAVE MORE POWER THAN THIS. GIVE YOURSELF TO IT. GIVE IN TO THE MAGIC IN YOUR UMBRELLA. BELIEVE! YOU MUST!
DON'T HOLD BACK! YOU HAVE THE VERY WIND AT YOUR COMMAND! AN ELEMENT OF THE EARTH IS AT YOUR BECK AND CALL! YOU CAN BE A GOD!
I DON'T KNOW HOW! WHAT DO YOU EVEN MEAN WHEN YOU SAY THAT?
BUT I DON'T–
STOP, LISTEN . . . NO!

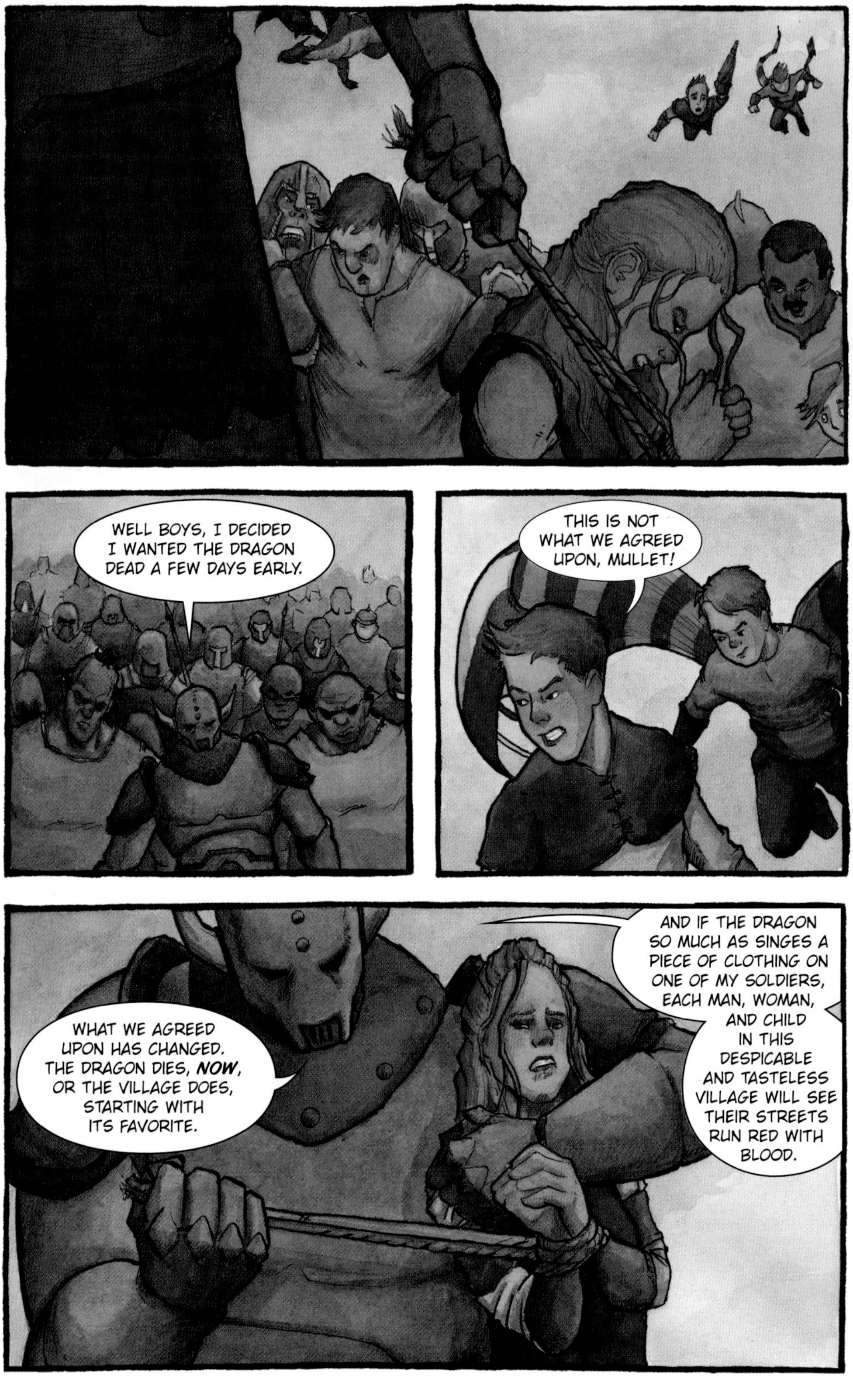
WELL BOYS, I DECIDED I WANTED THE DRAGON DEAD A FEW DAYS EARLY.
THIS IS NOT WHAT WE AGREED UPON, MULLET!
WHAT WE AGREED UPON HAS CHANGED. THE DRAGON DIES, ***NOW***, OR THE VILLAGE DOES, STARTING WITH ITS FAVORITE.
AND IF THE DRAGON SO MUCH AS SINGES A PIECE OF CLOTHING ON ONE OF MY SOLDIERS, EACH MAN, WOMAN, AND CHILD IN THIS DESPICABLE AND TASTELESS VILLAGE WILL SEE THEIR STREETS RUN RED WITH BLOOD.

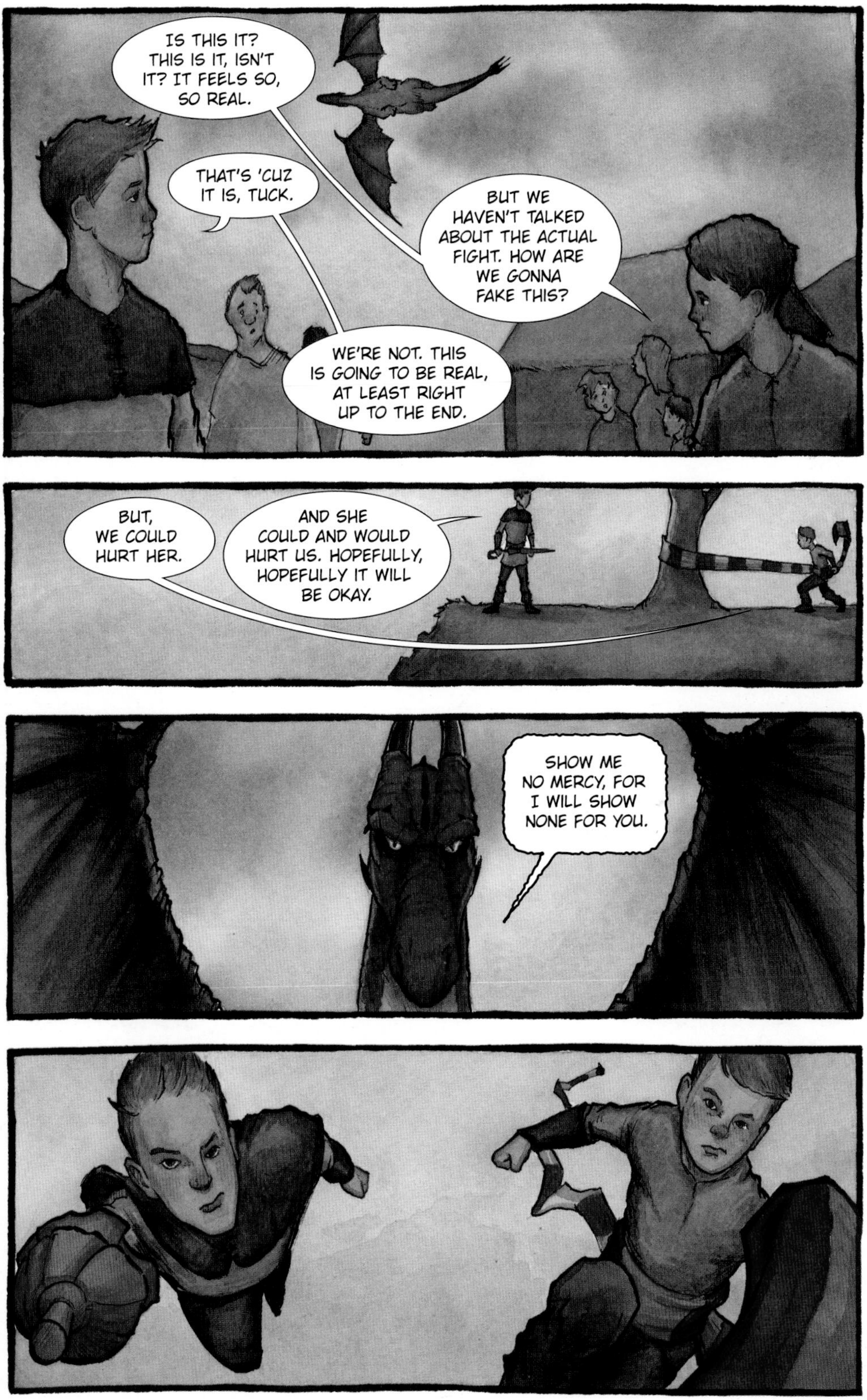
IS THIS IT? THIS IS IT, ISN'T IT? IT FEELS SO, SO REAL.
THAT'S 'CUZ IT IS, TUCK.
BUT WE HAVEN'T TALKED ABOUT THE ACTUAL FIGHT. HOW ARE WE GONNA FAKE THIS?
WE'RE NOT. THIS IS GOING TO BE REAL, AT LEAST RIGHT UP TO THE END.
BUT, WE COULD HURT HER.
AND SHE COULD AND WOULD HURT US. HOPEFULLY, HOPEFULLY IT WILL BE OKAY.
SHOW ME NO MERCY, FOR I WILL SHOW NONE FOR YOU.

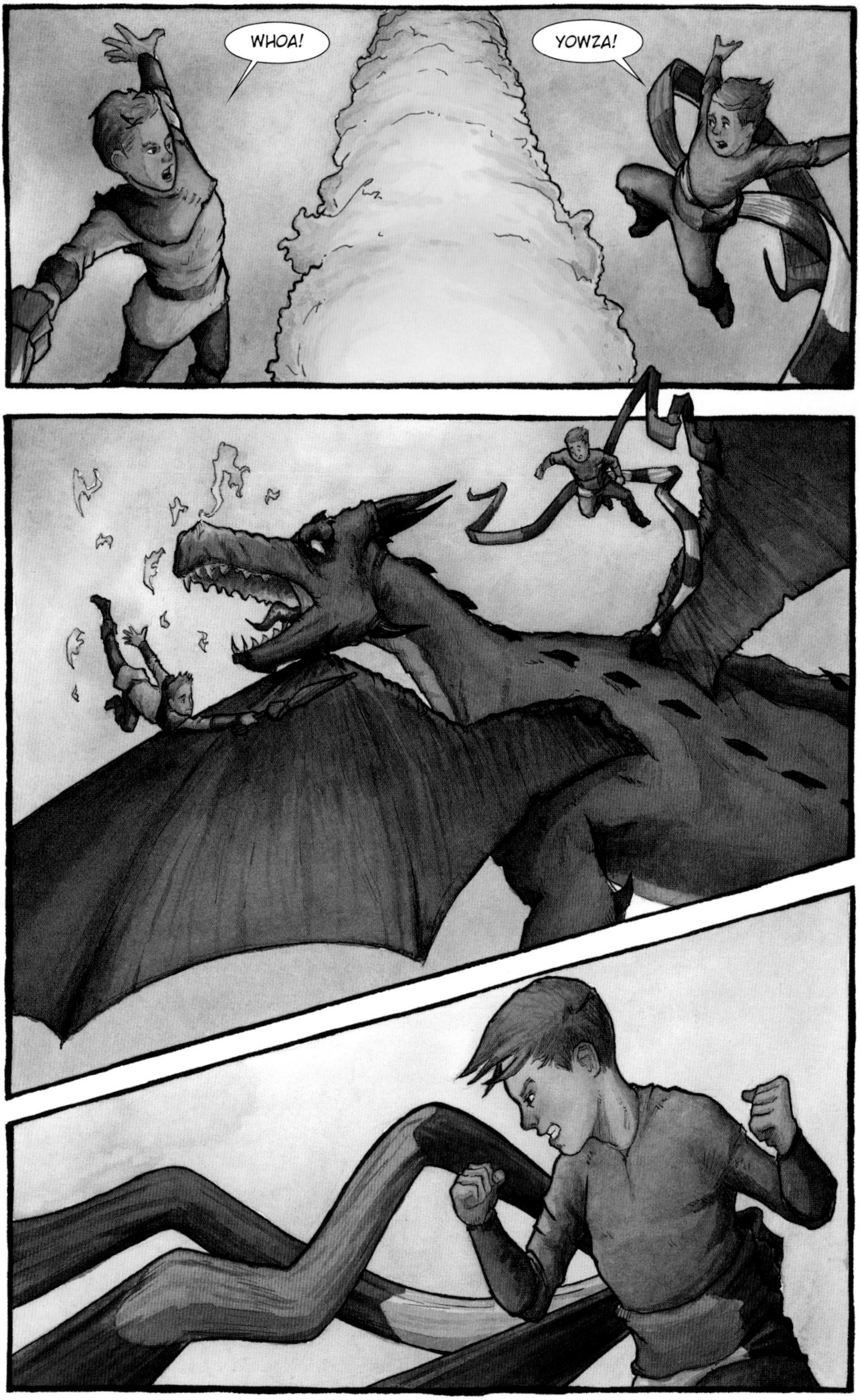
WHOA!
YOWZA!

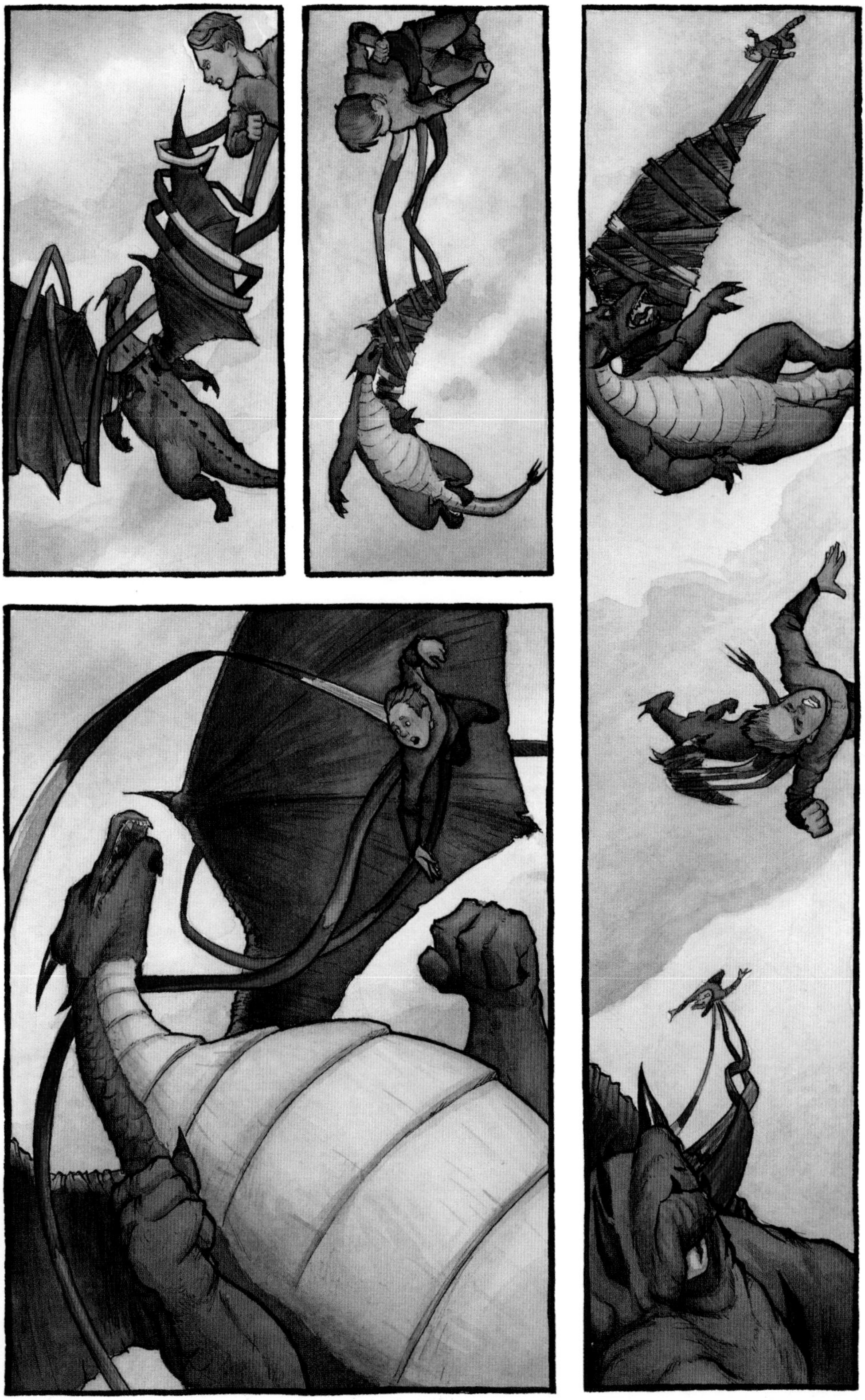

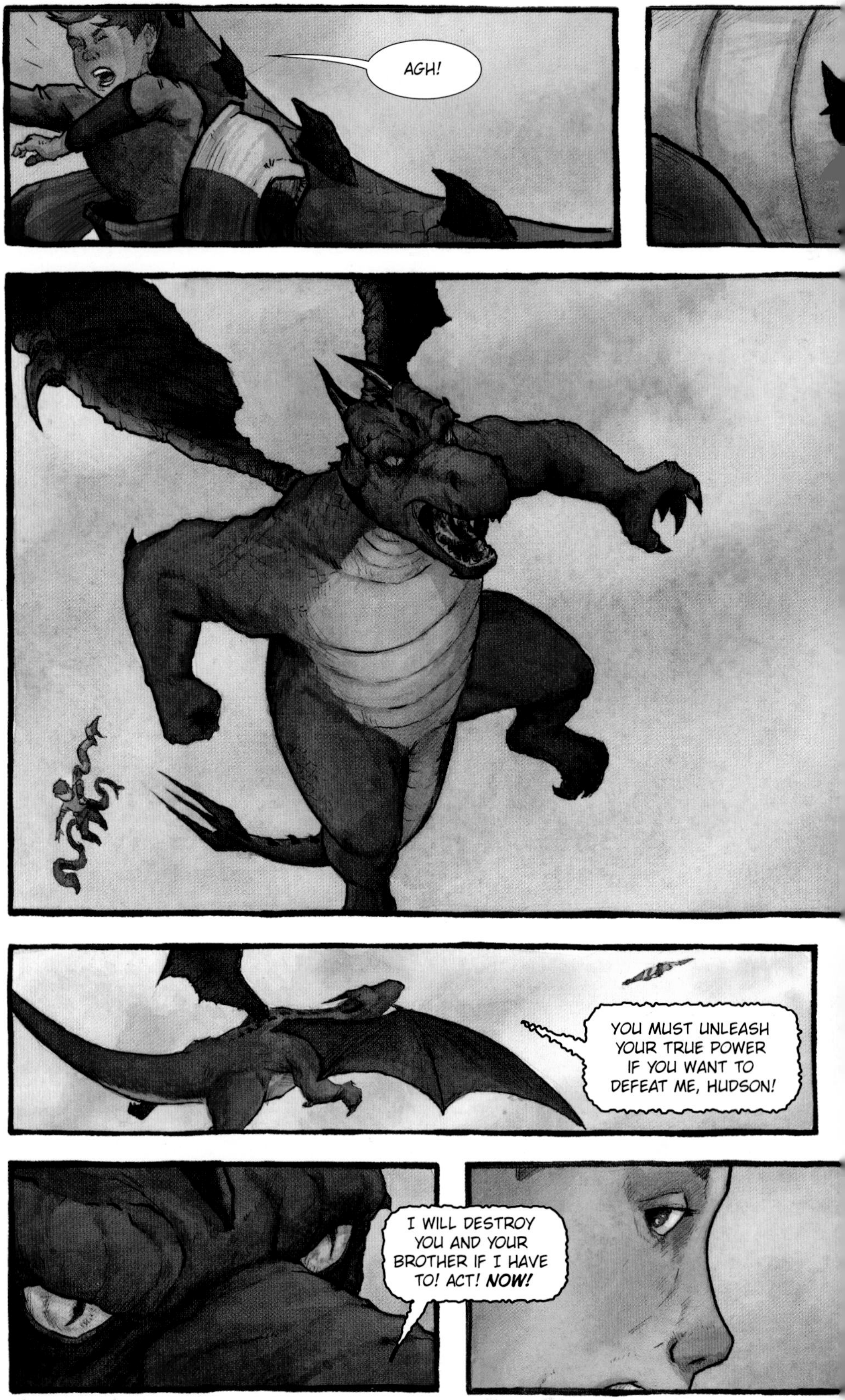
AGH!
YOU MUST UNLEASH YOUR TRUE POWER IF YOU WANT TO DEFEAT ME, HUDSON!
I WILL DESTROY YOU AND YOUR BROTHER IF I HAVE TO! ACT! **NOW!**

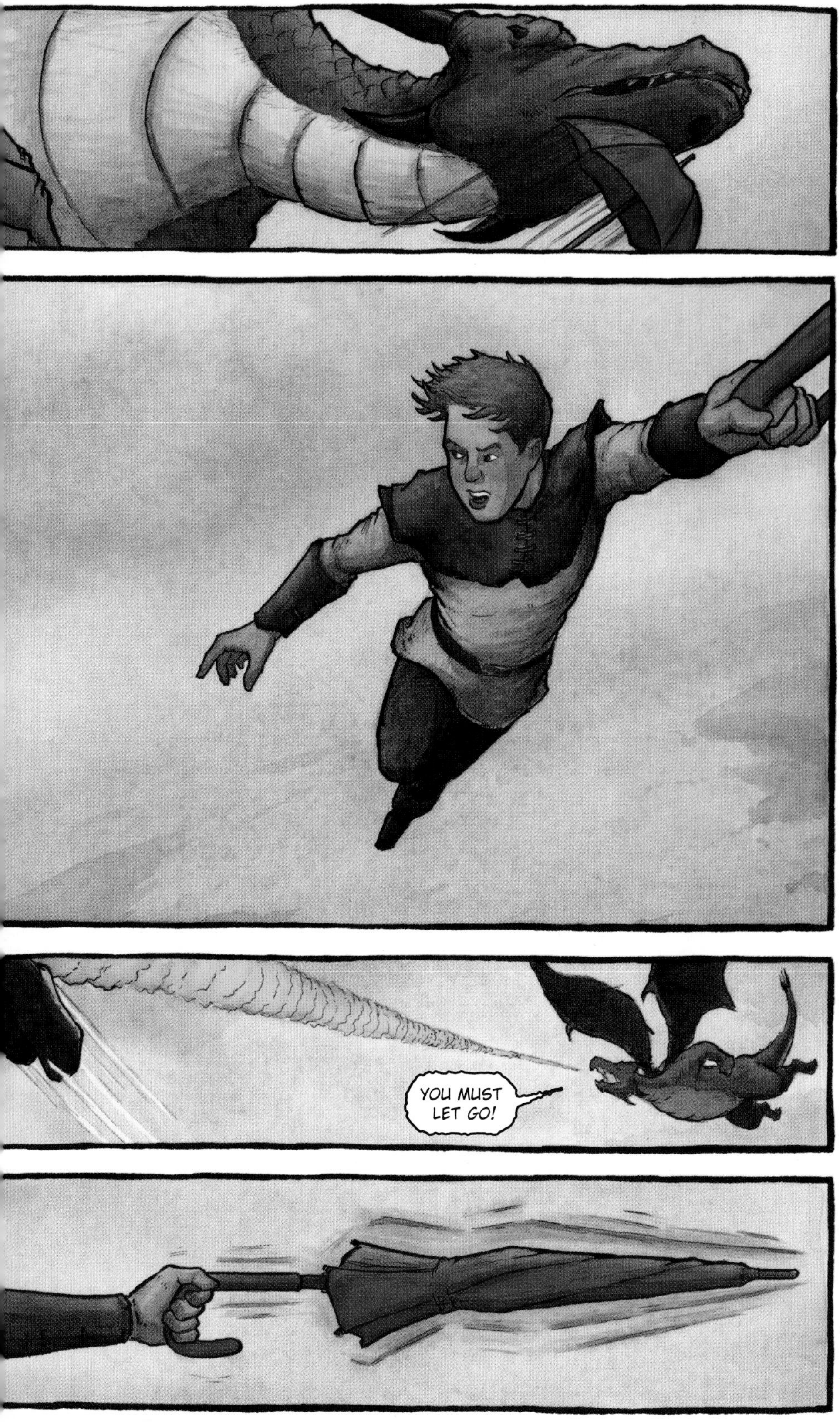
YOU MUST LET GO!

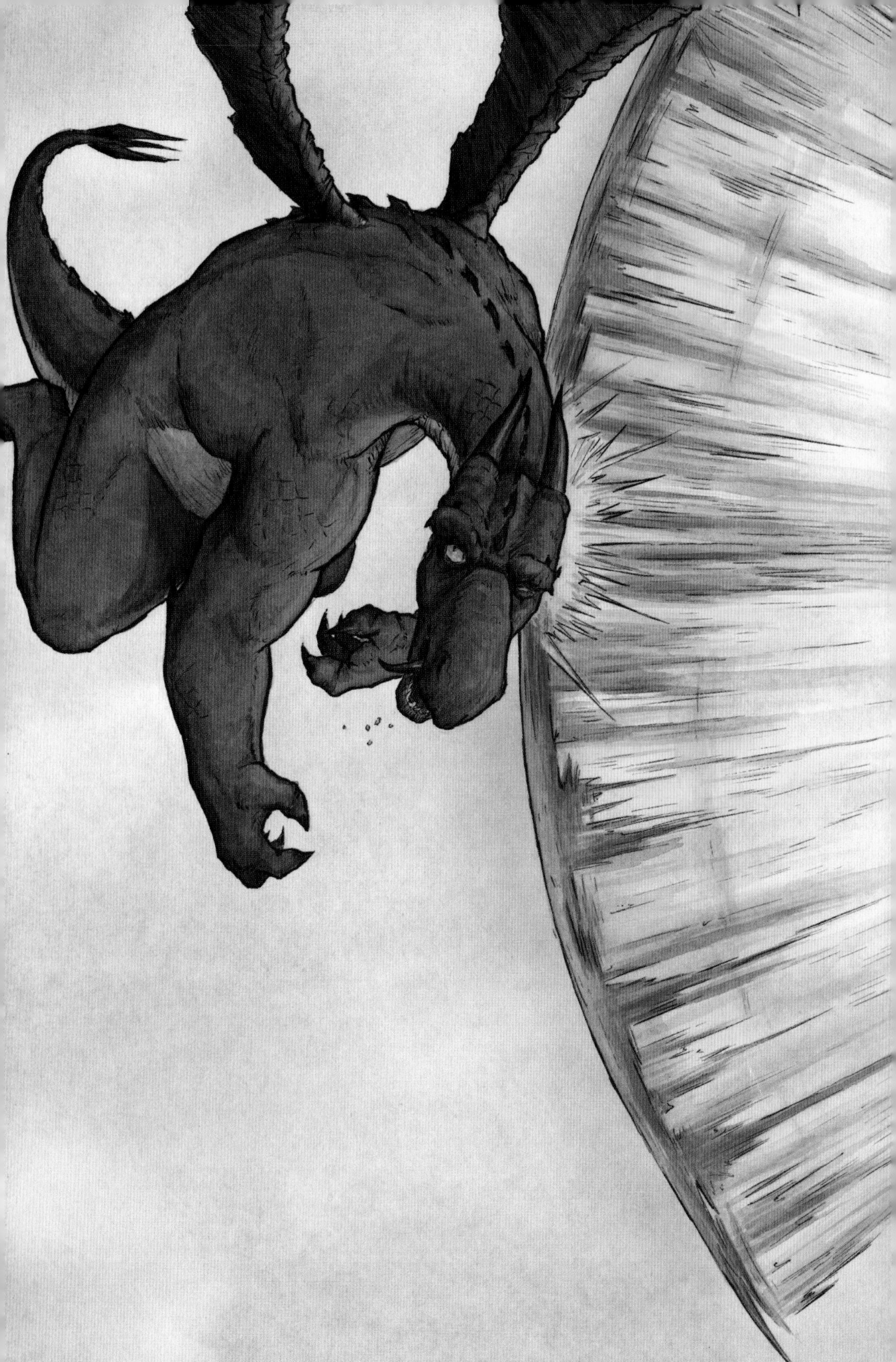

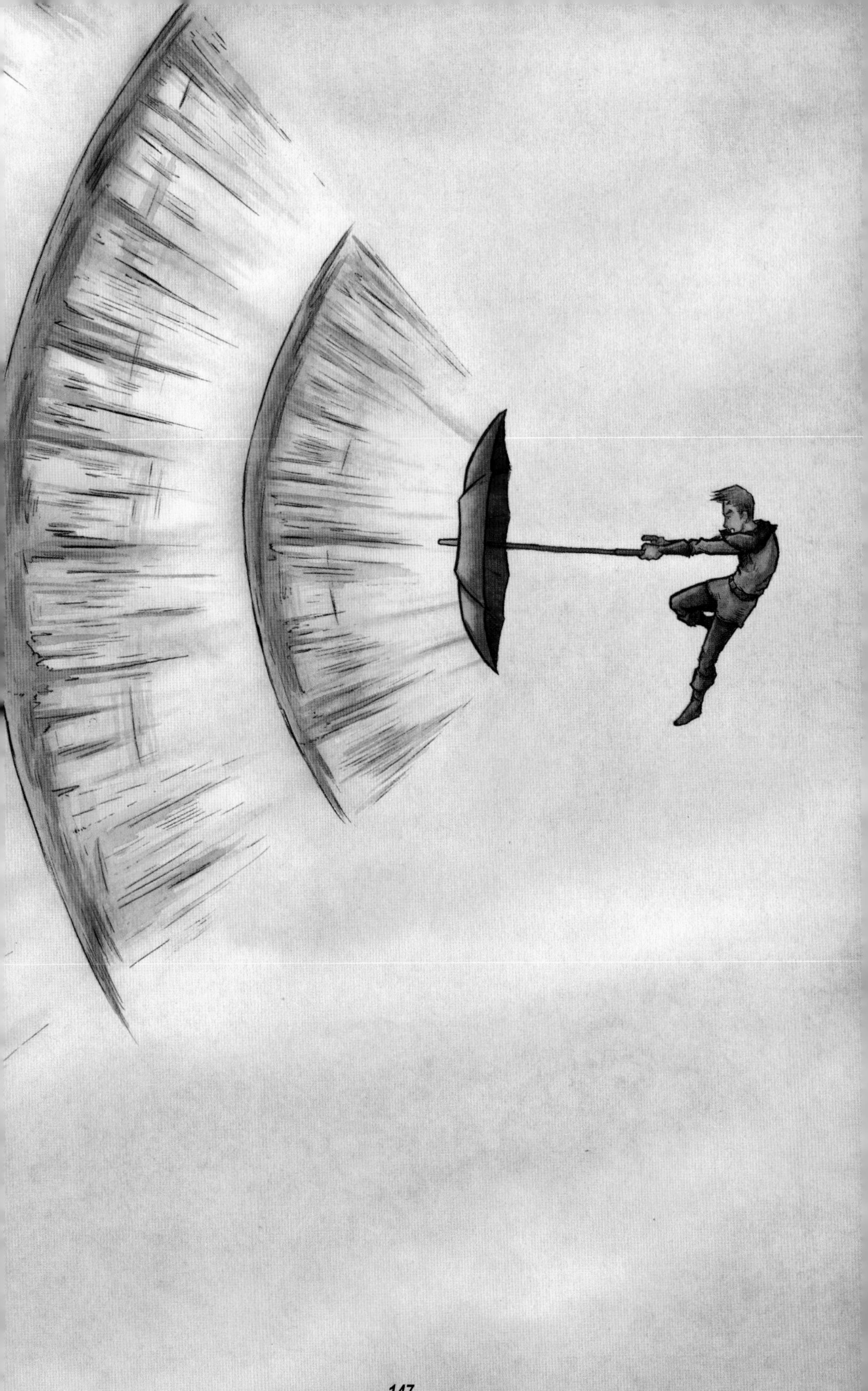

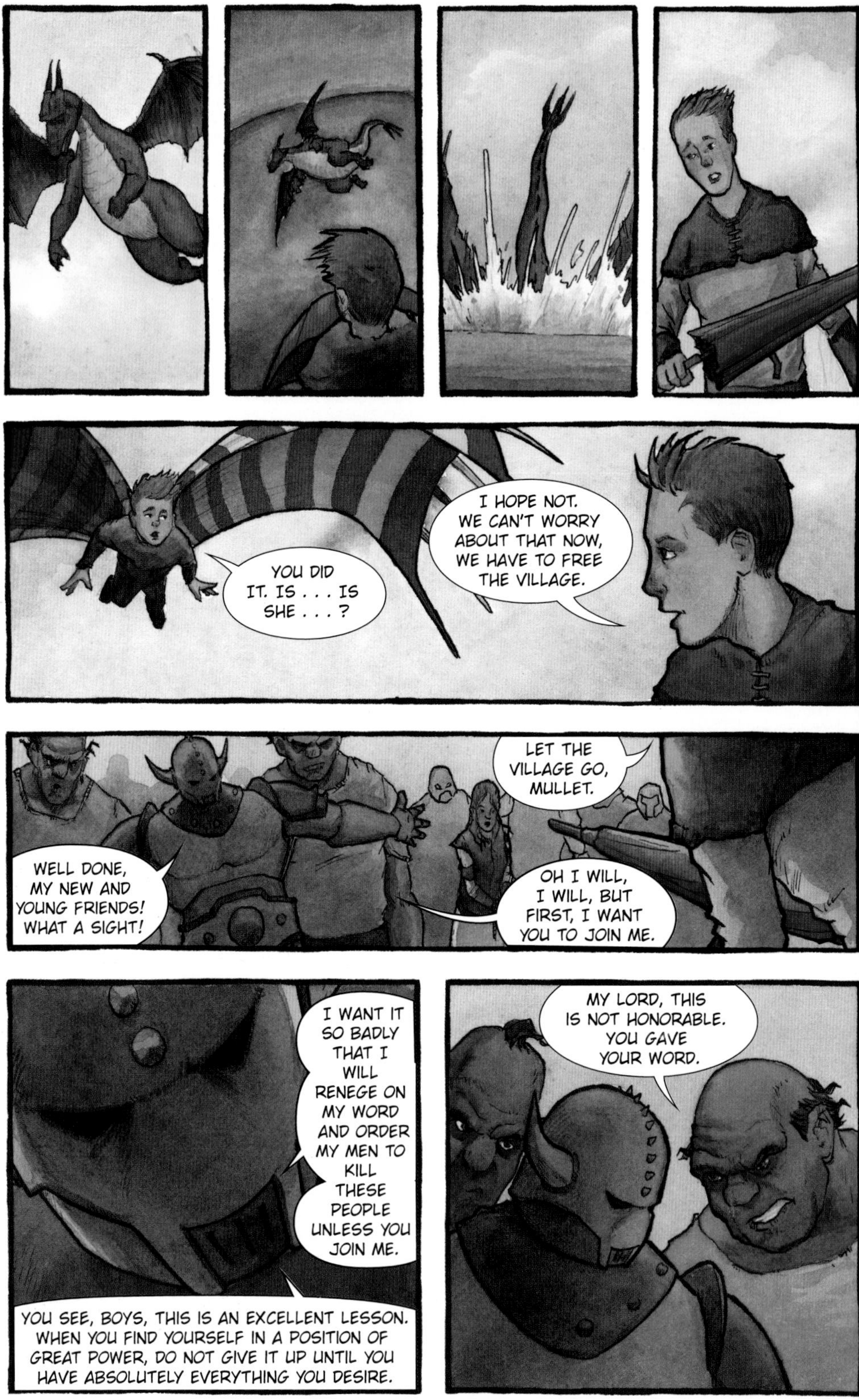
YOU DID IT. IS . . . IS SHE . . . ?
I HOPE NOT. WE CAN'T WORRY ABOUT THAT NOW, WE HAVE TO FREE THE VILLAGE.
WELL DONE, MY NEW AND YOUNG FRIENDS! WHAT A SIGHT!
LET THE VILLAGE GO, MULLET.
OH I WILL, I WILL, BUT FIRST, I WANT YOU TO JOIN ME.
I WANT IT SO BADLY THAT I WILL RENEGE ON MY WORD AND ORDER MY MEN TO KILL THESE PEOPLE UNLESS YOU JOIN ME.
YOU SEE, BOYS, THIS IS AN EXCELLENT LESSON. WHEN YOU FIND YOURSELF IN A POSITION OF GREAT POWER, DO NOT GIVE IT UP UNTIL YOU HAVE ABSOLUTELY EVERYTHING YOU DESIRE.
MY LORD, THIS IS NOT HONORABLE. YOU GAVE YOUR WORD.

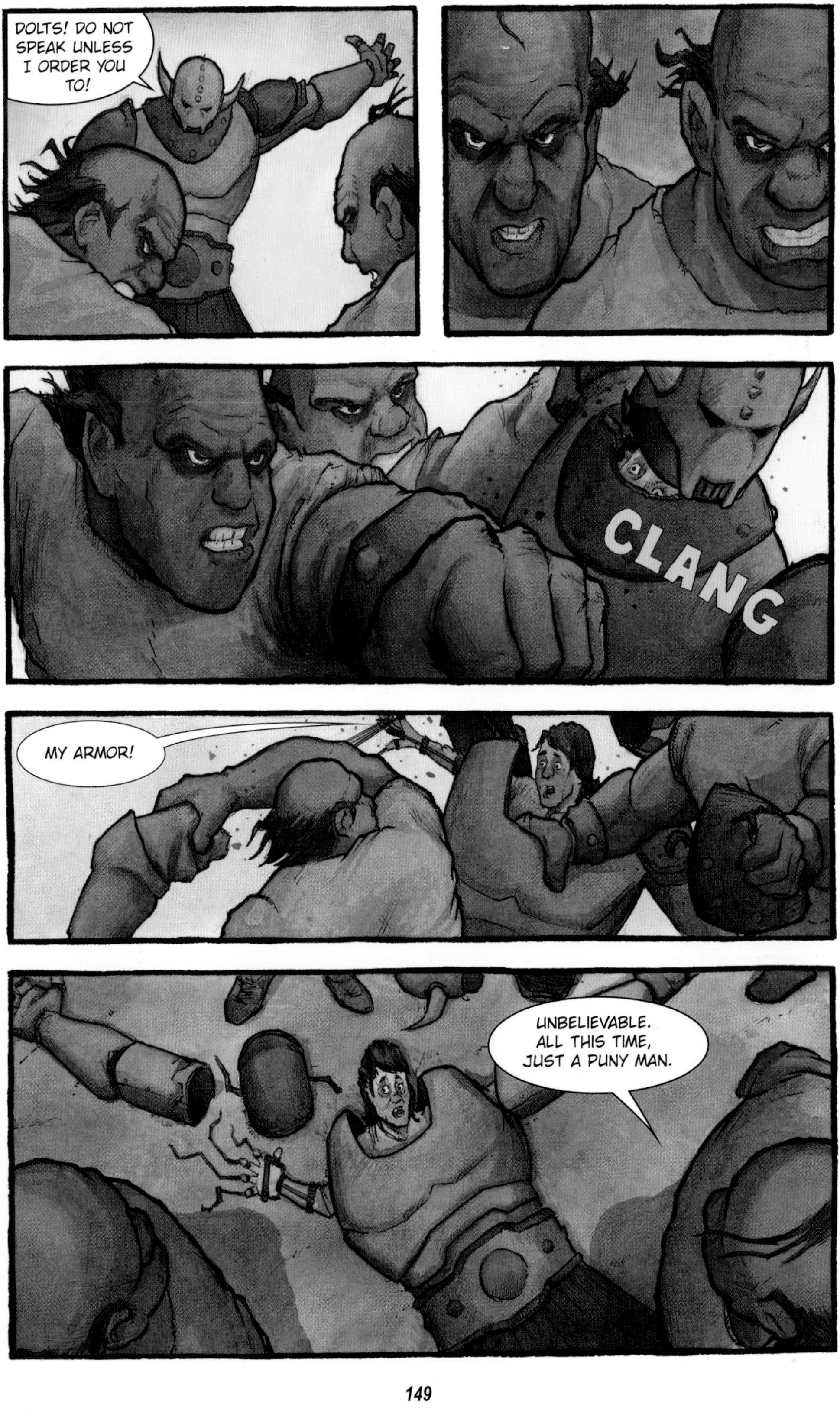
DOLTS! DO NOT SPEAK UNLESS I ORDER YOU TO!
CLANG
MY ARMOR!
UNBELIEVABLE. ALL THIS TIME, JUST A PUNY MAN.

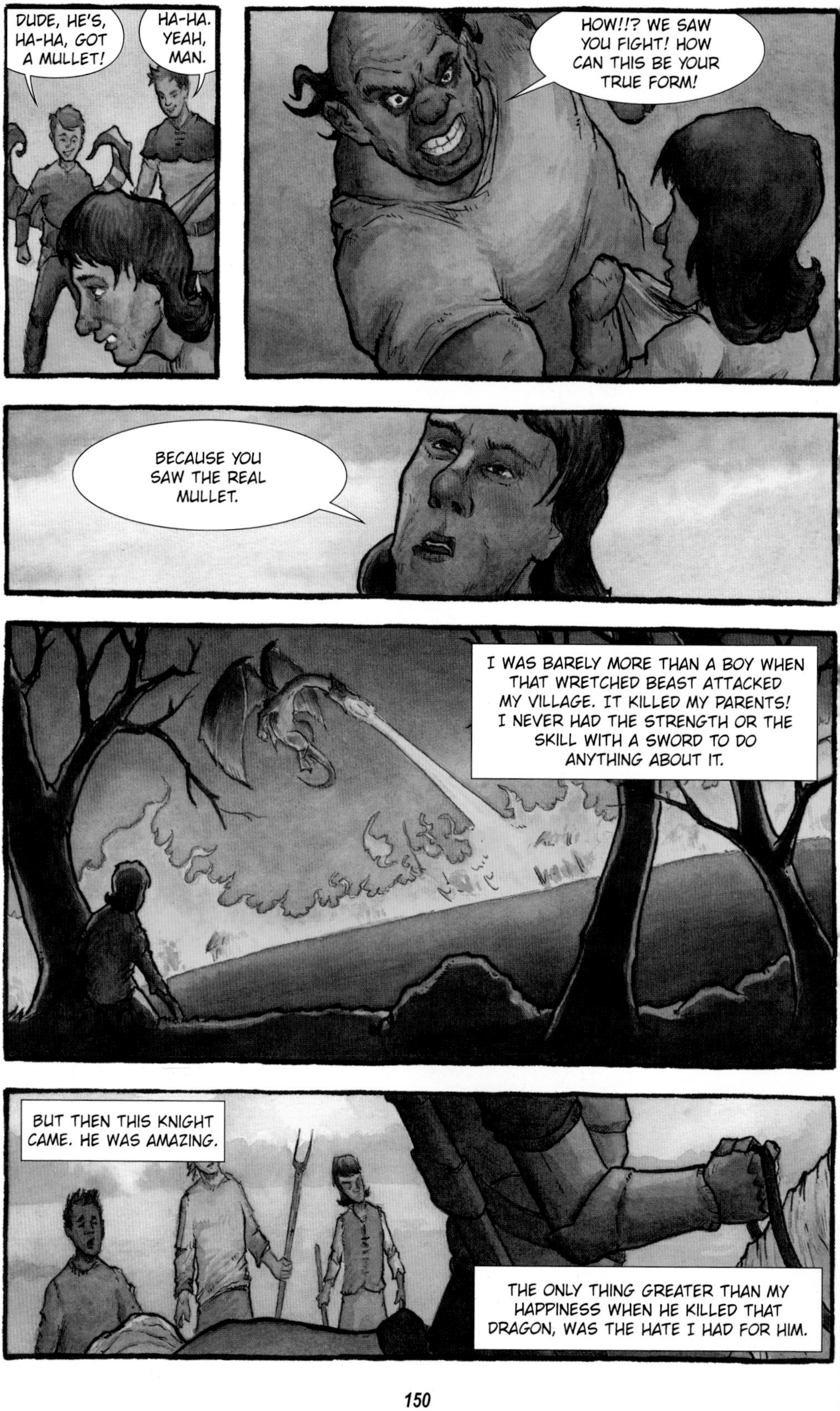
DUDE, HE'S, HA-HA, GOT A MULLET!
HA-HA. YEAH, MAN.
HOW!!? WE SAW YOU FIGHT! HOW CAN THIS BE YOUR TRUE FORM!
BECAUSE YOU SAW THE REAL MULLET.
I WAS BARELY MORE THAN A BOY WHEN THAT WRETCHED BEAST ATTACKED MY VILLAGE. IT KILLED MY PARENTS! I NEVER HAD THE STRENGTH OR THE SKILL WITH A SWORD TO DO ANYTHING ABOUT IT.
BUT THEN THIS KNIGHT CAME. HE WAS AMAZING.
THE ONLY THING GREATER THAN MY HAPPINESS WHEN HE KILLED THAT DRAGON, WAS THE HATE I HAD FOR HIM.

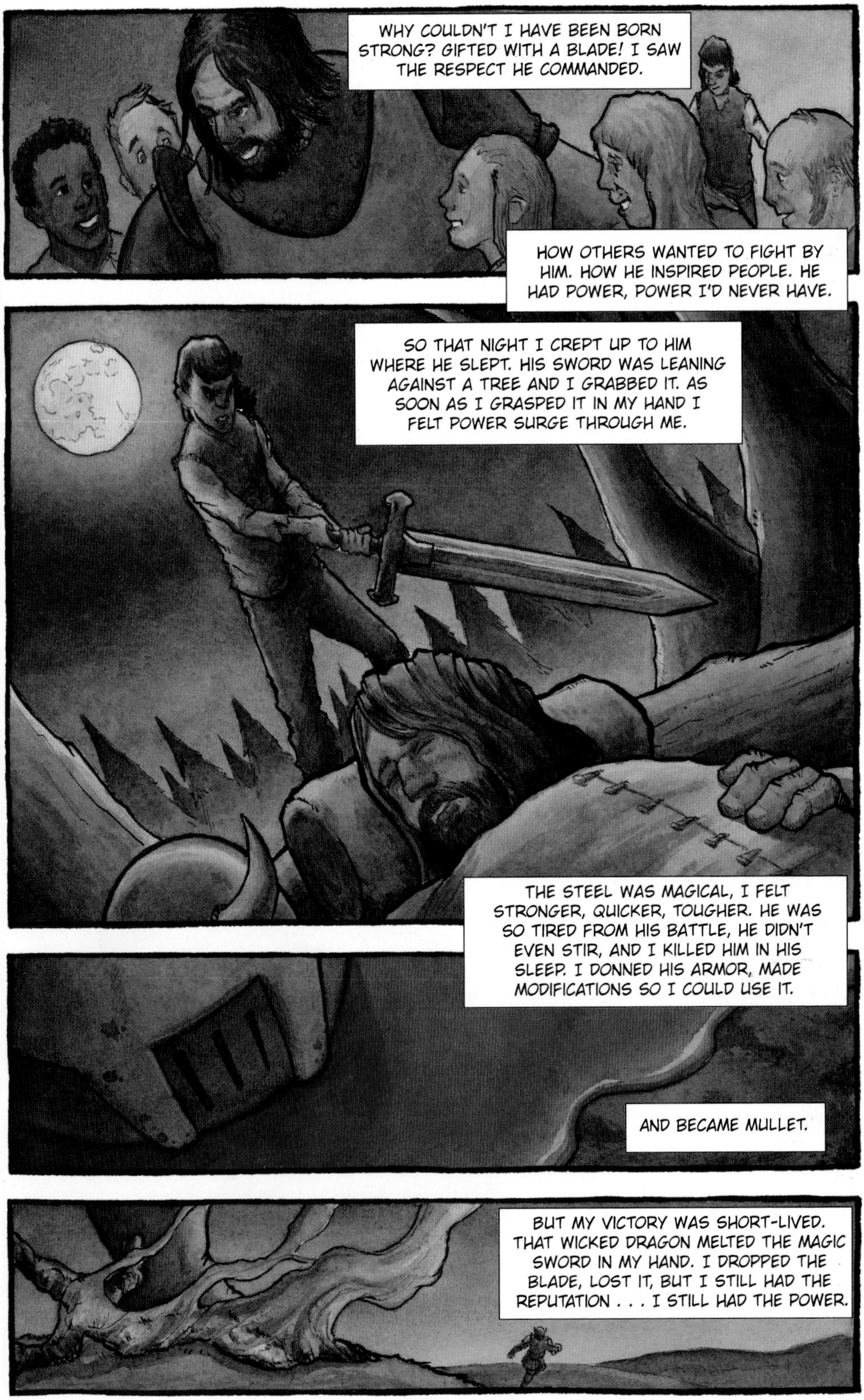
WHY COULDN'T I HAVE BEEN BORN STRONG? GIFTED WITH A BLADE! I SAW THE RESPECT HE COMMANDED.
HOW OTHERS WANTED TO FIGHT BY HIM. HOW HE INSPIRED PEOPLE. HE HAD POWER, POWER I'D NEVER HAVE.
SO THAT NIGHT I CREPT UP TO HIM WHERE HE SLEPT. HIS SWORD WAS LEANING AGAINST A TREE AND I GRABBED IT. AS SOON AS I GRASPED IT IN MY HAND I FELT POWER SURGE THROUGH ME.
THE STEEL WAS MAGICAL, I FELT STRONGER, QUICKER, TOUGHER. HE WAS SO TIRED FROM HIS BATTLE, HE DIDN'T EVEN STIR, AND I KILLED HIM IN HIS SLEEP. I DONNED HIS ARMOR, MADE MODIFICATIONS SO I COULD USE IT.
AND BECAME MULLET.
BUT MY VICTORY WAS SHORT-LIVED. THAT WICKED DRAGON MELTED THE MAGIC SWORD IN MY HAND. I DROPPED THE BLADE, LOST IT, BUT I STILL HAD THE REPUTATION . . . I STILL HAD THE POWER.

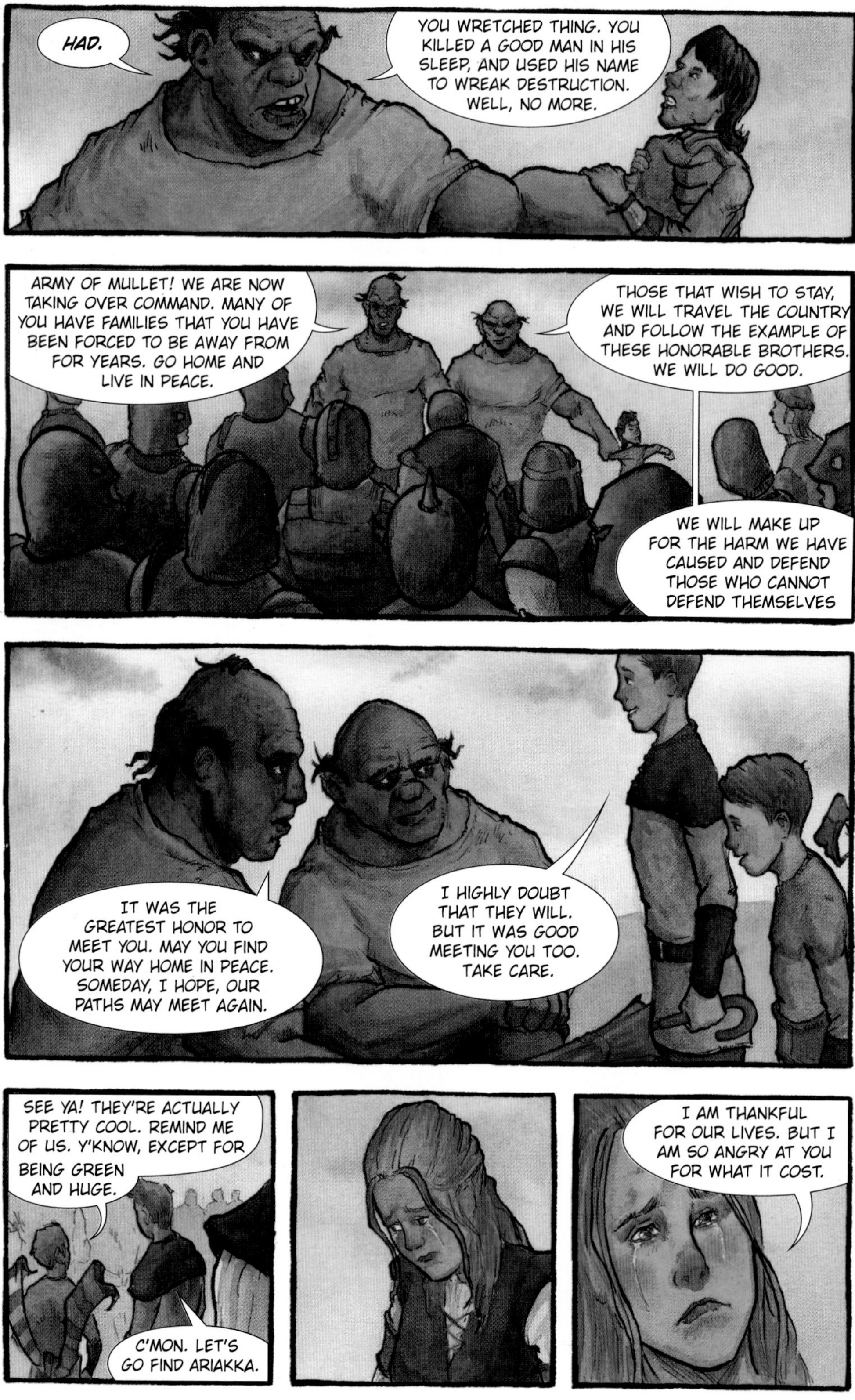
HAD.
YOU WRETCHED THING. YOU KILLED A GOOD MAN IN HIS SLEEP, AND USED HIS NAME TO WREAK DESTRUCTION. WELL, NO MORE.
ARMY OF MULLET! WE ARE NOW TAKING OVER COMMAND. MANY OF YOU HAVE FAMILIES THAT YOU HAVE BEEN FORCED TO BE AWAY FROM FOR YEARS. GO HOME AND LIVE IN PEACE.
THOSE THAT WISH TO STAY, WE WILL TRAVEL THE COUNTRY AND FOLLOW THE EXAMPLE OF THESE HONORABLE BROTHERS. WE WILL DO GOOD.
WE WILL MAKE UP FOR THE HARM WE HAVE CAUSED AND DEFEND THOSE WHO CANNOT DEFEND THEMSELVES
IT WAS THE GREATEST HONOR TO MEET YOU. MAY YOU FIND YOUR WAY HOME IN PEACE. SOMEDAY, I HOPE, OUR PATHS MAY MEET AGAIN.
I HIGHLY DOUBT THAT THEY WILL. BUT IT WAS GOOD MEETING YOU TOO. TAKE CARE.
SEE YA! THEY'RE ACTUALLY PRETTY COOL. REMIND ME OF US. Y'KNOW, EXCEPT FOR BEING GREEN AND HUGE.
C'MON. LET'S GO FIND ARIAKKA.
I AM THANKFUL FOR OUR LIVES. BUT I AM SO ANGRY AT YOU FOR WHAT IT COST.

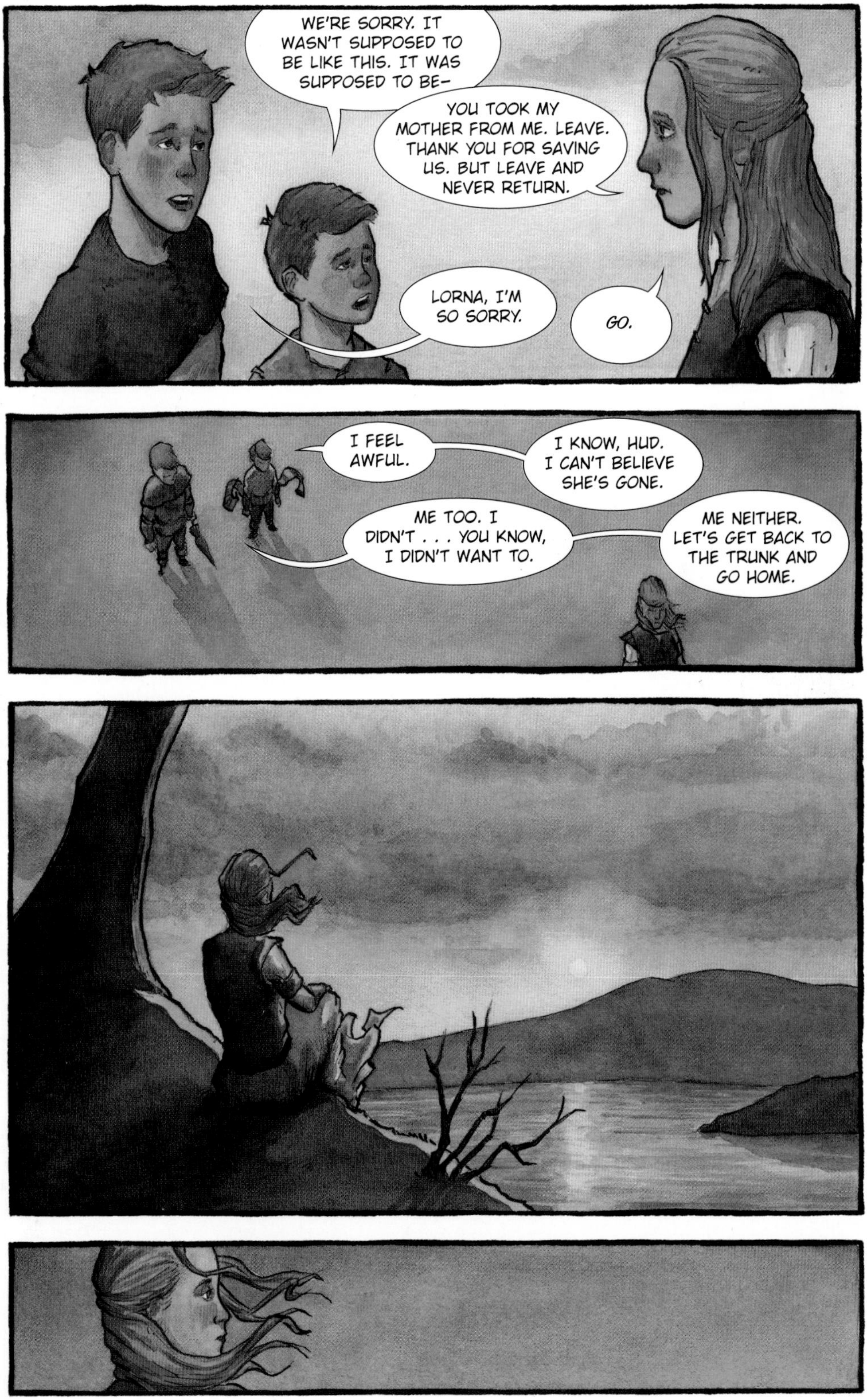
WE'RE SORRY. IT WASN'T SUPPOSED TO BE LIKE THIS. IT WAS SUPPOSED TO BE-
YOU TOOK MY MOTHER FROM ME. LEAVE. THANK YOU FOR SAVING US. BUT LEAVE AND NEVER RETURN.
LORNA, I'M SO SORRY.
GO.
I FEEL AWFUL.
I KNOW, HUD. I CAN'T BELIEVE SHE'S GONE.
ME TOO. I DIDN'T . . . YOU KNOW, I DIDN'T WANT TO.
ME NEITHER. LET'S GET BACK TO THE TRUNK AND GO HOME.

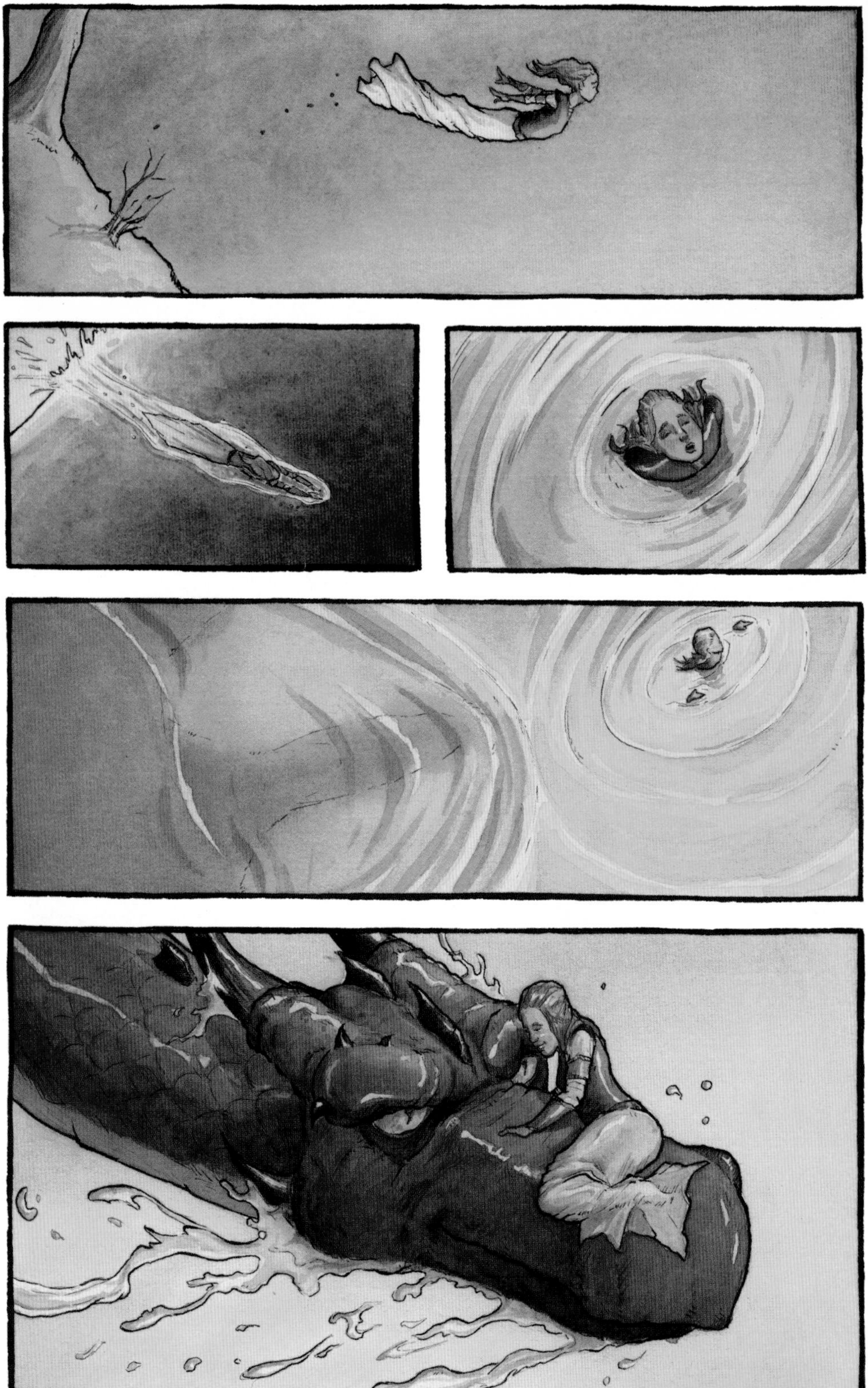

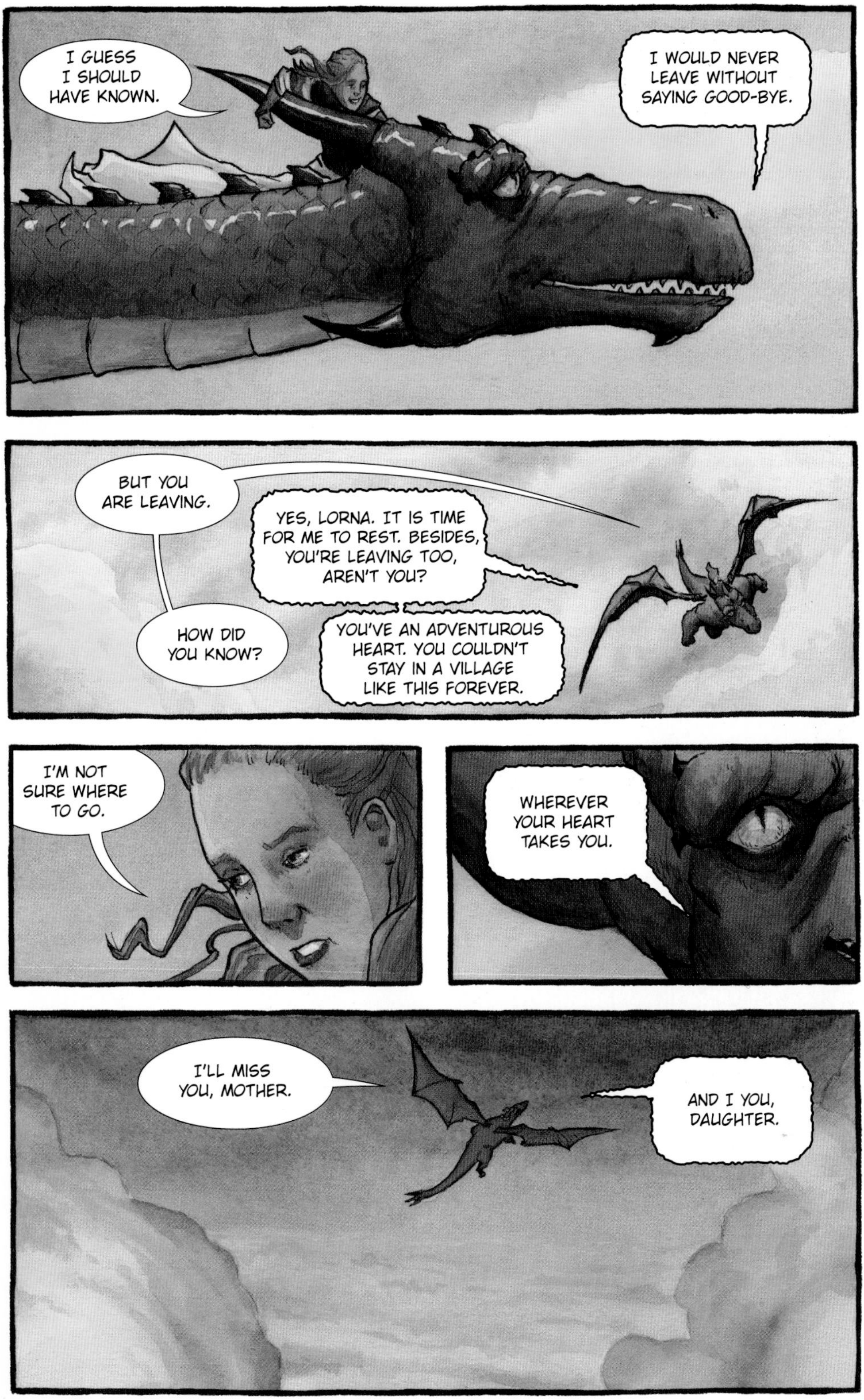
I GUESS I SHOULD HAVE KNOWN.
I WOULD NEVER LEAVE WITHOUT SAYING GOOD-BYE.
BUT YOU ARE LEAVING.
YES, LORNA. IT IS TIME FOR ME TO REST. BESIDES, YOU'RE LEAVING TOO, AREN'T YOU?
HOW DID YOU KNOW?
YOU'VE AN ADVENTUROUS HEART. YOU COULDN'T STAY IN A VILLAGE LIKE THIS FOREVER.
I'M NOT SURE WHERE TO GO.
WHEREVER YOUR HEART TAKES YOU.
I'LL MISS YOU, MOTHER.
AND I YOU, DAUGHTER.

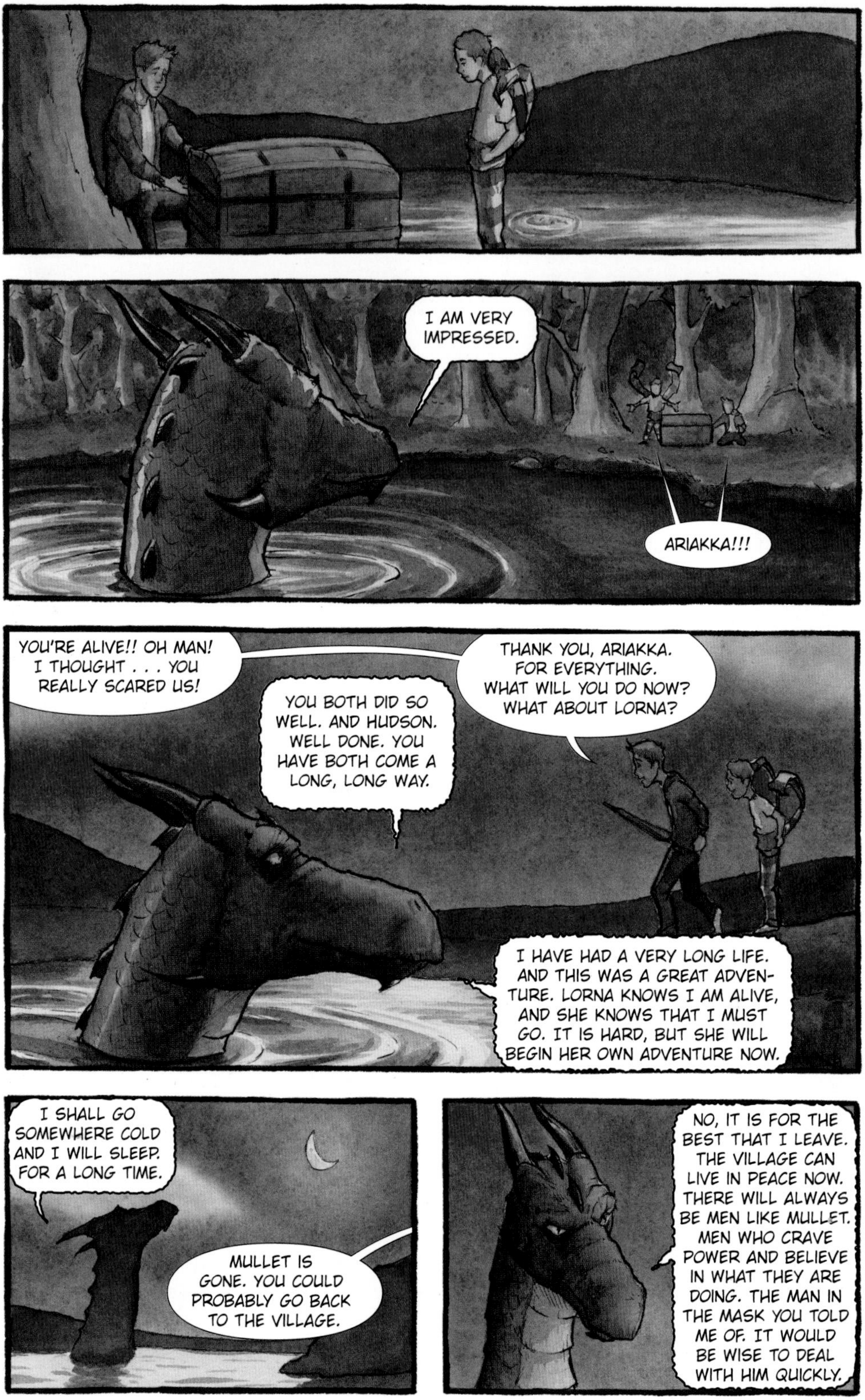
I AM VERY IMPRESSED.
ARIAKKA!!!
YOU'RE ALIVE!! OH MAN! I THOUGHT . . . YOU REALLY SCARED US!
THANK YOU, ARIAKKA. FOR EVERYTHING. WHAT WILL YOU DO NOW? WHAT ABOUT LORNA?
YOU BOTH DID SO WELL. AND HUDSON. WELL DONE. YOU HAVE BOTH COME A LONG, LONG WAY.
I HAVE HAD A VERY LONG LIFE. AND THIS WAS A GREAT ADVENTURE. LORNA KNOWS I AM ALIVE, AND SHE KNOWS THAT I MUST GO. IT IS HARD, BUT SHE WILL BEGIN HER OWN ADVENTURE NOW.
I SHALL GO SOMEWHERE COLD AND I WILL SLEEP. FOR A LONG TIME.
MULLET IS GONE. YOU COULD PROBABLY GO BACK TO THE VILLAGE.
NO, IT IS FOR THE BEST THAT I LEAVE. THE VILLAGE CAN LIVE IN PEACE NOW. THERE WILL ALWAYS BE MEN LIKE MULLET. MEN WHO CRAVE POWER AND BELIEVE IN WHAT THEY ARE DOING. THE MAN IN THE MASK YOU TOLD ME OF. IT WOULD BE WISE TO DEAL WITH HIM QUICKLY.

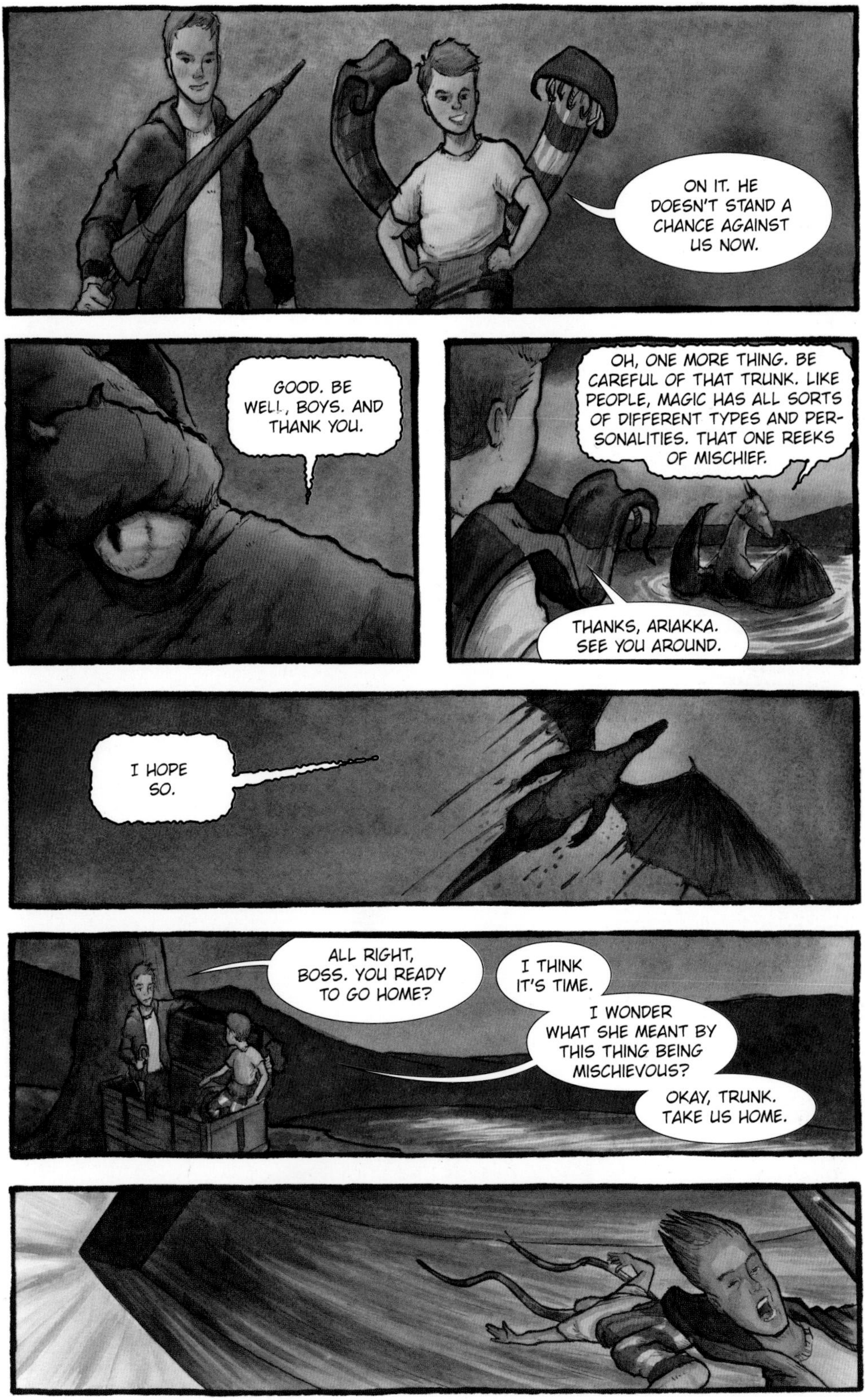
ON IT. HE DOESN'T STAND A CHANCE AGAINST US NOW.
GOOD. BE WELL, BOYS. AND THANK YOU.
OH, ONE MORE THING. BE CAREFUL OF THAT TRUNK. LIKE PEOPLE, MAGIC HAS ALL SORTS OF DIFFERENT TYPES AND PERSONALITIES. THAT ONE REEKS OF MISCHIEF.
THANKS, ARIAKKA. SEE YOU AROUND.
I HOPE SO.
ALL RIGHT, BOSS. YOU READY TO GO HOME?
I THINK IT'S TIME.
I WONDER WHAT SHE MEANT BY THIS THING BEING MISCHIEVOUS?
OKAY, TRUNK. TAKE US HOME.

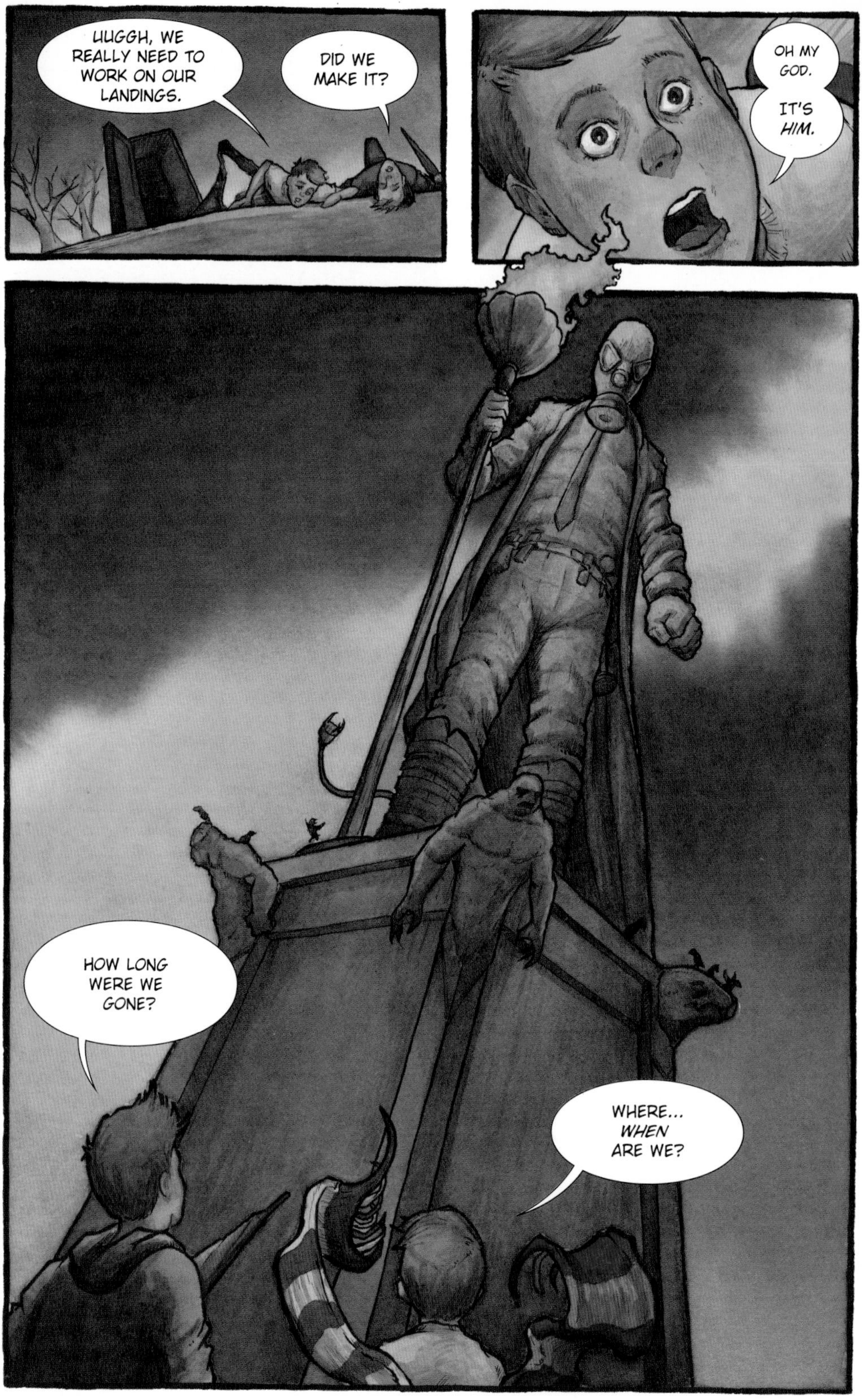
UUGGH, WE REALLY NEED TO WORK ON OUR LANDINGS.
DID WE MAKE IT?
OH MY GOD.
IT'S *HIM.*
HOW LONG WERE WE GONE?
WHERE... *WHEN* ARE WE?

ACKNOWLEDGMENTS

I'D LIKE TO THANK THE FAMILY, FRIENDS, AND COLLEAGUES WHO HAVE BEEN SO SUPPORTIVE AND PATIENT AS I COMPLETED THIS PROJECT. THANKS TO MY PARENTS, MY GRANDPARENTS, AND MY WHOLE FAMILY, THE TOWNS AND FRIENDS OF CATAUMET, MILLIS, AND NANTUCKET THAT MERGED TOGETHER AND BECAME SCRAGGY NECK ISLAND. THANKS TO SARAH WARNER, RICH JOHNSON, MEAGAN VINCENT, JESSE MARTINEZ, THE PAC HOUSE, KATHLEEN OWEN, JASMIN RUBERO, LILY MALCOM, LAURI HORNIK, DANA CHIDIAC, DAVID USLAN, AND MOST OF ALL THANK YOU RAYDENE SALINAS FOR YOUR CONSTANT ENCOURAGEMENT. THANKS SO MUCH TEAM.